The
BROKEN WINDOW

Jeffery
DEAVER

HODDER

First published in the United States of America in 2008 by Simon & Schuster, Inc.
First published in Great Britain in 2008 by Hodder & Stoughton
An Hachette UK company

First published in paperback in 2009

11

A CIP catalogue record for this title is available from the British Library

ISBN 978 0 340 99370 5

Typeset in Fairfield Light by
Palimpsest Book Production Limited, Grangemouth, Stirlingshire

Printed and bound by Clays Ltd, St Ives plc

Hodder & Stoughton policy is to use papers that are natural, renewable and
recyclable products and made from wood grown in sustainable forests.
The logging and manufacturing processes are expected to conform to the
environmental regulations of the country of origin.

Hodder & Stoughton Ltd
338 Euston Road
London NW1 3BH

www.hodder.co.uk

To a dear friend, the written word

I

SOMETHING IN COMMON

THURSDAY, MAY 12

Most privacy violations are not going to be caused by the exposure of huge personal secrets but by the publication of many little facts . . . As with killer bees, one is an annoyance but a swarm can be deadly.

—ROBERT O'HARROW, JR.,
No Place to Hide

Chapter
ONE

Something nagged, yet she couldn't quite figure out what.

Like a faint recurring ache somewhere in your body.

Or a man on the street behind you as you near your apartment . . . Was he the same one who'd been glancing at you on the subway?

Or a dark dot moving toward your bed but now vanished. A black widow spider?

But then her visitor, sitting on her living room couch, glanced at her and smiled and Alice Sanderson forgot the concern – if concern it was. Arthur had a good mind and a solid body, sure. But he had a great smile, which counted for a lot more.

'How 'bout some wine?' she asked, walking into her small kitchen.

'Sure. Whatever you've got.'

'So, this's pretty fun – playing hooky on a weekday. Two grown adults. I like it.'

'Born to be wild,' he joked.

Outside the window, across the street, were rows of painted and natural brownstones. They could also see part of the Manhattan skyline, hazy on this pleasant spring weekday.

Air – fresh enough for the city – wafted in, carrying the scents of garlic and oregano from an Italian restaurant up the street. It was their favorite type of cuisine – one of the many common interests they'd discovered since they'd met several weeks ago at a wine tasting in SoHo. In late April, Alice had found herself in the crowd of about forty, listening to a sommelier lecture about the wines of Europe, when she'd heard a man's voice ask about a particular type of Spanish red wine.

She had barked a quiet laugh. She happened to own a case of that very wine (well, *part* of a case now). It was made by a little-known vineyard. Perhaps not the best Rioja ever produced but the wine offered another bouquet: that of fond memory. She and a French lover had consumed plenty of it during a week in Spain – a perfect liaison, just the thing for a woman in her late twenties who'd recently broken up with her boyfriend. The vacation fling was passionate, intense and, of course, doomed, which made it all the better.

Alice had leaned forward to see who'd mentioned the wine: a nondescript man in a business suit. After a few glasses of the featured selections she'd grown braver and, juggling a plate of finger food, had made her way across the room and asked him about his interest in the wine.

He'd explained about a trip he'd taken to Spain a few years ago with an ex-girlfriend. How he'd come to enjoy the wine. They'd sat at a table and talked for some time. Arthur, it seemed, liked the same food she did, the same sports. They both jogged and spent an hour each morning in overpriced health clubs. 'But,' he said, 'I wear the cheapest JCPenney shorts and T-shirts I can find. No designer garbage for me . . .' Then he'd blushed, realizing he'd possibly insulted her.

But she'd laughed. She took the same approach to workout clothes (in her case, bought at Target when visiting her family in Jersey). She'd quashed the urge to tell him this, though, worried about coming on too strong. They'd played that popular urban dating game: what we have in common. They'd rated restaurants, compared *Curb Your Enthusiasm* episodes and complained about their shrinks.

A date ensued, then another. Art was funny and courteous. A little stiff, shy at times, reclusive, which she put down to what he described as the breakup from hell – a long-term girlfriend in the fashion business. And his grueling work schedule – he was a Manhattan businessman. He had little free time.

Would anything come of it?

He wasn't a boyfriend yet. But there were far worse people to spend time with. And when they'd kissed on their most recent date, she'd felt the low ping that meant, oh, yeah: chemistry. Tonight might or might not reveal exactly how much. She'd noticed that Arthur had furtively – *he* thought – been checking out the tight pink little number she'd bought at Bergdorf's especially for their date. And Alice had made some preparations in the bedroom in case kissing turned into something else.

Then the faint uneasiness, the concern about the spider, returned.

What *was* bothering her?

Alice supposed it was nothing more than a residue of unpleasantness she'd experienced when a deliveryman had dropped off a package earlier. Shaved head and bushy eyebrows, smelling of cigarette smoke and speaking in a thick Eastern European accent. As she'd signed the papers, he'd looked her over – clearly flirting – and then asked for a glass of water. She brought it to him reluctantly and found him in the middle of her living room, staring at her sound system.

She'd told him she was expecting company and he'd left, frowning, as if angry over a snub. Alice had watched out the window and noted that nearly ten minutes had passed before he got into the double-parked van and left.

What had he been doing in the apartment building all that time? Checking out—

'Hey, Earth to Alice . . .'

'Sorry.' She laughed, continued to the couch, then sat next to Arthur, their knees brushing. Thoughts of the deliveryman vanished. They touched glasses, these two people who were compatible in all-important areas – politics (they contributed virtually the same amount to the Dems and gave money during NPR pledge drives), movies, food, traveling. They were both lapsed Protestants.

When their knees touched again, his rubbed seductively. Then Arthur smiled and asked, 'Oh, that painting you bought, the Prescott? Did you get it?'

Her eyes shone as she nodded. 'Yep. I now own a Harvey Prescott.'

Alice Sanderson was not a wealthy woman by Manhattan standards but she'd invested well and indulged her true passion. She'd followed the career of Prescott, a painter from Oregon who specialized in photorealistic works of families – not existing people but ones he himself made up. Some traditional, some not so – single parent, mixed race or gay. Virtually none of his paintings were on the market in her price range but she was on the mailing lists of the galleries that occasionally sold his work. Last month she'd learned from one out west that a small early canvas might be coming available for $150,000. Sure enough, the owner decided to sell and she'd dipped into her investment account to come up with the cash.

That was the delivery she'd received today. But the pleasure of owning the piece now diminished again with a flare-up of concern about the driver. She recalled his smell, his lascivious eyes. Alice rose, on the pretense of opening the curtains wider, and looked outside. No delivery trucks, no skinheads standing on the street corner and staring up at her apartment. She thought about closing and locking the window, but that seemed too paranoid and would require an explanation.

She returned to Arthur, glanced at her walls and told him she wasn't sure where to hang the painting in her small apartment. A brief fantasy played out: Arthur's staying over one Saturday night and on Sunday, after brunch, helping her find the perfect place for the canvas.

Her voice was filled with pleasure and pride as she said, 'You want to see it?'

'You bet.'

They rose and she walked toward the bedroom, believing that she heard footsteps in the corridor outside. All the other tenants should have been at work, this time of day.

Could it be the deliveryman?

Well, at least she wasn't alone.

They got to the bedroom door.

Which was when the black widow struck.

With a jolt Alice now understood what had been bothering her, and it had nothing to do with the deliveryman. No, it was about *Arthur*. When they'd spoken yesterday he'd asked when the Prescott would be arriving.

She'd told him she was getting *a* painting but had never mentioned the artist's name. Slowing now, at the bedroom door. Her hands were sweating. If he'd learned of the painting without her telling him, then maybe he'd found other facts about her life. What if all of the many things they had in common were lies? What if he'd known about her love of the Spanish wine ahead of time? What if he'd been at the tasting just to get close to her? All the restaurants they knew, the travel, the TV shows . . .

My God, here she was leading a man she'd known for only a few weeks into her bedroom. All her defenses down . . .

Breathing hard now . . . Shivering.

'Oh, the painting,' he whispered, looking past her. 'It's beautiful.'

And, hearing his calm, pleasant voice, Alice laughed to herself. Are you crazy? She *must* have mentioned Prescott's name to Arthur. She tucked the uneasiness away. Calm down. You've been living alone too long. Remember his smiles, his joking. He thinks the way you think.

Relax.

A faint laugh. Alice stared at the two-by-two-foot canvas, the muted colors, a half dozen people at a dinner table looking out, some amused, some pensive, some troubled.

'Incredible,' he said.

'The composition is wonderful but it's their expressions that he captures so perfectly. Don't you think?' Alice turned to him.

Her smile vanished. 'What's that, Arthur? What are you doing?' He'd put on beige cloth gloves and was reaching into his pocket. And then she looked into his eyes, which had hardened into dark pinpricks beneath furrowed brows, in a face she hardly recognized at all.

▋▋ TRANSACTIONS

SUNDAY, MAY 22

You often hear the old legend that our body is worth $4.50, stripped for parts. Our digital identity is worth far more.

—ROBERT O'HARROW, JR.,
No Place to Hide

Chapter
TWO

The trail had led from Scottsdale to San Antonio to a rest area in Delaware off Interstate 95, filled with truckers and restless families, then finally to the improbable destination of London.

And the prey who'd taken this route? A professional killer Lincoln Rhyme had been pursuing for some time, a man he'd been able to stop from committing a terrible crime, but who'd managed to escape from the police with only minutes to spare, 'waltzing,' as Rhyme had put it bitterly, 'out of the city like a goddamn tourist who had to be back at work Monday morning.'

The trail had dried up like dust and the police and FBI could learn nothing about where he was hiding or what he might be planning next. But a few weeks earlier Rhyme had heard from contacts in Arizona that this very man was the likely suspect in the murder of a U.S. Army soldier in Scottsdale. Leads suggested he'd headed east – to Texas, then Delaware.

The name of the perp, which might have been real or a cover, was Richard Logan. It was likely that he came from the western portion of the United States or Canada. Intense searches turned up a number of Richard Logans, but none fit the profile of the killer.

Then in a burst of happenstance (Lincoln Rhyme would never use the word 'luck'), he'd learned from Interpol, the European criminal-information clearinghouse, that a professional killer from America had been hired for a job in England. He'd killed someone in Arizona to gain access to some military identification and information, met with associates in Texas and been given a down payment on his fee at some truck stop on the East Coast. He had flown to Heathrow and was now somewhere in the U.K., the exact location unknown.

The subject of Richard Logan's 'well-funded plot which originated at high levels' – Rhyme could only smile when he read the polished Interpol description – was a Protestant minister from Africa, who'd run a refugee camp and stumbled on a massive scam in which AIDS drugs were stolen and sold and the money used to purchase arms. The minister was relocated by security forces to London, having survived three attempts on his life in Nigeria and Liberia and even one in a transit lounge at Malpensa airport in Milan, where the Polizia di Stato, armed with stubby machine guns, scrutinize much and miss very little.

The Reverend Samuel G. Goodlight (a better name for a man of the cloth Rhyme couldn't imagine) was now in a safe house in London, under the watchful eye of officers from Scotland Yard, the home of the Metropolitan Police Service, and was presently helping British and foreign intelligence connect the dots of the drugs-for-arms plan.

Via encrypted satellite calls and e-mails flying around several continents, Rhyme and an Inspector Longhurst of the Metropolitan Police had set up a trap to catch the perp. Worthy of the precise plots that Logan himself crafted, the plan involved look-alikes and the vital assistance of a larger-than-life former arms broker from South Africa who came with a network of curried informants. Danny Krueger had made hundreds of thousands selling weapons as efficiently and dispassionately as other businessmen sell air conditioners and cough syrup. But a trip to Darfur last year had shaken him badly, seeing the carnage his toys caused. He'd given up the arms trade cold and had resettled in England. Others on the task force included officers from MI5, as well as personnel from the London office of the FBI and an agent from France's version of the CIA: La Direction Générale de la Sécurité Extérieure.

They hadn't known even the region of Britain in which Logan was in hiding, planning his hit, but the boisterous Danny Krueger had heard that the killer would be making his move in the next few days. The South African still had many contacts in the international underground and had put out hints about a 'secret' location where the meetings between Goodlight and the authorities would take place. The building had an exposed courtyard that was a perfect shooting zone for the killer to assassinate the minister.

It was also an ideal place to spot and take down Logan. Surveillance was in place and armed police, MI5 and FBI agents were on twenty-four-hour alert.

Rhyme was now sitting in his red battery-powered wheel-chair on the first floor of his Central Park West town house – no longer the quaint Victorian parlor it had once been, but a well-equipped forensic laboratory, larger than many labs in medium-size towns. He found himself doing what he'd done frequently over the past several days: staring at the phone, whose number-two speed-dial button would call a line in England.

'The phone's working, right?' Rhyme asked.

'Is there any reason for it not to be?' Thom, his caregiver, asked this in a measured tone, which Rhyme heard as a belabored sigh.

'I don't know. Circuits overload. Phone lines get hit by lightning. All kinds of things can go wrong.'

'Then maybe you should try it. Just to make sure.'

'Command,' Rhyme said, getting the attention of the voice-recognition system hooked to his ECU – the computerized environmental control unit that substituted in many ways for his physical functioning. Lincoln Rhyme was a quadriplegic; he had only limited movement below the place where his neck was broken in a crime-scene accident years before – the fourth cervical vertebra, near the base of the skull. He now ordered, 'Dial directory assistance.'

The dial tone filled the speakers, followed by *beep beep beep*. This irritated Rhyme more than a nonperforming phone would have. Why hadn't Inspector Longhurst called? 'Command,' he snapped. 'Disconnect.'

'Seems to be fine.' Thom placed a coffee mug in the cup holder of Rhyme's wheelchair and the criminalist sipped the strong brew through a straw. He looked at a bottle of Glenmorangie eighteen-year-old single-malt whisky on a shelf – it was nearby but, of course, always just out of Rhyme's reach.

'It's morning,' Thom said.

'Obviously it's morning. I can *see* it's morning. I don't want any . . . It's just . . .' He'd been waiting for a reason to ride the young man on the issue. 'I seem to recall being cut off rather early last night. Two tumblers. Virtually nothing.'

'It was three.'

'If you were to add up the contents, the cubic centimeters, I'm speaking of, it was the same as two small ones.' Pettiness, like liquor, could be intoxicating in its own right.

'Well, no scotch in the morning.'

'It helps me think more clearly.'

'No, it doesn't.'

'It does. And more creatively.'

'Doesn't do that either.'

Thom was wearing a perfectly ironed shirt, tie and slacks.

His clothes were less wrinkled than they used to be. Much of the job of a quadriplegic's caregiver is physical. But Rhyme's new chair, an Invacare TDX, for 'total driving experience,' could fold out into a virtual bed, and had made Thom's job much easier. The chair could even climb low stairs and speed along as fast as a middle-aged jogger.

'I'm saying I want some scotch. There. I've articulated my desire. How's that?'

'No.'

Rhyme scoffed and stared at the phone again. 'If he gets away . . .' His voice faded. 'Well, aren't you going to do what everybody does?'

'What do you mean, Lincoln?' The slim young man had been working with Rhyme for years. He'd been fired on occasion and had quit too. But here he still was. A testament to the perseverance, or perverseness, of both principals.

'I say, "If he gets away," and you say, "Oh, but he won't. Don't worry." And I'm supposed to be reassured. People do that, you know: They give reassurance when they have no idea what they're talking about.'

'But I didn't say that. Are we having an argument about something I didn't say but could have? Isn't that like a wife being mad at her husband because she saw a pretty woman on the street and thought he *would* have stared at her if he'd been there?'

'I don't know what it's like,' Rhyme said absently, his mind mostly on the plan in Britain to capture Logan. Were there holes in it? How was security? Could he trust the informants not to leak information the killer might pick up on?

The phone rang and a caller-ID box opened on the flat-screen monitor near Rhyme. He was disappointed to see the number wasn't a London exchange but closer to home – in the Big Building, cop-speak for One Police Plaza in downtown Manhattan.

'Command, answer phone.' *Click.* Then: 'What?'

From five miles away a voice muttered, 'Bad mood?'

'No word from England yet.'

'What're you, on call or something?' Detective Lon Sellitto asked.

'Logan's disappeared. He could make a move at any time.'

'Like having a baby,' Sellitto said.

'If you say so. What do you need? I don't want to keep the line tied up.'

'All that fancy equipment and you don't have call waiting?'

'Lon.'

'Okay. Something you oughta know about. There was a burglary-murder a week ago Thursday. Vic was a woman lived in the Village. Alice Sanderson. Perp stabbed her to death and stole some painting. We got the doer.'

Why was he calling about this? A mundane crime and the perp in custody. 'Evidence problem?'

'Nope.'

'So I'd be interested *why*?'

'The supervising detective just got a call a half hour ago?'

'The chase, Lon. The chase.' Rhyme was staring at the whiteboard that detailed the plan to catch the killer in England. The scheme was elaborate.

And fragile.

Sellitto brought him out of his reflection. 'Look, I'm sorry, Linc, but I gotta tell you, the perp's your cousin, Arthur Rhyme. It's murder one. He's looking at twenty-five years, and the D.A. says it's an airtight case.'

Chapter
THREE

'It's been quite a while.'

Judy Rhyme sat in the lab. Hands together, face ashen, she fiercely avoided looking at anything except the criminalist's eyes.

Two responses to his physical condition infuriated Rhyme: when visitors struggled agonizingly to pretend his disability didn't exist, and when they considered it a reason to be his best friend, joking and slinging around tough talk as if they'd been through the war together. Judy fell into the first category, measuring her words carefully before she set them delicately in front of Rhyme. Still, she was family, of sorts, and he remained patient as he tried to keep from glancing at the telephone.

'A long time,' the criminalist agreed.

Thom was picking up the social details to which Rhyme was forever oblivious. He'd offered Judy coffee, which now sat untouched, a prop, on the table in front of her. Rhyme had glanced at the whisky once more, a longing peek that Thom had no trouble ignoring.

The attractive, dark-haired woman seemed in better shape, solid and more athletic, than the last time he'd seen her – about two years before his accident. Judy risked a look at the criminalist's face. 'I'm sorry we never got here. Really. I wanted to.'

Meaning not a social visit before he was injured but a sympathy call after. Survivors of catastrophes can read what is unsaid in conversations as clearly as the words themselves.

'You got the flowers?'

Back then, after the accident, Rhyme had been dazed – medication, physical trauma, and the psychological wrestling match with the inconceivable: the fact that he would never walk again. He didn't remember any flowers from them but he was sure the family had sent them. A lot of people had. Flowers are easy, visits are hard. 'Yes. Thanks.'

Silence. An involuntary, lightning-fast glance at his legs. People think if you can't walk there's something wrong with your legs. No, they're fine. The problem was telling them what to do.

'You're looking good,' she said.

Rhyme didn't know whether he did or not. Never really considered it.

'And you're divorced, I heard.'

'That's right.'

'I'm sorry.'

Why? he wondered. But that was a cynical thought and he gave a nod, acknowledging her sympathy.

'What's Blaine up to?'

'She's out on Long Island. Remarried. We don't stay in touch much. Without kids, that usually happens.'

'I enjoyed that time in Boston, when you two came up for the long weekend.' A smile that wasn't really a smile. Painted on, a mask.

'It was nice, yes.'

A weekend in New England. Shopping, a drive south to Cape Cod, a picnic by the water. Rhyme remembered thinking how lovely the place was. Seeing the green rocks by the shore, he'd had a brainstorm and decided to start a collection of algae from around the New York City area for the NYPD crime lab database. He'd spent a week driving around the metro area, taking samples.

And, on the trip to see Arthur and Judy, he and Blaine hadn't fought once. Even the drive home, with a stop at a Connecticut inn, was nice. He remembered making love on the back deck of their room, the smell of honeysuckle overwhelming.

That visit was the last contact with his cousin in person. They'd had one other brief conversation but only via the phone. Then came the accident, and silence.

'Arthur kind of fell off the face of the earth.' She laughed, an embarrassed sound. 'You know we moved to New Jersey?'

'Really?'

'He was teaching at Princeton. But he got laid off.'

'What happened?'

'He was an assistant and a research fellow. They decided not to offer him a full professor's contract. Art says politics was behind it. You know how that is in colleges.'

Henry Rhyme, Art's father, was a renowned professor of physics at the University of Chicago; academia was an esteemed pursuit in that branch of the Rhyme family. In high school Arthur and Lincoln would debate the virtues of university research and teaching versus a private-sector job. 'In academia, you can make a serious contribution to society,' Art had said as the boys shared two somewhat illegal beers, and managed to keep a straight face when Lincoln supplied the requisite follow-up line: 'That, and the teaching assistants can be pretty hot.'

Rhyme wasn't surprised that Art had gone for a university job.

'He could've continued to be an assistant but he quit. He

was pretty angry. Assumed he'd get another job right away, but that didn't happen. He was out of work for a while. Ended up at a private company. A medical-equipment manufacturer.' Another automatic glance – this time at the elaborate wheelchair. She blushed as if she'd committed a Don Imus. 'It wasn't his dream job and he hasn't been real happy. I'm sure he wanted to come see you. But probably he was ashamed he hadn't done so well. I mean, with you being a celebrity and all.'

Finally, a sip of coffee. 'You both had so much in common. You two were like brothers. I remember Boston, all the stories you told. We were up half the night, laughing. Things I never knew about him. And my father-in-law, Henry – when he was alive he'd talk about you all the time.'

'Did he? We wrote quite a bit. In fact, I had a letter from him a few days before he died.'

Rhyme had dozens of indelible memories of his uncle, but one particular image stood out. The tall, balding, ruddy-faced man is rearing back, braying a laugh, embarrassing every one of the dozen or so family members at the Christmas Eve dinner table – embarrassing all, that is, except Henry Rhyme himself, his patient wife and young Lincoln, who is laughing right along. Rhyme liked his uncle very much and would often go to visit Art and the family, who lived about thirty miles away, on the shores of Lake Michigan in Evanston, Illinois.

Now, though, Rhyme was in no mood for nostalgia and was relieved when he heard the door open and the sound of seven firm footsteps, from threshold to carpet, the stride telling Rhyme who it was. A moment later a tall, slim redhead wearing jeans and a black T-shirt under a burgundy blouse entered the lab. The shirt was loose and the stern angle of a black Glock pistol was visible high on her hip.

As Amelia Sachs smiled and kissed Rhyme on the mouth, the criminalist was aware, in his periphery, of Judy's body language response. The message was clear and Rhyme wondered what had dismayed her: that she'd made the slip of not asking if he was seeing someone, or that she'd assumed a crip couldn't have a romantic partner – at least not one as disarmingly attractive as Sachs, who'd been a model before going to the police academy.

He introduced them. Sachs listened with concern to the story of Arthur Rhyme's arrest, and asked how Judy was coping with the situation. Then: 'Do you have children?'

Rhyme realized that while he'd been noting Judy's faux pas, he'd committed one himself, neglecting to ask about their son, whose name he'd forgotten. And, it turned out, the family had grown. In addition to Arthur Junior, who was in high school, there were two others. 'A nine-year-old, Henry. And a daughter, Meadow. She's six.'

'Meadow?' Sachs asked in surprise, for reasons Rhyme couldn't deduce.

Judy gave an embarrassed laugh. '*And* we live in Jersey. But it's got nothing to do with the TV show. She was born before I'd ever seen it.'

TV show?

Judy broke the brief silence. 'I'm sure you're wondering why I called that officer to get your number. But first I have to tell you Art doesn't know I'm here.'

'No?'

'In fact, to tell you the truth, I wouldn't have thought of it on my own. I've been so upset, not getting any sleep, not thinking straight. But I was talking to Art a few days ago in the detention center and he said, "I know what you're thinking, but don't call Lincoln. It's a case of mistaken identity or some-thing. We'll get it straightened out. Promise me you won't." He didn't want to burden you . . . You know how Art is. Just so kind, always thinking of everybody else.'

Rhyme nodded.

'But the more I got to thinking about it, the more sense it made. I wouldn't ask you to pull strings or do anything that wasn't right, but I thought maybe you could just make a call or two. Tell me what you thought.'

Rhyme could imagine how *that* would go over at the Big Building. As a forensic consultant for the NYPD, his job was getting to the truth, wherever that journey led, but the brass definitely preferred him to help convict, not exonerate, defendants.

'I went through some of your clippings—'

'Clippings?'

'Art keeps family scrapbooks. He has clippings about your cases from the newspapers. Dozens. You've done some amazing things.'

Rhyme said, 'Oh, I'm just a civil servant.'

Finally Judy delivered some unvarnished emotion: a smile, as she looked into his eyes. 'Art said he never believed your modesty for a minute.'

'Is that right?'

'But only because *you* never believed it either.'

Sachs chuckled.

Rhyme snorted a laugh that he thought would pass for sincere. Then he grew serious. 'I don't know how much I can do. But tell me what happened.'

'It was a week ago Thursday, the twelfth. Art always takes off early every Thursday. He goes for a long run in a state park on the way home. He loves to run.'

Rhyme recalled dozens of times when the two boys, born within months of each other, would race along sidewalks or through the green-yellow fields near their Midwestern homes, grasshoppers fleeing, gnats sticking to their sweaty skin when they stopped for breath. Art always seemed to be in better shape but Lincoln had made his school's varsity track team; his cousin hadn't been interested in trying out.

Rhyme pushed aside the memories and concentrated on what Judy was saying.

'He left work about three-thirty and went for his run, then came home about seven, seven-thirty. He didn't seem any different, wasn't acting odd. He took a shower. We had dinner. But the next day the police came to the house, two from New York and a New Jersey trooper. They asked him questions and looked through the car. They found some blood, I don't know . . .' Her voice conveyed traces of the shock she would have felt on that difficult morning. 'They searched the house and took away some things. And then they came back and arrested him. For murder.' She had trouble saying the word.

'What was he supposed to have done exactly?' Sachs asked.

'They claimed he killed a woman and stole a rare painting from her.' She scoffed bitterly. 'Stole a painting? What on earth for? And murder? Why, Arthur never hurt a single soul in his life. He isn't capable of it.'

'The blood that was found? Have they run a DNA test?'

'Well, yes, they did. And it seemed to match the victim. But those tests can be wrong, can't they?'

'Sometimes,' Rhyme said, thinking, Very, very rarely.

'Or the real killer could have planted the blood.'

'This painting,' Sachs asked, 'did Arthur have any particular interest in it?'

Judy played with thick black and white plastic bracelets on her left wrist. 'The thing is, yes, he used to own one by the same artist. He liked it. But he had to sell it when he lost his job.'

'Where was the painting found?'

'It wasn't.'

'But how did they know it was taken?'

'Somebody, a witness, said they saw a man carrying it from the woman's apartment to the car around the time she was killed. Oh, it's all just a terrible mix-up. Coincidences . . .

That's what it has to be, just a weird series of coincidences.'
Her voice cracked.

'Did he know her?'

'At first Art said he didn't but then, well, he thought they might've met. At an art gallery he goes to sometimes. But he said he never talked to her that he can remember.' Her eyes now took in the whiteboard containing the schematic of the plan to capture Logan in England.

Rhyme was remembering other times he and Arthur had spent together.

Race you to that tree . . . No, you wimp . . . the maple way over there. Touch the trunk! On three. One . . . two . . . go!

You didn't say three!

'There's more, isn't there, Judy? Tell us.' Sachs had seen something in the woman's eyes, Rhyme supposed.

'I'm just upset. For the kids too. It's a nightmare for them. The neighbors're treating us like terrorists.'

'I'm sorry to push but it's important for us to know all the facts. Please.'

The blush had returned and she was gripping her knees. Rhyme and Sachs had a friend who worked as an agent for the California Bureau of Investigation, Kathryn Dance. She was a kinesics, or body language, expert. Rhyme considered such skills secondary to forensic science but he'd come to respect Dance and had learned something about her specialty. He now could see easily that Judy Rhyme was a fountain of stress.

'Go on,' Sachs encouraged.

'It's just that the police found some other evidence – well, it wasn't really evidence. Not like clues. But . . . it made them think maybe Art and the woman were seeing each other.'

Sachs asked, 'What's your opinion of that?'

'I don't think he was.'

Rhyme noted the softened verb. Not as adamant a denial as with the murder and theft. She desperately wanted the answer to be no, though she'd probably come to the same conclusion Rhyme just had: that the woman's being his lover worked in Arthur's favor. You were more likely to rob a stranger than someone you were sleeping with. Still, as a wife and mother, Judy was crying out for one particular answer.

Then she glanced up, less cautious now about looking at Rhyme, the contraption he sat in and the other devices that defined his life. 'Whatever else was going on, he did *not* kill that woman. He couldn't have. I *know* it in my soul . . . Is there anything you can do?'

Rhyme and Sachs shared a look. He said, 'I'm sorry, Judy, we're in the midst of a big case right now. We're real close to catching a very dangerous killer. I can't drop that.'

'I wouldn't want you to. But, just *something*. I don't know what else to do.' Her lip was trembling.

He said, 'We'll make some calls, find out what we can. I can't give you information you couldn't otherwise get through your lawyer but I'll tell you honestly what I think about the D.A.'s chance of success.'

'Oh, thank you, Lincoln.'

'Who's his lawyer?'

She gave them the name and phone number. A high-profile, and -priced, criminal defense attorney Rhyme knew. But he'd be a man with a lot on his plate and more experience with financial than violent crimes.

Sachs asked about the prosecutor.

'Bernhard Grossman. I can get you his number.'

'That's all right,' Sachs said. 'I have it. I've worked with him before. He's reasonable. I assume he offered your husband a plea bargain?'

'He did, and our lawyer wanted to take it. But Art refused. He keeps saying this is just a mistake, it'll all get straightened out. But that doesn't always happen, does it? Even if people are innocent they go to jail sometimes, don't they?'

They do, yes, Rhyme thought, then said, 'We'll make a few phone calls.'

She rose. 'I can't tell you how sorry I am that we let things slide. Inexcusable.' Surprising him, Judy Rhyme strode directly to the wheelchair and bent down, brushing her cheek against his. Rhyme smelled nervous sweat and two distinct scents, perhaps deodorant and hair spray. No perfume. She didn't seem the perfume type. 'Thank you, Lincoln.' She walked to the door and paused. To them both she said, 'Whatever else you find, about that woman and Arthur, it's all right. All I care about is that he doesn't go to jail.'

'I'll do what I can. We'll give you a call if we find something concrete.'

Sachs saw her out.

When she returned Rhyme said, 'Let's check with the lawyers first.'

'I'm sorry, Rhyme.' He frowned, and she added, 'I just mean, it's got to be hard on *you*.'

'How's that?'

'Thinking a close relative got busted for murder.'

Rhyme shrugged, one of the few gestures he could manage. 'Ted Bundy was somebody's son. Maybe a cousin too.'

'But still.' Sachs lifted the receiver. Eventually she tracked down the defense lawyer, got his answering service and left a message. Rhyme wondered which hole of which golf course he was on at that moment.

She then got in touch with the assistant district attorney, Grossman, who wasn't enjoying the day of rest but was in his office downtown. He'd never connected the last name of the perp to the criminalist. 'Hey, I'm sorry, Lincoln,' he said sincerely. 'But I have to say, it's a good case. I'm not blowing smoke. I'd tell you if there were gaps. But there aren't. A jury's going to nail him. If you can talk him into a plea, you'd be doing him a huge favor. I could probably go down to twelve solid.'

Twelve years, with no parole. It would kill Arthur, Rhyme reflected.

'Appreciate that,' Sachs said.

The A.D.A. added that he had a complicated trial starting tomorrow so he couldn't spend any more time talking to them now. He'd call later in the week, if they liked.

He did, however, give them the name of the lead detective in the case, Bobby LaGrange.

'I know him,' she said, dialing him at home too. She got his voice mail but when she tried his cell he answered immediately.

'LaGrange.'

The hiss of wind and the sound of slapping water explained what the detective was up to on this clear-sky, warm day.

Sachs identified herself.

'Oh, sure. Howya doin', Amelia? I'm waiting for a call from a snitch. We've got something going down in Red Hook anytime now.'

So, not on his fishing boat.

'I may have to hang up fast.'

'Understood. You're on speaker.'

'Detective, this is Lincoln Rhyme.'

A hesitation. 'Oh. Yeah.' A call from Lincoln Rhyme got people's full attention pretty fast.

Rhyme explained about his cousin.

'Wait . . . "Rhyme." You know, I thought it was a funny name. I mean, unusual. But I never put it together. And he never said anything about you. Not in any of the interviews. Your cousin. Man, I'm sorry.'

'Detective, I don't want to interfere with the case. But I said I'd call and find out what the story is. It's gone to the A.D.A., I know. Just talked to him.'

'I gotta say the collar was righteous. I've run homicides for five years and short of somebody from Patrol witnessing a gang clip, this was the cleanest wrap I've seen.'

'What's the story? Art's wife only gave me the bones.'

In the stiff voice that cops fall into when recounting details of a crime – stripped of emotion: 'Your cousin left work early. He went to the apartment of a woman named Alice Sanderson, down in the Village. She'd gotten off work early too. We aren't sure how long he was there but sometime around six she was knifed to death and a painting was stolen.'

'Rare, I understand?'

'Yeah. But not like Van Gogh.'

'Who was the artist?'

'Somebody named Prescott. Oh, and we found some direct-mail things, flyers, you know, that a couple of galleries'd sent your cousin about Prescott. That didn't look so good.'

'Tell me more about May twelfth,' Rhyme said.

'At about six a witness heard screams and a few minutes later saw a man carrying a painting out to a light blue Mercedes parked on the street. It left the scene fast. The wit only got the first three letters on the tag – couldn't tell the state but we ran everything in the metro area. Narrowed the list down and interviewed the owners. One was your cousin. My partner and me went out to Jersey to talk to him, had a trooper with us, for protocol, you know. We saw what looked like blood on the back door and in the backseat. A bloody washcloth was under the seat. It matched a set of linens in the vic's apartment.'

'And DNA was positive?'

'Her blood, yeah.'

'The witness identified him in a lineup?'

'Naw, was anonymous. Called from a pay phone and wouldn't give their name. Didn't want to get involved. But we didn't need any wits. Crime Scene had a field day. They lifted a shoeprint from the vic's entryway – same kind of shoe your cousin wore – and got some good trace.'

'Class evidence?'

'Yeah, class. Traces of shave cream, snack food chips, lawn fertilizer from his garage. Exactly matched what was at the vic's apartment.'

No, it didn't *match*, Rhyme reflected. Evidence falls into several categories. 'Individuating' evidence is unique to a single source, like DNA and fingerprints. 'Class' evidence shares certain characteristics with similar materials but they don't necessarily come from the same source. Carpet fibers, for instance. A DNA test of blood at a crime scene can definitely 'match' the criminal's blood. But a comparison of carpet fiber at a scene can only be 'associated with' fibers found in the suspect's house, allowing the jury to infer he was at the scene.

'What was your take on whether or not he knew her?' Sachs asked.

'He claimed he didn't, but we found two notes she'd written. One at her office and one at home. One was "Art – drinks." The other just said "Arthur." Nothing else. Oh, and we found his name in her phonebook.'

'His number?' Rhyme was frowning.

'No. Prepaid mobile. No record.'

'So you figure they were more than friends?'

'Crossed our minds. Why else only give her a prepaid number and not his home or office?' He gave a laugh. 'Apparently she didn't care. You'd be surprised what people accept without asking questions.'

Not that surprised, Rhyme thought.

'And the phone?'

'Toast. Never found it.'

'And you think he killed her because she was pressuring him to leave the wife?'

'That's what the prosecutor'll argue. Something like that.'

Rhyme compared what he knew of his cousin, whom he hadn't seen in more than a decade, against this information; he could neither confirm nor deny the allegation.

Sachs asked, 'Anybody else have a motive?'

'Nope. Family and friends said she dated some, but real casual. No terrible breakups. I was even wondering if the wife did it – Judy – but she was accounted for at the time.'

'Did Arthur have any alibi?'

'None. Claims he went for a run but nobody could confirm seeing him. Clinton State Park. Big place. Pretty deserted.'

'I'm curious,' Sachs said, 'what his demeanor was during interrogation?'

LaGrange laughed. 'Funny you bring that up – the weirdest part of the whole case. He looked like he was dazed. Just blown away by seeing us there. I've collared a lot of people in my day, some of 'em pros. Connected guys, I mean. And he was, hands down, the best at playing the innocent-me game. Great actor. You remember that about him, Detective Rhyme?'

The criminalist didn't reply. 'What happened to the painting?'

A pause. 'That's the other thing. Never recovered. Wasn't in his house or garage, but the crime-scene folks found dirt in the backseat of the car and his garage. It matched the dirt in the state park where he went jogging every night near his house. We figured he buried it somewhere.'

'One question, Detective,' Rhyme said.

A pause at the other end of the line, during which a voice spoke indecipherable words and the wind howled again. 'Go on.'

'Can I see the file?'

'The file?' Not really a question. Just stalling to consider. 'It's a solid case. We ran it by the book.'

Sachs said, 'We don't doubt that for a minute. The thing is, though, we understand he's rejected a plea.'

'Oh. You want to talk him into one? Yeah, I get it. That's the best thing for him. Well, all I have is copies, the A.D.A.'s got everything else and the evidence. But I can get you the reports. A day or two okay?'

Rhyme shook his head. Sachs said to the detective, 'If you could talk to Records and okay it I'll go down there and pick up the file myself.'

The wind filled the speakers again, then stopped abruptly. LaGrange must have moved into shelter.

'Yeah, okay, I'll give 'em a call now.'

'Thanks.'

'No problem. Good luck.'

After they'd disconnected, Rhyme gave a brief smile. 'That was a nice touch. The plea bargain thing.'

'You gotta know your audience,' Sachs said and slung her purse over her shoulder, heading out of the door.

Chapter
FOUR

Sachs returned from her trip to Police Plaza a lot faster than
if she'd taken public transportation – or paid attention to stop-
lights. Rhyme knew that she'd slapped a flashing light on the
dash of her car, a 1969 Camaro SS, which she'd had painted
fiery red a few years ago to match Rhyme's preferred shade for
his wheelchairs. Like a teenager, she still looked for any excuse
to fire up the massive engine and sear rubber off the tires.

'Copied everything,' she said, carrying a thick folder into
the room. She winced as she set it on an examining table.

'You okay?'

Amelia Sachs suffered from arthritis, she had all her life, and
popped glucosamine, chondroitin and Advil or Naprosyn like jelly
beans but she rarely acknowledged the condition, fearful that the
brass might stick her behind a desk on a medical if they found
out. Even when she and Rhyme were alone she downplayed the
pain. But today she admitted, 'Some twinges're worse than others.'

'Want to sit?'

A shake of the head.

'So. What've we got?'

'Report, evidence inventory and copies of the photos. No
videos. They're with the D.A.'

'Let's get everything on the board. I want to see the primary crime scene and Arthur's house.'

She walked to a whiteboard – one of the dozens in the lab – and transcribed information as Rhyme watched.

ALICE SANDERSON HOMICIDE

ALICE SANDERSON APARTMENT:

- Traces of Edge Advanced Gel shave cream, with aloe
- Crumbs determined to be Pringles, fat free, barbecue flavor
- Chicago Cutlery knife (MW)
- TruGro fertilizer
- Shoeprint of Alton EZ-Walk, size 10 1⁄2
- Fleck of latex glove
- References to 'Art' and a prepaid mobile number in phonebook, now no longer active. Untraceable (Possible affair?)
- Two notes: 'Art – drinks' (office) and 'Arthur' (home)
- Wit saw light blue Mercedes, partial tag NLP

ARTHUR RHYME'S CAR:

- 2004 light blue Mercedes sedan, C Class, New Jersey license NLP 745, registered to Arthur Rhyme

- Blood on door, rear floor (DNA match to victim's)
- Bloody washcloth, matching set found in victim's apartment (DNA match to victim's)
- Dirt with composition similar to dirt in Clinton State Park

ARTHUR RHYME'S HOUSE:

- Edge Advanced Gel with aloe, shave cream, associated with that from primary crime scene
- Pringles barbecue-flavored chips, fat free
- TruGro fertilizer (garage)
- Spade containing dirt similar to dirt in Clinton State Park (garage)
- Chicago Cutlery knives, same type as the MW
- Alton EZ-Walk shoes, size 10 1⁄2, tread similar to that at primary crime scene

- Direct-mail flyers from Wilcox Gallery, Boston, and Anderson-Billings Fine Arts, Carmel, about shows of Harvey Prescott paintings
- Box of Safe-Hand latex gloves, rubber composition similar to that of fleck found at primary crime scene (garage)

'Man, it's pretty incriminating, Rhyme,' Sachs said, standing back, hand on her hips.

'And using a prepaid cell? And references to "Art." But no address where he lives or works. That *would* suggest an affair . . . Any other details?'

'No. Other than the pictures.'

'Tape them up,' he instructed while scanning the chart, regretting that he hadn't searched the scene himself – vicariously, that was, with Amelia Sachs, as they often did, via a microphone/headset or a high-definition video camera she wore. It seemed like a competent CS job, but not stellar. No photos of the nonscene rooms. And the knife . . . He saw the picture of the bloody weapon, beneath the bed. An officer was lifting a flap of dust ruffle to get a good shot. Was it invisible with the cloth down (which meant the perp might logically have missed it in the frenzy of the moment) or was it visible, suggesting it had been left intentionally as planted evidence?

He studied the picture of packing material on the floor, apparently what the Prescott painting had been wrapped in.

'Something's wrong,' he whispered.

Sachs, standing at the whiteboard, glanced his way.

'The painting,' Rhyme continued.

'What about it?'

'LaGrange suggested two motives. One, Arthur stole the Prescott as a cover because he wanted to kill Alice to get her out of his life.'

'Right.'

'But,' Rhyme went on, 'to make a homicide seem incidental to a burglary, a smart perp wouldn't steal the one thing in the apartment that could be connected to him. Remember, Art had owned a Prescott. And he had direct-mail flyers about them.'

'Sure, Rhyme, that doesn't make any sense.'

'And say he really *did* want the painting and couldn't afford it. Well, it's a hell of a lot safer and easier to break in and cart it off during the day when the owner's at work, rather than murder them for it.' His cousin's demeanor too, though not high in Rhyme's arsenal when he assessed guilt or innocence, nagged. 'Maybe he wasn't playing innocent. Maybe he *was* innocent . . . Pretty incriminating, you said? No. *Too* incriminating.'

He thought to himself: Let's just postulate that he didn't do it. If not, then the consequences were significant. Because this wasn't simply a case of mistaken identity; the evidence matched too closely – including a conclusive connection between her blood and his car. No, if Art was innocent, then someone had gone to a great deal of trouble to set him up.

'I'm thinking he was framed.'

'Why?'

'Motive?' he muttered. 'We don't care at this point. The relevant question now is *how*. We answer that, it can point us to *who*. We might get *why* along the way, but that's not our priority. So we start with a premise that someone else, Mr X, murdered Alice Sanderson and stole the painting, then framed Arthur. Now, Sachs, how could he have done it?'

A wince – her arthritis again – and she sat. She thought for several moments, then said, 'Mr X followed Arthur and followed Alice. He saw they had an interest in art, put them together at the gallery and found their identities.'

'Mr X knows she owns a Prescott. He wants one but can't afford it.'

'Right.' Sachs nodded at the evidence chart. 'Then he breaks into Arthur's house, sees that he owns Pringles, Edge shave cream, TruGro fertilizer, and Chicago Cutlery knives. He steals some to plant. He knows what shoes Arthur wears, so he can leave the footprint, and he gets some of the dirt from the state park on Arthur's shovel . . .

'Now, let's think about May twelfth. Somehow Mr X knows that Art always leaves work early on Thursdays and goes running in a deserted park – so he doesn't have an alibi. He goes to the vic's apartment, kills her, steals the painting and calls from a pay phone to report the screams and seeing a man take the painting to a car that looks a lot like Arthur's, with a partial tag number. Then he heads out to Arthur's house in New Jersey and leaves the traces of blood, the dirt, the washcloth, the shovel.'

The phone rang. The caller was Arthur's defense lawyer. The man sounded harried as he reiterated everything that the assistant district attorney had explained. He offered nothing that might help them and, in fact, tried several times to talk them into pressuring Arthur to take a plea. 'They'll nail him up,' the man said. 'Do him a favor. I'll get him fifteen years.'

'That'll destroy him,' Rhyme said.

'It won't destroy him as much as a life sentence.'

Rhyme said a chilly good-bye and hung up. He stared again at the evidence board.

Then something else occurred to him.

'What is it, Rhyme?' Sachs had noticed that his eyes were rising to the ceiling.

'Think maybe he's done this before?'

'How do you mean?'

'Assuming the goal – the *motive* – was to steal the painting, well, it's not exactly a onetime score. Not like a Renoir you fence for ten million and disappear forever. The whole thing smells like an enterprise. The perp's hit on a smart way to get away with a crime. And he's going to keep at it until somebody stops him.'

'Yeah, good point. So we should look for thefts of other paintings.'

'No. Why should he steal just paintings? It could be anything. But there's one common element.'

Sachs frowned then provided the answer. 'Homicide.'

'Exactly. Since the perp frames somebody else, he has to murder the victims – because they could identify him. Call somebody at Homicide. At home if you need to. We're looking for the same scenario: an underlying crime, maybe a theft, the vic murdered and strong circumstantial evidence.'

'And maybe a DNA link that might've been planted.'

'Good,' he said, excited at the thought they might be on to something here. 'And if he's sticking to his formula, there'll be an anonymous witness who gave nine-one-one some specific identifying information.'

She walked to a desk in the corner of the lab, sat and placed the call.

Rhyme leaned his head back in his wheelchair and observed his partner on the phone. He noticed dried blood in her thumbnail. A mark was just visible above her ear, half hidden by her straight red hair. Sachs did this frequently, scratching her scalp, teasing her nails, damaging herself in small ways – both a habit and an indicator of the stress that drove her.

She was nodding, and her eyes took on a focused gaze, as she wrote. His own heart – though he couldn't feel it directly – had speeded up. She'd learned something significant. Her pen dried up. She tossed it onto the floor and whipped out another as quickly as she drew her pistol in combat shooting competitions.

After ten minutes she hung up.

'Hey, Rhyme, get this.' She sat next to him, in a wicker chair. 'I talked to Flintlock.'

'Ah, good choice.'

Joseph Flintick, his nickname intentionally or otherwise a reference to the old-time gun, had been a homicide detective when Rhyme was a rookie. The testy old guy was familiar with nearly every murder that had been committed in New York City – and many nearby – during his lengthy tenure. At an age when he should have been visiting his grandchildren, Flintlock was working Sundays. Rhyme wasn't surprised.

'I laid it all out for him and he came back with two cases that might fit our profile right off the top of his head. One was a theft of rare coins, worth about fifty G. The other a rape.'

'Rape?' This added a deeper, and much more disturbing, element to the case.

'Yep. In both of them an anonymous witness called to report the crime and gave some information that was instrumental in ID'ing the perp – like the wit calling about your cousin's car.'

'Both male callers, of course.'

'Right. And the city offered a reward but neither of them came forward.'

'What about the evidence?'

'Flintlock didn't remember it too clearly. But he did say that the trace and circumstantial connections were right on. Just what happened to your cousin – five or six types of associated class evidence at the scene and in the perps' houses. And in both cases the victims' blood was found on a rag or article of clothing in the suspects' residence.'

'And I'll bet there weren't any fluid matches in the rape case.' Most rapists are convicted because they leave behind traces of the Three S's – semen, saliva or sweat.

'Nope. None.'

'And the anonymous callers – did they leave *partial* license plate numbers?'

She glanced at her notes. 'Yeah, how did you know?'

'Because our perp needed to buy some time. If he left the whole tag number, the cops'd head right to the fall guy's house and he wouldn't have time to plant the evidence there.' The killer had thought out everything. 'And the suspects denied everything?'

'Yep. Totally. Rolled the dice with the jury and lost.'

'No, no, no, this's all too coincidental,' Rhyme muttered. 'I want to see—'

'I asked somebody to pull the files from the disposed cases archives.'

He laughed. One step ahead of him, as often. He recalled when they'd first met, years ago, Sachs a disillusioned patrol officer ready to give up her career in policing, Rhyme ready to give up more than that. How far they'd both come since then.

Rhyme spoke into his stalk mike. 'Command, call Sellitto.' He was excited now. He could feel that unique buzz – the thrill of a budding hunt. Answer the damn phone, he thought angrily, and for once he wasn't thinking about England.

'Hey, Linc.' Sellitto's Brooklyn-inflected voice filled the room. 'What's—'

'Listen. There's a problem.'

'I'm kinda busy here.' Rhyme's former partner, Lieutenant Detective Lon Sellitto, hadn't been in the best of moods himself lately. A big task force case he'd worked on had just tanked. Vladimir Dienko, the thug of a Russian mob boss from Brighton Beach, had been indicted last year for racketeering and murder. Rhyme had assisted with some of the forensics. To everyone's shock the case against Dienko and three of his associates had been dismissed, just last Friday, after witnesses had stonewalled or vanished. Sellitto and agents from the Bureau had been working all weekend, trying to track down new witnesses and informants.

'I'll make it fast.' He explained what he and Sachs found about his cousin and the rape and coin-theft cases.

'*Two* other cases? Friggin' weird. What's your cousin say?'

'Haven't talked to him yet. But he denies everything. I want to have this looked into.'

'"Looked into." The fuck's that mean?'

'I don't think Arthur did it.'

'He's your cousin. Of *course* you don't think he did it. But whatta you have concrete?'

'Nothing yet. That's why I want your help. I need some people.'

'I'm up to my ass in the Dienko situation in Brighton Beach. Which, I gotta say, you'd be helping on except, no, you're too busy sipping fucking tea with the Brits.'

'This could be big, Lon. Two other cases that stink of planted evidence? I'll bet there are more. I know how much you love your clichés, Lon. Doesn't "getting away with murder" move you?'

'You can throw all the clauses you want at me, Linc, I'm busy.'

'That's a phrase, Lon. A clause has a subject and predicate.'

'What-fucking-ever. I'm trying to salvage the Russian Connection. Nobody at City Hall or the Federal Building's happy about what happened.'

'And they have my deepest sympathies. Get reassigned.'

'It's homicide. I'm Major Cases.'

The Major Cases Division of the NYPD didn't investigate murders, but Sellitto's excuse brought a cynical laugh to Rhyme's lips. 'You work homicides when you *want* to work them. When the hell have department protocols meant anything to you?'

'Tell you what I'll do,' the detective mumbled. 'There's a captain working today. Downtown. Joe Malloy. Know him?'

'No.'

'I do,' said Sachs. 'He's solid.'

'Hey, Amelia. You surviving the cold front today?'

Sachs laughed. Rhyme snarled, 'Funny, Lon. Who the hell's this guy?'

'Smart. No compromises. And no sense of humor. You'll appreciate that.'

'Lots of comedians round here today,' Rhyme muttered.

'He's good. And a crusader. His wife was killed in a B and E five, six years ago.'

Sachs winced. 'I didn't know that.'

'Yeah, and he gives the job a hundred fifty percent. Word is he's headed for a corner office upstairs some day. Or maybe even next door.'

Meaning City Hall.

Sellitto continued, 'Give him a call and see if he can get a few people released for you.'

'I want *you* released.'

'Not gonna happen, Linc. I'm running a fucking stakeout. It's a nightmare. But keep me posted and—'

'Gotta go, Lon . . . Command, disconnect phone.'

'You hung up on him,' Sachs pointed out.

Rhyme grunted and placed a call to Malloy. He'd be furious if he got voice mail.

But the man answered on the second ring. Another senior cop working on Sunday. Well, Rhyme had done so pretty often too and had the divorce to show for it.

'Malloy here.'

Rhyme identified himself.

A brief hesitation. Then: 'Well, Lincoln . . . I don't believe we've ever met. But I know about you, of course.'

'I'm here with one of your detectives, Amelia Sachs. We're on speaker, Joe.'

'Detective Sachs, afternoon,' said the stiff voice. 'What can I do for you two?' Rhyme explained about the case and how he believed Arthur was being set up.

'Your cousin? I'm sorry to hear that.' But he didn't sound

particularly sorry. Malloy would be worried that Rhyme wanted him to intervene and get the charges reduced. Uh-oh, appearance of impropriety at the most innocent. Or, at the worst, an internal-affairs investigation and the media. Weighed against that, of course, was the bad form of not helping out a man who provided invaluable service to the NYPD. *And* one who was a gimp. Political correctness thrives in city government.

But Rhyme's request, of course, was more complicated. He added, 'I think there's a good chance that this same perp committed other crimes.' He gave the details of the coin theft and the rape.

So not one but three individuals had been wrongly arrested by Malloy's NYPD. Which meant that three crimes had in fact gone unsolved and the real perp was still at large. This portended a major public-relations nightmare.

'Well, it's pretty odd. Irregular, you know. I understand your loyalty to your cousin—'

'I have a loyalty to the truth, Joe,' Rhyme said, not caring if he sounded pompous.

'Well . . .'

'I just need a couple of officers assigned to us. To look over the evidence in these cases again. Maybe do some legwork.'

'Oh, I see . . . Well, sorry, Lincoln. We just don't have the resources. Not for something like this. But I'll bring it up tomorrow with the deputy commissioner.'

'Actually, think we could call him now?'

Another hesitation. 'No. He's got something going on today.'

Brunch. Barbecue. A Sunday-matinee performance of *Young Frankenstein* or *Spamalot*.

'I'll raise the issue tomorrow at the briefing. It's a curious situation. But you won't do anything until you hear from me. Or someone.'

'Of course not.'

They disconnected. Rhyme and Sachs were both silent for a few long seconds.

A curious situation . . .

Rhyme gazed at the whiteboard – on which sat the corpse of an investigation shot dead just as it had lurched to life.

Snapping the quiet, Sachs asked, 'Wonder what Ron's up to.'

'Let's find out, why don't we?' He gave her a genuine – and rare – smile.

She pulled out her phone, hit a speed dial number, then SPEAKER.

A youthful voice crackled, 'Yes, ma'am, Detective.'

Sachs had been after young patrolman Ron Pulaski to call her Amelia for years but usually he couldn't bring himself to do it.

'You're on speaker, Pulaski,' Rhyme warned.

'Yes, sir.'

And the 'sir' bothered Rhyme, but he had no inclination to correct the young man now.

'How are you?' Pulaski asked.

'Does it matter?' Rhyme responded. 'What're you doing? Right now. And is it important?'

'Right now?'

'I think I just asked that.'

'Washing dishes. Jenny and I just had Sunday brunch with my brother and his wife. We went to the farmers' market with the kids. It's a blast. Do you and Detective Sachs ever get to – ?'

'You're at home then. And not doing anything.'

'Well. The dishes.'

'Leave 'em. Get over here.' Rhyme, a civilian, had no authority to order anybody in the NYPD, even traffic cops, to do anything.

But Sachs was a detective third-class; while she couldn't order him to help them, she could formally request a shift in assignment. 'We need you, Ron. And we might need you tomorrow too.'

Ron Pulaski worked regularly with Rhyme, Sachs and Sellitto. Rhyme had been amused to learn that his assignments for the quasi-celeb forensic detective elevated the status of the young officer within the department. He was sure that the supervisor would agree to hand over Pulaski for a few days – as long as he didn't call Malloy or anyone else downtown and learn that the case wasn't a case at all.

Pulaski gave Sachs the name of the commander at the precinct house. Then asked, 'Oh, sir? Is Lieutenant Sellitto working on this one? Should I call and coordinate with him?'

'No,' blurted both Rhyme and Sachs.

A brief silence followed, then Pulaski said uncertainly, 'Well, then, I guess I'll be there as soon as I can. Just, can I dry the glasses first? Jenny hates water spots.'

Chapter
FIVE

Sundays are the best.

Because most Sundays I'm free to do what I love.

I collect things.

Everything you can imagine. If it appeals to me and I can get it into my backpack, or into my trunk, I'll collect it. I'm not a pack rat like some people might say. Those rodents leave something in place of what they've taken. Once I find something, it's mine. I never let go. Ever.

Sunday's my favorite day. Because it's the day of rest for the masses, the sixteens who call this amazing city home. Men, women, children, lawyers, artists, cyclists, cooks, thieves, wives and lovers (I collect DVDs too), politicians, joggers and curators . . . It's amazing the number of things that sixteens do for enjoyment.

They roam like happy antelope through the city and the parks of New Jersey and Long Island and upstate New York.

And I'm free to hunt them.

Which is what I'm up to right now, having deflected all the other boring distractions of Sunday: brunch, movies and even an invitation to go play golf. Oh, and worship – always popular with the antelope, provided, of course, that a visit to church is followed by the aforementioned brunch or nine holes of smack-the-ball.

Hunting . . .

Right now I'm thinking of my most recent transaction, the memory tucked away in my mental collection – the transaction with young Alice Sanderson, 3895-0967-7524-3630, who was looking fine, very fine. Until the knife, of course.

Alice 3895 in that nice pink dress, accentuating her breasts, flirting at the hip (I also think of her as 38-26-36, but that's a joke on my part). Pretty enough, perfume the scent of Asian flowers.

My plans for her had only partly to do with the Harvey Prescott painting that she was lucky enough to snatch off the market (or unlucky, as it turned out for her). Once I was sure she'd received the delivery, out would come the duct tape and I'd spend the next few hours with her in the bedroom. But she'd ruined it all. Just as I was coming up behind her she turned and gave that nightmare scream. I had no choice but to slice her neck like tomato skin, grab my beautiful Prescott and sneak out – through the window, so to speak.

No, I can't stop thinking about pretty-enough Alice 3895, in a skimpy pink dress, her skin floral-scented like a tea house. So, bottom line, I need a woman.

Strolling along these sidewalks, glancing at the sixteens through my sunglasses. They, on the other hand, don't really see me. As I intend; I groom myself to be invisible and there's no place like Manhattan to be invisible.

I turn corners, slip along an alleyway, make a purchase – cash, of course – then plunge into a deserted area of the city, formerly industrial, becoming residential and commercial, near SoHo. Quiet here. That's good. I want it peaceful for my transaction with Myra Weinburg, 9834-4452-6740-3418, a sixteen I've had my eye on for a while.

Myra 9834, I know you very well. The data have told me

everything. (Ah, that debate again: data . . . plural or singular? Data *has told* or data *have told*? *Merriam-Webster's* assures us either is correct. By myself, I tend to be purist: data plural. But in public I try hard to treat the word as singular, like most of society, and hope I don't slip up. Language is a river; it goes where it will and if you swim against that current you get noticed. And that, of course, is the last thing in the world I want.)

Now, the data on Myra 9834: She lives on Waverly Place, Greenwich Village, in a building the owner wants to sell as co-op units via an eviction plan. (*I* know this, though the poor tenants don't yet, and judging from incomes and credit histories, most of them are totally screwed.)

The beautiful, exotic, dark-haired Myra 9834 is a graduate of NYU and has worked in New York for several years at an advertising agency. Her mother's still alive, but her father's dead. Hit and run, the John Doe warrant still outstanding after all these years. Police don't pull out the stops for crimes like that.

At the moment Myra 9834 is between boyfriends, and friendships must be problematic because her recent thirty-second birthday was marked with a single order of moo shu pork from Hunan Dynasty on West Fourth (not a bad choice) and a Caymus Conundrum white ($28 from overpriced Village Wines). A subsequent trip to Long Island on Saturday, coinciding with local travel by other family members and acquaintances and a large bill, with copious Brunello, at a Garden City restaurant of which *Newsday* speaks highly, made up for the solitary evening, I imagine.

Myra 9834 sleeps in a Victoria's Secret T, a fact I deduce because she owns five of them in a size too big to wear out in public. She wakes early to the thought of an Entenmann's danish pastry (never low-fat, I'm proud of her for that) and home-brewed Starbucks; she rarely goes to the coffee shops. Which is a shame, since I *do* like to observe in person the antelope I've had my eye on, and Starbucks is among the best places on the veldt to do so. Around eight-twenty she leaves her apartment and heads for work in Midtown – Maple, Reed & Summers advertising, where she's a junior account executive.

Onward and upward. I continue on my way this Sunday, wearing a nondescript baseball cap (they account for 87.3 percent of all men's headgear in the metro area). And, as always, eyes down. If you think a satellite can't record your smiling face from thirty miles up in space, think again; somewhere in a dozen servers around the world there are hundreds of pictures of you taken from on high, and let's hope all you were doing when they snapped the shutter was squinting away the sun while you glanced up at the Goodyear blimp or a cloud shaped like a lamb.

My passion for collecting includes not only these daily facts but the *minds* of the sixteens I'm interested in, and Myra 9834 is no exception. She goes for drinks with friends after work with some frequency and I've noticed that she picks up the tab often, too often, in my opinion. Clearly she's buying their love – right, Dr Phil? Possibly had acne during the *adolescence terrible*; she still sees a dermatologist once in a while, though the bills are low, as if she's just debating dermabrasion (completely unnecessary from what I've seen) or checking to make sure the zits aren't returning like ninjas in the night.

Then, after the three rounds of Cosmopolitans with the gals, or a visit to a fit-and-start health club, it's home to phone calls, the ubiquitous computer and basic, not premium, cable. (I enjoy tracking her viewing habits; her show selections suggest extreme loyalty; she changed networks when *Seinfeld* did, and she blew off two dates to spend the night with Jack Bauer.)

Bedtime follows, and she sometimes enjoys a bit of distraction (buying double-A batteries in bulk tells the tale, her digital camera and iPod being rechargeable).

Of course, those are the data on her weekday life. But today's a glorious Sunday, and Sundays are different. This is when Myra 9834 climbs aboard her beloved, and very expensive, bicycle, and heads out to cruise the streets of her city.

The routes vary. Central Park might figure, as does Riverside Park and Prospect Park in Brooklyn. But whatever the path, Myra 9834 makes one particular stop without fail toward the end of her journey: Hudson's Gourmet Deli on Broadway. And then, food and shower beckoning, she takes the fastest bike route home – which, owing to the madness of downtown traffic, is right past the very spot where I'm standing at the moment.

I'm in front of a courtyard leading to a ground-floor loft, owned by Maury and Stella Griszinski (imagine – buying ten years ago for $278,000). The Griszinskis aren't home, though, because they're enjoying a springtime cruise in Scandinavia. They've stopped the mail and have hired no plant waterers or pet sitters. And there's no alarm system.

No sign of her yet. Hm. Has something intervened? I might be wrong.

But I rarely am.

Five agonizing minutes pass. I pull images of the Harvey Prescott painting out of my mental collection. I enjoy them for a time and tuck them back. I glance around and I resist a salivating urge to go through the fat trash bin here to see what treasures it might hold.

Stay in the shadows . . . Stay off the grid. Especially at times like this. And avoid the windows at all costs. You'd be amazed at the lure of voyeurism and how many people are watching you from the other side of the glass, which, to you, is only a reflection or glare.

Where is she? Where?

If I don't get my transaction soon—

And then, ah, I feel the slam within me as I see her: Myra 9834.

Moving slowly, low gear, beautiful legs pumping away. A $1,020 bike. More than my first car cost.

Ah, the bicycle outfit is tight. My breath is fast. I need her so badly.

A glance up and down the street. Empty, except for the approaching woman, who's now getting close, thirty feet away. Cell phone off but flipped open and up to my ear, Food Emporium bag dangling. I glance at her once. Stepping to the curb, as I carry on an animated and entirely fictitious conversation. I pause to let her pass. Frowning, looking up. Then smiling. 'Myra?'

She slows. Biking outfit so tight. Control it, control it. Act casual.

Nobody in the empty windows facing the street. No traffic.

'Myra Weinburg?'

The squeal of bike brakes. 'Hi.' The greeting and attempted flash of recognition are due solely to the fact that people would rather do almost anything than be embarrassed.

I'm totally in the role of the mature businessman as I walk toward her, telling my invisible friend I'll call back and close the phone.

She replies, 'I'm sorry.' A smiling frown. 'You're . . . ?'

'Mike. I'm the AE from Ogilvy? I think we met at . . . yeah, that's it. The National Foods shoot at David's. We were in the second studio. I came by and met you and – what's his name? Richie. You guys had a better caterer than we did.'

Now a hearty smile. 'Oh, sure.' She remembers David and National Foods and Richie and the photo studio's caterer. But she can't remember me because I was never there. And *nobody* named Mike was there either but she won't focus on that because it happens to be the name of her dead father.

'Good seeing you,' I say, giving her my best how's-this-for-a-coincidence grin. 'You live around here?'

'Village. You?'

A nod to the Griszinskis. 'There.'

'Wow, a loft. Sweet.'

I ask about her job, she asks about mine. Then I wince. 'Better get inside. I just ran out for lemons.' Holding up the citrus prop. 'Got some people over.' My voice fades as a brilliant idea comes to mind. 'Hey, I don't know if you have plans but we're having a late brunch. You want to join us?'

'Oh, thanks, but I'm a mess.'

'Please . . . we were out all day on a Walk for the Cure, my partner and me.' Nice touch, I think. And wholly improvised. 'We're sweatier than you, believe me. This is way casual. It'll be fun. There's a senior AE from Thompson there. And a couple guys from Burston. Cute but straight.' I shrug mournfully. 'And we've got a surprise actor too. I won't tell you who.'

'Well . . .'

'Oh, come on. You look like you need a Cosmo . . . At the photo shoot, didn't we both decide that was our favorite drink?'

Chapter
SIX

The Tombs.

Okay, it wasn't the Tombs any longer, the original one from the 1800s. That building was long gone, but everybody still used the name when describing this place: the Manhattan Detention Center, downtown, in which Arthur Rhyme was now sitting, his heart doing the same despairing *thud, thud, thud* it had regularly since he was arrested.

But whether the place was called the Tombs, the MDC or the Bernard Kerik Center (as it had been temporarily until the former police chief and corrections head went down in flames) to Arthur the place was simply hell.

Absolute hell.

He was in an orange jumpsuit like everyone else but there the similarity with his fellow cons ended. The five-foot-eleven man, 190 pounds, with corporate-clipped brown hair was as different as could be from the other souls awaiting trial here. No, he wasn't big and inked (he'd learned that meant tattooed) or shaved or stupid or black or Latino. The sort of criminal Arthur would resemble – businessmen charged with white-collar crimes – didn't reside in the Tombs until trial; they were out on bond. Whatever sins they'd committed, the infractions didn't warrant the two-million-dollar bail set for Arthur.

So the Tombs had been his home since May 13 – the longest and most wrenchingly difficult period of his life.

And bewildering.

Arthur might have met the woman he was supposed to have killed, but he couldn't even recall her. Yes, he'd been to that gallery in SoHo, where apparently she'd browsed too, though he couldn't remember talking to her. And, yes, he loved the work of Harvey Prescott and had been sick at heart when he'd had to sell his canvas after losing his job. But stealing one? Killing someone? Were they fucking mad? Do I *look* like a killer?

It was a hopeless mystery to him, like Fermat's theorem, the mathematical proof that, even after learning the explanation, he still didn't get. Her blood in his car? He was being framed, of course. Even thinking the police might have done it themselves.

After ten days in the Tombs, O.J.'s defense seems a bit less *Twilight Zone*.

Why, why, why? Who was behind this? He thought of the angry letters he'd written when Princeton passed him over. Some were stupid and petty and threatening. Well, there were plenty of unstable people in the academic field. Maybe they wanted revenge for the stink he'd made. And then that student in his class who'd come on to him. He'd told her, no, he didn't want to have an affair. She'd gone ballistic.

Fatal Attraction . . .

The police had checked her out and decided she wasn't behind the killing but how hard had they worked to verify her alibi?

He looked around the large common area now, the dozens of nearby cons – the inside word for prisoners. At first he'd been regarded as a curiosity. His stock seemed to rise when they'd learned he'd been arrested for murder but then it fell at the news that the victim hadn't tried to steal his drugs or cheat on him – two acceptable reasons for killing a woman.

Then when it was clear he was just one of those white guys who'd fucked up, life got ugly.

Jostling, challenges, taking his milk carton – just like in middle school. The sex thing wasn't what people thought. Not here. These were all new arrestees and everybody could keep their dicks in their jumpsuits for a time. But he'd been assured by a number of his new 'friends' that his virginity wouldn't last long once he got to one of the long hauls, like Attica, especially if he earned a quarter-pounder – twenty-five to life.

He'd been punched in the face four times, tripped twice and pinned to the floor by psycho Aquilla Sanchez, who dripped sweat into his face as he screamed in Spanglish until some bored hacks (that is, guards) pulled him off.

Arthur had peed his pants twice and puked a dozen times. He was a worm, scum, not worth fucking.

Until later.

And the way his heart kept thudding, he expected it to pop apart at any moment. As had happened to Henry Rhyme, his father, though the famed professor had died not in an ignoble place like the Tombs, of course, but on an appropriately stately collegiate sidewalk in Hyde Park, Illinois.

How had this happened? A witness and evidence . . . It made no sense.

'Take the plea, Mr Rhyme,' the assistant district attorney had said. 'I'd recommend it.'

His attorney had too. 'I know the ins and outs, Art. It's like I'm reading a fucking GPS map. I can tell you exactly where this is going – and it's not the needle. Albany can't write a death penalty law to save its life. Sorry, bad joke. But you're still looking at twenty-five years. I can get you fifteen. Go for it.'

'But I didn't *do* it.'

'Uh-huh. That doesn't really mean a whole lot to anybody, Arthur.'

'But I *didn't*!'

'Uh-huh.'

'Well, I'm *not* taking a plea. The jury'll understand. They'll see me. They'll know I'm not a killer.'

Silence. Then: 'Fine.' Though it wasn't fine. Clearly he was pissed off, despite the six hundred plus an hour he was racking up – and where the hell was *that* kind of money going to come from? He—

Then suddenly Arthur looked up to see two cons studying him, Latinos. They were regarding him now with no expression whatsoever on their faces. Not friendly, not challenging, not tough. They seemed curious.

As they approached him, he debated whether to get up or to stay put.

Stay.

But look down.

He looked down. One of the men stood in front of him, putting his scuffed running shoes right in Arthur's line of vision.

The other went around to the back.

He was going to die. Arthur Rhyme knew it. Just do it fast and get it fucking over with.

'Yo,' the man behind him said in a high voice.

Arthur looked up at the second, in front. He had blood-shot eyes and a large earring, bad teeth. Arthur couldn't speak.

'Yo,' came the voice again.

Arthur swallowed. Didn't want to but couldn't help himself.

'We talking to you, me an' my friend. You no be civil. Why you a prick?'

'Sorry. I just . . . Hello.'

'Yo. Whatchu do for work, man?' High Voice asked his back.

'I'm . . .' His mind froze. What should I say? 'I'm a scientist.'

Earring Man: 'Fuck. Scientist? Whatchu do, like, make rockets?'

They both laughed.

'No, medical equipment.'

'Like that shit, you know, they say "clear," and electrocute you? Like, *ER*?'

'No, it's complicated.'

Earring Man frowned.

'I didn't mean that,' Arthur said quickly. 'It's not that you couldn't understand it. It's just hard to explain. Quality-control systems for dialysis. And—'

High Voice: 'Make good money, huh? Hear you had a nice suit when you got prossed.'

'I got . . . ?' Oh, *processed*. 'I don't know. I got it at Nordstrom.'

'Nordstrom. The fuck is Nordstrom?'

'A store.'

As Arthur looked back down at Earring Man's feet the con continued, 'I saying, good money? How much you make?'

'I—'

'You going to say you don't know?'

'I—' Yes, he was.

'How much you make?'

'I don't . . . I'd guess about six figures.'

'Fuck.'

Arthur didn't know if this meant the amount was a lot or a little to them.

Then High Voice laughed. 'You got a family?'

'I'm not telling you anything about them.' This was defiant.

'You got a *family*?'

Arthur Rhyme was looking away, at the wall nearby, where a nail protruded from mortar between cinder blocks, meant to hold a sign, he assumed, that had been taken down or stolen years ago. 'Leave me alone. I don't want to talk to you.'

He tried to make his voice forceful. But he sounded like a girl approached by a nerd at a dance.

'We trying to make civil conversation, man.'

He actually said that? *Civil conversation?*

Then he thought, Hell, maybe they *are* just trying to be pleasant. Maybe they could've been friends, watched his back for him. Christ knew he needed all the friends he could get. Could he salvage this? 'I'm sorry. It's just, this's a really weird thing for me. I've never been in any trouble before. I'm just—'

'What you wife do? She a scientist too? She a smart girl?'

'I . . .' The intended words evaporated.

'She got big titties?'

'You fuck her in the ass?'

'Listen up, Science Fuck, here's how it gonna work. You smart wife, she goin' to get some money from the bank. Ten thousand. And she gonna take a drive up to my cousin in the Bronx. An'—'

The tenor voice faded.

A black prisoner, six-two, massive with muscle and fat, his jumpsuit sleeves rolled up, approached the trio. He was gazing at the two Latinos and squinting mean.

'Yo, Chihuahuas. Get the fuck outa here.'

Arthur Rhyme was frozen. He couldn't have moved if someone had started shooting at him, which wouldn't have surprised him, even here in the realm of the magnetometers.

'Fuck you, nigger,' Earring Man said.

'Piece of shit.' From High Voice, drawing a laugh from the black guy, who put an arm around Earring Man and led him away, whispering something to him. The Latino's eyes glazed and he nodded to his buddy, who joined him. The two walked to the far corner of the area, feigning indignity. If Arthur weren't so frightened he would have thought this was amusing – faced-down bullies from his children's school.

The black man stretched and Arthur heard a joint pop. His heart was thudding even harder. A half-formed prayer crossed his mind: for the coronary to take him away now, right now.

'Thanks.'

The black guy said, 'Fuck you. Them two, they pricks. They gotta know the way it is. You unnerstand what I'm saying?'

No, no clue. But Arthur Rhyme said, 'Still. My name's Art.'

'I know the fuck yo' name. Ever'body know ever'thing round here. 'Cept you. You don' know shit.'

But one thing Arthur Rhyme knew, and knew it with certainty: He was dead. And so he said, 'Okay, then tell me who the fuck you are, asshole.'

The huge face turned toward him. Smelling sweat and smoky breath, Arthur thought of his family, his children first and then Judy. His parents, mother first, then father. Then, surprisingly, he thought of his cousin, Lincoln. Recalling a footrace through a hot Illinois field one summer when they were teenagers.

Race you to that oak tree. See it, that one over there. On three. You ready? One . . . two . . . three . . . go!

But the man just turned away and stalked across the hall to another black prisoner. They tapped fists together and Arthur Rhyme was forgotten.

He sat watching their camaraderie, feeling more and more forlorn. Then he closed his eyes and lowered his head. Arthur Rhyme was a scientist. He believed that life advanced via the process of natural selection; divine justice played no role.

But now, sunk in a depression as relentless as winter tides, he couldn't help wondering if some system of retribution, as real and invisible as gravity, existed and was now at work, punishing him for the bad he'd done in his life. Oh, he'd done much good. Raised children, taught them open-minded values and tolerance, been a good companion to his wife, helped her through a cancer incident, contributed to the great body of science that enriched the world.

Yet there was bad too. There always is.

Sitting here in his stinking orange jumpsuit, he struggled to believe that by the right thoughts and vows – and faith in the system he dutifully supported every election day – he could work his way back to the other side of the scale of justice and be reunited with his family and life.

That with the right spirit and intention he could outrun fate through the same breathless effort with which he'd beaten Lincoln in that hot, dusty field, charging all out toward the oak tree.

That maybe he could be saved. It might—

'Move.'

He jumped at the word, though the speaker's voice was soft. Another prisoner, white, shaggy hair, full of tats but light on teeth and twitchy as the drugs leached from his system, had come up behind him. He stared at the bench where Arthur sat, though he could have picked anywhere. His eyes were just plain mean.

And Arthur's momentary hope – in some measurable and scientific system of moral justice – vanished. One word from this small but damaged and dangerous man killed it.

Move . . .

Struggling to hold back tears, Arthur Rhyme moved.

Chapter
SEVEN

The phone rang and Lincoln Rhyme was irritated by the distraction. He was thinking about their Mr X and the mechanics of planting the evidence, if in fact that was what had happened, and wanted no distractions.

But then reality struck; he saw the 44 in the caller ID, the country code that included England. 'Command, answer phone,' he ordered instantly.

Click.

'Yes, Inspector Longhurst?' He'd given up on first names. Relations with Scotland Yard required a certain propriety.

'Detective Rhyme, hello,' she said. 'We have some movement here.'

'Go on,' Rhyme said.

'Danny Krueger heard from one of his former gun-runners. It seems that the reason Richard Logan left London was to collect something in Manchester. We aren't sure what, but we do know that Manchester's got more than its share of black-market weapons dealers.'

'Any idea where he is exactly?'

'Danny's still trying to find out. It would be lovely if we could take him there, rather than wait till London.'

'Is Danny being subtle?' Rhyme remembered from the video-conference a big, tanned, loud South African with a belly and a gold pinkie ring that both jutted outward alarmingly. Rhyme had had a case involving Darfur, and he and Krueger had spent some time talking about the country's tragic conflict.

'Oh, he knows what he's doing. He's subtle when he needs to be. Fierce as a hound when the situation calls for it. He'll get the details if there's any way. We're working with our counterparts in Manchester to get an assault team ready. We'll call you back when we know something more.'

He thanked her and they disconnected.

'We'll get him, Rhyme,' Sachs said, not simply for his benefit. She too had an interest in finding Logan; Sachs herself had nearly died in one of his plots.

Sachs took a call. She listened and said she'd be there in ten minutes. 'The files in those other cases Flintlock mentioned? They're ready. I'll go get them. . . . Oh, and Pam might stop by.'

'What's she up to?'

'Studying with a friend in Manhattan – a *boy*friend.'

'Good for her. Who?'

'Some kid from school. Can't wait to meet him. He's all she talks about. She sure deserves somebody decent in her life. But I just don't want her getting too close too fast. I'll feel better when I've met him and given him the third degree in person.'

Rhyme nodded as Sachs left, but his mind was elsewhere. He was staring at the whiteboard containing the information on the Alice Sanderson case as he ordered the phone to make another call.

'Hello?' a soft male voice answered as a waltz played in the background. Loud.

'Mel. Is that you?'

'Lincoln?'

'What's that goddamn music? Where are you?'

'New England Ballroom Competition,' answered Mel Cooper.

Rhyme sighed. Washing dishes, theater matinees, ballroom dancing. He hated Sundays. 'Well, I need you. I've got a case. It's unique.'

'They're all unique with you, Lincoln.'

'This one's more unique than others, if you'll forgive the grammatical misdemeanor. Can you come in? You mentioned New England. Don't tell me you're in Boston or Maine.'

'Midtown. And I guess I'm free – Gretta and I were just eliminated. Rosie Talbot and Bryan Marshall are going to win. It's all the scandal.' He said this with some significance. 'How soon?'

'Now.'

Cooper chuckled. 'How long will you need me?'

'Maybe a while.'

'As in six o'clock tonight? Or as in Wednesday?'

'Better call your supervisor and tell him you're being reassigned. I hope it won't be longer than Wednesday.'

'I'll have to give him a name. Who's running the investigation? Lon?'

'Let me put it this way: Be a little vague.'

'Well, Lincoln, you *do* remember being a cop, don't you? "Vague" doesn't fly. "Very specific" does.'

'There isn't exactly a lead detective.'

'You're on your own?' His voice was uncertain.

'Not exactly. There's Amelia, there's Ron.'

'That's all?'

'You.'

'I see. Who's the perp?'

'Actually, the perps're already in jail. Two are convicted, one's awaiting trial.'

'And you have your doubts that we got the right parties.'

'Something like that.'

A detective with the NYPD Crime Scene Unit, Mel Cooper specialized in lab work and he was one of the most brilliant officers on the force, as well as one of the most savvy. 'Oh. So you want me to help you find out how my bosses screwed up and arrested the wrong people, then talk them into opening three new and expensive investigations against the real perps, who, by the way, probably won't be real tickled either when they learn that they're not getting off scot-free after all. This is sort of a lose-lose-lose situation, isn't it, Lincoln?'

'Apologize to your girlfriend for me, Mel. Be here soon.'

Sachs was halfway to her crimson Camaro SS when she heard, 'Hey, Amelia!'

She turned to see a pretty teenage girl, with long chestnut hair, streaked with red, and a few tasteful piercings in both ears. She was lugging two canvas bags. Her face, dusted with delicate freckles, was radiant with happiness. 'You're leaving?' she asked Sachs.

'Big case. I'm going downtown. Want a ride?'

'Sure. I'll get the train at City Hall.' Pam climbed into the car.

'How was studying?'

'You know.'

'So where's your friend?' Sachs was looking around.

'You just missed him.'

Stuart Everett was a student at the Manhattan high school Pam was attending. She'd been going out with him for several months. They'd met in class and immediately discovered a mutual love of books and music. They were in the school's Poetry Club, which reassured Sachs; at least he wasn't a biker or a knuckle-dragging jock.

Pam tossed one of her bags, containing schoolbooks, into the backseat and opened the other one. A fuzzy-headed dog looked out.

'Hey, Jackson,' Sachs said, petting his head.

The tiny Havanese grabbed the Milk-Bone the detective offered from an add-on cup holder, whose sole purpose was as a reservoir of dog treats; Sachs's acceleration and cornering habits weren't conducive to keeping liquids contained.

'Stuart couldn't walk you here? What kind of gentleman is that?'

'He's got this soccer game. He's way into sports. Are most guys like that?'

Pulling into traffic, Sachs gave a wry laugh. 'Yup.'

It seemed an odd question from a girl this age, most of whom would know all about boys and sports. But Pam Willoughby wasn't like most girls. When she was very young her father died on a U.N. peacekeeping mission and her unstable mother had flung herself into the political and religious right-wing underground, growing more and more militant. She was now serving a life sentence for murder (she was responsible for the U.N. bombing some years ago in which six people died). Amelia Sachs and Pam had met back then, when the detective had saved the girl from a serial kidnapper. She then disappeared but, by sheer coincidence, Sachs had rescued her again, not long ago.

Liberated from her sociopath family, Pam had been placed with a foster family in Brooklyn – though not before Sachs had checked out the couple like a Secret Service agent planning a presidential visit. Pam enjoyed life with the family. But she and Sachs continued to hang out together and were close. With Pam's foster mother often fully occupied with taking care of five younger children, Sachs took on the role of older sister.

This worked for them both. Sachs had always wanted children. But complications existed. She'd planned on a family with her first serious live-in boyfriend, though he, a fellow cop, proved to be about the worst choice in the world (extortion, assault and eventually prison, for a start). After him she'd been alone until she'd met Lincoln Rhyme and had been with him ever since. Rhyme didn't quite get children, but he was a good man, fair and smart, and could separate his stony professionalism from his home life; a lot of men couldn't.

But starting a family would be difficult at this point in their lives; they had to contend with the dangers and demands of policing and the restless energy they both felt – and the uncertainty about Rhyme's future health. They also had a certain physical barrier to be overcome, though the problem, they'd learned, was Sachs's, not Rhyme's (he was perfectly capable of fathering a family).

So, for now, the relationship with Pam was enough. Sachs enjoyed her role and took it seriously; the girl was lowering her reticence to trust adults. And Rhyme genuinely enjoyed her company. Presently he was helping her outline a book about her experiences in the right-wing underground to be called *Captivity*. Thom had told her that she had a chance of getting on *Oprah*.

Speeding around a taxi, Sachs now said, 'You never answered. How was studying?'

'Great.'

'You set for that test on Thursday?'

'Got it down. No problem.'

Sachs gave a laugh. 'You didn't even crack a book today, did you?'

'Amelia, come on. It was such a neat day! The weather's been sucky all week. We *had* to get outside.'

Sachs's instinct was to remind her of the importance of getting good scores on her finals. Pam was smart, with a high IQ and a voracious appetite for books, but after her bizarre schooling she'd find it tough to get into a good college. The girl, though, looked so happy that Sachs relented. 'So what'd you do?'

'Just walked. All the way up to Harlem, around the re-servoir. Oh, and there was this concert by the boathouse, just a cover band, you know, but they *totally* nailed Coldplay. . . .' Pam thought back. 'Mostly, like, Stuart and I just talked. About nothing. That's the best, you ask me.'

Amelia Sachs couldn't disagree. 'Is he cute?'

'Oh, yeah. Way cute.'

'Have a picture?'

'Amelia! That'd be so uncool.'

'After this case is over, how 'bout we have dinner, the three of us?'

'Yeah? You really want to meet him?'

'Any boy going out with you better know that you've got somebody watching your back. Somebody who carries a gun and handcuffs. Okay, hold on to the dog; I'm in the mood to drive.'

Sachs downshifted hard, pumped the gas and left two exclamation points of rubber on the dull black asphalt.

Chapter
EIGHT

Since Amelia Sachs had begun spending occasional nights and weekends here at Rhyme's, certain changes had occurred around the Victorian town house. When he'd lived here alone, after the accident and before Sachs, the place had been more or less neat – depending on whether or not he'd been firing aides and housekeepers – but 'homey' wasn't a word that described it. Nothing personal had graced the walls – none of the certificates, degrees, commendations and medals he'd received during his celebrated tenure as head of the NYPD crime-scene operation. Nor any pictures of his parents, Teddy and Anne, or his uncle Henry's family.

Sachs hadn't approved. 'It's important,' she lectured, 'your past, your family. You're purging your history, Rhyme.'

He'd never seen her apartment – the place wasn't disabled accessible – but he knew that the rooms were chockablock with evidence of *her* history. He'd seen many of the pictures, of course: Amelia Sachs as a pretty young girl (with freckles that had long since vanished) who didn't smile a lot; as a high school student with mechanics tools in hand; as a college-age daughter flanked on holidays by a grinning cop father and a stern mother; as a magazine and advertising model, her eyes offering the chic frigidity that was au courant (but which Rhyme knew was contempt for the way models were considered mere coat hangers).

Hundreds of other pix too, shot mostly by her father, the man with a quick-draw Kodak.

Sachs had studied Rhyme's bare walls and had gone where the aides – even Thom – did not: the boxes in the basement, scores of cartons containing evidence of Rhyme's prior life, his life in the Before, artifacts hidden away and as unmentioned as first wife to second. Many of these certificates and diplomas and family pictures now filled the walls and mantelpiece.

Including the one he was presently studying – of himself as a lean teenager, in a track uniform, taken after he'd just competed in a varsity meet. It depicted him with unruly hair and a prominent Tom Cruise nose, bending forward with his hands on his knees, having just finished what was probably a mile run. Rhyme was never a sprinter; he liked the lyricism, the elegance of the longer distances. He considered running 'a process.' Sometimes he would not stop running even after crossing the finish line.

His family would have been in the stands. Both father and uncle resided in suburbs of Chicago, though some distance apart. Lincoln's home was to the west, in the flat, balding sprawl that was then still partly farmland, a target of both thoughtless developers and frightening tornados. Henry Rhyme and his family were somewhat immune to both, being on the lakefront in Evanston.

Henry commuted twice a week to teach his advanced physics courses at the University of Chicago, a long, two-train trek through the city's many social divides. His wife, Paula, taught at Northwestern. The couple had three children, Robert, Marie and Arthur, all named after scientists, Oppenheimer and Curie being the most famous. Art was named after Arthur Compton, who in 1942 ran the famed Metallurgic Lab at the

University of Chicago, the cover for the project to create the world's first controlled nuclear chain reaction. All the children had attended good schools. Robert, Northwestern Medical. Marie, UC-Berkeley. Arthur went to M.I.T.

Robert had died years earlier in an industrial accident in Europe. Marie was working in China on environmental issues. As for the Rhyme parents, only one remained of the four: Aunt Paula now lived in an assisted-care facility, amid vivid, coherent memories of sixty years ago, while experiencing the present in bewildering fragments.

Rhyme now continued to stare at the picture of himself. He was unable to look away, recalling the track meet . . . In his college classes Professor Henry Rhyme signified approval with a subtle, raised eyebrow. But on the playing field, he was always leaping to his feet in the bleachers, whistling and bellowing for Lincoln to *push, push, push, you can do it!* Encouraging him over the finish line first (he often was).

Following the meet, Rhyme supposed he'd gone off with Arthur. The boys spent as much time together as they could, filling the sibling gap. Robert and Marie were considerably older than Arthur, and Lincoln was an only child.

So Lincoln and Art adopted each other. Most weekends and every summer the surrogate brothers would go off on their adventures, often in Arthur's Corvette (Uncle Henry, even as a professor, made several times what Rhyme's father did; Teddy was a scientist too, though he was more comfortable out of the spotlight). The boys' outings were typical teenage venture – girls, ball games, movies, arguing, eating burgers and pizza, sneaking beer and explaining the world. And more girls.

Now, sitting in the new TDX wheelchair, Rhyme wondered where exactly he and Arthur had gone after the meet.

Arthur, his surrogate brother . . .

Who never came to see him after his spine was cracked like a piece of defective wood.

Why, Arthur? Tell me why . . .

But these memories were derailed by the ringing doorbell in his town house. Thom veered toward the hallway and a moment later, a slightly built, balding man wearing a tuxedo strode into the room. Mel Cooper shoved his thick glasses up on his thin nose and nodded to Rhyme. 'Afternoon.'

'Formal?' Rhyme asked, glancing at the tux.

'The dance competition. If we'd been finalists, you know I wouldn't have come.' He took off jacket and bow tie, then rolled up the sleeves of the frilly shirt. 'So what do we have, this *unique* case you were telling me about?'

Rhyme filled him in.

'I'm sorry about your cousin, Lincoln. I don't think you ever mentioned him.'

'What do you think of the M.O.?'

'If it's true it's brilliant.' Cooper gazed at the evidence chart of the Alice Sanderson homicide.

'Thoughts?' Rhyme asked.

'Well, half the evidence at your cousin's was in the car or the garage. A lot easier to plant it there than in the house.'

'Exactly what I was thinking.'

The doorbell rang again. A moment later Rhyme heard his aide's footsteps returning solo. Rhyme was wondering if someone had delivered a package. But then his mind jumped: Sunday. A visitor could be in street clothes and running shoes, which would make no sound on the entryway floor.

Of course.

Young Ron Pulaski turned the corner and nodded shyly. He wasn't a rookie any longer, having been a uniformed patrolman for several years. But he looked like a rookie and so, to Rhyme, that's what he was. And probably would always be.

The shoes were indeed quiet Nikes but he was wearing a very loud Hawaiian shirt over blue jeans. His blond hair was stylishly spiked and a scar prominently marked his forehead – a remnant from a nearly fatal attack during his first case with Rhyme and Sachs. The assault was so vicious that he'd suffered a brain injury and nearly quit the force. The young man had decided to fight his way through rehab and stay on the NYPD, inspired largely by Rhyme (a fact he shared only with Sachs, of course, not the criminalist himself; she relayed the news).

He blinked at Cooper's tux and then nodded hello to both men.

'Your dishes spotless, Pulaski? Your flowers watered? Your leftovers tucked away in freezer bags?'

'I left right away, sir.'

The men were going over the case when they heard Sachs's voice from the doorway. 'A costume party.' She was looking at Cooper's tuxedo and Pulaski's brash shirt. To the lab man she said, 'You're looking pretty smart. That's the word for somebody in a tux, right? "Smart"?'

'Sadly, "semifinalist" is the only thing that comes to my mind.'

'Is Gretta taking it well?'

His beautiful Scandinavian girlfriend was, he reported, 'hanging out with her friends and drowning her sorrows with Aquavit. Her homeland's beverage. But, if you ask me, it's undrinkable.'

'How's your mom?'

Cooper lived with his mother, a feisty lady who was a long-term Queensean.

'She's doing well. Out for brunch at the Boat House.'

Sachs also asked about Pulaski's wife and two young children. Then added, 'Thanks for coming in on Sunday.' To Rhyme: 'You did tell him how much we appreciate it, didn't you?'

'I'm sure I did,' he muttered. 'Now, if we could get to

work . . . So what've you got?' He eyed the large brown folder she carried.

'Evidence inventory and photos from the coin theft and rape.'

'Where's the actual P.E.?'

'Archived in the evidence warehouse on Long Island.'

'Well, let's take a look.'

As she had with his cousin's file, Sachs picked up a marker and began writing on another whiteboard.

HOMICIDE/THEFT – MARCH 27

March 27

Crime: Homicide, theft of six boxes of rare coins
COD: Blood loss, shock, due to multiple stab wounds
Location: Bay Ridge, Brooklyn
Victim: Howard Schwartz
Suspect: Randall Pemberton

EVIDENCE LOG FROM VICTIM'S HOUSE:

- Grease
- Flecks of dried hair spray
- Polyester fibers
- Wool fibers
- Shoeprint of size 9 1/2 Bass walker

Witness reported man in tan-colored vest fleeing to black Honda Accord

EVIDENCE INVENTORY FROM SUSPECT'S HOUSE AND CAR:

- Grease on umbrella on patio, matching what was found at victim's house
- Pair of 9 1/2 Bass walkers
- Clairol hair spray, matching fleck found at scene
- Knife/Trace embedded in handle:
- Dust matching nothing at either crime scene or suspect's house
- Flecks of old cardboard
- Knife/Trace on blade:
- Victim's blood. Positive match
- Suspect owned 2004 black Honda Accord
- One coin identified as coming from the collection of victim

- A Culberton Outdoor Company vest, tan. Polyester fiber found at the scene matches
- A wool blanket in the car. The wool fiber at the scene matches

Note: Prior to trial, investigators canvassed major coin dealers in metro area or on the Internet. No one attempted to fence the particular stolen coins.

'So if our perp stole the coins he's kept them. And "dust matching nothing at either crime scene" . . . That means it probably came from the perp's house. But what the hell kind of dust is it? Didn't they analyze it?' Rhyme shook his head. 'Okay, I want to see the pictures. Where are they?'

'I'm getting them. Hold on.'

Sachs found some tape and mounted printouts on a third whiteboard. Rhyme maneuvered closer and squinted up at the dozens of photos of the crime scenes. The coin collector's living space was tidy, the perp's less so. The kitchen, where the coin and knife had been found, under the sink, was cluttered, the table covered with dirty dishes and food cartons. On the table was a pile of mail, most of it apparently junk.

'Next one,' he announced. 'Let's go.' He tried to keep his voice from tipping into impatience.

HOMICIDE/RAPE – APRIL 18

April 18

Crime: Homicide, rape
COD: Strangulation
Location: Brooklyn
Victim: Rita Moscone
Suspect: Joseph Knightly

EVIDENCE FROM SUSPECT'S HOUSE:

- Durex condoms containing lubricant identical to that found on victim
- Coil of rope, fibers matching those found at crime scene

EVIDENCE FROM VICTIM'S APARTMENT:

- Traces of Colgate-Palmolive Softsoap hand soap
- Condom lubricant
- Rope fibers
- Dust adhering to duct tape, matching no samplars in apartment
- Duct tape, American Adhesive brand
- Fleck of latex
- Wool/polyester fibers, black
- Tobacco on victim (see note below)
- Two-foot length of same rope, victim's blood on it, along with two-inch strand of BASF B35 nylon 6, most likely source a doll's hair
- Colgate-Palmolive Softsoap
- Duct tape, American Adhesive brand
- Latex gloves, matching the fleck found at the scene
- Men's socks, wool-polyester blend, matching fiber found at scene. Another identical pair in the garage, containing traces of victim's blood
- Tobacco from Tareyton cigarettes (see note below)

'The supposed perp *saved* his socks with blood on them and took them home with him? Bullshit. Planted evidence.' Rhyme read through the material again. 'What's the "note below"?'

Sachs found it: a few paragraphs to the prosecutor from the lead detective about possible problems with this case. She showed it to Rhyme.

Stan:

A couple potential glitches the defense might try to bring up:

—Possible contamination issue: Similar tobacco flakes found at crime scene and perp's home, but neither the victim or the suspect smoked. Arresting officers and crime scene staff questioned, but assured lead detective that they were not the source.

– Found no DNA linking material, other than victim's blood.

– Suspect has an alibi, eyewitness who placed him outside his own house – about four miles away, at around the time of the crime. Alibi witness is a homeless man who suspect gives money to occasionally.

'Had an alibi,' Sachs pointed out. 'Who the jury didn't believe. Obviously.'

'What do you think, Mel?' Rhyme asked.

'I'm sticking to my story. It all lines up too conveniently.'

Pulaski nodded. 'The hair spray, the soap, the fibers, the lubricant . . . everything.'

Cooper continued, 'They're obvious choices for planted evidence. And look at the DNA – it's not the *suspect*'s at the crime scene; it's the *victim*'s at the suspect's home. That's a lot easier to plant.'

Rhyme continued to examine the charts, scanning slowly.

Sachs added, 'But not all of the evidence matches. The old cardboard and the dust – those aren't related to either scene.'

Rhyme said, 'And the tobacco. Neither the vic nor the fall guy smoked. That means those might be from the real perp.'

Pulaski asked, 'What about the doll's hair? Does that mean he has kids?'

Rhyme ordered, 'Tape up *those* pictures. Let's take a look.'

Like the other scenes, the victim's apartment and the perp's house and garage had been well documented by the Crime Scene Unit. Rhyme scanned the photos. 'No dolls. No toys at all. Maybe the real killer has children or some contact with toys. And he smokes or has some access to cigarettes or tobacco. Good. Oh, we're on to something here.

'Let's do a profile chart. We've been calling him "Mr X." But we need something else for our perp . . . What's today's date?'

'May twenty-second,' Pulaski said.

'Okay. Unknown subject Five Twenty-Two. Sachs, if you would . . .' He nodded toward a whiteboard. 'Let's start the profile.'

UNSUB 522 PROFILE	NONPLANTED EVIDENCE
• Male	• Dust
• Possibly smokes or lives/works with someone who does, or near source of tobacco	• Old cardboard
	• Hair from doll, BASF B35 nylon 6
• Has children or lives/works near them or near source of toys	• Tobacco from Tareyton cigarettes
• Interest in art, coins?	

Well, it was a start, he reflected, if a pretty lame one.

'Should we call Lon and Malloy?' Sachs asked.

Rhyme scoffed. 'And tell them *what*?' He nodded at the chart. 'I think our little clandestine operation'd get closed down pretty fast.'

'You mean, this isn't official?' Pulaski asked.

'Welcome to the underground,' Sachs said.

The young officer digested this information.

'That's why we're in disguise,' Cooper added, pointing at the black satin strip on his tuxedo trousers. He might have winked but Rhyme couldn't tell through his dense glasses. 'What're our next steps?'

'Sachs, call Crime Scene in Queens. We can't get our hands on the evidence in my cousin's case. With the trial coming up, all the P.E.'ll be in custody at the prosecutor's office. But see if anybody at the warehouse can send us the evidence from these earlier crimes – the rape and the coin theft. I want the dust, cardboard and rope. And, Pulaski, you go down to the Big Building. I want you to look through the files of every murder in the past six months.'

'*Every* murder?'

'The mayor's cleaned up the city, didn't you hear? Be thankful we're not in Detroit or Washington. Flintlock thought of these *two* cases. I'll bet there are others. Look for an underlying crime, maybe theft, maybe rape, ending in homicide. Clear class evidence and an anonymous call right after the crime. Oh, and a suspect who swears he's innocent.'

'Okay, sir.'

'And us?' Mel Cooper asked.

'We wait,' Rhyme muttered, as if the word were an obscenity.

Chapter
NINE

A wonderful transaction.

I'm satisfied now. Walking down the street, happy, content. Flipping through the images I've just slipped into my collection. Images of Myra 9834. The visual ones are stored in my memory. The digital tape recorder has the others.

Walking down the street, watching sixteens around me.

I see them streaming down sidewalks. In cars, buses, taxis, trucks.

I see them through windows, oblivious to me as I study them.

Sixteens . . . Ah, I'm not the only one who refers to human beings like this, of course. Not at all. It's a common short-hand in the industry. But I'm probably the only one who *prefers* to think of people as sixteens, who feels comforted by the thought.

A sixteen-digit number is far more precise and efficient than a name. Names make me edgy. I don't like that. It's not good for me, not good for anybody, when I'm edgy. Names . . . ah, *terrible*. For instance, the surnames Jones and Brown each account for roughly .6 percent of the population of the United States. Moore is .3 percent, and as for everyone's favorite,

Smith – a whopping 1 percent. Nearly 3,000,000 of them in the country. (And given names, if you're interested: John? Nope. It comes in number two – 3.2 percent. James is the winner at 3.3 percent.)

So think of the implications: I hear someone say, 'James Smith.' Well, *which* James Smith does he mean when there are hundreds of thousands? And those are just the living ones. Tally up all the James Smiths in history.

Oh, my God.

Drives me crazy just to think about.

Edgy . . .

And the consequences of mistakes can be serious. Say, it's 1938 Berlin. Is Herr Wilhelm Frankel the Jewish Wilhelm Frankel or the gentile one? Made a big difference and, whatever else you feel about them, those brown-shirted boys were absolute geniuses at tracking identities (and they used computers to do it!).

Names lead to mistakes. Mistakes are noise. Noise is contamination. Contamination must be eliminated.

There could be dozens of Alice Sandersons, but only one Alice 3895, who sacrificed her life that I might own an American Family painting by dear Mr Prescott.

Myra Weinburgs? Ah, not many, surely. But more than one. Yet only Myra 9834 sacrificed herself so that I might be satisfied.

I'll bet there are plenty of DeLeon Williams, but only 6832-5794-8891-0923 is going to jail forever for raping and killing her so that I might remain free to do it all over again.

I'm en route to his house at the moment (technically his girlfriend's, I've learned), carrying enough evidence to make sure the poor man is convicted of the rape/murder in about one hour of deliberation.

DeLeon 6832 . . .

I've already called 911, a transaction in which I reported

an old beige Dodge – his model of car – speeding away from the scene, a man inside, a black man. 'I could see his hands! They were all bloody! Oh, get somebody there now! The screaming was terrible.'

What a perfect suspect you'll be, DeLeon 6832. About half of the perpetrators commit rape under the influence of alcohol or drugs (he drinks beer in moderation now, but was in AA several years ago). The majority of rape victims know their assailant (DeLeon 6832 had once done some carpentry for the grocery store where the late Myra 9834 regularly shopped so it was logical to assume that they knew each other, though they probably didn't).

Most rapists are thirty or under (the exact age of DeLeon 6832, as it turns out). Unlike drug dealers and users, they don't have many prior arrests except for domestic abuse – and my boy has a conviction for assaulting a girlfriend; how perfect is *that*? Most rapists are from the lower social classes and economically disadvantaged (he's been out of work for months).

And now, ladies and gentlemen of the jury, please note that two days prior to the rape the defendant bought a box of Trojan-Enz condoms, just like the two found near the victim's body. (As for the two actually used – my own – they're long gone, of course. That DNA stuff is very dangerous, especially now that New York is collecting samples from all felonies, not just rapes. And in Britain you'll soon get swabbed when you get a citation because your dog messes the sidewalk or you make a dicey U-turn.)

There's another fact that the police might take into account if they do their homework. DeLeon 6832 was a combat vet who'd served in Iraq, and there was some question about what happened to his .45-caliber sidearm when he left the service. He had none to turn in. It had been 'lost' in combat.

But curiously he bought .45-caliber ammunition a few years ago.

If the police learn this, which they easily can, they might conclude that their suspect is armed. And digging a bit deeper, they'll find that he was treated at a Veterans Administration hospital – for post-traumatic stress syndrome.

An unstable, armed suspect?

What police officer *wouldn't* be inclined to shoot first?

Let's hope. I'm not always completely confident about the sixteens I pick. You never know about unexpected alibis. Or idiotic juries. Maybe DeLeon 6832'll end today in a body bag. Why not? Don't I deserve a *little* good luck in compensation for the edginess God gave me? It's not always an easy life, you know.

It should take about a half hour or so on foot to get to his house here in Brooklyn. Still warmly satisfied from my transaction with Myra 9834, I'm enjoying the walk. The backpack rides heavy on my spine. Not only does it contain the evidence to plant and the shoe that left DeLeon 6832's telltale footprint, but it's filled with some treasures I've found prowling the streets today. In my pocket is, sadly, only a small trophy from Myra 9834, a portion of her fingernail. I'd like something more personal but deaths in Manhattan are a big deal, and missing parts draw a lot of attention.

I pick up my pace a bit, enjoying the triplet beat of the backpack. Enjoying the clear spring Sunday and the memories of my transaction with Myra 9834.

Enjoying the complete comfort of knowing that, though I am probably the most dangerous person in the city of New York, I am also invulnerable, virtually invisible to all the sixteens who would do me harm.

The light caught his attention.

A flash from the street.

Red.

Another flash. Blue.

The phone sagged in DeLeon Williams's hand. He was calling a friend, trying to find the man he used to work for, the man who skipped town after his carpentry business went under and left only debt behind, including more than $4,000 owed to his most dependable employee, DeLeon Williams.

'Leon,' the guy on the other end of the line was saying, 'I myself don't know where the prick is. He left *me* holding—'

'Call you back.'

Click.

The big man's palms were sweating as he glanced through the curtain that he and Janeece had just put up Saturday (Williams feeling bad, bad, bad that she'd had to pay for them – oh, he hated being unemployed). He noticed that the flashes were from the grille lights of two unmarked police cars. A couple of detectives climbed out, unbuttoning their coats, and not because the spring day was so warm. The cars sped off to block the intersections.

They looked around cautiously, then – destroying the last hope that this was some strange coincidence – walked to Williams's beige Dodge, noted the tag, glanced inside. One spoke into his radio.

Williams's lids lowered in despair as a disgusted sigh eased from his lungs.

She was at it again.

She . . .

Last year Williams had been involved with a woman who was not only sexy but smart and kind. Or so it had seemed at first. Not long after they started going out seriously, though, she'd turned into a raging witch. Moody, jealous, vindictive. Unstable . . . He was with her about four months and they were the worst of his life. And he'd spent much of that time protecting her own children from their mother.

His good deeds, in fact, had landed him in jail. One evening Leticia had swung a fist at her daughter for not scrubbing a pot clean enough. Williams instinctively grabbed the woman's arm, while the sobbing girl fled. He'd calmed her mother down and the matter seemed settled. But several hours later he had been sitting on the porch debating how he could get the children away from her, perhaps back to their father, when the police arrived and he was arrested.

Leticia had pressed assault charges, displaying the arm bruised by his restraint. Williams was appalled. He explained what had happened but the officers had no choice but to arrest him. The case went to trial, but Williams wouldn't let the daughter take the stand in his defense, though the girl wanted to. He was found guilty of misdemeanor assault, the sentence community service.

But during the trial he'd testified to Leticia's cruelty. The prosecutor believed him and gave the woman's name to the Department of Social Services. A social worker showed up at her house to investigate the welfare of the children and they were removed and placed in the custody of their father.

Leticia began harassing Williams. It had persisted for a long time but then she'd disappeared, months ago, and Williams was just thinking recently that he was safe. . . .

But now this. He knew she was behind it.

Jesus, our Lord, how much can a man put up with?

He looked again. No! The detectives had their guns out!

A wave of horror zipped through him. Had she actually hurt one of her kids and claimed that he'd done it? He wouldn't be surprised.

Williams's hands shook and he cried big tears, which streamed down his broad face. He felt the same panic that had slammed him in the desert war when he'd turned to his buddy just in time to see the grinning Alabaman turned into a red mass of nothing, thanks to an Iraqi's rocket-propelled grenade. Until that moment Williams had been more or less fine. Been shot at, spattered with sand from bullets, passed out from the heat. But seeing Jason turn into a *thing* had affected him fundamentally. The post-traumatic stress syndrome he'd wrestled with since was now kicking into high gear.

Utter, helpless fear.

'No, no, no, no.' Gasping, struggling to breathe. He'd stopped taking his meds months ago, believing he was better.

Now, watching the detectives fan out around the house, DeLeon Williams thought blindly: Get the hell out, run!

He had to distance himself. To show that Janeece had no connection to him, to save her and her son – two people he truly loved – he'd vanish. The man slipped the chain on the front door, the deadbolt too, and ran upstairs for a bag, tossed into it whatever he thought of. Nothing made sense: shave cream but no razors, underwear but no shirts, shoes but no socks.

And he took one other thing from the closet.

His military pistol, a Colt .45. The weapon was unloaded – he wouldn't think of shooting anyone – but he could use it to bluff his way past the police, or hijack a car if he had to.

All he could think was: Run! Go!

Williams took a last look at the picture of Janeece and him together, with her son, on a trip to Six Flags. He started to cry again, then wiped his eyes, slung the bag over his shoulder and, kneading the grip of the heavy pistol, started down the stairs.

Chapter
TEN

'The forward sniper's in position?'

Bo Haumann, former drill sergeant and now head of the city's Emergency Service Unit – NYPD's SWAT team – gestured at a building that provided a perfect shooting location, covering the tiny backyard of the detached house where DeLeon Williams was living.

'Yes, sir,' an officer standing nearby said. 'And Johnny's got the back covered.'

'Good.'

A graying man, crew cut and tough as leather, Haumann ordered the two ESU takedown teams into position. 'And stay out of sight.'

Haumann had been in his own backyard not far from here, coaxing last year's charcoal to ignite, when a call came in about a rape/murder and a solid lead to the suspect. He turned over the incendiary mission to his son, donned his gear and sped out, thanking the good Lord that he hadn't popped that first beer. Haumann would drive after he'd had a couple of brews, but he never fired a weapon within eight hours of imbibing.

And there was now a chance, on this fine Sunday, that they would see some gunplay.

His radio crackled and through the headset earpiece he heard, 'S and S One to Base, K.' A Search and Surveillance team was across the street, along with the second sniper.

'Base. Go ahead, K.'

'Getting some thermals. Somebody could be inside. No audible.'

Could be, Haumann thought, irritated. He'd seen the budget for the equipment. It ought to be able to say for sure if somebody was inside – if not report their goddamn shoe size and whether they'd flossed that morning.

'Check again.'

After what seemed like forever, he heard, 'S and S One. Okay, we've got only one person inside. And a visual through a window. It's definitely DeLeon Williams, from the DMV pic you passed out, K.'

'Good. Out.'

Haumann called the two tactical teams, which were moving into position around the house now, remaining nearly invisible. 'Now, we didn't have much time for a briefing. But listen up. This perp is a rapist and a killer. We want him alive but he's too dangerous to let get away. If he makes any hostile gesture, you're green-lighted.'

'B leader. Roger that. Be advised, we're in position. Alley and streets to the north are covered and back door, K.'

'A leader to Base. Roger the green light. We're in position on front door, and covering all streets to the south and east.'

'Snipers,' Haumann radioed. 'You copy the green light?'

'Roger.' They added that they were locked and loaded. (The phrase was a pet peeve of Haumann's, since it was unique to the old M-1 army rifle, with which you had to *lock* the bolt back and *load* a clip of bullets through the top; you didn't have to lock a modern rifle to load it. But now wasn't the time for lectures.)

Haumann unsnapped the thong on his Glock and slipped

into the alley behind the house, where he was joined by yet more officers, whose plans on this idyllic spring Sunday, like his, had changed so fast and dramatically.

At that moment a voice clattered into his earpiece, 'S and S Two to Base. I think we've got something.'

On his knees DeLeon Williams carefully looked through a crack in the door – an actual crack in the wood that he'd been meaning to fix – and could see that the officers were no longer there.

No, he corrected himself, they're no longer *visible*. Big difference. He saw a glint of metal or glass in the bushes. Maybe from one of those weird elves or deer lawn ornaments the neighbor collected.

Or it might be a cop with a gun.

Lugging the bag, he crawled to the back of the house. Another peek. This time, risking a look through the window, struggling hard to control the panic.

The backyard and the alley beyond were empty.

But once again he corrected: *seemed* to be empty.

He felt another shiver of PTSD panic and an urge to race out the door, pull the gun and charge down the alley, threatening anybody he saw, screaming for them to stand back.

Impulsively, his mind whirling, he reached for the knob.

No . . .

Be smart.

He sat back, head against the wall, working to slow his breathing.

After a moment he calmed and decided to try something else. In the basement was a window that led into the tiny side yard. Across eight feet of anemic grass a similar window opened into his neighbor's basement. The Wongs were away for the weekend – he was watering their plants for them – and Williams figured he could sneak inside, then upstairs and through their back door. If he was lucky the police wouldn't be covering the side yard. Then he'd take the alley up to the main street and jog to the subway.

The plan wasn't great but it gave him more of a chance than just waiting here. Tears again. And panic.

Stop it, soldier. Come on.

He rose and staggered down the stairs into the basement.

Just get the hell out. The cops'd be at the front door at any minute, kicking it in.

He unlatched the window and climbed up and out. Starting to crawl toward the Wongs' basement window, he glanced to his right. He froze.

Oh, Jesus Lord . . .

Police, a male and a female detective, holding guns in their right hands, were crouching in the narrow side yard. They weren't looking his way, but staring out, toward the back door and the alley.

The panic again slammed hard. He'd pull out the Colt and threaten them. Make them sit down, cuff themselves and throw away their radios. He hated to do it; that would be a *real* crime. But he didn't have any choice. They were obviously convinced he'd done something terrible. Yes, he'd get their guns and flee. Maybe they had an unmarked car nearby. He'd take their keys.

Was somebody covering them, somebody he couldn't see? A sniper maybe?

Well, he'd just have to take that chance.

He quietly set the bag down and began to reach for the gun.

Which was when the woman detective turned his way. Williams gasped. I'm dead, he thought.

Janeece, I love you. . . .

But the woman glanced at a piece of paper and then squinted as she looked him over. 'DeLeon Williams?'

His voice gurgled. 'I—' He nodded, shoulders falling. He

could only stare at her pretty face, her red hair in a ponytail, her cold eyes.

She held up the badge that was hanging around her neck. 'We're police officers. How'd you get out of your house?' Then she noted the window and nodded. 'Mr Williams, we're in the middle of an operation here. Could you go back inside? You'll be safer there.'

'I—' Panic was shattering his voice. 'I—'

'Now,' she said insistently. 'We'll be with you as soon as everything's resolved. Be quiet. Don't try to leave again. Please.'

'Sure. I . . . Sure.'

He left the bag and started to ease through the window.

She said into her radio, 'This's Sachs. I'd expand the perimeter, Bo. He's going to be real cautious.'

What the hell was going on? Williams didn't waste time speculating. He awkwardly climbed back into the basement and walked upstairs. Once there he headed straight into the bathroom. He lifted the lid off the back of the toilet and dropped the gun in. He walked to the window, going to peek out once more. But then paused and ran back to the toilet just in time to be painfully sick.

A curious thing to say, given this fine day – and given what I've been up to with Myra 9834 – but I miss being in the office.

First, I enjoy working, always have. And I enjoy the atmosphere, the camaraderie with the sixteens around you, almost like a family.

Then there's the feeling of being productive. Being involved in fast-paced New York business. ('Cutting edge' one hears, and *that*'s something I do hate, the corporate-speak – a phrase that is itself corporate-speak. No, the great leaders – FDR, Truman, Caesar, Hitler – didn't need to wrap themselves in the cloak of simple-minded rhetoric.)

Most important, of course, is how my job helps me with my hobby. No, it's more than that. It's vital.

My particular situation is good, very good. I can usually get away when I want to. With some juggling of commitments I can find time during the week to pursue my passion. And given who I am in public – my professional face, you could say – it would be very unlikely for someone to suspect that I'm a very different person at heart. To put it mildly.

I'm often at work on weekends too, and that's one of my favorite times – if, of course, I'm not engaging in a transaction with a beautiful girl like Myra 9834 or acquiring a painting or comic books or coins or a rare piece of china. Even when there are few other sixteens present at the office, on a holiday, Saturday or Sunday, the halls hum with the white noise of wheels moving society slowly forward – into a bold new world.

Ah, here's an antiques store. I pause to look into the window. There are some pictures and souvenir plates, cups and posters that appeal to me. Sadly I won't be able to return here to shop because it's too close to DeLeon 6832's house. The odds of anyone making a connection between me and the 'rapist' are quite minimal, but . . . why take chances? (I only shop in stores or scavenge. eBay is fun to look at, but buying something online? You'd have to be mad.) For the time being cash is still good. But soon it'll be tagged, like everything else. RFIDs in the bills. It's already done in some countries. The bank will know which $20 bill was dispensed to you from which ATM or bank. And they'll know you spent it on coke or a bra for your mistress or as a down payment to a hit man. We should go back to gold, I sometimes think.

Off. The. Grid.

Ah, poor DeLeon 6832. I know his face, from the driver's license picture, a benign gaze at the civil-servant camera. I can imagine his expression when the police knock on his door and display the warrant for his arrest on rape and murder charges. I can see too the horrified look he'll give to his girl-friend, Janeece 9810, and her ten-year-old son if they're home when it happens. Wonder if he's a crier.

I'm three blocks away. And—

Ah, wait . . . Here's something unusual.

Two new Crown Victorias parked on this tree-filled side street. Statistically it's unlikely that this sort of car, in such pristine shape, would be seen in this neighborhood. Two identical cars are particularly unlikely, and factor in that they're parked in tandem, with no flecks of leaves or pollen, unlike the others. They've arrived recently.

And, yes, a casual look inside, normal passerby curiosity, reveals that they're police cars.

Not predicted procedure for a domestic dispute or break-in. Yes, statistically those infractions occur pretty frequently in this part of Brooklyn, but rarely, the data show, at this time of day – before the six-packs appear. And you'd probably never see hidden unmarkeds, only blue-and-white squad cars in full view. Let's think. They're three blocks away from DeLeon 6832 . . . Have to consider this. It wouldn't be inconceivable for their commander to tell the officers, 'He's a rapist. He's dangerous. We're going to go in in ten minutes. Park the car three blocks away and get back here. Pronto.'

I casually glance down the closest alley. Okay, getting worse. Parked there in the shade is an NYPD ESU truck. Emergency Service. They often back up police arrests of people like DeLeon 6832. But how did they get here so soon? I dialed 911 only a half hour ago. (That's always a risk but if you call too long after a transaction, the cops might wonder why you were only now reporting screams or that you'd seen a suspicious man earlier.)

Now, there are two explanations for the police's presence. The most logical is that after my anonymous call they did a database search of every beige Dodge over five years old in the city (1,357 of them as of yesterday) and that somehow they lucked out with this one. They're convinced, even without the evidence I was going to plant in his garage, that DeLeon 6832 is the rapist and murderer of Myra 9834 and they're arresting him right now, or lying in wait for him to return.

The other explanation is far more troubling. The police have decided that he's being set up. And they're lying in wait for *me*.

I'm sweating now. This is not good this is not good not good . . .

But don't panic. Your treasures are safe, your Closet is safe. Relax.

Still, whatever's happened I *have* to find out. If the police presence here is just a perverse coincidence, having nothing to do with DeLeon 6832 or with me, then I'll plant the evidence and get the hell back to my Closet.

But if they've found out about me they could find out about the others. Randall 6794 and Rita 2907 and Arthur 3480 . . .

Cap down a little more over the eyes — the sunglasses pushed high on my nose – I change course completely, circling well around the house, moving through alleys and gardens and backyards. Keeping the three-block perimeter, which they helpfully established as my safety zone by parking the Crown Vic beacons there.

This takes me in a semicircle to a grassy embankment leading up to the highway. Climbing up it, I'm able to see the tiny backyards and porches of the houses on DeLeon 6832's block. I begin to count dwellings to find his.

But I don't need to. I see clearly a police officer on the roof of a two-story house behind the alley from his place. He has a rifle. A sniper! There's another, with a pair of binoculars too. And several more, in suits or street clothes, crouching in bushes right next to the structure.

Then two cops are pointing in my direction. I see that yet

another officer was on the top of the house across the street. He's pointing my way too. And since I'm not six feet three, 230 pounds, with skin dark as ebony, they *aren't* waiting for DeLeon 6832. They've been waiting for *me*.

My hands are beginning to shake. Imagine if I'd blundered right into the middle of that, with the evidence in my backpack.

A dozen other officers are running to their cars or jogging fast in my direction. Running like wolves. I turn and scrabble up the embankment, breathing hard, panicked. I'm not even to the top when I hear the first of the sirens.

No, no!

My treasures, my Closet . . .

The highway, four lanes total, is crowded, which is good because the sixteens have to drive slowly. I can dodge pretty well, even with my head down; I'm sure nobody gets a good look at my face. Then I vault the barrier and stumble down the other embankment. My collecting, and other activities, keep me in good shape and soon I'm sprinting fast toward the closest subway station. I pause only once, to pull on cotton gloves and rip from my backpack the plastic bag containing the evidence I was going to plant, then shove it into a trash can. I can't be caught with it. I *can't*. A half block closer to the subway, I dodge into an alley behind a restaurant. I turn my reversible jacket inside out, swap hats and emerge again, my backpack now stuffed into a shopping bag.

Finally, I'm at the subway station, and – thank you – I can feel the musty tunnel breath preceding a train as it approaches. Then the thunder of the bulky car, the squeal of metal on metal.

But before I get to the turnstile I pause. The shock is now gone, but it's been replaced by the edgy. I understand I can't leave just yet.

The significance of the problem crashes down on me. They

might not know my identity but they've figured out what I was doing.

Which means they want to take something away from me. My treasures, my Closet . . . everything.

And that, of course, is unacceptable.

Making sure I stay clear of the CCTV camera, I casually walk back up the stairs, digging in my bag, as I leave the subway station.

'Where?' Rhyme's voice filled Amelia Sachs's earphone. 'Where the hell is he?'

'He spotted us, took off.'

'You're sure it was him?'

'Pretty sure. Surveillance saw somebody a few blocks away. Looks like he spotted some of the detectives' cars and changed his route. We saw him watching us, and he ran. We've got teams after him.'

She was in DeLeon Williams's front yard with Pulaski, Bo Haumann and a half dozen other ESU officers. Some Crime Scene Unit techs and uniformed patrolmen were searching the escape route for evidence and canvassing for witnesses.

'Any sign he has a car?'

'Don't know. He was on foot when we saw him.'

'Christ. Well, let me know when you find something.'

'I'll—'

Click.

She grimaced at Pulaski, who was holding his Handi Talkie up to his ear, listening to the pursuit. Haumann was monitoring it too. The progress, from what she could hear, didn't seem fruitful. Nobody on the highway had seen him or was willing to admit it, if they had. Sachs turned to the house and saw a very concerned, and very confused, DeLeon Williams looking out through a curtained window.

Saving the man from being yet another fall guy of 522 had involved both happenstance and good police work.

And they had Ron Pulaski to thank for it. The young officer in the brash Hawaiian shirt had done what Rhyme had requested: immediately gone to One Police Plaza and started looking for other cases that matched 522's modus operandi. He found none but as he was talking to a Homicide detective the unit got a report from Central about an anonymous phone call. A man had heard screams from a loft near SoHo and seen a black man fleeing in an old beige Dodge. A patrolman had responded and found that a young woman, Myra Weinburg, had been raped and murdered.

Pulaski was struck by the anonymous call, echoing the earlier cases, and immediately called Rhyme. The criminalist figured that if 522 was in fact behind the crime he was probably sticking to his plan: he would plant evidence blaming a fall guy and they needed to find which of the more than 1,300 older beige Dodges was the one 522 might pick. Sure, maybe the man wasn't 522 but even if not, they had the chance to collar a rapist and killer.

At Rhyme's instruction, Mel Cooper cross-matched Department of Motor Vehicle records with criminal records and came up with seven African-American men who had convictions for crimes more serious than traffic violations. One, though, was the most likely: an assault charge against a woman. DeLeon Williams was a perfect choice as a fall guy.

Happenstance and police work.

To authorize a tactical takedown, a lieutenant or higher was required. Captain Joe Malloy still had no clue about the clandestine 522 operation, so Rhyme called Sellitto, who grumbled but agreed to call Bo Haumann and authorize an ESU op.

Amelia Sachs had joined Pulaski and the team at Williams's house, where they'd learned from Search and Surveillance that only Williams was inside, not 522. There, they deployed to take the killer when he arrived to plant the evidence. The plan was tricky, improvised on the fly – and obviously hadn't worked, though they'd saved an innocent man from being arrested for rape and murder and perhaps had discovered some good evidence to lead to the perp.

'Anything?' she asked Haumann, who'd been conferring with some of his officers.

'Nope.'

Then his radio clattered again and Sachs heard the loud transmission. 'Unit One, we're on the other side of the highway. Looks like he's rabbited clean. He must've made it to the subway.'

'Shit,' she muttered.

Haumann grimaced but said nothing.

The officer continued, 'But we've followed the route he probably took. It's possible he ditched some evidence in a trash can on the way.'

'That's something,' she said. 'Where?' She jotted the address the officer recited. 'Tell them to secure the area. I'll be there in ten.' Sachs then walked up the steps and knocked on the door. DeLeon Williams answered, and she said, 'Sorry I haven't had a chance to explain. A man we were trying to catch was headed to your house.'

'Mine?'

'We think so. But he got away.' She explained about Myra Weinburg.

'Oh, no – she's dead?'

'I'm afraid so.'

'I'm sorry, real sorry.'

'Did you know her?'

'No, never heard of her.'

'We think the perp might've been trying to blame you for the crime.'

'Me? Why?'

'We have no idea. After we investigate a little more we may want to interview you.'

'Sure thing.' He gave her his home and mobile numbers. Then frowned. 'Can I ask? You seem pretty certain I didn't do it. How'd you know I was innocent?'

'Your car and garage. Officers searched them and didn't find any evidence from the murder scene. The killer, we're pretty sure, was going to plant some things there to implicate you. Of course, if we'd gotten here *after* he'd done that, you'd've had a problem.'

Sachs added, 'Oh, one more thing, Mr Williams?'

'What's that, Detective?'

'Just some trivia you might be interested in. Do you know owning an unregistered handgun in New York City is a very serious crime?'

'I think I heard that somewhere.'

'And some more trivia is that there's an amnesty program at your local precinct. No questions asked if you turn in a weapon . . . Okay, you take care. Enjoy the rest of your weekend.'

'I'll try.'

Chapter
ELEVEN

I'm watching the policewoman as she searches the trash can where I dumped the evidence. I was dismayed at first but then I realized I shouldn't have been. If They were smart enough to figure out about me, They're smart enough to find the trash.

I doubt They got a good look at me but I'm being very careful. Of course, I'm not at the scene itself; I'm in a restaurant across the street, forcing down a hamburger and sipping water. The police have this outfit called the 'Anti-crime' detail, which has always struck me as absurd. As if other details are pro-crime. Anti-crime officers wear street clothes and they circulate at crime scenes to find witnesses and, occasionally, even the perps, who have returned. Most criminals do so because they're stupid or behave irrationally. But I'm here for two specific reasons. First, because I've realized I have a problem. I can't live with it so I need a solution. And you can't solve a problem without knowledge. I've already learned a few things.

For instance, I know some of the people who are after me. Like this redheaded policewoman in a white plastic jumpsuit concentrating on the crime scene the way I concentrate on my data.

I see her step out of the area, surrounded by yellow tape, with several bags. She sets these in gray plastic boxes and strips off the white suit. Despite the lingering horror from the disaster of this afternoon, I feel that twinge inside as I see her tight jeans, the satisfaction from my transaction with Myra 9834 earlier today wearing off.

As the police head back to their cars she makes a phone call.

I pay the bill and walk nonchalantly out the door, acting like any other patron on this fine late-afternoon Sunday.

Off. The. Grid.

Oh, the second reason I'm here?

Very simple. To protect my treasures, to protect my life, which means doing whatever's necessary to make Them go away.

'What'd Five Twenty-Two leave in that trash can?' Rhyme was speaking into the hands-free phone.

'There's not much. We're sure it's his stuff, though. Bloody paper towel and some wet blood in plastic bags – so he could leave some in Williams' car or garage. I've already sent a sample to the lab for a preliminary DNA match. Computer printout of the vic's picture. Roll of duct tape – Home Depot house brand. And a running shoe. It looked new.'

'Just one?'

'Yep. The right.'

'Maybe he stole it from Williams' place to leave a print at the scene. Anybody get a look at him?'

'A sniper and two guys from the S and S team. But he wasn't very close. Probably white or light-skinned ethnic, medium build. Tan cap and sunglasses, backpack. No age, no hair color.'

'That's it?'

'Yep.'

'Well, get the evidence here stat. Then I want you to walk the grid at the Weinburg rape scene. They're preserving it till you get there.'

'I've got another lead, Rhyme.'

'You do? What's that?'

'We found a Post-it note stuck to the bottom of the plastic bag with the evidence in it. Five Twenty-Two wanted to ditch the bag; I'm not sure he wanted to pitch out the note.'

'What is it?'

'A room number of a residence hotel, Upper East Side, Manhattan. I want to check it out.'

'You think it's Five Twenty-Two's?'

'No, I called the front desk and they say the tenant's been in the room all day. Somebody named Robert Jorgensen.'

'Well, we need the rape scene searched, Sachs.'

'Send Ron. He can handle it.'

'I'd rather you ran it.'

'I really think we need to see if there's any connection between this Jorgensen and Five Twenty-Two. And fast.'

He couldn't dispute her point. Besides, both of them had ridden Pulaski hard in teaching him how to walk the grid – Rhyme's coined expression for searching a crime scene, a reference to looking over the area according to the grid pattern, the most comprehensive way of discovering evidence.

Rhyme, feeling both like a boss and a parent, knew that the kid would have to run his first homicide scene solo sooner or later. 'All right,' he grumbled. 'Let's hope this Post-it lead pays off.' He couldn't help adding, 'And isn't a complete waste of time.'

She laughed. 'Don't we always hope that, Rhyme?'

'And tell Pulaski not to screw up.'

They disconnected and Rhyme told Cooper the evidence was on its way.

Staring at the evidence charts, he muttered, 'He got away.'

He ordered Thom to put the sparse description of 522 on the whiteboard.

Probably white or light-skinned . . .

How helpful is *that*?

Amelia Sachs was in the front seat of her parked Camaro, the door open. Late-afternoon spring air was wafting into the car, which smelled of old leather and oil. She was jotting notes for her crime-scene report. She always did this as soon as possible after searching a scene. It was amazing what one could forget in a short period of time. Colors changed, left became right, doors and windows moved from one wall to another or vanished altogether.

She paused, distracted once again by the odd facts of the case. How had the killer managed to come so close to blaming an innocent man for an appalling rape and murder? She'd never run into a perp like this; planting evidence to mislead the police wasn't unusual but this guy was a genius at pointing them in the wrong direction.

The street where she'd parked was two blocks away from the trash-can crime scene, shadowed and deserted.

Motion caught her eye. Thinking of 522, she felt a throb of uneasiness. She glanced up and in the rearview mirror saw somebody walking her way. She squinted, studying him carefully, though the man seemed harmless: a clean-cut businessman. He was carrying a take-out bag in one hand and talking on his cell phone, a smile on his face. A typical resident out to get Chinese or Mexican for dinner.

Sachs returned to her notes.

Finally she was finished and tucked them into her briefcase. But then something struck her as strange. The man on the sidewalk should have passed the Camaro by now. But he hadn't. Had he gone into one of the buildings? She turned to the sidewalk where he'd been.

No!

She was staring at the take-out bag, sitting on the sidewalk to the left and behind the car. It was just a prop!

Her hand went for her Glock. But before she could draw, the right side door was ripped open and she was staring into the face of the killer, eyes narrowed, lifting a pistol toward her face.

The doorbell rang and a moment later Rhyme heard yet another distinctive footfall. Heavy ones.

'In here, Lon.'

Detective Lon Sellitto nodded a greeting. His stocky figure was encased in blue jeans and a dark purple Izod shirt, and he was wearing running shoes, which surprised Rhyme. The criminalist rarely saw him in casual clothes. He was also struck by the fact that, while Sellitto didn't seem to own a suit that wasn't fiercely wrinkled, this outfit looked hot off the ironing board. The only disfigurements were a few stretch marks in the cloth where his belly jutted past his waistband, and the bulge in the back where his off-duty pistol was not efficiently hidden.

'He rabbited, I heard.'

Rhyme spat out, 'Gone completely.'

The floor creaked under the big man's weight as he ambled to the evidence charts and looked them over. 'That's what you're calling him? Five Twenty-Two?'

'May twenty-second. What happened with the Russian case?'

Sellitto didn't answer. 'Mr Five Twenty-Two leave anything behind?'

'We're about to find out. He ditched a bag of evidence he was going to plant. It's on its way.'

'That was courteous.'

'Iced tea, coffee?'

'Yeah,' the detective muttered to Thom. 'Thanks. Coffee. You have skim milk?'

'Two percent.'

'Good. And any of those cookies from last time? The chocolate chip ones?'

'Just oatmeal.'

'Those're good too.'

'Mel?' Thom asked. 'You want something?'

'If I eat or drink near an examining table, I get yelled at.'

Rhyme snapped, 'It's hardly my fault if defense lawyers have this *thing* about excluding contaminated evidence. I didn't make the rules.'

Sellitto observed, 'See your mood hasn't improved. What's going on in London?'

'Now *that*'s a subject I don't want to talk about.'

'Well, just to improve your spirits we got another problem.'

'Malloy?'

'Yep. He heard Amelia was running a scene and I okayed an ESU action. He got all happy thinking it was the Dienko case, then all sad when he found out it wasn't. He asked if it was connected with you. I'll take a fist on the chin for you, Linc, but not a bullet. I dimed you out . . . Oh, thanks.' Nodding as Thom brought him the refreshments. The aide set a similar offering on a table not far from Cooper, who pulled on latex gloves and started on a cookie.

'Some scotch, if you please,' Rhyme said quickly.

'No.' Thom was gone.

Scowling, Rhyme said, 'I figured Malloy'd bust us as soon as ESU was involved. But we need brass on our side now that it's a hot case. What do we do?'

'Better think of something fast 'cause he wants us to call. Like a half hour ago.' He sipped more coffee and, with some reluctance, set down the remaining quarter of his cookie with the apparent resolve not to finish it.

'Well, I need the brass on board. We've got to have people out there looking for this guy.'

'Then let's call. You ready?'

'Yeah, yeah.'

Sellitto dialed a number. Hit SPEAKER.

'Lower the volume,' Rhyme said. 'I suspect this could be loud.'

'Malloy here.' Rhyme could hear the sounds of the wind, voices and the clink of dishes or glassware. Maybe he was at an outdoor café.

'Captain, you're on speaker with Lincoln Rhyme and me.'

'Okay, what the hell is going on? You could've told me that the ESU operation was what Lincoln called me about earlier. Did you know I deferred the decision about any operation till tomorrow?'

'No, he didn't,' Rhyme said.

The detective blurted, 'Yeah, but I knew enough to figure it out.'

'I'm touched you're both taking the heat for each other but the question is why didn't you tell me?'

Sellitto said, "Cause we had a good chance to collar a rapist-murderer. I decided we couldn't afford any delays.'

'I'm not a child, Lieutenant. *You* make your case to me and *I'll* make the judgment. That's how it's supposed to work.'

'Sorry, Captain. It seemed like the right decision at the time.'

Silence. Then: 'But he got away.'

'Yes, he did,' Rhyme said.

'How?'

'We got a team together as fast as we could but the cover wasn't the best. The UNSUB was closer than we thought. He saw an unmarked or one of the team, I guess. He took off. But he ditched some evidence that could be helpful.'

'Which is on its way to the lab in Queens? Or to you?'

Rhyme glanced at Sellitto. People rise in rank in institutions like the NYPD based on experience, drive and quick minds. Malloy was a good half-step ahead of them.

'I've asked for it to come here, Joe,' Rhyme said.

No silence this time. The sound from the speaker was a resigned sigh. 'Lincoln, you understand the problem, don't you?'

Conflict of interest, Rhyme thought.

'There's a clear conflict of interest with you as an advisor to the department and trying to exonerate your cousin. And beyond that, the implication is that there's been a wrongful arrest.'

'But that's exactly what happened. And two wrongful *convictions*.' Rhyme reminded Malloy about the rape and coin-theft cases that Flintlock had told them about. 'And I wouldn't be surprised if this's happened other times too. . . . You know Locard's Principle, Joe?'

'That was in your book, the one from the academy, right?'

The French criminalist Edmond Locard stated that whenever a crime occurs there's always a transfer of evidence between the perpetrator and the crime scene or the victim. He was referring specifically to dust but the rule applies to many substances and types of evidence. The connection may be difficult to find but it exists.

'Locard's Principle guides what *we* do, Joe. But here's a perp who's using it as a *weapon*. It's his M.O. He kills and gets away because somebody else is convicted of the crime. He knows exactly when to strike, what kind of evidence to plant and when to plant it. The crime-scene teams, the detectives, the lab people, the prosecutors and judges . . . he's used *everybody*, made them accomplices. This has nothing to do with my cousin, Joe. This has to do with stopping a very dangerous man.'

A sighless silence now.

'Okay, I'll sanction it.'

Sellitto was lifting an eyebrow.

'With caveats. You keep me informed of every development in the case. I mean everything.'

'Sure.'

'And, Lon, you try not being straight with me again and I'll transfer you to Budgets. Understand me?'

'Yeah, Captain. Absolutely.'

'And since you're at Lincoln's, Lon, I assume you want a reassignment from the Vladimir Dienko case.'

'Petey Jimenez's up to speed. He's done more of the legwork than I have and he's set up the stings personally.'

'And Dellray's running the snitches, right? And the federal jurisdiction?'

'That's right.'

'Okay, you're off it. *Temporarily*. Open a file on this UNSUB – I mean, send out a memo about the file you've *already* started on the sly. And listen to me: I'm not raising any issues of innocent people being convicted wrongly. Not raising it with anybody. And you're not going to either. That issue is not on the table. The only crime you're running is a single rape-murder that occurred this afternoon. Period. As part of his M.O. this UNSUB might have tried to shift the blame to somebody else but that's all you can say and *only* if the subject comes up. Don't raise the issue yourself and, for God's sake, don't say anything to the press.'

'I don't talk to the press,' Rhyme said. Who did, if they could avoid it? 'But we'll need to look into the other cases to get an idea of how he operates.'

'I didn't say you couldn't,' the captain said, firm but not strident. 'Keep me posted.' He hung up.

'Well, we got ourselves a case,' Sellitto said, surrendering to the abandoned quarter of a cookie and washing it down with the coffee.

* * *

Standing on the curb with three other men in street clothes, Amelia Sachs was talking to the compact man who'd ripped open the door of her Camaro and leveled his weapon at her. He'd turned out not to be 522 but a federal agent who worked for the Drug Enforcement Administration.

'We're still trying to put it together,' he said, and glanced at his boss, an assistant special agent in charge of the Brooklyn DEA office.

The ASAC said, 'We'll know more in a few minutes.'

Not long before, at gunpoint in the car, Sachs had lifted her hands slowly and identified herself as a police officer. The agent had taken her weapon and had checked her ID twice. He'd returned the gun, shaking his head. 'I don't get it,' he said. He apologized but his face didn't seem to suggest he was sorry. Mostly the expression said that, well, he just didn't get it.

A moment later his boss and two other agents had arrived.

Now the ASAC got a call and listened for a few minutes. He then snapped his mobile shut and explained what seemed to have happened. Not long before somebody had made an anonymous call from a pay phone reporting that an armed woman fitting Sachs's description had just shot somebody in what seemed to be a drug dispute.

'We've got an operation going on here at the moment,' he said. 'Looking into some dealer and supplier assassinations.' He nodded toward his agent, the one who'd tried to arrest Sachs. 'Anthony lives a block away. The operations director sent him here to assess the sit while he scrambled the troops.'

Anthony added, 'I thought you were leaving so I grabbed some old take-out bags and moved in. Man . . .' Now the import of what he'd nearly done was sinking in. He was now ashen and Sachs reflected that Glocks have a very light trigger pull. She wondered just how close she'd come to being shot.

'What were you doing here?' the ASAC asked.

'We had a homicide-rape.' She didn't explain about 522's setting up innocent people to take the fall. 'I'm guessing our perp spotted me and made a call to slow up pursuit.'

Or get me killed in a friendly fire incident.

The federal agent shook his head, frowning.

'What?' Sachs asked.

'Just thinking this guy is pretty sharp. If he called NYPD – which most people would've – they'd know about your operation and who you were. So he called us instead. All we'd know was that you were a shooter and we'd approach with caution, ready to take you out if you pulled a weapon.' A frown. 'That's smart.'

'Pretty fucking scary too,' Anthony said, his face still white.

The agents left and she made a call.

When Rhyme answered she told him about the incident.

The criminalist digested this, then he said, 'He called the Feds?'

'Yep.'

'It's almost as if he knew they were in the middle of a drug op. And that the agent who tried to collar you lived nearby.'

'He couldn't know that,' she countered.

'Maybe not. But he sure as hell knew one thing.'

'What's that?'

'He knew exactly where you were. Which means he was watching. Be careful, Sachs.'

Rhyme was explaining to Sellitto how the perp had set up Sachs in Brooklyn.

'He did that?'

'Looks like it.'

The men were discussing how he might've gotten the information – and coming to no helpful conclusions – when the phone trilled. Rhyme glanced at caller ID and answered quickly. 'Inspector.'

Longhurst's voice filled the speaker. 'Detective Rhyme, how are you?'

'Good.'

'Excellent. Just wanted to let you know: We've found Logan's safe house. It wasn't in Manchester after all. It was in Oldham, nearby. East of the city.' She then explained that Danny Krueger had learned from some of his people that a man believed to be Richard Logan had inquired about purchasing some parts for guns. 'Not guns themselves, mind. But if you have the parts to repair guns, presumably you could also make one.'

'Rifles?'

'Yes. Large caliber.'

'Any identity?'

'No, though they thought Logan was U.S. military. Apparently he promised he could get them some discount ammunition in bulk in the future. He seemed to have official army documents about inventories and specifications.'

'So, the shooting zone in London's in play.'

'It would seem. Now, about the safe house: We have contacts in the Hindi community in Oldham. They're quite impeccable. They heard about an American who's rented an old house on the outskirts of town. We managed to track it down. We haven't searched yet. Our team could have done it but we thought it best to talk to you first.'

Longhurst continued, 'Now, Detective, my sense is that he doesn't know we found out about the safe house. And I suspect there may be some rather helpful evidence inside it. I've rung up some fellows at MI5 and borrowed a bit of an expensive toy from them. It's a high-definition video camera. We'd like to have one of our officers wear it and have you guide him through the scene, tell us what you think. We should have the equipment on site in forty minutes or so.'

To do a proper search of the safe house, including the exits and entrances, the drawers, the toilets, closets, mattresses . . . it would consume the better part of the night.

Why was this happening now? He was convinced that 522 was a real threat. In fact, given the time line – with the earlier cases, his cousin's and the murder today – the crimes seemed to be accelerating. And he was particularly troubled by the latest event: 522's turning on them, and nearly getting Sachs shot.

Yes, no?

After a moment of agonizing debate, he said, 'Inspector, I'm sorry to say, something's come up here. We've had a series of homicides. I need to focus on them.'

'I see.' Unflappable British reserve.

'I'll have to hand over the case to your command.'

'Of course, Detective. I understand.'

'You're free to make any and all decisions.'

'I appreciate the vote of confidence. We'll get it sorted out and I'll keep you informed. I better ring off now.'

'Good luck.'

'And to you.'

This was hard for Lincoln Rhyme, stepping away from a hunt, especially when the quarry was this particular perp.

But the decision had been made. Five Twenty-Two was now his only prey.

'Mel, get on the phone and find out where the hell that evidence from Brooklyn is.'

Chapter
TWELVE

Okay, this is a surprise.

The Upper East Side address and the fact that Robert Jorgensen was an orthopedic surgeon had led Amelia Sachs to expect that the Henderson House Residence, the address on the Post-it note, would be a lot nicer than this.

But it was a disgusting dive, a transients' hotel inhabited by druggies and drunks. The flyblown lobby, filled with mismatched and moldy furniture, stank of garlic, cheap disinfectant, useless air freshener and sour human odor. Most homeless shelters were more pleasant.

Standing in the grimy doorway, she paused and turned. Still uneasy about 522's surveillance and the ease with which he'd set up the federal officers in Brooklyn, she looked carefully around the street. Nobody seemed to be paying much attention to her, but then the killer would have been nearby at DeLeon Williams's house too and she'd missed him completely. She studied an abandoned building across the street. Was somebody gazing at her from one of the grime-covered windows?

Or there! On the second floor was a large broken window and she was sure she saw motion in the darkness. Was it a face? Or light from a hole in the roof?

Sachs stepped closer and examined the building carefully. But she found no one and decided her eyes had played tricks on her. She turned back to the hotel and, breathing shallowly, stepped inside. At the front desk she flashed her badge to the hopelessly overweight clerk. He didn't seem the least bit surprised, or troubled, that a cop was here. She was directed toward the elevator. It opened to a foul stench. Okay, the stairs.

Wincing from the strain on her arthritic joints, she pushed through the door on the sixth floor and found room 672. She knocked, then stepped aside. 'Police. Mr Jorgensen? Please open the door.' She didn't know what connection this man might have to the killer so her hand hovered near the grip of her Glock, a fine weapon, as dependable as the sun.

No answer but she believed she heard the sound of the metal cover of the peephole.

'Police,' she repeated.

'Put your ID under the door.'

She did.

A pause, then several chains were undone. And a deadbolt. The door opened a short way but was stopped by a security bar. The gap was bigger than that left by a chain but not large enough for someone to get through.

The head of a middle-aged man appeared. His hair was long and unwashed, his face marred with an unruly beard. The eyes were twitchy.

'You're Robert Jorgensen?'

He peered at her face, then at her ID again, turning the card over and holding it up to the light, though the laminated rectangle was opaque. He handed it back and unhooked the security bar. The door swung open. He examined the hall behind her, then gestured her in. Sachs entered cautiously, hand still near her weapon. She checked the room and closets. The place was otherwise unoccupied and he was unarmed. 'You're Robert Jorgensen?' she repeated.

He nodded.

She then looked over the sad room more carefully. It contained a bed, desk and chair, armchair and ratty couch. The dark gray carpet was stained. A single pole lamp cast dim yellow light, and the shades were drawn. He was living, it seemed, out of four large suitcases and a gym bag. He had no kitchen but a portion of the living room contained a miniature fridge and two microwaves. A coffeepot too. His diet was largely soup and ramen noodles. A hundred manila file folders were carefully lined up against the wall.

His clothes were from a different time in his life, a better time. They seemed expensive but were threadbare and stained. The heels of the rich-looking shoes were worn down. Guessing: He lost his medical practice due to a drug or drinking problem.

At the moment he was occupied by an odd task: dissecting a large hardcover textbook. A chipped magnifying glass on a gooseneck stand was clamped to the desk and he'd been slicing out pages and cutting them into strips.

Maybe mental illness had led to his downfall.

'You're here about the letters. It's about time.'

'Letters?'

He studied her suspiciously. 'You're not?'

'I don't know about any letters.'

'I sent them to Washington. But you *do* talk, don't you? All you law enforcers. You *public-safety* people. Sure you do. You have to, everybody talks. Criminal databases and all that . . .'

'I really don't know what you mean.'

He seemed to believe her. 'Well, then—' His eyes went wide, looking down at her hip. 'Wait, is your cell phone on?'

'Well, yes.'

'Jesus Christ in heaven! What's wrong with you?'

'I—'

'Why don't you run down the street naked and tell every

stranger you see your address? Take the battery out. Not just shut it off. The battery!'

'I'm not doing that.'

'Take it out. Or you can get the hell out right now. The PDA too. And pager.'

This seemed to be a deal breaker. But she said firmly, 'I'm not dumping my memory. I'll do the phone and the pager.'

'Okay,' he grumbled and leaned forward as she slipped the batteries out of the two devices and shut off the PDA.

Then she asked for his ID. He debated and dug out a driver's license. The address was Greenwich, Connecticut, one of the ritziest towns in the metro area. 'I'm not here about any letters, Mr Jorgensen. I just have some questions. I won't take much of your time.'

He gestured her toward the gamy couch and sat down on a wobbly chair at the desk. As if he couldn't help himself he turned to the book and with a razor knife cut a piece off the spine. He handled the knife expertly, fast and sure. Sachs was glad the desk was between them and her gun un-obstructed.

'Mr Jorgensen, I'm here about a crime that was committed this morning.'

'Ah, sure, of course.' Lips pursing, he glanced at Sachs again and his expression was clear: resignation and disgust. 'And what was I supposed to have done *this* time?'

This time?

'The crime was a rape and murder. But we know you weren't involved. You were here.'

A cruel grin. 'Ah, keeping track of me. Sure.' Then a grimace. 'Goddamnit.' This was in response to something he found, or didn't find, in the bit of book spine he was dissecting. He tossed it into the trash. Sachs noticed half-open garbage bags containing remnants of clothes, books, newspapers and small boxes that had also been cut apart.

Then she glanced into the larger microwave and saw that it contained a book.

Germ phobic, she supposed.

He noticed her gaze. 'Microwaving's the best way to destroy them.'

'Bacteria? Viruses?'

He laughed at the question as if she were joking. He nodded at the volume in front of him. 'But sometimes they're really hard to find. You have to, though. You need to see what the enemy looks like.' Now a nod at the microwave. 'And pretty soon they'll start making ones that you can't even nuke. Ah, you better believe it.'

They . . . them . . . Sachs had been a beat cop in the Patrol Division for some years – a portable, they were called in cop slang. She'd worked Times Square back when it was, well, Times Square, before the place became Disneyland North. Patrolwoman Sachs had had lots of experience with the homeless and emotionally disturbed. She recognized signs of paranoid personality, maybe even schizophrenia.

'Do you know a DeLeon Williams?'

'No.'

She offered the names of the other victims and fall guys, including Rhyme's cousin.

'No, never heard of any of them.' He seemed to be answering truthfully. The book took all his attention for a long thirty seconds. He removed a page and held it up, grimacing again. He pitched it out.

'Mr Jorgensen, this room number was found on a note near the crime scene today.'

The hand with the knife froze. He looked at her with scary, burning eyes. Breathlessly he asked, '*Where*? Where the hell did you find it?'

'In a trash bin in Brooklyn. It was stuck to some evidence. It's possible this killer discarded it.'

In a ghastly whisper he asked, 'You have a name? What does he look like? Tell me!' He half rose and his face grew bright red. His lips trembled.

'Take it easy, Mr Jorgensen. Calm down. We're not positive he's the one who left the note.'

'Oh, he's the one. You bet he is. That motherfucker!' He leaned forward. 'You have a *name*?'

'No.'

'Tell me, goddamnit! Do something *for* me for a change. Not *to* me!'

She said firmly, 'If I can help you, I will. But you have to stay calm. Who are you talking about?'

He dropped the knife and sat back, shoulders slumped. A bitter smile spread across his face. 'Who? Who? Why, God, of course.'

'God?'

'And I'm Job. You know Job? The innocent man God tormented. All the trials he inflicted? That's nothing compared to what *I've* been through. . . . Oh, it's him. He found out where I am now and wrote it down on that note of yours. I thought I'd escaped. But he's got me again.'

Sachs thought she saw tears. She asked, 'What's this all about? Please, tell me.'

Jorgensen rubbed his face. 'Okay . . . A few years ago I was a practicing doctor, lived in Connecticut. Had a wife and two wonderful children. Money in the bank, retirement plan, vacation house. A comfortable life. I was happy. But then a strange thing happened. No big deal, not at first. I applied for a new credit card – to get miles in my frequent-flier program. I was making three hundred thousand a year. I'd never missed a credit card or mortgage payment in my life. But I was rejected. Some mistake, I thought. But the company said that I was a credit risk since I'd moved three times in the past six months. Only I hadn't moved at all. Somebody had gotten my name,

Social Security number and credit information and rented apartments as me. Then he defaulted on the rent. But not before he'd bought nearly a hundred thousand dollars' worth of merchandise and had it delivered to those addresses.'

'Identity theft?'

'Oh, the mother lode of identity theft. God opened credit cards in my name, ran up huge bills, had the statements sent to different addresses. Never paid them, of course. As soon as I'd get one straightened out he'd do something else. And he kept getting all this information on me. God knew everything! My mother's maiden name, her birthday, my first dog's name, my first car – all the things companies want to know for passwords. He got my phone numbers – and my calling card number. He ran up a ten-thousand-dollar phone bill. How? He'd call time and temperature in Moscow or Singapore or Sydney and leave the phone off the hook for hours.'

'Why?'

'Why? Because he's God. And I'm Job . . . The son of a bitch bought a house in my name! A whole house! And then defaulted on it. I only found out when a lawyer working for a collection agency tracked me down at my clinic in New York and asked about making payment arrangements for the three hundred and seventy thousand dollars I owed. God also ran up a quarter million in online gambling debts.

'He made bogus insurance claims in my name and my malpractice carrier dropped me. I couldn't work at my clinic without insurance, and nobody would insure me. We had to sell the house and, of course, every penny went to the debt quote *I* had run up – which was by then about two million dollars.'

'Two *million*?'

Jorgensen closed his eyes briefly. 'And then things got worse. My wife was hanging in there throughout all of this. It was hard but she was with me . . . until God had presents – expensive ones – sent in my name to some former nurses at the clinic, bought with my credit card, and that included invitations and suggestive comments. One of the women left a message at home thanking me and saying she'd *love* to go away for the weekend. My daughter got it. She was crying uncontrollably when she told my wife. I think she believed I was innocent. But she still left me four months ago and moved in with her sister in Colorado.'

'I'm sorry.'

'Sorry? Oh, well, thank you very much. But I'm not through yet. Oh, no. Just after my wife left, the arrests started. It seems guns purchased with a credit card and fake driver's license in my name were used in armed robberies in East New York, New Haven and Yonkers. One clerk was seriously wounded. The New York Bureau of Investigation arrested me. They finally let me go but I've still got an arrest on my record. That'll be there forever. Along with the time the Drug Enforcement Agency arrested me because a check of mine was traced to the purchase of illegally imported prescription drugs.

'Oh, and I was actually in prison for a while – well, not me: somebody that *God* sold fake credit cards to and a driver's license in my name. Of course, the prisoner was somebody altogether different. Who knows what his real name is? But as far as the world is concerned, government records show that Robert Samuel Jorgensen, Social Security number nine two three, six seven, four one eight two, formerly of Greenwich, Connecticut, was a prisoner. It's on my record too. For-*ever*.'

'You must've followed up, called the police.'

He scoffed. 'Oh, please. You're a cop. You know where something like this falls in the priority of police work? Just above jaywalking.'

'Did *you* learn anything that might help us? Anything about him? Age, race, education, location?'

'No, nothing. Everywhere I looked there was only one person: me. He took me away from myself. . . . Oh, they say there are safeguards, there are protections. Bullshit. Yes, if you lose a credit card, maybe you're protected to a point. But if somebody wants to destroy your life, there's nothing you can do about it. People believe what computers tell us. If they say you owe money, you owe money. If it says you're a bad insurance risk, you're a bad risk. The report says you have no credit, then you have no credit, even if you're a multimillionaire. We believe the *data*; we don't care about the truth.

'Ah, want to see what my most recent job was?' He jumped up and opened his closet, displaying a fast food franchise uniform. Jorgensen returned to his desk and set to work on the book again, muttering, 'I'll find you, you fucker.' He glanced up. 'And do you want to know the worst part of all?'

She nodded.

'God never lived in the apartments he rented in my name. He never took delivery of the illegal drugs. Or got any of the merchandise he had shipped. The police recovered everything. And he never lived in the beautiful house he bought. Get it? His only point was to torment me. He's God, I'm Job.'

Sachs noticed a picture on his desk. It was of Jorgensen and a blond woman about his age, their arms around a teenage girl and young boy. The house in the background was very nice. She wondered why 522 would go to all the trouble to destroy a man's life, if in fact their perp was behind this. Was he testing out techniques to use to get close to victims and to implicate fall guys? Was Robert Jorgensen a guinea pig?

Or was 522 a cruel sociopath? What he'd done to Jorgensen might be called a nonsexual rape.

'I think you should find another place to live, Mr Jorgensen.'

A resigned smile. 'I know. It's safer that way. Always be harder to find.'

Sachs thought to herself of an expression her father had

used. She thought it described her own life view pretty well. 'When you move they can't getcha . . .'

He nodded at the book. 'You know how he found me here? This, I've got a feeling. Everything started to go bad just after I bought it. I keep thinking it's got the answer. I nuked it but that didn't work – obviously. There's got to be an answer inside. There's *got* to be!'

'What *are* you looking for exactly?'

'Don't you know?'

'No.'

'Well, tracking devices, of course. They put them in books. And clothes. Pretty soon they'll be in almost everything.'

So not germs.

'Microwaves destroy tracking devices?' she asked, playing along.

'Most of them. You can break the antennae too but they're so small nowadays. Almost microscopic.' Jorgensen fell silent and she realized he was staring at her intently as he considered something. He announced. 'You take it.'

'What?'

'The book.' His eyes were dancing madly around the room. 'It's got the answer in it, the answer to everything that's happened to me . . . Please! You're the first one who hasn't rolled their eyes when I told them my story, the only one who hasn't looked at me like I'm mad.' He sat forward. '*You* want to get him as much as I do. You have all sorts of equipment, I'll bet. Scanning microscopes, sensors . . . You can find it! And it'll lead you to him. Yes!' He thrust it toward her.

'Well, I don't know what we're looking for.'

He nodded sympathetically. 'Oh, you don't have to tell me. That's the problem. They change things all the time. They're always one step ahead of us. But please . . .'

They . . .

She took the book, debating about slipping it into a plastic evidence bag and attaching a chain-of-custody card. She wondered how loud the ridicule would be in Rhyme's town house. Probably better just to carry it.

He leaned forward and pressed her hand hard. 'Thank you.' He was crying again.

'So you'll move?' she asked.

He said he would and gave her the name of another transient hotel, one down on the Lower East Side. 'Don't write it down. Don't tell anybody. Don't mention me on the phone. They're listening all the time, you know.'

'Call me if anything else comes to mind about . . . God.' She gave him her card.

He memorized the information on it, then tore the cardboard up. He stepped into the bathroom, flushed half down the toilet. He noticed her curiosity. 'I'll flush the other half later. Flushing something all at once is as stupid as leaving bills in your mailbox with the red flag up. People are such fools.'

He walked her to the door, leaned close. The stink of unwashed clothing hit her. His red-rimmed eyes gazed fiercely at her. 'Officer, listen to me. I know you have that big gun on your hip. But that won't do any good against somebody like him. You have to get close before you can shoot him. But he doesn't have to get close at all. He can sit in a dark room somewhere, sip a glass of wine and bring your life down in pieces.' Jorgensen nodded at the book in her hand. 'And now that you've got that, you're infected too.'

Chapter
THIRTEEN

I've been checking the news — there are so many efficient ways to get information nowadays — and I've heard nothing about any redheaded police officers gunned down by fellow law enforcers in Brooklyn.

But at the least They're afraid.

They'd be edgy now.

Good. Why should I be the only one?

As I walk I reflect: How did this happen? How could it *possibly* have happened?

This isn't good, this isn't good this this . . .

They seemed to know *exactly* what I was doing, who my victim was.

And that I was on the way to DeLeon 6832's house at *just that moment*.

How?

Running through the data, permutating them, analyzing them. No, I can't understand how They did it.

Not yet. Have to think some more.

I don't have enough information. How can I draw conclusions if I don't have the *data*? How?

Ah, slow down, slow down, I tell myself. When sixteens

walk quickly they shed data, revealing all sorts of information, at least to those who are smart, who can make good deductions.

Up and down the gray, urban streets, Sunday no longer beautiful. An ugly day, ruined. The sunlight's harsh and tainted. The city's cold, its edges ragged. The sixteens are mocking and snide and pompous.

I hate them all!

But keep your head down, pretend to enjoy the day.

And, most of all, *think*. Be analytical. How would a computer, confronted with a problem, analyze the data?

Think. Now, how could They have found out?

One block, two blocks, three blocks, four . . .

No answers. Only the conclusion: They're good. And another question: Who exactly *are* They? I suppose—

I'm struck with a terrible thought. Please, no . . . I stop and dig through my backpack. No, no, no, it's gone! The Post-it, stuck to the evidence bag, and I forgot to pull it off before I threw everything out. The address of my favorite sixteen: 3694-8938-5330-2498, my pet – known to the world as Dr Robert Jorgensen. I'd just found where he'd fled to, trying to hide, and jotted it on a Post-it. I'm furious I didn't memorize it and throw away the note.

I *hate* myself, hate everything. How could I be so careless?

I want to cry, to scream.

My Robert 3694! For two years he's been my guinea pig, my human experiment. Public records, identity theft, credit cards . . .

But, most of all, ruining him was a huge high. Orgasmic, indescribable. Like coke or heroin. Taking a perfectly normal, happy family man, a good, caring doctor, and destroying him.

Well, I can't take any chances. I have to assume someone will find the note and call him. He'll flee . . . and I'll have to let him go.

Something else has been taken away from me today. I can't describe how I feel when that happens. It's pain like fire, it's fear like blind panic, it's falling and knowing you'll collide with the blurring earth at any moment but not . . . quite . . . yet.

I blunder through the herds of antelope, these sixteens roaming on their day of rest. My happiness is destroyed, my comfort gone. Whereas just hours ago I looked at everyone with benign curiosity or lust, but now I simply want to storm up to someone and slice his pale flesh, thin as tomato skin, with one of my eighty-nine straight razors.

Maybe my Krusius Brothers model from the late 1800s. It has an extra-long blade, a fine stag's horn handle and is the pride of my collection.

'Evidence, Mel. Let's look it over.'

Rhyme was referring to what had been collected in the trash can near DeLeon Williams's house.

'Friction ridges?'

The first items Cooper examined for fingerprints were the plastic bags – the one holding the evidence 522 had presumably intended to plant and the bags inside, containing some still-wet blood and a bloody paper towel. But there were no prints on the plastic – a disappointment, since it preserves them so well. (Often they're visible, not latent, and can be observed without any special chemicals or lighting.) Cooper did find indications that the UNSUB had touched the bags with cotton gloves – the sort experienced criminals prefer to latex gloves, which retain the perp's prints *inside* the fingers very efficiently.

Using various sprays and alternative light sources, Mel Cooper examined the rest of the items and found no prints on these either.

Rhyme realized that this case, like the others he suspected 522 was behind, was different from most in that it presented two categories of evidence. First, false evidence that the killer intended to plant to implicate DeLeon Williams; he'd undoubtedly made sure that none of this would lead back to himself personally. Second, real evidence that he'd left accidentally and that could very well lead to his home – such as the tobacco and the doll's hair.

The bloody paper towel and wet blood were in the first category, intended to be left. Similarly the duct tape, meant to be slipped into Williams's garage or car, would undoubtedly match strips used to gag or bind Myra Weinburg. But it would have been kept carefully protected from 522's dwelling so it didn't pick up any trace.

The size-13 Sure-Track running shoe probably wasn't going to be stashed at Williams's house but it was still 'planted' evidence in the sense that 522 had undoubtedly used it to leave a print of a shoe similar to one of Williams's. Mel Cooper tested the shoe anyway and found some trace: beer on the tread. According to the database of fermented beverage ingredients, created for the NYPD by Rhyme years ago, it was most likely Miller brand. That could be in either category – planted or real. They'd have to see what Pulaski recovered from the Myra Weinburg crime scene to know for sure.

The bag also contained a computer printout of Myra's photo, probably included to suggest Williams had been stalking her online; it was therefore meant to be planted as well. Still, Rhyme had Cooper check it carefully but a ninhydrin test revealed no fingerprints. Microscopic and chemical analyses revealed generic, untraceable paper, printed with Hewlett-Packard laser toner, also untraceable beyond the brand name.

But they did make a discovery that might prove helpful. Rhyme and Cooper found something embedded in the paper: traces of *Stachybotrys Chartarum* mold. This was the infamous 'sick building' mold. Since the amounts found in the paper were so small, it was unlikely that 522 meant it to be planted.

More likely it came from the killer's residence or place of work. The presence of this mold, which was found indoors almost exclusively, meant that at least part of his home or workplace would be dark and humid. Mold can't grow in a dry location.

The Post-it note, also probably not intended to be planted, was a 3M brand, not the cheaper generic but still impossible to source. Cooper had found no trace in the note other than a few more spores of the mold, which at least told them that the Post-it's source probably was 522. The ink was from a disposable pen sold in countless stores around the country.

And that was it for the evidence, though as Cooper was jotting the results, a tech from the outside lab Rhyme used for expedited medical analysis called and reported that the preliminary test confirmed the blood found in the bags was that of Myra Weinburg.

Sellitto took a phone call, had a brief conversation then hung up. 'Zip . . . The DEA traced the call about Amelia to a pay phone. Nobody saw the caller. And nobody on the expressway saw anyone running. The canvass at the two closest subway stations didn't turn up anything suspicious around the time he got away.'

'Well, he's not going to do anything *suspicious,* now, is he? What did the canvassers think? An escaping murderer would jump a turnstile or strip his clothes off and change into a superhero outfit?'

'Just telling you what they said, Linc.'

Grimacing, he asked Thom to write the results of the search up on the whiteboard.

The doorbell rang and Ron Pulaski walked briskly into the room, carrying two milk crates containing plastic bags, evidence from the scene where Myra Weinburg had been killed.

Rhyme noted immediately that his expression had changed. His face was still. Pulaski often cringed or seemed perplexed

STREET NEAR DELEON WILLIAMS'S HOUSE

- Three plastic bags, ZipLoc freezer style, one-gallon
- One right size-13 Sure-Track running shoe, dried beer in tread (probably Miller brand), no wear marks. No other discernible trace. Bought to leave imprint at scene of crime?
- Paper towel with blood in plastic bag. Preliminary test confirms it's the victim's
- 2 ccs blood in plastic bag. Preliminary test confirms it's the victim's
- Post-it with address of the Henderson House Residence, Room 672, occupied by Robert Jorgensen. Note and pen untraceable. Paper untraceable. Evidence of Stachybotrys Chartarum mold in paper
- Picture of victim, apparently computer printout, color. Hewlett-Packard printer ink. Otherwise untraceable. Paper untraceable. Evidence of Stachybotrys Chartarum mold in paper
- Duct tape, Home Depot house brand, not traceable to particular location.
- No friction-ridge prints

or occasionally looked proud – he even blushed – but now his eyes seemed hollow, not at all like the determined gaze of earlier. He glanced at Rhyme with a nod, walked sullenly to the examination tables, handed off the evidence to Cooper and gave him the chain-of-custody cards, which the tech signed.

The rookie stepped back, looking over the whiteboard chart Thom had created. Hands in his jeans pockets, Hawaiian shirt untucked, he wasn't seeing a single word.

'You all right, Pulaski?'

'Sure.'

'You don't look all right,' Sellitto said.

'Naw, it's nothing.'

But that wasn't true. Something about running his first solo homicide scene had upset him.

Finally he said, 'She was just lying there, faceup, staring at the ceiling. It's like she was alive and looking for something. Frowning, kind of curious. I guess I expected her to be covered up.'

'Yeah, well, you know we don't do that,' Sellitto muttered.

Pulaski looked out the window. 'The thing is . . . okay, it's crazy. It's just she looked a little like Jenny.' His wife. 'Kind of weird.'

Lincoln Rhyme and Amelia Sachs were similar in many ways when it came to their work. They felt you needed to summon empathy in searching crime scenes, which allowed you to feel what the perp, and the victim, experienced. This helped to better understand the scene and find evidence you otherwise might not.

Those who had this skill, as harrowing as its consequences might be, were masters at walking the grid.

But Rhyme and Sachs differed in one important aspect. Sachs believed it was important never to become numb to the horror of crime. You needed to feel it every time you went to a scene, and afterward. If you didn't, she said, your heart grew hard, you moved closer to the darkness within the people you pursued. Rhyme, on the other hand, felt you should be as dispassionate as possible. Only by coldly putting aside the tragedy could you be the best police officer you could – and more efficiently stop future tragedies from occurring. ('It's not a human being anymore,' he'd lectured his new recruits. 'It's a source of evidence. And a damn good one.')

Pulaski had the potential to be more like Rhyme, the criminalist believed, but at this early stage of his career he fell into Amelia Sachs's camp. Rhyme felt for the young man now but they had a case to solve. At home tonight Pulaski could hold his wife close and silently mourn the death of the woman she resembled.

He asked gruffly, 'You with us, Pulaski?'

'Yes, sir. I'm fine.'

Not exactly, but Rhyme had made his point. 'You processed the body?'

A nod. 'I was there with the M.E.'s tour doctor. We did it together. I made sure he wore rubber bands on his booties.'

To avoid confusion when it came to footprints Rhyme had a policy of his crime scene searchers' putting rubber bands around their feet, even when they were in the hooded plastic jumpsuits worn to prevent contamination from their own hair, skin cells and other trace.

'Good.' Rhyme then glanced eagerly at the milk crates. 'Let's get going. We ruined one plan of his. Maybe he's mad about it and is out targeting somebody else. Maybe he's buying a ticket to Mexico. Either way, I want to move fast.'

The young cop flipped open his notebook. 'I—'

'Thom, come on in here. Thom, where the hell are you?'

'Oh, sure, Lincoln,' said the aide with a cheerful smile, walking into the room. 'Always happy to drop everything in the face of such polite requests.'

'We need you again – another chart.'

'Do you?'

'Please.'

'You don't mean it.'

'*Thom.*'

'All right.'

'"Myra Weinburg Crime Scene."'

The aide wrote the heading and stood ready with the marker, as Rhyme asked, 'Now, Pulaski, I understand it wasn't her apartment?'

'That's right, sir. A couple owned it. They're on vacation,

on a cruise ship. I managed to get through to them. They'd never heard of Myra Weinburg. Man, you should've heard them; they were *way* upset. They didn't have any idea who it might've been. And to get in he broke the lock.'

'So he knew it was empty and that there was no alarm,' Cooper said. 'Interesting.'

'Whatta you think?' Sellitto was shaking his head. 'He just picked it for location?'

'It was real deserted around there,' Pulaski put in.

'And what was she doing, do you think?'

'I found her bike outside – she had a Kryptonite key in her pocket and it fit.'

'Biking. Could be that he'd checked out her route and knew she'd be by there at a certain time. And somehow he knew the couple were going to be away so he wouldn't have any disturbances . . . Okay, rookie, run through what you found. Thom, if you would be so kind as to write this down.'

'You're trying too hard.'

'Ha. Cause of death?' Rhyme asked Pulaski.

'I told the doctor to have the medical examiner expedite the autopsy results.'

Sellitto laughed gruffly. 'And what'd he say to that?'

'Something like "Yeah, right." And a couple other things too.'

'You need a bit more starch in your collar before you can make requests like that. But I appreciate the effort. What was the *preliminary*?'

He looked over his notes. 'Suffered several blows to the head. To subdue her, the M.E. thought.' The young officer paused, perhaps recalling his own, similar injury a few years ago. He continued, 'Cause of death was strangulation. There were petechiae in the eyes and inside the eyelids – pinpoint hemorrhages—'

'I know what they are, rookie.'

'Oh, sure. Right. And venous distention in the scalp and face.

This is the probable murder weapon.' He held up a bag containing a length of rope about four feet long.

'Mel?'

Cooper took the rope and carefully opened it over a large sheet of clean newsprint, dusting to dislodge trace. He then examined what he'd found and took a few samples of the fibers.

'What?' Rhyme asked impatiently.

'Checking.'

The rookie took refuge in his notes again. 'As far as the rape, it was vaginal and anal. Postmortem, the tour doctor thought.'

'Posing of the body?'

'No . . . but one thing I noticed, Detective,' Pulaski said. 'All her fingernails were long, except one. It was cut really short.'

'Blood?'

'Yes. It was cut right down to the quick.' He hesitated. 'Probably premortem.'

So 522's a bit of a sadist, Rhyme reflected. 'He likes pain.'

'Check the other crime-scene photos, from the earlier rape.'

The young officer hurried off to find the pictures. He shuffled through them and found one, squinting. 'Look at this, Detective. Yeah, he cut off a fingernail there too. The same finger.'

'Our boy likes trophies. That's good to know.'

Pulaski nodded enthusiastically. 'And think about it – the wedding ring finger. Probably something about his past. Maybe his wife left him, maybe he was neglected by his mother or a mother figure—'

'Good point, Pulaski. Reminds me – we forgot something else.'

'What's that, sir?'

'Did you check your horoscope this morning before we started the investigation?'

'My . . . ?'

'Oh, and who got the tea-leaf-reading assignment? I forget.'

Sellitto was chuckling. Pulaski was blushing.

Rhyme snapped, 'Psychological profiling isn't helpful. What's *helpful* about the nail is knowing that Five Twenty-Two now has in his possession a DNA connection to the crime. Not to mention that if we can decide what kind of implement he used to remove the trophy, we might be able to trace the purchase and *find* him. Evidence, rookie. Not psychobabble.'

'Sure, Detective. Got it.'

'"Lincoln" is fine.'

'Okay. Sure.'

'The rope, Mel?'

Cooper was scrolling through the fiber database. 'Generic hemp. Available in thousands of retail outlets around the country.' He ran a chemical analysis. 'No trace.'

Crap.

'What else, Pulaski?' Sellitto asked.

He went through the list. Fishing line, binding her hands, and cutting through the skin, which resulted in the bleeding. Duct tape covered her mouth. The tape was Home Depot brand, of course, torn off the roll 522 had ditched; the ragged ends matched perfectly. Two unopened condoms were discovered near the body, the young officer explained, holding up the bag. They were Trojan-Enz brand.

'And here are the swabs.'

Mel Cooper took the plastic evidence bags and checked the vaginal and rectal swabs. The M.E.'s office would give a more detailed report but it was clear that among the substances were traces of a spermicidal lubricant similar to that used with the condoms. There was no semen anywhere at the scene.

Another swab, from the floor, where Pulaski found the

treadmark of a running shoe, revealed beer. It proved to be Miller brand. The electrostatic image of the tread was, naturally, a size-13 Sure-Track right shoe – the same that 522 had ditched in the trash can. 'And the owners of the loft had no beer, right? You did search the kitchen and pantry?'

'Right, yes, sir. And I didn't find any.'

Lon Sellitto was nodding. 'Bet you ten bucks that Miller is DeLeon's brew of choice.'

'I won't take you up on that one, Lon. What else was there?'

Pulaski held up a plastic bag containing a brown fleck that he'd found just above the victim's ear. Analysis revealed it to be tobacco. 'What's the story with that, Mel?'

The tech's examination revealed that it was a fine-cut piece, the sort used in cigarettes, but it was not the same as the Tareyton sampler in the database. Lincoln Rhyme was one of the few nonsmokers in the country who decried the bans on smoking; tobacco and ash were wonderful forensic links between criminal and crime scene. Cooper couldn't tell the brand. He decided, though, that because the tobacco was so desiccated it was probably old.

'Did Myra smoke? Or the people in the loft?'

'I didn't see any evidence of it. And I did what you're always telling us. I smelled the scene when I got there. No smell of smoking.'

'Good.' Rhyme was pleased with the search so far. 'What's the friction-ridge situation?'

'Checked fingerprint samples of the homeowners – from the medicine cabinet and things in the bedside table.'

'So you weren't fudging. You really did read my book.' Rhyme had devoted a number of paragraphs in his forensic text to the importance of collecting control prints at crime scenes and where to best find them.

'Yes, sir.'

'I'm so pleased. Did I make any royalties?'

'I borrowed my brother's.' Pulaski's twin was a cop down at the Sixth Precinct in Greenwich Village.

'Let's hope *he* paid for it.'

Most of the prints found in the loft were the couples' – which they determined from the samples. The others were probably from visitors but it wasn't impossible that 522 had been careless. Cooper scanned all of them into the Integrated Automated Fingerprint Identification System. The results would be available soon.

'Okay, tell me, Pulaski, what was your impression of the scene?'

The question seemed to throw him. 'Impression?'

'Those are the trees.' Rhyme lowered his eyes toward the evidence bags. 'What did you think of the forest?'

The young officer thought. 'Well, I *did* have a thought. It's stupid, though.'

'You know I'll be the first one to say if you've come up with a stupid theory, rookie.'

'It's just, when I first got there my impression was that the struggle seemed off.'

'How do you mean?'

'See, her bike was chained to a lamppost outside the loft. Like she'd parked it, not thinking anything was wrong.'

'So he didn't just grab her on the street.'

'Right. And to get into the loft you went through a gate and then down a long corridor to the front door. It was real narrow and it was packed with things the couple stored outside – jars and cans, sports things, some stuff to be recycled, tools for their garden. But nothing was disturbed.' He tapped another photo. 'But look inside – that's where the struggle began. The table and the vases. Right by the front door.' His voice went soft again. 'Looks like she fought real hard.'

Rhyme nodded. 'All right. So Five Twenty-Two lures her to the loft, smooth-talking her. She locks up the bike, walks down the corridor and they go into the loft. She stops in the entryway, sees he's lying and tries to get out.'

He considered this. 'So he must've known enough about Myra to put her at ease, and make her feel that she could trust him . . . Sure, think about it: He's got all this information – about who people are, what people buy, when they're on vacation, whether they have alarms, where they're going to be . . . Not bad, rookie. Now we know something concrete about him.'

Pulaski struggled to keep a smile off his face.

Cooper's computer dinged. He read the screen. 'No hits on the prints. Zero.'

Rhyme shrugged, not surprised. 'I'm interested in this idea – that he knows so much. Somebody give DeLeon Williams a call. Was Five Twenty-Two right about all the evidence?'

Sellitto's brief conversation revealed that, yes, Williams wore size-13 Sure-Track shoes, he regularly bought Trojan-Enz brand condoms, he had forty-pound fishing line, he drank Miller beer and he'd recently been to Home Depot for duct tape and hemp rope to use as a tie-down.

Looking at the evidence chart of the earlier rape, Rhyme noted that the condoms used by 522 in that crime were Durex. The killer had used those because Joseph Knightly bought that brand.

On the speakerphone he asked Williams, 'Is one of your shoes missing?'

'No.'

Sellitto said, 'So he bought a pair. Same type, same size as you've got. How'd he know that? Have you seen anybody on your property recently, maybe in your garage, going through your car or trash? Or have you had a break-in recently?'

'No, we sure haven't. I'm out of work and here most days taking care of the house. I'd know. And it's not the best neighborhood in the world; we've got an alarm. We always put it on.'

Rhyme thanked him and they disconnected.

He stretched his head back and gazed at the chart, as he dictated to Thom what to write.

MYRA WEINBURG CRIME SCENE

- COD: Strangulation. Awaiting final M.E. report
- No mutilation or arranging of body but ring fingernail, left hand, was cut short. Possible trophy. Premortem most likely
- Condom lubricant, from Trojan-Enz
- Unopened condoms (2), Trojan-Enz
- No used condoms, or body fluids
- Traces of Miller beer on floor (source other than crime scene)
- Fishing line, 40-pound monofilament, generic brand
- Four-foot length of brown hemp rope (MW)
- Duct tape on mouth
- Tobacco flake, old, from unidentified brand
- Footprint, Sure-Track man's running shoe, size 13
- No fingerprints

Rhyme asked, 'Our boy called nine-one-one, right? To report the Dodge?'

'Yeah,' Sellitto confirmed.

'Find out about the call. What he said, what his voice sounded like.'

The detective added, 'The earlier cases too – your cousin's and the coin theft and earlier rape.'

'Good, sure. I didn't think about that.'

Sellitto got in touch with central dispatch. Nine-one-one calls are recorded and kept for varying periods of time. He requested the information. Ten minutes later he received a callback. The 911 reports from Arthur's case and today's murder were still in the system, the dispatch supervisor reported, and had been sent to Cooper's e-mail address as .wav files. The earlier cases had been sent to archives on CD. It could take days to find them but an assistant had sent in a request for them.

When the audio files arrived, Cooper opened and played them. They were of a male voice telling the police to hurry to an address where he'd heard screaming. He described the get-away vehicles. The voices sounded identical.

'Voice print?' Cooper asked. 'If we get a suspect, we can compare it.'

Voice prints were more highly regarded in the forensic world than lie detectors, and were admissible in some courts, depending on the judge. But Rhyme shook his head. 'Listen to it. He's talking through a box. Can't you tell?'

A 'box' is a device that disguises a caller's voice. It doesn't produce a weird, Darth Vader sound; the timbre is normal, if a little hollow. Many directory assistance and customer service operations use them to make employees' voices uniform.

It was then that the door opened and Amelia Sachs strode into the parlor, carrying a large object under her arm. Rhyme couldn't tell what it was. She nodded, then gazed at the evidence chart, saying to Pulaski, 'Looks like a good job.'

'Thanks.'

Rhyme noted that what she held was a book. It seemed half disassembled. 'What the hell is that?'

'A present from our doctor friend, Robert Jorgensen.'

'What is it? Evidence?'

'Hard to say. It was really an odd experience, talking to him.'

'Whatta you mean by odd, Amelia?' Sellitto asked.

'Think Batboy, Elvis and aliens behind the Kennedy assassination. *That* sort of odd.'

Pulaski exhaled a fast laugh, drawing a withering look from Lincoln Rhyme.

Chapter
FOURTEEN

She told a story of a troubled man whose identity had been stolen and his life ruined. A man who described his nemesis as God, and himself as Job.

Clearly he was unhinged; 'odd' didn't go far enough. Yet if even partly true, his story was moving and hard to listen to. A life completely in tatters, and the crime pointless.

But then Sachs caught Rhyme's complete attention when she said, 'Jorgensen claims the man behind it's been keeping track of him ever since he bought this book two years ago. He seems to know everything he's doing.'

'Knows everything,' Rhyme repeated, looking at the evidence charts. 'Just what we were talking about a few minutes ago. Getting all the information he needs on the victims and the fall guys.' He filled her in on what they'd learned.

She handed the book to Mel Cooper and told him Jorgensen believed it held a tracking device.

'Tracking device?' Rhyme scoffed. 'He's been watching too many Oliver Stone movies . . . All right, search it if you want. But let's not neglect the real leads.'

Sachs's calls to the police in the various jurisdictions where Jorgensen had been victimized weren't productive. Yes, there'd been identity theft, no question. 'But,' one cop in Florida asked, 'you know how much of this goes on? We find a fake residence and raid it but by the time we get there it's empty. They've taken all the merch they'd charged to the vic's account and headed off to Texas or Montana.'

Most of them had heard of Jorgensen ('He sure writes a lot of letters') and were sympathetic. But none had any specific leads to an individual or gang who might have been behind the crimes and they couldn't devote nearly enough time to the cases as they would have liked. 'We could have another hundred people on staff and still not be able to make any headway.'

After she'd hung up, Sachs explained that since 522 knew Jorgensen's address, she'd told the residence hotel clerk to let her know immediately if anyone called or came around asking about him. If the clerk agreed, Sachs would neglect to bring up the residence hotel with the city's building inspection office.

'Nicely done,' Rhyme said. 'You knew there were violations?'

'Not until he agreed at, oh, about the speed of light.' Sachs walked to the evidence that Pulaski had gotten from the loft near SoHo, looking it over.

'Any thoughts, Amelia?' Sellitto asked.

She stood, staring at the boards, one fingernail taking on another as she tried to make sense out of the disparate collection of clues.

'Where'd he get this?' She picked up the bag containing the printout of Myra Weinburg's face – looking sweet and amused, her eyes on the camera that had snapped her picture. 'We should find out.'

Good point. Rhyme hadn't considered the source of the picture, merely that 522 had downloaded it from a Web site somewhere. He'd been more interested in the paper as a source of clues.

In the photo Myra Weinburg was standing beside a flowering

tree, gazing back at the camera, a smile on her face. She was holding a pink drink in a martini glass.

Rhyme noticed Pulaski gazing at the picture too, his eyes troubled again.

The thing is . . . she looked a little like Jenny.

Rhyme noted distinctive borders and what appeared to be the strokes of some letters to the right, disappearing out of frame. 'He'd've got it online. To make it look like DeLeon Williams was checking her out.'

Sellitto said, 'Maybe we could trace him through the site he downloaded it from. How can we tell where he got it?'

'Google her name,' Rhyme suggested.

Cooper tried this and found a dozen hits, several referring to a different Myra Weinburg. The ones that related to the victim were all professional organizations. But none of the photos of her was similar to the one that 522 had printed out.

Sachs said, 'Got an idea. Let me call my computer expert.'

'Who, that guy at Computer Crimes?' Sellitto asked.

'No, somebody even better than him.'

She picked up the phone and dialed a number. 'Pammy, hi. Where are you? . . . Good. I've got an assignment. Go online for a Web chat. We'll do audio by phone.'

Sachs turned to Cooper. 'Can you boot up your webcam, Mel?'

The tech typed and a moment later his monitor filled with an image of Pam's room at her foster parents' house in Brooklyn. The face of the pretty teenager appeared as she sat down. The image was slightly distorted by the wide-angle lens.

'Hi, Pam.'

'Hi, Mr Cooper' came the lilting voice through the speakerphone.

'I'll take over,' Sachs said and replaced Cooper at the keyboard. 'Honey, we've found a picture and we think it came from the Internet. Could you take a look and tell us if you know where?'

'Sure.'

Sachs held up the sheet to the webcam.

'It's kind of glary. Can you take it out of the plastic?'

The detective pulled on latex gloves and carefully slipped the sheet out, held it up again.

'That's better. Sure, it's from OurWorld.'

'What's that?'

'You know, a social-networking site. Like Facebook and MySpace. It's the hot new one. Everybody's on it.'

'You know about those, Rhyme?' Sachs asked.

He gave a nod. Curiously, he'd been thinking about this recently. He'd read an article in *The New York Times* about networking sites and virtual existence worlds like Second Life. He'd been surprised to learn that people were spending less time in the outside world and more in the virtual – from avatars to these social-networking sites to telecommuting. Apparently teenagers today spent less time out of doors than in any other period in U.S. history. Ironically, thanks to an exercise regimen that was improving his physical condition and his changing attitudes, Rhyme himself was becoming *less* virtual and was venturing out more. The dividing line between abled and disabled was blurring.

Sachs now asked Pam, 'You can tell for sure it's from that site?'

'Yeah. They've got that special border. If you look close it's not just a line; it's little globes, like the earth, over and over again.'

Rhyme squinted. Yes, the border was just as she'd described it. He thought back, recalling OurWorld from the article. 'Hello, Pam . . . there are a lot of members, aren't there?'

'Oh, hi, Mr Rhyme. Yeah. Like, thirty or forty million people. Whose realm is that one?'

'Realm?' Sachs asked.

'That's what they call your page. Your "realm." Who is she?'

'I'm afraid she was killed today,' Sachs said evenly. 'That's the case I told you about earlier.'

Rhyme wouldn't have mentioned the murder to a teenager. But this was Sachs's call; she'd know what to share and what not to.

'Oh, I'm sorry.' Pam was sympathetic but not shocked or dismayed by the hard truth.

Rhyme asked, 'Pam, can anybody log on and get into your realm?'

'Well, you're supposed to join. But if you don't want to post anything or host your own realm you can crack in just to look around.'

'So you'd say that the man who printed this out knows computers.'

'Yeah, he'd have to, I guess. Only he didn't print it out.'

'What?'

'You can't print or download anything. Even with the print screen command. There's a filter on the system – to prevent stalkers, you know. And you can't crack it. It's like what protects copyrighted books online.'

'Then how did he get the picture?' Rhyme asked.

Pam laughed. 'Oh, he probably did what we all do at school if we want a shot of a cute guy or some weird Goth chick. We just take a picture of the screen with a digital camera. Everybody does that.'

'Sure,' Rhyme said, shaking his head. 'Never occurred to me.'

'Oh, don't worry, Mr Rhyme,' the girl said. 'A lot of times people miss the obvious answer.'

Sachs glanced at Rhyme, who smiled at the girl's reassurance. 'Okay, Pam. Thanks. I'll see you later.'

''Bye!'

'Let's fill in the portrait of our friend.'

Sachs picked up the marker and stepped to the whiteboard.

UNSUB 522 PROFILE

- Male
- Possibly smokes or lives/works with someone who does, or near source of tobacco
- Has children or lives/works near them or near source of toys
- Interest in art, coins?
- Probably white or light-skinned ethnic
- Medium build
- Strong – able to strangle victims
- Access to voice-disguise equipment
- Possibly computer literate; knows OurWorld. Other social-networking sites?
- Takes trophies from victims. Sadist?
- Portion of residence/workplace dark and moist

NONPLANTED EVIDENCE

- Dust
- Old cardboard
- Hair from doll, BASF B35 nylon 6
- Tobacco from Tareyton cigarettes
- Old tobacco, not Tareyton, but brand unknown
- Evidence of Stachybotrys Chartarum mold

Rhyme was looking over the details when he heard Mel Cooper laugh. 'Well, well, well.'

'What?'

'This is interesting.'

'Be specific. I don't need interesting. I need facts.'

'It's still interesting.' The lab man had been shining a bright light on the slit-open spine of Robert Jorgensen's book. 'You were thinking the doctor was crazy, talking about tracking devices? Well, guess what? Oliver Stone *may* have a movie here – there *is* something implanted in it. In the spine tape.'

'Really?' Sachs said, shaking her head. 'I thought he was nuts.'

'Let me see,' Rhyme said, his curiosity piqued and skepticism on temporary hold.

Cooper moved a small high-definition camera closer to the examining table and hit the book with an infrared light. It revealed underneath the tape a tiny rectangle of crisscrossed lines.

'Take it out,' Rhyme said.

Carefully Cooper slit the spine tape and removed what appeared to be an inch-long piece of plasticized paper printed with what looked like computer circuit lines. Also, a series of numbers and the manufacturer's name, DMS, Inc.

Sellitto asked, 'The fuck is it? Really a tracking device?'

'I don't see how. There's no battery or power source that I can find,' Cooper said.

'Mel, look up the company.'

A fast business search revealed it was Data Management Systems, based outside Boston. He read a description of the outfit, one division of which manufactured these little devices – known as RFID tags, for radio frequency identification.

'I've heard about those,' Pulaski said. 'It was on CNN.'

'Oh, the definitive source for forensic knowledge,' Rhyme said cynically.

'No, that's *CSI*,' Sellitto said, drawing another aborted laugh from Ron Pulaski.

Sachs asked, 'What does it do?'

'This is interesting.'

'Again, interesting.'

'Essentially it's a programmable chip that can be read by a radio scanner. They don't need a battery; the antenna picks up the radio waves and that gives them enough juice to work.'

Sachs said, 'Jorgensen was talking about breaking off antennas to disable them. He also said you could destroy some of them in a microwave. But that one' – she gestured – 'he couldn't nuke. Or so he said.'

Cooper continued, 'They're used for inventory control by manufacturers and retailers. In the next few years nearly every product sold in the U.S. will have its own RFID tag. Some major retailers already require them before they'll stock a product line.'

Sachs laughed. 'That's just what Jorgensen was telling me. Maybe he wasn't as *National Enquirer* as I thought.'

'Every product?' Rhyme asked.

'Yep. So stores know where the stuff in inventory is, how much stock they have, what's selling faster than other things, when to restock the shelves, when to reorder. They're also used for baggage handling by airlines so they know where your luggage is without having to visually scan the bar code. And they're used in credit cards, driver's licenses, employee IDs. They're called "smart cards" then.'

'Jorgensen wanted to see my department ID. He looked it over real carefully. Maybe that's what he was interested in.'

'They're all over the place,' Cooper continued. 'In those discount cards you use in grocery stores, in frequent-flier cards, in tollbooth smart pass transponders.'

Sachs nodded at the evidence boards. 'Think about it, Rhyme. Jorgensen was talking about this man he called God knowing all about his life. Enough to steal his identity, to buy things in his name, take out loans, get credit cards, find out where he was.'

Rhyme felt the excitement of moving forward in the hunt. 'And Five Twenty-Two knows enough about his victims to get close to them, get inside their defenses. He knows enough about the fall guys to plant evidence that's identical to what they have at home.'

'And,' Sellitto added, 'he knows exactly where they were at the time of the crime. So they won't have an alibi.'

Sachs looked over the tiny tag. 'Jorgensen said his life started to fall apart around the time he got that book.'

'Where'd he buy it? Any receipts or price stickers, Mel?'

'Nope. If there were he cut them out.'

'Call Jorgensen back. Let's get him in here.'

Sachs pulled out her phone and called the transient hotel where she'd just met with him. She was frowning. 'Already?' she asked the clerk.

Doesn't bode well, Rhyme reflected.

'He's moved out,' she said after hanging up. 'But I know where he's going.' She found a slip of paper, placed another call. Though after a brief conversation she hung up, sighing. Jorgensen wasn't at that hotel either, she said; he hadn't even called to make a reservation.

'Do you have a cell number?'

'He doesn't have a phone. He doesn't trust them. But he knows my number. If we're lucky he'll call.' Sachs walked closer to the tiny device. 'Mel. Cut the wire off. The antenna.'

'What?'

'Jorgensen said now that we've got the book, we're infected too. Cut it off.'

Cooper shrugged and glanced at Rhyme, who thought the idea was absurd. Still, Amelia Sachs didn't spook easily. 'Sure, go ahead. Just make a notation on the chain-of-custody card. "Evidence rendered safe."'

A phrase usually reserved for bombs and handguns.

Rhyme then lost interest in the RFID. He looked up. 'All right. Until we hear from him, let's speculate . . . Come on, folks. Be ballsy. I need some thoughts here! We've got a perp who can get his hands on all this goddamn information about people. How? He knows *everything* the fall guys bought. Fishing line, kitchen knives, shave cream, fertilizer, condoms, duct tape, rope, beer. There've been four victims and four fall guys – at least. He can't follow everybody around, he doesn't break into their houses.'

'Maybe he's a clerk at one of those big discount stores,' Cooper suggested.

'But DeLeon bought some of the evidence at Home Depot – you can't buy condoms and snack food there.'

'Maybe Five Twenty-Two works for a credit card company?' Pulaski suggested. 'He can see what people buy that way.'

'Not bad, rookie, but some of the time the vics must've paid cash.'

It was Thom, surprisingly, who provided one answer. He fished out his keys. 'I heard Mel mention the discount cards earlier.' He displayed several small plastic cards on his key chain. One for A&P, one for Food Emporium. 'I swipe the card and get a discount. Even if I pay cash the store still knows what I bought.'

'Good,' Rhyme said. 'But where do we go from there? We're still looking at dozens of different sources the victims and fall guys shopped at.'

'Ah.'

Rhyme looked at Sachs, who was staring at the evidence board with a faint smile on her face. 'I think I've got it.'

'What?' Rhyme asked, expecting the clever application of a forensic principle.

'Shoes,' she said simply. 'The answer's shoes.'

Chapter
FIFTEEN

'It's not just about knowing *generally* what people buy,' Sachs explained. 'It's knowing the *specifics* about *all* the vics and the fall guys. Look at three of the crimes. Your cousin's case, the Myra Weinburg case and the coin theft. Five Twenty-Two not only knew the kind of shoe the fall guys wore. He knew the sizes.'

Rhyme said, 'Good. Let's find out where DeLeon Williams and Arthur buy their footwear.'

A fast call to Judy Rhyme and one to Williams revealed that the shoes were bought mail order – one through a catalog, one through a Web site, but both directly from the companies.

'All right,' Rhyme said, 'pick one, give them a call and find out how the shoe business works. Flip a coin.'

Sure-Track won. And it took only four phone calls to reach somebody connected with the company, the president and CEO, no less.

Water was sounding in the background, splashing, children laughing, as the man asked uncertainly, 'A crime?'

'Nothing to do with you directly,' Rhyme reassured him. 'One of your products is evidence.'

'But not like that guy who tried to blow up the airplane with a bomb in his shoe?' He stopped talking, as if even bringing this up was a breach of national security.

Rhyme explained the situation – the killer's getting personal information about the victims, including specifics about Sure-Track shoes, as well as his cousin's Altons and the other fall guy's Bass walkers. 'Do you sell through retail locations?'

'No. Only online.'

'Do you share information with your competitors? Information about customers?'

A hesitation.

'Hello?' Rhyme asked the silence.

'Oh, we can't share information. That would be an antitrust violation.'

'Well, how could somebody have gotten access to information about customers of Sure-Track shoes?'

'That's a complicated situation.'

Rhyme grimaced.

Sachs said, 'Sir, the man we're after is a killer and rapist. Do you have *any* thoughts about how he could've learned about your customers?'

'Not really.'

Lon Sellitto barked, 'Then we'll get a fucking warrant and take your records apart line by line.'

Not the subtle way Rhyme would have handled it but the sledge-hammer approach worked just fine. The man blurted, 'Wait, wait, wait. I might have an idea.'

'Which is?' Sellitto snapped.

'Maybe he . . . okay, if he had information from *different* companies maybe he got it from a data miner.'

'What's that?' Rhyme asked.

This pause was one of surprise, it seemed. 'You never heard of them?'

Rhyme rolled his eyes. 'No. What are they?'

'What it sounds like. Information service companies – they dig through data about consumers, their purchases and houses and cars, credit histories, everything about them. They analyze it and sell it. You know, to help companies spot market trends, find new customers, target direct-mail pieces and plan advertising. Things like that.'

Everything about them . . .

Rhyme thought: Maybe we're on to something here. 'Do they get information from RFID chips?'

'Sure they do. That's one of the big sources for data.'

'What data miner does your company use?'

'Oh, I don't know. Several of them.' His voice was reticent.

'We really need to know,' Sachs said, playing good cop to Sellitto's bad. 'We don't want anybody else to get hurt. This man is very dangerous.'

A sigh floated over the man's debate. 'Well, I suppose SSD is the main one. They're pretty big. But if you're thinking that somebody from there was involved in a crime, impossible. They're the greatest guys in the world. And there's security, there's—'

'Where are they based?' Sachs asked.

Another hesitation. Come on, damnit, Rhyme thought.

'In New York City.'

Five Twenty-Two's playground. The criminalist caught Sachs's eye. He smiled. This was looking promising.

'Any others in the area?'

'No. Axciom, Experian and Choicepoint, the other big ones, aren't around here. But, believe me, nobody from SSD could be involved. I swear.'

'What does SSD stand for?' Rhyme asked.

'Strategic Systems Datacorp.'

'Do you have a contact there?'

'Not anybody in particular exactly.' He said this fast. Too fast.

'You don't?'

'Well, there are sales reps we deal with. I can't recall their names at the moment. I could check it and find out.'

'Who runs the company?'

Another pause. 'That would be Andrew Sterling. He's the founder and CEO. Look, I guarantee nobody there would do anything illegal. Impossible.'

Then Rhyme realized something: The man was scared. Not of the police. Of SSD itself. 'What are you worried about?'

'It's just . . .' In a confessional tone he said, 'We couldn't function without them. We're really . . . partnered with them.'

Though, from his tone, the spurious verb seemed to mean 'desperately dependent on.'

'We'll be discreet,' Sachs said.

'Thank you. Really. Thank you.' The relief was obvious.

Sachs politely thanked him for his cooperation, drawing an eye roll from Sellitto.

Rhyme disconnected. 'Data mining? Anybody heard of it?'

Thom said, 'I don't know SSD but I've heard of data miners. It's *the* business of the twenty-first century.'

Rhyme glanced at the evidence chart. 'So if Five Twenty-Two works for SSD or is one of their customers he could find out everything he'd need about who bought shave cream, rope, condoms, fishing line – all the evidence he could plant.' Then another idea struck him. 'The head of the shoe company said that they sell the data for mailing lists. Arthur had gotten some direct mail about that Prescott painting, remember? Five Twenty-Two could have found out about it from their mailing lists. Maybe Alice Sanderson was on a list too.'

'And look – the crime-scene photos.' Sachs walked to the whiteboards and pointed to several pictures from the coin-theft scene. Direct-mail pieces sat prominently on the tables and floor.

Pulaski said, 'And, sir? Detective Cooper mentioned E-ZPass. If this SSD mines their data, then the killer might've been able to find out exactly when your cousin was in the city and when he headed home.'

'Jesus,' Sellitto muttered. 'If it's true, this guy's stumbled on one hell of an M.O.'

'Check out this data mining, Mel. Google it. I want to know for sure if SSD is the only one in the area.'

A few keystrokes later: 'Hmm. I got over twenty million hits for "data mining."'

'Twenty *million*?'

Over the next hour, the team watched as Cooper narrowed the list of the top data miners in the country – about a half dozen. He downloaded hundreds of pages of information from their sites and other details. Comparing the various data miners' client lists with the products used as evidence in the 522 case, it appeared that SSD was the most likely single source of all the information and was, in fact, the only one based in or near New York.

'If you want,' Cooper said, 'I can download their sales brochure.'

'Oh, we want, Mel. Let's see it.'

Sachs sat next to Rhyme and they looked over the screen as the SSD Web site appeared, topped by the company's logo: a watchtower with a window, from which radiated lines of illumination.

'Knowledge is Power' . . . The most valuable commodity in the 21st Century is information, and SSD is the number-one leader in using knowledge to hand-craft your strategies, to redefine your goals and to help you structure solutions to meet the myriad challenges you'll be facing in today's world. With more than 4,000 clients in the U.S. and abroad, SSD sets the industry standard as the pre-eminent Knowledge Service Provider on earth.

THE DATABASE

innerCircle® is the largest private database in the world, with key information on 280 million Americans and 130 million citizens of other countries. innerCircle® resides on our proprietary Massively Parallel Computer Array Network (MPCAN®), the most powerful commercial computer system ever assembled.

innerCircle® presently holds more than 500 petabytes of information – that equals trillions of pages of data – and we anticipate that soon the system will grow to an exabyte of data, an amount so vast that it would take only five exabytes to store the transcript of every word spoken by every human being in history!

We have troves of personal and public information: telephone numbers, addresses, vehicle registration, licensing information, buying histories and preferences, travel profiles, government records and vital statistics, credit and income histories and much, much more. We get these data into your hands at the speed of light, in a form that's easily accessible and instantly usable, uniquely tailored to your specific needs.

innerCircle® grows at the rate of hundreds of thousands of entries a day.

THE TOOLS

- Watchtower DBM®, the most comprehensive database management system in the world. Your partner in strategic planning, Watchtower® helps you target your goals, extracts the most meaningful data from innerCircle® and delivers a winning strategy directly to your desk, 24/7, via our light-ning-fast and super-secure servers. Watchtower® meets and exceeds the standards that SQL set years ago.

- Xpectation® predictive behavior software, based on the latest artificial intelligence and modeling technology. Manufacturers, service providers, wholesalers and retailers . . . want to know where your market is going and what your customers will want in the future? Then this is the product for you. And, law enforcers, take note: With Xpectation® you can predict where and when crimes will occur, and most important, who is likely to commit them.

- FORT® (Finding Obscure Relationships Tool), a unique and revolutionary product which analyzes millions of seem-ingly unrelated facts to determine connections human beings couldn't possibly discover on their own. Whether you're a commercial company wishing to know more about the marketplace (or about your competitors) or a law enforcement organization faced with a difficult criminal case, FORT® will give you the edge!

- ConsumerChoice® monitoring software and equipment allows you to determine consumers' accurate responses to advertising, marketing programs and new or proposed products. Forget subjective focus group opinions. Now, through biometric monitoring, you can gather and analyze individuals' true feelings about your potential plans – often without their awareness that they're being observed!

- Hub Overvue® information consolidation software. This easy-to-use product allows you to control every database within your organization – and, in appropriate circumstances, within other companies' operations as well.

- SafeGard®, security and identity verification software and services. Whether your concerns are terrorist threats, corporate kidnapping, industrial espionage or employee or customer theft, SafeGard® assures that your facilities will remain secure, letting you concentrate on your core business. This division includes the world's leading background verification, security and substance-screening companies, used by corporate and government clients throughout the world. The SafeGard® Division of SSD is also home to the industry leader in biometric hardware and software, Bio-Chek®.

- NanoCure® medical research software and services. Welcome to the world of microbiologic intelligent systems for the diagnosis and treatment of illness. Working with M.D.'s, our nanotechnologists are crafting solutions to the common health problems facing today's populace. From monitoring genetic issues to developing injectible tags to help in detecting and curing persistent, deadly illnesses, our NanoCure® Division is working to create a healthy society.

- On-Trial® civil litigation support systems and services. From products liability to anti-trust cases, On-Trial® streamlines document handling and deposition and evidence control.

- PublicSure® law enforcement support software. This is THE system for the consolidation and management of criminal and allied public records stored in international, federal, state and local databases. Through PublicSure® search results can be downloaded to offices, patrol car computers, PDA's or cell phones within seconds of the request, helping investigators bring cases to speedy conclusions and enhancing the preparedness and security of officers in the field.

- EduServe®, scholastic support software and services. Managing what children learn is vital in a successful society. EduServe® helps school boards and teachers in facilities from K to 12 most efficiently utilize their resources and offer services that guarantee the best education per tax dollar spent.

Rhyme laughed in disbelief. 'If Five Twenty-Two can get his hands on all this information . . . well, he's the man who knows everything.'

Mel Cooper said, 'Okay, listen to this. I was looking at the companies that SSD owns. Guess one of them.'

Rhyme replied, 'I'll go with whatever the hell their initials were – DMS. The maker of that RFID tag in the book, right?'

'Yep. You got it.'

No one said anything for some moments. Rhyme noticed

everyone in the room was looking at the glowing window logo of SSD on the computer screen.

'So,' Sellitto muttered, eyes on the chart. 'Where do we go from here?'

'Surveillance?' suggested Pulaski.

'That makes sense,' Sellitto said. 'I'll give S and S a call, set up some teams.'

Rhyme gave a cynical glance. 'Surveillance at a company with, what? A thousand employees?' He shook his head, then asked, 'You know Occam's razor, Lon?'

'Who the fuck is Occam? A barber?'

'A philosopher. The razor's a metaphor – cutting away unnecessary explanations for a phenomenon. His theory was that when you have multiple possibilities the simplest is almost always the correct one.'

'So what's your simple theory, Rhyme?'

Staring at the brochure, the criminalist answered Sachs, 'I think you and Pulaski should go pay a visit to SSD tomorrow morning.'

'And do what?'

He gave a shrug. 'Ask if anybody who works there is the killer.'

Chapter
SIXTEEN

Ah, home at last.

I close the door.

And lock out the world.

I breathe deeply and, setting my backpack on the couch, go into the spotless kitchen and drink some pure water. No stimulants for me at the moment.

That edgy thing again.

The town house is a nice one. Prewar, huge (it would have to be when you live the way I do, given my collections). Not easy to find the perfect place. It took me some time. But here I am, largely unnoticed. It's obscenely easy to be virtually anonymous in New York. What a marvelous city! Here, the default mode of existence is life off the grid. Here, you have to fight to be noticed. Many sixteens do that, of course. But then, the world's always had more than its share of fools.

Still, listen, you need to keep up appearances. The front rooms of my town house are simple and tastefully decorated (thank you, Scandinavia). I don't socialize here much but you need a façade to seem normal. You have to function in the real world. If you don't, sixteens begin to wonder if there's something going on, if you're someone other than you seem.

And it's a short step from that to someone coming round, poking into your Closet and taking everything away from you. Everything you've worked so hard for.

Everything.

And that's the worst of the worst.

So you make sure your Closet is secret. You make sure your treasures are hidden behind curtained or blocked windows, while you maintain your other life in full view, the sunlit side of the moon. To stay off the grid it's best to have a second living space. You do what I've done: keep this Danish modern patina of normalcy clean and ordered, even if it grates on your nerves like steel on slate to be there.

You have a normal house. Because that's what everybody has.

And you maintain a pleasant connection with associates and friends. Because that's what everyone does.

And you date occasionally and entice her to spend the night and you go through the motions.

Because that too is what everyone does. No matter that she doesn't get you as hard as when you've smooth talked your way into a girl's bedroom, smiling, aren't we soul mates, look at everything we have in common, with a tape recorder and a knife in your jacket pocket.

Now, I pull the shades in the bay windows and head to the back of the living room.

'Wow, this is like a really neat place . . . It looks bigger from the outside.'

'Yeah, funny how that happens.'

'Hey, you've got a door in your living room. What's through there?'

'Oh, that. Just storage. A closet. Nothing to see. Want some wine?'

Well, what's through there, Debby Sandra Susan Brenda, is where I'm headed right now. My *real* home. My Closet, I call it. It's like a keep – that last defensible spot of a medieval castle – the sanctuary in the center. When all else failed, the king and his family would retreat to the keep.

I enter mine through that magic doorway. It actually *is* a closet, a walk-in, and inside you'll see hanging clothes and shoe boxes. But push them aside and you'll find a second door. It opens on to the rest of the house, which is far, far bigger than the façade's horrifying blond Swedish minimalism.

My Closet . . .

I enter it now and lock the doors behind me and turn on the light.

Trying to relax. But after today, after the disaster, I'm having trouble shaking the edgy.

This isn't good this isn't good this . . .

I drop into my desk chair and boot up the computer as I stare at the Prescott painting in front of me, courtesy of Alice 3895. What a touch he had! The eyes of the family members are fascinating. Prescott managed to give each one a different gaze. It's clear they're all related; the expressions are similar in that way. Yet they're also different, as if each is imagining a different aspect of life as a family: happy, troubled, angry, mystified, controlling, controlled.

It's what a family is all about.

I suppose.

I open the backpack and take out the treasures I've acquired today. A tin canister, a pencil set, an old cheese grater. Why would somebody throw these away? I also unload some practical items I'll use in the next few weeks: some preapproved credit mailings that people carelessly discarded, credit card vouchers, phone bills . . . Fools, I was saying.

There's another item for my collection, of course, but I'll get to the tape recorder later. It's not as great a find as it could be, since Myra 9834's throaty screams while I detached the fingernail had to be muted by duct tape (I was worried about passersby). Still, everything in a collection can't be a crown jewel; you need the mundane to make the special soar.

I then wander through my Closet, depositing the treasures in the appropriate places.

It looks bigger from the outside . . .

As of today, I have 7,403 newspapers, 3,234 magazines (*National Geographic*s being the cornerstone, of course), 4,235 matchbooks . . . and, forgoing the numbers: coat hangers, kitchen utensils, lunch boxes, soda pop bottles, empty cereal boxes, scissors, shaving gear, shoe horns and trees, buttons, cuff links boxes, combs, wristwatches, clothes, tools useful and tools long outmoded. Phonograph records in colors, records in black. Bottles, toys, jam jars, candles and holders, candy dishes, weapons. It goes on and on and on.

The Closet consists of, what else? *Sixteen* galleries, like a museum's, ranging from those holding cheerful toys (though that Howdy Doody is pretty damn scary) to rooms of some things that *I* treasure but most people would find, oh, unpleasant. Hair and nail clippings and some shriveled mementoes from various transactions. Like this afternoon's. I deposit Myra 9834's fingernail in a prominent spot. And while this would normally give me enough pleasure to make me hard again, now the moment is dark and spoiled.

I hate Them so much . . .

With quivering hands I close the cigar box, taking no pleasure from my treasures at the moment.

Hate hate hate . . .

Back at the computer, I'm reflecting: Maybe there's no threat. Maybe it's just an odd set of coincidences that led Them to DeLeon 6832's house.

But I can't take any chances.

The problem: The risk that my treasures will be taken from me, which is consuming me now.

The solution: To do what I started in Brooklyn. To fight back. To eliminate any threats.

What most sixteens, including my pursuers, don't understand and what puts Them at a pathetic disadvantage is this: I believe in the immutable truth that there is absolutely nothing morally wrong with taking a life. Because I know that there is eternal existence completely independent of these bags of skin and organ we cart around temporarily. I have proof: Just look at the trove of data about your life, built up from the moment you're born. It's all permanent, stored in a thousand places, copied, backed up, invisible and indestructible. After the body goes, as all bodies must, the data survive forever.

And if that's not the definition of an immortal soul, I don't know what is.

Chapter
SEVENTEEN

The bedroom was quiet.

Rhyme had sent Thom home to spend Sunday night with Peter Hoddins, the caregiver's longtime partner. Rhyme gave the aide a lot of crap. He couldn't help that and sometimes he felt bad about it. But he tried to compensate and when Amelia Sachs was staying with him, as tonight, he shooed Thom off. The young man needed more of a life outside the town house here, taking care of a feisty old crip.

Rhyme heard tinkering in the bathroom. The sounds of a woman getting ready for bed. Clinks of glass and snaps of plastic lids, aerosol hisses, water running, fragrances escaping on humid bathroom air.

He liked moments like these. They reminded him of his life in the Before.

Which in turn brought to mind the pictures downstairs in the laboratory. Beside the one of Lincoln in his tracksuit was another, in black and white. It showed two men wearing suits on their lanky frames, in their twenties, standing side by side. Their arms hung straight, as if they were wondering whether to embrace.

Rhyme's father and uncle.

He thought often of Uncle Henry. His father not so much. This had been true throughout his life. Oh, there was nothing objectionable about Teddy Rhyme. The younger of the two siblings was simply retiring, often shy. He loved his nine-to-five job crunching numbers in various labs, loved to read, which he did every evening while lounging in a thick, well-worn armchair, while his wife, Anne, sewed or watched TV. Teddy favored history, especially the American Civil War, an interest that, Rhyme supposed, was the source of his own given name.

The boy and his father coexisted pleasantly, though Rhyme recalled many awkward silences present when father and son were alone. What troubles also engages. What challenges you makes you feel alive. And Teddy never troubled or challenged.

Uncle Henry did, though. In spades.

You couldn't be in the same room with him for more than a few minutes without his attention turning to you like a searchlight. Then came the jokes, the trivia, recent family news. And always the questions – some asked because he was genuinely curious to learn. Most, though, asked as a call to debate with you. Oh, how Henry Rhyme loved intellectual jousting. You might cringe, you might blush, you might grow furious. But you'd also burn with pride at one of the rare compliments he offered because you knew you'd earned it. No false praise or unwarranted encouragement ever slipped from Uncle Henry's lips.

'You're close. Think harder! You've got it in you. Einstein had done all his important work when he was just a little older than you.'

If you got it right, you were blessed with a raised eyebrow of approval, tantamount to winning the Westinghouse Science Fair prize. But all too often your arguments were fallacious, your premises straw, your criticisms emotional, your facts skewed . . . At issue, though, wasn't his victory over you; his only goal was arriving at the truth and making sure you understood the route. Once he'd diced your argument to fine chop, and made sure you saw why, the matter was over.

So you understand where you went wrong? You calculated the temperature with an incorrect set of assumptions. Exactly! Now, let's make some calls – get some people together and go see the White Sox on Saturday. I need a ballpark hot dog and we sure as hell won't be able to buy one at Comiskey Park in October.

Lincoln had enjoyed the intellectual sparring, often driving all the way to Hyde Park to sit in on his uncle's seminars or informal discussion groups at the university; in fact, he had gone more frequently than Arthur, who was usually busy with other activities.

If his uncle were still alive, he'd undoubtedly stroll into Rhyme's room now without a glance at his motionless body, point at the gas chromatograph and blurt, 'Why are you still running that piece of crap?' Then settling down across from the evidence whiteboards, he'd start questioning Rhyme about his handling of the 522 case.

Yes, but is it logical *for this individual to behave in this manner? State your givens once more for me.*

He thought back to the night he'd recalled earlier: the Christmas Eve of his senior year in high school, at his uncle's house in Evanston. Present were Henry and Paula and their children, Robert, Arthur and Marie; Teddy and Anne with Lincoln; some aunts and uncles, other cousins. A neighbor or two.

Lincoln and Arthur had spent much of the evening playing pool downstairs and talking about plans for the next fall and college. Lincoln's heart was set on M.I.T. Arthur, too, planned to go there. They were both confident of admission and that night were debating rooming together in a dorm or finding an off-campus apartment (male camaraderie versus a babe lair).

The family then assembled at the massive table in his uncle's dining room, Lake Michigan churning nearby, the wind hissing through bare, gray branches in the backyard. Henry presided over the table the way he presided over his class, in charge and aware, a faint smile below quick eyes taking in all the conversations around him. He'd tell jokes and anecdotes and ask about his guests' lives. He was interested, curious – and sometimes manipulative. 'So, Marie, now that we're all here, tell us about that fellowship at Georgetown. I think we agreed it'd be excellent for you. And Jerry can come visit on weekends in that fancy new car of his. By the way, when's the deadline for the application? Coming up, I seem to recall.'

And his wispy-haired daughter avoided his eyes and said what with Christmas and final exams, she hadn't quite finished the paperwork. But she would. Definitely.

Henry's mission, of course, was to get his daughter to commit in front of witnesses, no matter that she'd be separated from her fiancé for another six months.

Rhyme had always believed that his uncle would have made an excellent trial lawyer or politician.

After the remnants of the turkey and mincemeat pie were cleared away and the Grand Marnier, coffee and tea had appeared, Henry ushered everyone into the living room, dominated by a massive tree, busy fireplace flames and a stern painting of Lincoln's grandfather – a triple doctorate and a professor at Harvard.

It was time for the competition.

Henry would throw out a science question and the first to answer it would win a point. The top three players would receive prizes picked by Henry and meticulously wrapped by Paula.

Tensions were palpable – they always were when Henry was in charge – and people competed seriously. Lincoln's father could be counted on to nail more than a few chemistry questions. If the topic involved numbers his mother, a part-time math teacher, answered some before Henry had even finished asking. The front runners throughout the contest, though, were the cousins – Robert, Marie, Lincoln and Arthur – and Marie's fiancé.

Toward the end, nearly 8 P.M., the contestants were literally on the edge of their chairs. The rankings changed with every question. Palms were sweaty. With only minutes remaining on timekeeper Paula's clock, Lincoln answered three questions in a row and nosed ahead for the first-place win. Marie was second, Arthur third.

Amid the clapping, Lincoln took a theatrical bow and accepted the top prize from his uncle. He still remembered his surprise as he unwrapped the dark green paper: a clear plastic box containing a one-inch cube of concrete. It wasn't a joke prize, though. What Lincoln held was a piece of Stagg Field at the University of Chicago, where the first atomic chain reaction had occurred, under the direction of his cousin's namesake, Arthur Compton, and Enrico Fermi. Henry had apparently acquired one of the pieces when the stadium was torn down in the 1950s. Lincoln had been very touched by the historic prize and suddenly glad he'd played seriously. He still had the rock somewhere, tucked away in a cardboard box in the basement.

But Lincoln had no time to admire his award.

Because that night he had a late date with Adrianna.

Like his family, unexpectedly thrust into his thoughts today, the beautiful, red-haired gymnast had figured in his memories too.

Adrianna Waleska – pronounced with a soft V, echoing her second-generation Gdansk roots – worked in the college counselor's office in Lincoln's high school. Early in his senior year, delivering some applications to her, he'd spotted *Stranger in a Strange Land* on her desk, the Heinlein novel well-thumbed. They'd spent the next hour discussing the book, agreeing often, arguing some, with the result that Lincoln realized he'd missed his chemistry class. No matter. Priorities were priorities.

She was tall, lean, had invisible braces and an appealing

figure under her fuzzy sweaters and flared jeans. Her smile ranged from ebullient to seductive. They were soon dating, the first foray into serious romance for both of them. They'd attend each other's sports meets, go to the Thorne Rooms at the Art Institute, the jazz clubs in Old Town and, occasionally, visit the backseat of her Chevy Monza, which was hardly any back-seat at all and therefore just the ticket. Adrianna lived a short run from his house, by Lincoln's track-and-field standards, but that would never do – can't show up sweaty – so he'd borrow the family car when he could and head over to see her.

They'd spend hours talking. As with Uncle Henry, he and Adie *engaged*.

Obstacles existed, yes. He was leaving next year for college in Boston; she, for San Diego to study biology and work in the zoo. But those were mere complications and Lincoln Rhyme, then as now, would not accept complications as excuses.

Afterward – after the accident, and after he and Blaine divorced – Rhyme often wondered what would have happened if he and Adrianna had stayed together and pursued what they'd started. That Christmas Eve night, in fact, he'd come very close to proposing. He'd considered offering her not a ring but, as he'd cleverly rehearsed, 'a different kind of rock' – his uncle's prize from the science trivia contest.

But he'd balked, thanks to the weather. As they'd sat, clutching each other on a bench, the snow had begun to tumble suicidally from the silent Midwest sky and in minutes their hair and coats were covered with a damp white blanket. She'd just made it back to her house and Lincoln to his before the roads were blocked. He lay in bed that night, the plastic box containing the concrete beside him, and practiced a proposal speech.

Which was never delivered. Events intruded in their lives, sending them on different paths, seemingly minute events, though small in the way of invisible atoms tricked to fission in a chilly sports stadium, changing the world forever.

Everything would've been different . . .

Rhyme now caught a glimpse of Sachs brushing her long red hair. He watched her for some moments, glad she'd be staying tonight – more pleased than usual. Rhyme and Sachs weren't inseparable. They were staunchly independent people, preferring often to spend time apart. But tonight he wanted her here. Enjoying the presence of her body next to his, the sensation – in those few places he was able to feel – all the more intense for its rarity.

His love for her was one of the motivators for his exercise regimen, working on a computerized treadmill and Electrologic bike. If medical science crept past that finishing line – allowing him to walk again – his muscles were going to be ready. He was also considering a new operation that might improve his condition until that day arrived. Experimental, and controversial, it was known as peripheral nerve rerouting, a technique that had been talked about – and occasionally tried – for years without many positive results. But recently foreign doctors had been performing the operation with some success, despite the reservation of the American medical community. The procedure involved surgically connecting nerves above the site of the injury to nerves below it. A detour around a washed-out bridge, in effect.

The successes were mostly in bodies less severely damaged than Rhyme's but the results were remarkable: return of bladder control, movement of limbs, even walking. The latter would not be the result in Rhyme's case but discussions with a Japanese doctor who'd pioneered the procedure and with a colleague at an Ivy League university teaching hospital gave some hope of improvement. Possibly sensation and movement in his arms, hands and bladder.

Sex too.

Paralyzed men, even quads, are perfectly capable of having sex. If the stimulus is mental – seeing a man or woman who appeals to us – then, no, the message doesn't make it past the site of the damaged spinal cord. But the body is a brilliant mechanism and there's a magic loop of nerve that operates on its own, below the injury. A little local stimulus, and even the most severely disabled men can often make love.

The bathroom light clicked out and he watched her silhouette join him and climb into what she'd announced long ago was the most comfortable bed in the world.

'I—' he began, and his voice was immediately muffled by her mouth as she kissed him hard.

'What did you say?' she whispered, moving her lips along his chin, then to his neck.

He'd forgotten. 'I forgot.'

He gripped her ear with his lips and was then aware of the blankets being pulled down. This took some effort on her part; Thom made up the bed like a soldier afraid of his drill sergeant. But soon he could see that the blankets were bunched up at the foot. Sachs's T-shirt had joined them.

She kissed him again. He kissed her back hard.

Which is when her phone rang.

'Uh-uh,' she whispered. 'I didn't hear that.' After four rings, blessed voice mail took over. But a moment later it rang again.

'Could be your mother,' Rhyme pointed out.

Rose Sachs had been undergoing some treatments for a cardiac problem. The prognosis was good but she'd had some recent setbacks.

Sachs grunted and flipped it open, bathing both of their bodies in a blue light. Looking at caller ID, she said, 'Pam. I better take it.'

'Of course.'

'Hey, there. What's up?'

As the one-sided conversation continued, Rhyme deduced that something was wrong.

'Okay . . . Sure . . . But I'm at Lincoln's. You want to come over here?' She glanced at Rhyme, who was nodding agreement. 'Okay, honey. We'll be awake, sure.' She snapped the phone shut.

'What is it?'

'I don't know. She wouldn't say. She just said Dan and Enid had two emergency placements tonight. So all the older kids had to room together. She had to get out. And she doesn't want to be at my place alone.'

'It's fine with me. You know that.'

Sachs lay back down and her mouth explored energetically. She whispered, 'I did the math. She's got to pack a bag, get her car out of the garage . . . it'll take her a good forty-five minutes to be here. We've got a little time.'

She leaned forward and kissed him again.

Just as the doorbell rang jarringly and the intercom clattered, 'Mr Rhyme? Amelia? Hi, it's Pam. Can you buzz me in?'

Rhyme laughed. 'Or she might've called from the front steps.'

They sat in one of the upstairs bedrooms, Pam and Sachs.

The room was the girl's for whenever she wished to stay. A stuffed animal or two sat neglected on the shelf (when your mother and stepfather are running from the FBI, toys don't figure much in your childhood) but she had several hundred books and CDs. Thanks to Thom there always were plenty of clean sweats and T-shirts and socks. A Sirius satellite radio set and a disk player. Her running shoes too; Pam loved to speed along the 1.6-mile path surrounding the Central Park reservoir. She ran from love of running and she ran from hungry need.

The girl now sat on the bed, carefully painting gold polish on her toenails, cotton balls separating the canvases. Her mother had forbidden this, as well as makeup ('out of respect for Christ,' however that was supposed to work), and once sprung from the far-right underground she took up small, comforting additions to her persona, like this, some ruddy hair tint and the three ear piercings. Sachs was relieved she didn't go overboard; if anybody had a reason to slingshot herself into the weird, it was Pamela Willoughby.

Sachs was lounging in a chair, feet up, her own toenails bare. A breeze carried into the small room the complicated mix of spring scents from Central Park: mulch, earth, dew-damp foliage, vehicle exhaust. She sipped her hot chocolate. 'Ouch. Blow on it first.'

Pam whistled into her cup and tasted it. 'It's good. Yeah, hot.' She returned to her nails. In contrast to her visage earlier in the day, the girl's face was troubled.

'You know what those are called?' Sachs was pointing.

'Feet? Toes?'

'No, the bottoms?'

'Sure. The bottoms of feet and the bottoms of toes.' They laughed.

'Plantars. And they have prints too, just like fingerprints. Lincoln convicted somebody once because the perp kicked somebody unconscious with his bare foot. But he missed once and whacked the door. Left a print on it.'

'That's cool. He should write another book.'

'I'm after him to,' Sachs said. 'So what's up?'

'Stuart.'

'Go on.'

'Maybe I shouldn't've come. It's stupid.'

'Come on. I'm a cop, remember. I'll sweat it out of you.'

'Just, Emily called and it was weird her calling on Sunday, like, she never does, and I'm thinking, okay, something's going on. And it's like she really doesn't want to say anything but then she does. And she said she saw Stuart today with somebody else. This girl from school. After the soccer game. Only he told me he was going right home.'

'Well, what are the facts? Were they just talking? Nothing wrong with that.'

'She said she wasn't sure but it, you know, kind of looked like he was hugging her. And then when he saw somebody looking at him, he kind of walked away real fast with her. Like he was trying to hide.' The toenail project came to a stop, halfway done. 'I really, really like him. It'd suck if he didn't want to see me anymore.'

Sachs and Pam had been to a counselor together – and, with Pam's agreement, Sachs had spoken to the woman alone. Pam would be undergoing a lengthy period of post-traumatic stress, not only from her lengthy captivity with a sociopath parent but from a particular episode in which her stepfather had nearly sacrificed her life while trying to murder police officers. Incidents like this one with Stuart Everett, small to most people, were amplified in the girl's mind and could have devastating effects. Sachs had been told not to add to her fears but not to downplay them either. To look at each one carefully and try to analyze it.

'Have you guys talked about seeing other people?'

'He said . . . well, a month ago he said he wasn't. I'm not either. I told him that.'

'Any other intelligence?' Sachs asked.

'Intelligence?'

'I mean, have any of your other friends said anything?'

'No.'

'Do you know any of *his* friends?'

'Kind of. But not like I could ask them anything about it. That'd be way uncool.'

Sachs smiled. 'So spies aren't going to work. Well, what you should do is just ask him. Point-blank.'

'You think?'

'I think.'

'What if he says he *is* seeing her?'

'Then you should be thankful he's honest with you. That's a good sign. And then you convince him to dump the bimbo.' They laughed. 'What you do is say that you just want to date one person.' The start-up mother in Sachs added quickly, 'We're not talking about getting married, not moving in. Just dating.'

Pam nodded quickly. 'Oh, absolutely.'

Relieved, Sachs continued, 'And he's the one you want to see. But you expect the same thing from him. You have something important, you relate to each other, you can talk, you've got a connection and you don't see that very much.'

'Like you and Mr Rhyme.'

'Yeah, like that. But if he doesn't want it, then okay.'

'No, it's not.' Pam frowned.

'No, I'm just telling you what you say. But then tell him *you're* going to be dating other people too. He can't have it both ways.'

'I guess. But what if he says fine?' Her face was dark at the thought.

A laugh. Sachs shook her head. 'Yep, it's a bummer when they call your bluff. But I don't think he will.'

'All right. I'm going to see him tomorrow after class. I'll talk to him.'

'Call me. Let me know.' Sachs rose, lifted away the polish and capped it. 'Get some sleep. It's late.'

'But my nails. I'm not finished.'

'Don't wear open-toed.'

'Amelia?'

She paused at the doorway.

'Are you and Mr Rhyme going to get married?'

Sachs smiled and closed the door.

III

THE FORTUNE TELLER

MONDAY, MAY 23

With uncanny accuracy, computers predict behavior by sifting through mountains of data about customers collected by businesses. Called predictive analytics, this automated crystal ball gazing has become a $2.3 billion industry in the United States and is on track to reach $3 billion by 2008.

—CHICAGO TRIBUNE

Chapter
EIGHTEEN

They're pretty big . . .

Amelia Sachs sat in Strategic Systems Datacorp's sky-high lobby and reflected that the shoe company president's description of SSD's data mining operation was, well, *pretty* understated.

The Midtown building was thirty stories high, a gray spiky monolith, the sides smooth granite flashing with mica. The windows were narrow slits, which was surprising given the stunning views of the city from this location and elevation. She was familiar with the building, dubbed the Gray Rock, but had never known who owned it.

She and Ron Pulaski – no longer in play clothes but wearing a navy suit and navy uniform, respectively – sat facing a massive wall on which were printed the locations of the SSD offices around the world, among them London, Buenos Aires, Mumbai, Singapore, Beijing, Dubai, Sydney and Tokyo.

Pretty big . . .

Above the list of satellite offices was the company logo: the window in the watchtower.

Her gut twisted slightly as she recalled the windows in the abandoned building across the street from Robert

Jorgensen's residence hotel. She recalled Lincoln Rhyme's words about the incident with the federal agent in Brooklyn.

He knew exactly where you were. Which means he was watching. Be careful, Sachs . . .

Looking around the lobby, she saw a half dozen business-people waiting here, many of them uneasy, it seemed, and she recalled the shoe company president and his concern about losing SSD's services. She then saw, almost en masse, their heads swivel, looking past the receptionist. They were watching a short man, youthful, enter the lobby and walk directly toward Sachs and Pulaski over the black-and-white rugs. His posture was perfect and his stride long. The sandy-haired man nodded and smiled, offering a fast greeting – by name – to nearly everybody here.

A presidential candidate. That was Sachs's first impression.

But he didn't stop until he came to the officers. 'Good morning. I'm Andrew Sterling.'

'Detective Sachs. This is Officer Pulaski.'

Sterling was shorter than Sachs by several inches but he seemed quite fit and had broad shoulders. His immaculate white shirt featured a starched collar and cuffs. His arms seemed muscular; the jacket was tight-fitting. No jewelry. Crinkles radiated from the corners of his green eyes when that easy smile crossed his face.

'Let's go to my office.'

The head of such a big company . . . yet he'd come to them, rather than having an underling escort them to his throne room.

Sterling walked easily down the wide, quiet halls. He greeted every employee, sometimes asking questions about their weekends. They ate up his smiles at reports of an enjoy-able weekend and his frowns at word of ill relatives or canceled games. There were dozens of them, and he made a personal comment to each.

'Hello, Tony,' he said to a janitor, who was emptying the contents of shredded documents into a large plastic bag. 'Did you see the game?'

'No, Andrew, I missed it. Had too much to do.'

'Maybe we should start three-day weekends,' Sterling joked.

'I'd vote for that, Andrew.'

And they continued down the hall.

Sachs didn't think she *knew* as many in the NYPD as Sterling said hello to in their five-minute walk.

The decor of the company was minimal: some small, tasteful photographs and sketches – none in color – overwhelmed by the spotless white walls. The furniture, also black or white, was simple – expensive Ikea. It was a statement of some kind, she guessed, but she found it bleak.

As they walked, she ran through what she'd learned last night, after saying good night to Pam. The man's bio, patched together from the Web, was sparse. He was an intensely reclusive man – a Howard Hughes, not a Bill Gates. His early life was a mystery. She'd found no references at all to his childhood, or his parents. A few sketchy pieces in the press had put him on the radar at age seventeen, when he'd had his first jobs, mostly in sales, working door-to-door and telemarketing, moving up to bigger, more expensive products. Finally computers. For a kid with '7/8 of a bachelor's degree from a night school,' Sterling told the press, he found himself a successful salesman. He'd gone back to college, finishing the last one-eighth of the degree and completing a master's in computer science and engineering in short order. The stories were all very Horatio Alger and included only details that boosted his savvy and status as a businessman.

Then, in his twenties, had come the 'great awakening,' he said, sounding like a Chinese communist dictator. Sterling was selling a lot of computers but not enough to satisfy him. Why wasn't he more successful? He wasn't lazy. He wasn't stupid.

Then he realized the problem: He was inefficient.

And so were a lot of other salesmen.

So Sterling learned computer programming and spent weeks of eighteen-hour days, in a dark room, writing software. He hocked everything and started a company, one based on a concept that was either foolish or brilliant: Its most valuable asset wouldn't be owned by his company but by millions of other people, much of it free for the taking – information about themselves. Sterling began compiling a database that included potential customers in a number of service and manufacturing markets, the demographics of the area in which they were located, their income, marital status, the good or bad news about their financial and legal and tax situations, and as much other information – personal and professional – as he could buy, steal or otherwise find. 'If there's a fact out there, I want it,' he was quoted as saying.

The software he wrote, the early version of the Watchtower database management system, was revolutionary at the time, an exponential leap over the famed SQL – pronounced 'sequel,' Sachs had learned – program. In minutes Watchtower would decide which customers would be worthwhile to call on and how to seduce them, and which weren't worth the effort (but whose names might be sold to other companies for their own pitches).

The company grew like a monster in a science fiction film. Sterling changed the name to SSD, moved it to Manhattan and began to collect smaller companies in the information business to add to his empire. Though unpopular with privacy rights organizations, there'd never been a hint of a scandal at SSD, à la Enron. Employees had to earn their salaries – no one received obscenely high Wall Street bonuses – but if the company profited, so did they. SSD offered tuition and home-purchasing assistance, internships for children, and parents were given a year of maternity or paternity leave. The company was known for the familial way it treated its workers and Sterling encouraged hiring spouses, parents and children. Every month he sponsored motivational and team-building retreats.

The CEO was secretive about his personal life, though Sachs learned that he didn't smoke or drink and that no one had ever heard him utter an obscenity. He lived modestly, took a surprisingly small salary and kept his wealth in SSD stock. He shunned the New York social scene. No fast cars, no private jets. Despite his respect for the family unit among SSD employees, Sterling was twice divorced and unmarried at the moment. There were conflicting reports about children he'd fathered in his youth. He had several residences but he kept their whereabouts out of the public record. Perhaps because he knew the power of data, Andrew Sterling appreciated its dangers too.

Sterling, Sachs and Pulaski now came to the end of a long corridor and entered an exterior office, where two assistants had their desks, both of which were filled with perfectly ordered stacks of papers, file folders, printouts. Only one assistant was in at the moment, a young man, handsome, in a conservative suit. His nameplate read *Martin Coyle*. His area was the most ordered – even the many books behind him were arranged in descending order of size, Sachs was amused to see.

'Andrew.' He nodded a greeting to his boss, ignoring the officers as soon as he noted that they hadn't been introduced. 'Your phone messages are on your computer.'

'Thank you.' Sterling glanced at the other desk. 'Jeremy's going to look over the restaurant for the press junket?'

'He did that this morning. He's running some papers over to the law firm. About that other matter.'

Sachs marveled that Sterling had *two* personal assistants – apparently one for the inside work, the other handling out-of-the-office matters. At the NYPD detectives shared, if they had help at all.

They continued on to Sterling's own office, which wasn't much bigger than any other she'd seen in the company. And its walls were free of decoration. Despite the SSD logo of the voyeuristic window in the watchtower, Andrew Sterling's were curtained, cutting off what would be a magnificent view of the city. A ripple of claustrophobia coursed through her.

Sterling sat in a simple wooden chair, not a leather swivel throne. He gestured them into similar ones, though padded. Behind him were low shelves filled with books but, curiously, they were stacked with spines facing up, not outward. Visitors to his office couldn't see his choice of reading matter without walking past the man and looking down or pulling out a volume.

The CEO nodded at a pitcher and a half dozen inverted glasses. 'That's water. But if you'd like some coffee or tea, I can have some fetched.'

Fetched? She didn't think she'd ever heard anyone actually use the word.

'No, thank you.'

Pulaski shook his head.

'Excuse me. Just one moment.' Sterling picked up his phone, dialed. 'Andy? You called.'

Sachs deduced from the tone that it was someone close to him, though it was clearly a business call about a problem of some sort. Yet Sterling spoke emotionlessly. 'Ah. Well, you'll have to, I think. We need those numbers. You know, they're not sitting on *their* hands. They'll make a move any day now . . . Good.'

He hung up and noticed Sachs watching him closely. 'My son works for the company.' A nod at a photo on his desk, showing Sterling with a handsome, thin young man who resembled the CEO. Both were wearing SSD T-shirts at some employee outing, maybe one of the inspirational retreats. They were next to each other but there was no physical contact between them. Neither was smiling.

So one question about his personal life had been answered.

'Now,' he said, turning his green eyes on Sachs, 'what's this all about? You mentioned some crime.'

Sachs explained, 'There've been several murders in the past few months in the city. We think that someone might've used information in your computers to get close to the victims, kill them and then used that and other information to frame innocent people for the crimes.'

The man who knows everything . . .

'Information?' His concern seemed genuine. He was perplexed too, though. 'I'm not sure how that could happen but tell me more.'

'Well, the killer knew exactly what personal products the victims used and he planted traces of them as evidence at an innocent person's residence to connect them to the killing.' From time to time the eyebrows above Sterling's emerald irises narrowed. He seemed genuinely troubled as she gave him the details about the theft of the painting and coins and the two sexual assaults.

'That's terrible . . .' Troubled by the news, he glanced away from her. 'Rapes?'

Sachs nodded grimly and then explained how SSD seemed to be the only company in the area that had access to all the information the killer had used.

He rubbed his face, nodding slowly.

'I can see why you're concerned . . . But wouldn't it be easier for this killer just to follow the people he victimized and find out what they bought? Or even hack into their computers, break into their mailboxes, their homes, jot down their license plate numbers from the street?'

'But see, that's the problem: He could. But he'd have to do *all* of those things to get the information he needed. There've been four crimes at a minimum – we think there could probably be more – and that means up-to-date information on the four victims and four men he's setting up. The most efficient way to get that information would be to go through a data miner.'

Sterling gave a smile, a delicate wince.

Sachs frowned and cocked her head.

He said, 'Nothing wrong with that term, "data miner." The press has latched on to it and you see it everywhere.'

Twenty million search-engine hits . . .

'But I prefer to call SSD a knowledge service provider – a KSP. Like an Internet service provider.'

Sachs had a strange sensation; he seemed almost hurt by what she'd said. She wanted to tell him she wouldn't do it again.

Sterling smoothed a stack of papers on his organized desktop. At first she thought they were blank but then she noticed they were all turned facedown. 'Well, believe me, if anyone at SSD is involved, I want to find out as much as you do. This could look very bad for us – knowledge service providers haven't been doing very well in the press or in Congress lately.'

'First of all,' Sachs said, 'the killer would have bought most of the items with cash, we're pretty sure.'

Sterling nodded. 'He wouldn't want to leave any trace of himself.'

'Right. But the shoes he bought mail order or online. Would you have a list of people who bought these shoes in these sizes in the New York area?' She handed him a list of the Altons, the Bass and the Sure-Tracks. 'The same man would have bought all of them.'

'What time period?'

'Three months.'

Sterling made a phone call. He had a brief conversation and no more than sixty seconds later he was looking at his computer screen. He swiveled it so Sachs could see, though she wasn't sure what she was looking at – strings of product information and codes.

The CEO shook his head. 'Roughly eight hundred Altons sold, twelve hundred Bass, two hundred Sure-Tracks. But no one person bought all three. Or even two pairs.'

Rhyme had suspected that the killer, if he used information from SSD, would cover his tracks but they'd hoped this lead would pay off. Staring at the numbers, she wondered if the killer had used the identity-theft techniques he'd perfected on Robert Jorgensen to order the shoes.

'Sorry.'

She nodded.

Sterling uncapped a battered silver pen and pulled a notepad toward him. In precise script he wrote several notes Sachs couldn't read, stared at it, nodded to himself. 'You're thinking, I'd imagine, that the problem is an intruder, an employee, one of our customers or a hacker, right?'

Ron Pulaski glanced at Sachs and said, 'Exactly.'

'All right. Let's get to the bottom of it.' He checked his Seiko watch. 'I want some other people in here. It may take a few minutes. We have our Spirit Circles every Monday around this time.'

'Spirit Circles?' Pulaski asked.

'Inspirational team meetings by the group leaders. They should be finished soon. We start at eight on the dot. But some go a little longer than others. Depending on the leader.' He said, 'Command, intercom, Martin.'

Sachs laughed to herself. He was using the same sort of voice-recognition system that Lincoln Rhyme had.

'Yes, Andrew?' The voice came from a tiny box on the desk.

'I want Tom – security Tom – and Sam. Are they in Spirit Circles?'

'No, Andrew, but Sam's probably going to be in Washington all week. He won't be back till Friday. Mark, his assistant's in.'

'Him, then.'

'Yes, sir.'

'Command, intercom, disconnect.' To Sachs he said, 'Should just be a moment.'

She imagined that when Andrew Sterling summoned you, you materialized pretty quickly. He jotted a few more notes. As he did, she glanced at the company logo on the wall. When he was through writing she said, 'I'm curious about that. The tower and the window. What's the significance of it?'

'On one level it just means observing data. But there's a second meaning.' He smiled, pleased to be explaining this. 'Do you know the concept of the broken window in social philosophy?'

'No.'

'I learned about it years ago and never forgot it. The thrust is that in order to improve society you should concentrate on the small things. If you control those – or fix them – then the bigger changes will follow. Take housing projects with a high-crime problem. You can sink millions into increased police patrols and security cameras but if the projects still look dilapidated and dangerous, they'll stay dilapidated and dangerous. Instead of millions of dollars, put thousands into fixing the windows, painting, cleaning the halls. It may seem cosmetic but people will notice. They'll take pride in where they live. They'll start to report people who are threats and who don't look after their property.

'As I'm sure you know, that was the thrust of crime prevention in New York in the nineties. And it worked.'

'Andrew?' came Martin's voice from the intercom. 'Tom and Mark are here.'

Sterling ordered, 'Send them in.' He set the paper he'd been jotting notes on directly in front of him. He gave Sachs a grim smile. 'Let's see if anybody's been peeking through our window.'

Chapter
NINETEEN

The doorbell rang and Thom ushered in a man in his early thirties, disheveled brown hair, jeans, a Weird Al Yankovic T-shirt under a shabby brown sports coat.

You couldn't be in the forensics game nowadays without being computer literate but both Rhyme and Cooper recognized their limitations. When it was clear that there were digital implications of the 522 case, Sellitto had requested some help from the NYPD Computer Crimes Unit, an elite group of thirty-two detectives and support staff.

Rodney Szarnek strode into the room, glanced at the nearest monitor and said, 'Hey,' as if he were speaking to the hardware. Similarly when he glanced toward Rhyme he expressed no interest in his physical condition whatsoever, only in the wireless environmental control unit attached to the armrest. He seemed impressed.

'Your day off?' Sellitto asked, glancing at the slim young man's outfit, his voice making it clear he didn't approve. Rhyme knew the detective was old school; police officers should dress appropriately.

'Day off?' Szarnek replied, missing the dig. 'No. Why would I have a day off?'

'Just wondering.'

'Heh. So, now, what's the story?'

'We need a trap.'

Lincoln Rhyme's theory about strolling into SSD and just plain asking about a killer wasn't as naive as it seemed. When he'd seen on the company Web site that SSD's PublicSure division supported police departments, his hunch was that NYPD was a customer. If that was the case, then the killer might have access to the department files. A fast call revealed that, yes, the department was a client. PublicSure software and SSD consultants provided data management services for the city, including consolidation of case information, reports and records. If a patrolman on the street needed a warrant check, or a detective new to a homicide needed the case's history, PublicSure helped get the information to his desk or squad-car computer or even his PDA or cell phone, in minutes.

By sending Sachs and Pulaski to the company and asking who might have accessed the data files about the victims and fall guys, 522 could learn they were on to him and try to get into the NYPD system through PublicSure to look at the reports. If he did, they might be able to trace who had accessed the files.

Rhyme explained the situation to Szarnek, who nodded knowingly – as if he set up traps like this every day. He was taken aback, though, when he learned what company the killer might have a connection to. 'SSD? The biggest data miner in the world. They got the scoop on all of God's children.'

'Is that a problem?'

His carefree geek image faltered and he answered softly, 'I hope not.'

And he set to work with their trap, explaining what he was doing. He stripped from the files any details about the case they didn't want 522 to know and manually transferred those sensitive files to a computer that had no Internet access.

He then put an alarmed visual traceroute program in front of the 'Myra Weinburg Sexual Assault/Homicide' file on the NYPD server. And added subfiles to tempt the killer, like 'Suspects' whereabouts,' 'Forensic analysis' and 'Witnesses,' all of which contained only general notes about crime-scene procedures. If anyone accessed it, either hacking in or through authorized channels, a notice of the person's ISP and physical location would be instantly sent to Szarnek. They could tell immediately if the one checking out the file was a cop with a legitimate inquiry or was somebody on the outside. If so, Szarnek would notify Rhyme or Sellitto, who'd have the ESU team head to the location immediately. Szarnek also included a large amount of material and background, such as public information on SSD, all of it encrypted, to make sure that the killer spent plenty of time in the system deciphering the data and giving them a better chance to find him.

'How long will it take?'

'Fifteen, twenty minutes.'

'Good. And when you've got that finished, I also want to see if somebody could have hacked in from the outside.'

'Cracked SSD?'

'Uh-huh.'

'Heh. They'll have firewalls on their firewalls on their firewalls.'

'Still, we need to know.'

'But if one of their people is the killer, I assume you don't want me to call the company up and coordinate with them?'

'Right.'

Szarnek's face clouded. 'I'll just try to break in, I guess.'

'You can do that legally?'

'Yes and no. I'll only test the 'walls. It's not a crime if I don't actually get into their system and bring it crashing down in a really embarrassing media event that lands us all in jail.' He added ominously, 'Or worse.'

'Okay, but I want the trap first. ASAP.' Rhyme glanced at the clock. Sachs and Pulaski were already spreading the word about the case down at the Gray Rock.

Szarnek pulled a heavy portable computer out of his satchel and set it on a table nearby. 'Any chance I could get a . . . Oh, thanks.'

Thom was bringing around a coffeepot and cups.

'Just what I was going to ask for. Extra sugar, no milk. You can't take the geek out of the geek, even when he's a cop. Never got in the habit of this thing called sleep.' He dumped in sugar, swirled it and drank half while Thom stood there. The aide refilled the cup. 'Thanks. Now, what've we got here?' He was looking over the workstation where Cooper was perched. 'Ouch.'

'Ouch?'

'You're running on a cable modem with one point five MBPs? You know they make computer screens in color now, and there's this thing called the Internet.'

'Funny,' Rhyme muttered.

'Talk to me when the case is over. We'll do some rewiring and LAN readjustment. Set you up with FE.'

Weird Al, FE, LAN . . .

Szarnek pulled on tinted glasses, plugged his computer into ports on Rhyme's computer and began pounding on the keys. Rhyme noticed certain letters were worn off and the touchpad was seriously sweat-stained. The keyboard seemed to be dusted with crumbs.

The look Sellitto shot Rhyme said, It takes all kinds.

The first of the two men who joined them in Andrew Sterling's office was slender, middle-aged, with an unrevealing face. He resembled a retired cop. The other, younger and cautious, was pure corporate junior exec. He looked like the blond brother on that sitcom, *Frazier*.

Regarding the first, Sachs was near the mark; he hadn't been blue but was a former FBI agent and was now head of SSD's security, Tom O'Day. The other was Mark Whitcomb, the assistant head of the company's Compliance Department.

Sterling explained, 'Tom and his security boys make sure people on the outside don't do anything bad to us. Mark's department makes sure *we* don't do anything bad to the general public. We navigate a minefield. I'm sure that the research you did on SSD showed you we're subject to hundreds of state and federal laws on privacy – the Graham-Leach-Bliley Act about misuse of personal information and pretexting, the Fair Credit Reporting Act, the Health Insurance Portability and Accountability Act, the Drivers Privacy Protection Act. A lot of state laws too. The Compliance Department makes sure we know what the rules are and stay within the lines.'

Good, she thought. These two would be perfect to spread the word about the 522 investigation and encourage the killer to sniff out the trap on the NYPD server.

Doodling on a yellow pad, Mark Whitcomb said, 'We want to make sure that when Michael Moore makes a movie about data purveyors we're not center stage.'

'Don't even joke,' Sterling said, laughing, though with genuine concern evident in his face. Then he asked Sachs, 'Can I share with them what you told me?'

'Sure, please.'

Sterling gave a succinct and clear account. He'd retained everything she'd told him, even down to the specific brands of the clues.

Whitcomb frowned as he listened. O'Day took it all in, unsmiling and silent. Sachs was convinced that FBI reserve was not learned behavior but originated in the womb.

Sterling said firmly, 'So. That's the problem we're facing. If there is any way SSD is involved I want to know about it, and I want solutions. We've identified four possible sources of the risk. Hackers, intruders, employees and clients. Your thoughts?'

O'Day, the former agent, said to Sachs, 'Well, let's deal with hackers first. We have the best firewalls in the business. Better than Microsoft and Sun. We use ICS out of Boston for Internet security. I can tell you we're a duck in an arcade game – every hacker in the world would like to crack us. And nobody's been able to do it since we moved to New York five years ago. We've had a few people get into our administrative servers for ten, fifteen minutes. But not a single breach of innerCircle, and that's what your UNSUB would have to get into to find the information he needed for these crimes. And he couldn't get in through a single breach; he'd have to hit at least three or four separate servers.'

Sterling added, 'As for an outside intruder, that'd be impossible too. We have the same physical perimeter protections used by the National Security Agency. We have fifteen full-time security guards and twenty part-time. Besides, no visitor could get near the innerCircle servers. We log everybody and don't let anyone roam freely, even customers.'

Sachs and Pulaski had been escorted to the sky lobby by one of those guards – a humorless young man whose vigilance wasn't diminished one bit by the fact they were police.

O'Day added, 'We had one incident about three years ago. But nothing since.' He glanced at Sterling. 'The reporter.'

The CEO nodded. 'Some hotshot journalist from one of the metro papers. He was doing an article on identity theft and decided we were the devil incarnate. Axciom and Choicepoint had the good sense not to let him into their headquarters. I believe in free press, so I talked to him . . . He went to the restroom and claimed he got lost. He came back here, cheerful as could be. But something didn't seem right. Our security people went through his briefcase and found a camera. On it were pictures of trade-secret-protected business plans and even pass codes.'

O'Day said, 'The reporter not only lost his job but was prosecuted under criminal trespass statutes. He served six months in state prison. And, as far as I know, he hasn't had a steady job as a journalist since.'

Sterling lowered his head slightly and said to Sachs, 'We take security very, very seriously.'

A young man appeared in the doorway. At first she thought it was Martin, the assistant, but she realized that was only because of the similarity in build and the black suit. 'Andrew, I'm sorry to interrupt.'

'Ah, Jeremy.'

So this was the second assistant. He looked at Pulaski's uniform, then at Sachs. Then, as with Martin, when he realized he wasn't being introduced he ignored everyone in the room except his boss.

'Carpenter,' Sterling said. 'I need to see him today.'

'Yes, Andrew.'

After he was gone, Sachs asked, 'Employees? Is there anyone you've had disciplinary problems with?'

Sterling said, 'We run extensive background checks on our people. I won't allow hiring anybody who's had any convictions other than traffic violations. And background checks are one of our specialties. But even if an employee wanted to get into innerCircle it would be impossible for him to steal any data. Mark, tell her about the pens.'

'Sure, Andrew.' To Sachs he said, 'We have concrete firewalls.'

'I'm not a technical person,' Sachs said.

Whitcomb laughed. 'No, no, it's very *low*-tech. Literally concrete. As in walls and floors. We divide up the data when we receive them and store them in physically separate places. You'll understand better if I tell you how SSD operates. We start with the premise that data is our main asset. If somebody was to duplicate innerCircle we'd be out of business in a week. So number one – 'protect our asset,' as we say here. Now, where does all this data come from? From thousands of sources: credit card companies, banks, government-records offices, retail stores, online operations, court clerks, DMV departments, hospitals, insurance companies. We consider each event that creates data a quote transaction, which could be a call to an eight hundred number, registering a car, a health insurance claim, filing a lawsuit, a birth, wedding, purchase, merchandise return, a complaint . . . In your business, a transaction could be a rape, a burglary, a murder – any crime. Also, the opening of a case file, selecting a juror, a trial, a conviction.'

Whitcomb continued, 'Any time data about a transaction comes to SSD it goes first to the Intake Center, where it's evaluated. For security we have a data masking policy – separating the person's name and replacing it with a code.'

'Social Security number?'

A flicker of emotion crossed Sterling's face. 'Ah, no. Those were created solely for government retirement accounts. Ages ago. It was a fluke that they became identification. Inaccurate, easy to steal or buy. Dangerous – like keeping a loaded gun unlocked around the house. Our code is a sixteen-digit number. Ninety-eight percent of adult Americans have SSD codes. Now, every child whose birth is registered – anywhere in North America – automatically gets a code.'

'Why sixteen digits?' Pulaski asked.

'Gives us room for expansion,' Sterling said. 'We never have to worry about running out of numbers. We can assign nearly one quintillion codes. The earth will run out of living space before SSD runs out of numbers. The codes make our system much more secure and it's far faster to process data than using a name or Social. Also, using a code neutralizes the human element and takes the prejudice out of the equation. Psychologically we have opinions about Adolf or Britney or

Shaquilla or Diego before we even meet them, simply because of their name. A number eliminates that bias. And improves efficiency. Please, go on, Mark.'

'Sure, Andrew. Once the name is swapped for the code, the Intake Center evaluates the transaction, decides where it belongs and sends it to one or more of three separate areas – our data pens. Pen A is where we store personal lifestyle data. Pen B is financial. That includes salary history, banking, credit reports, insurance. Pen C is public and government filings and records.'

'Then the data's cleansed.' Sterling took over once again. 'The impurities are weeded out and it's made uniform. For instance, on some forms your sex is given as "F." In others, it's "Female." Sometimes it's a one or a zero. You have to be consistent.

'We also remove the noise – that's impure data. It could be erroneous, could have too many details, could have too few details. Noise is contamination, and contamination has to be eliminated.' He said this firmly – another dash of emotion. 'Then the cleansed data sits in one of our pens until a client needs a fortune-teller.'

'How do you mean?' asked Pulaski.

Sterling explained, 'In the nineteen seventies, computer database software gave companies an analysis of past perform-ance. In the nineties the data showed how they were doing at any given moment. More helpful. Now we can predict what consumers are *going* to do and guide our clients to take advantage of that.'

Sachs said, 'Then you're not just predicting the future. You're trying to change it.'

'Exactly. But what other reason is there to go to a fortune-teller?'

His eyes were calm, almost amused. Yet Sachs felt uneasy, thinking back to the run-in with the federal agent yesterday in Brooklyn. It was as if 522 had done just what he was describing: predicted a shootout between them.

Sterling gestured to Whitcomb, who continued, 'Okay, so data, which contain no names but only numbers, go into these three separate pens on different floors in different security zones. An employee in the public records pen can't access the data in the lifestyle pen or the financial pen. And nobody in any of the data pens can access the information in the Intake Center, and link the name and address to the sixteen-digit code.'

Sterling said, 'That's what Tom meant when he said that a hacker would have to breach all of the data pens independently.'

O'Day added, 'And we monitor twenty-four/seven. We'd know instantly if someone unauthorized tried to physically enter a pen. They'd be fired on the spot and probably arrested. Besides, you can't download anything from the computers in the pens – there are no ports – and even if you managed to break into a server and hardwire a device, you couldn't get it out. Everybody's searched – every employee, senior executive, security guard, fire warden, janitor. Even Andrew. We have metal and dense-material detectors at every entrance and exit to the data pens and Intake – even the fire doors.'

Whitcomb took up the narrative. 'And a magnetic field generator that you have to walk through. It erases all digital data on any medium you're carrying – iPod, phone or hard drive. No, nobody gets out of those rooms with a kilobyte of information on them.'

Sachs said, 'So stealing the data from these pens – either by hackers outside or intruders or employees inside – would be almost impossible.'

Sterling was nodding. 'Data are our only asset. We guard them religiously.'

'What about the other scenario – somebody who works for a client?'

'Like Tom was saying, the way this man operates he'd have

to have access to the innerCircle dossiers of each of the victims and the men arrested for the crimes.'

'Right.'

Sterling lifted his hands, like a professor. 'But customers don't have access to dossiers. They wouldn't want them anyway. innerCircle contains raw data and wouldn't do them any good. What they want is our *analysis* of the data. Customers log on to Watchtower – that's our proprietary database management system – and other programs like Xpectation or FORT. The programs themselves search through innerCircle, find the relevant data and put them into usable form. If you want to think of the mining analogy, Watchtower sifts through tons of dirt and rock and finds gold nuggets.'

She said in response, 'But if a client bought a number of mailing lists, say, they could come up with enough data about one of our victims to commit the crimes, couldn't they?' She nodded at the evidence list she'd shown Sterling earlier. 'For instance, our perp could get lists of everyone who bought that kind of shave cream and condoms and duct tape and running shoes and so on.'

Sterling lifted an eyebrow. 'Hm. It would be a huge amount of work but it's theoretically possible . . . All right. I'll get a list of all our customers who've bought any data that included your victims' names – in the past, say, three months? No, maybe six.'

'That should do it.' She dug through her briefcase – considerably less organized than Sterling's desktop – and handed him a list of the victims and fall guys.

'Our client agreement gives us the right to share information about them. There won't be a problem legally but it will take a few hours to put together.'

'Thanks. Now, one final question about employees . . . Even if they're not allowed in the pens, could they download a dossier in their office?'

He was nodding, impressed by her question, it seemed,

even though it suggested an SSD worker might be the killer. 'Most employees can't – again, we have to protect our data. But a few of us have what's called "all-access permission."'

Whitcomb gave a smile. 'Well, but look who that is, Andrew.'

'If there's a problem here, we need to explore all possible solutions.'

Whitcomb said to Sachs and Pulaski, 'The thing is, the all-access employees are senior people here. They've been with the company for years. We're like a family. We have parties together, we have our inspirational retreats—'

Sterling held up a hand, cutting him off, and said, 'We have to follow up on it, Mark. I want this rooted out, whatever it takes. I want answers.'

'Who has all-access rights?' Sachs asked.

Sterling shrugged. 'I'm authorized. Our head of Sales, the head of Technical Operations. Our Human Resources director could put together a dossier, I suppose, though I'm sure he never has. And Mark's boss, our Compliance Department director.' He gave her the names.

Sachs glanced at Whitcomb, who shook his head. 'I don't have access.'

O'Day didn't either.

'Your assistants?' Sachs asked Sterling, referring to Jeremy and Martin.

'No . . . Now, as for the repair folks – the techies – the line people couldn't assemble a dossier but we have two service managers who could. One on the day shift, one at night.' He gave her their names too.

Sachs looked over the list. 'There's one easy way to tell whether or not they're innocent.'

'How?'

'We know where the killer was on Sunday afternoon. If they have alibis, they'll be off the hook. Let me interview them. Right now, if we can.'

'Good,' Sterling said and gave an approving look at her suggestion: a simple 'solution' to one of his 'problems.' Then she realized something: Every time he'd looked at her this morning his gaze had met her eyes. Unlike many, if not most, men Sachs met, Sterling hadn't once glanced over her body, hadn't offered a bit of flirt. She wondered what the bedroom story was. She asked, 'Could I see the security in the data pens for myself?'

'Sure. Just leave your pager, phone and PDA outside. And any thumbdrives. If you don't, all the data will be erased. And you'll be searched when you leave.'

'Okay.'

Sterling nodded to O'Day, who stepped into the hall and returned with the stern security guard who'd walked Sachs and Pulaski here from the massive lobby downstairs.

Sterling printed out a pass for her, signed it and handed it to the guard, who led her out into the halls.

Sachs was pleased that Sterling hadn't resisted her request. She had an ulterior motive for seeing the pens for herself. Not only could she make yet more people aware of the investigation – in the hope they'd go for the bait – but she could question the guard about the security measures, to verify what O'Day, Sterling and Whitcomb had told her.

But the man remained virtually silent, like a child told by his parents not to speak to strangers.

Through doorways, up corridors, down a staircase, up another one. She was soon completely disoriented. Her muscles shivered. The spaces were increasingly confined, narrow and dim. Her claustrophobia began to kick in; while the windows were small throughout the Gray Rock, here – approaching the data pens – they were nonexistent. She took a deep breath. It didn't help.

She glanced at his name badge. 'Say, John?'

'Yes, ma'am?'

'What's the story with the windows? They're either small – or there aren't any.'

'Andrew's concerned that people might try to photograph information from outside, like passcodes. Or business plans.'

'Really? Could somebody do that?'

'I don't know. We're told to check sometimes – scan nearby observation decks, windows of buildings facing the company. Nobody's ever seen something suspicious. But Andrew wants us to keep doing it.'

The data pens were eerie places, all color-coded. Personal lifestyle was blue, financial red, governmental green. They were huge spaces but that did nothing to allay her claustrophobia. The ceilings were very low, the rooms dim and aisles narrow between the rows of computers. A constant churning filled the air, a low tone like a growl. The air-conditioning was working like mad, given the number of computers and the electricity they'd require, but the atmosphere was close and stifling.

As for the computers, she'd never seen so many in her life. They were massive white boxes and were identified, curiously, not by numbers or letters but by decals depicting cartoon characters like Spider-Man, Batman, Barney, the Road Runner and Mickey Mouse.

'SpongeBob?' she asked, nodding at one.

John offered his first smile. 'It's another layer of security Andrew thought of. We have people looking online for anybody talking about SSD and innerCircle. If there's a reference to the company *and* a cartoon name, like Wile E. Coyote or Superman, it might mean somebody's a little too interested in the computers themselves. The names jump out more than if we just numbered the computers.'

'Smart,' she said, reflecting on the irony that Sterling preferred people to be numbered and his computers named.

They entered the Intake Center, painted a grim gray. It was

smaller than the data pens and boosted her claustrophobia even further. As in the pens, the only decorations here were the logo of the watchtower and illuminated window, and a large picture of Andrew Sterling, a posed smile on his face. Below it was the caption 'You're Number One!'

Maybe it referred to market share or to an award the company had won. Or maybe it was a slogan about the importance of employees. Still, to Sachs it seemed ominous, as if you were at the top of a list you didn't want to be on.

Her breathing was coming quickly as the sense of confinement grew.

'Gets to you, doesn't it?' the guard asked.

She gave a smile. 'A little.'

'We make our rounds but nobody spends more time in the pens than we have to.'

Now that she'd broken the ice and gotten John to answer in more than monosyllables, she asked him about the security, to verify if Sterling and the others were being straight.

They were, it seemed. John reiterated what the CEO had said: None of the computers or workstations in the rooms had a slot or port to download data, merely keyboards and monitors. And the rooms were shielded, the guard said; no wireless signals could get out. And he explained too what Sterling and Whitcomb had told her earlier about data from each pen being useless without the data from the others and from Intake. There wasn't much security on the computer monitors but to get into the pens you needed your ID card, a passcode and a biometric scan – or, apparently, a big security guard watching your every move (which was just what John had been doing, and not so subtly).

The security outside the pens was tight too, as the executives had told her. Both she and the guard were searched carefully when they left each one and had to walk through both a metal detector and a thick frame called a Data-Clear unit. The machine warned, *'Passing through this system permanently erases all digital data on computers, drives, cell phones and other devices.'*

As they returned to Sterling's office John told her that to his knowledge nobody had ever broken into SSD. Still, O'Day regularly had them run drills to prevent security intrusions. Like most of the guards, John didn't carry a gun but Sterling had a policy that at least two armed guards be present twenty-four hours a day.

Back in the CEO's office, she found Pulaski sitting on a huge leather sofa near Martin's desk. Though not a small man, he seemed dwarfed, a student who'd been sent to the principal's office. In her absence, the young officer had taken the initiative to check on the Compliance Department head, Samuel Brockton — Whitcomb's boss, who had all-access rights. He was staying in Washington, D.C.; hotel records showed he'd been at brunch in the dining room at the time of the killing yesterday. She noted this, then glanced over the all-access permission list.

Andrew Sterling, President, Chief Executive Officer
Sean Cassel, Director of Sales and Marketing
Wayne Gillespie, Director of Technical Operations
Samuel Brockton, Director, Compliance Department
    Alibi – hotel records confirm presence in Washington
Peter Arlonzo-Kemper, Director of Human Resources
Steven Shraeder, Technical Service and Support Manager, day shift
Faruk Mameda, Technical Service and Support Manager, night shift

She said to Sterling, 'I'd like to interview them as soon as possible.'

The CEO called his assistant and learned that, other than

Brockton, everyone was in town, though Shraeder was handling a hardware crisis in the Intake Center and Mameda would not be coming in until three that afternoon. He instructed Martin to have them come upstairs for interviews. He'd find a vacant conference room.

Sterling told the intercom to disconnect and said, 'All right, Detective. It's up to you now. Go clear our name . . . or find your killer.'

Chapter
TWENTY

Rodney Szarnek had their mousetrap in place and the young shaggy-haired officer was happily trying to hack into SSD's main servers. His knee bobbed and he whistled from time to time, which irritated Rhyme, but he let the kid alone. The criminalist had been known to talk to himself when searching crime scenes and considering possible approaches to a case.

Takes all kinds . . .

The doorbell rang; it was an officer from the CS lab in Queens with a present, some evidence from one of the earlier crimes: the murder weapon, a knife, used in the coin theft and killing. The rest of the physical evidence was 'in storage somewhere.' A request had been made but no one could say when, or if, it could be located.

Rhyme had Cooper sign the chain-of-custody form – even after trial, protocols must be followed.

'That's strange: Most of the other evidence is missing,' Rhyme remarked though he realized that, being a weapon, the knife would have been retained in a locked facility in the lab's inventory, rather than archived with nonlethal evidence.

Rhyme glanced at the chart about the crime. 'They found some of that dust in the knife handle. Let's see if we can figure out what it is. But, first, what's the story on the knife itself?'

Cooper ran the manufacturer's information through the NYPD weapons database. 'Made in China, sold in bulk to thousands of retail outlets. Cheap, so we can assume he paid cash for it.'

'Well, hadn't expected much. Let's move on to the dust.'

Cooper donned gloves and opened the bag. He carefully brushed the handle of the knife, whose blade was dark brown with the victim's blood, and it shed traces of white dust onto the examination paper.

Dust fascinated Rhyme. In forensics the term refers to solid particles less than five hundred micrometers in size and made up of fibers from clothing and upholstery, dander from human and animal skin, fragments of plants and insects, bits of dried excrement, dirt, and any number of chemicals. Some types are aerosol, others settle quickly on surfaces. Dust can cause health problems – like black lung – and be dangerously explosive (flour dust in grain elevators, for instance) and can even affect the climate.

Forensically, thanks to static electricity and other adhesive properties, dust is often transferred from perpetrator to crime scene and vice versa, which makes it extremely helpful to police. When Rhyme was running the Crime Scene division of the NYPD he'd created a large database of dust, gathered from all five boroughs of the city and parts of New Jersey and Connecticut.

Only small amounts adhered to the knife handle but Mel Cooper collected enough to run a sample through the gas chromatograph/mass spectrometer, which breaks substances down into their component parts, then identifies each one. This took some time. It wasn't Cooper's fault. His hands, surprisingly large and muscular for such a slight man, moved quickly and efficiently. It was the machines that plodded away slowly, performing their methodical magic. While they waited for the results Cooper ran additional chemical tests on another sample of the dust to reveal materials the GC/MS might not find.

Eventually the results were available and Mel Cooper explained the combined analysis as he wrote the details on the whiteboard. 'All right, Lincoln. We've got vermiculite, plaster, synthetic foam, glass fragments, paint particles, mineral wool fibers, glass fibers, calcite grains, paper fibers, quartz grains, low-temperature combustion material, metal flakes, chrysotile asbestos and some chemicals. Looks like polycyclic aromatic hydrocarbons, paraffin, olefin, napthene, octanes, polychlorinated biphenyls, dibenzodioxins – don't see those very often – and dibenzofurans. Oh, and some brominated diphenyl ethers.'

'The Trade Center,' Rhyme said.

'It is?'

'Yep.'

The dust from the collapsed World Trade Towers in 2001 had been the source of health problems for workers near Ground Zero, and variations of its composition had been in the news lately. Rhyme was well aware of its composition.

'So he's downtown?'

'Possibly,' Rhyme said. 'But you could find the dust all over the five boroughs. Let's leave it a question mark for the time being. . . .' He grimaced. 'So our profile so far: a man who *might* be white or a light-skinned ethnic. Who *might* collect coins and *might* like art. And his residence or place of work *might* be downtown. He *might* have children, *might* smoke.' Rhyme squinted at the knife. 'Let me see it up close.' Cooper brought the weapon to him and Rhyme stared at every millimeter of the handle. His body was defective but his eyesight was as good as a teenager's. 'There. What's that?'

'Where?'

'Between the hasp and the bone.'

It was a tiny fleck of something pale. 'You could see that?' the tech whispered. 'I missed it completely.' With a needle probe he worked it out and put it on an examination slide. He looked at it through a microscope. He started with lower magnifications, which are enough, 4 to 24 power, unless you need the magic of a scanning electron microscope. 'Crumb of food, looks like. Something baked. Orange tint. Spectrum suggests oil. Maybe junk food. Like Doritos. Or potato chips.'

'Not enough to run through the GC/MS.'

'No way,' Cooper confirmed.

'He wasn't going to plant something as small as that at the fall guy's house. It's some other bit of real information about Five Twenty-Two.'

What the hell was it? Something from his lunch the day of the killing?

'I want to taste it.'

'What? There's blood on it.'

'The handle, not the blade. Just where that fleck is. I want to find out what it is.'

'There's not enough to taste. This little chip? You can hardly see it. I *didn't* see it.'

'No, the knife itself. Maybe I can find a flavor or spice that'll tell us something.'

'You can't lick a murder weapon, Lincoln.'

'Where's that written down, Mel? I don't remember reading that. We need information about this guy!'

'Well . . . okay.' The tech held the knife close to Rhyme's face and the criminalist leaned forward and touched his tongue to the place where they'd found the fleck.

'Jesus Christ!' He reared his head back.

'What's wrong?' Cooper asked, alarmed.

'Get me some water!'

Cooper tossed the knife onto the examination table and

went to call Thom, as Rhyme spit on the floor. His mouth was on fire.

Thom came running. 'What's wrong?'

'Man . . . that hurts. I asked for water! I just ate some hot sauce.'

'Hot sauce, like Tabasco?'

'I don't know what kind!'

'Well, you don't want water. You want milk or yogurt.'

'Then get some!'

Thom came back with a carton of yogurt and fed Rhyme several spoonfuls. To his surprise the pain went away immediately. 'Phew. That hurt. . . . Okay, Mel, we've learned something else – maybe. Our boy likes his chips and salsa. Well, let's just go with a snack food and hot sauce. Put it on the chart.'

As Cooper wrote, Rhyme glanced at the clock and snapped, 'Where the hell is Sachs?'

'Well, she's at SSD.' Cooper looked confused.

'I know *that*. What I mean is why the hell isn't she back here? . . . And, Thom, I want some more yogurt!'

UNSUB 522 PROFILE

- Male
- Possibly smokes or lives/works with someone who does, or near source of tobacco
- Has children or lives/works near them or near source of toys
- Interest in art, coins?
- Probably white or light-skinned ethnic
- Medium build
- Strong – able to strangle victims
- Access to voice-disguise equipment
- Possibly computer literate; knows OurWorld. Other social-networking sites?
- Takes trophies from victims. Sadist?
- Portion of residence/work-place dark and moist
- Lives in/near downtown Manhattan?
- Eats snack food/hot sauce

NONPLANTED EVIDENCE

- Old cardboard
- Hair from doll, BASF B35 nylon 6
- Tobacco from Tareyton cigarettes
- Old tobacco, not Tareyton, but brand unknown
- Evidence of Stachybotrys Chartarum mold
- Dust, from World Trade Center attack, possibly indicating residence/job downtown Manhattan
- Snack food with hot sauce

Chapter
TWENTY-ONE

The conference room where Sachs and Pulaski had been led was as minimalist as Sterling's office. She decided a good way to describe the entire company would be 'austere deco.'

Sterling himself escorted them to the room and gestured to two chairs, beneath the logo of the window atop the watch-tower. He said, 'I don't expect to be treated any differently than anyone else. Since I have all-access rights I'm a suspect too. But I have an alibi for yesterday – I was on Long Island all day. I do that a lot – drive to some of the big discount stores and the membership shopping clubs to see what people are buying, how they buy, what times of day. I'm always looking for ways to make our business more efficient, and you can't do that unless you know our clients' needs.'

'Who were you meeting with?'

'Nobody. I never tell anyone who I am. I want to see the operation the way it actually works. Blemishes and everything. But my car's E-ZPass records should show that I went through the Midtown Tunnel tollbooth about nine A.M. eastbound and then came back through about five-thirty. You can check with DMV.' He recited his tag number. 'Oh, and yesterday? I called my son. He took the train up to Westchester to go hiking in some forest preserve. He went by himself and I wanted to check on him. I called about two in the afternoon. The phone records'll show a call from my Hampton house. Or you can take a look at the incoming call list on his mobile. It should have the date and time. His extension is seven one eight seven.'

Sachs wrote this down, along with the number of Sterling's summer house's phone. She thanked him, then Jeremy, the 'outside' assistant, arrived and whispered something to his boss.

'Have to take care of something. If there's anything you need, anything at all, just let me know.'

A few minutes later the first of their suspects arrived. Sean Cassel, the director of Sales and Marketing. He struck her as quite young, probably midthirties, but she'd seen very few people in SSD who were over forty. Data was perhaps the new Silicon Valley, a world of youthful entrepreneurs.

Cassel, with a long face, classically handsome, seemed athletic; solid arms, broad shoulders. He was wearing the SSD 'uniform,' in his case a navy suit. The white shirt was immaculate and the cuffs clasped with heavy gold links. The yellow tie was thick silk. He had curly hair, rosy skin and peered steadily at Sachs through glasses. She hadn't known Dolce & Gabbana made frames.

'Hi.'

'Hello. I'm Detective Sachs, this is Officer Pulaski. Have a seat.' She shook his hand, noting the firm grip that lingered longer than the clasp with Pulaski.

'So you're a detective?' The sales director had not a shred of interest in the patrolman.

'That's right. Would you like to see my ID?'

'No, that's okay.'

'Now, we're just getting information about some of the employees here. Do you know a Myra Weinburg?'

'No. Should I?'

'She was the victim of a murder.'

'Oh.' A flash of contrition, as the hip façade vanished momentarily. 'I heard something about a crime. I didn't know it was a murder, though. I'm sorry. Was she an employee here?'

'No. But the person who killed her might have had access to information in your company's computers. I know you have full access to innerCircle; is there any way somebody who works for you could assemble an individual's dossier?'

He shook his head. 'To get a closet you need three passcodes. Or a biomet and one.'

'Closet?'

He hesitated. 'Oh, that's what we call a dossier. We use a lot of shorthand in the knowledge service business.'

Like secrets in a closet, she assumed.

'But nobody could get my passcode. Everyone's very careful about keeping them secret. Andrew insists on it.' Cassel removed his glasses and polished them with a black cloth that appeared magically in his hand. 'He's fired employees who've used other people's passcodes even with their permission. Fired on the spot.' He concentrated on his glass-polishing task. Then looked up. 'But let's be honest. What you're *really* asking about isn't passcodes but alibis. Am I right?'

'We'd like to know that too. Where were you from noon to four P.M. yesterday?'

'Running. I'm training for a mini-triathlon . . . You look like you run too. You're pretty athletic.'

If standing still while punching holes in targets at twenty-five and fifty feet is athletic, then yes. 'Could anybody verify that?'

'That you're athletic? It's pretty obvious to me.'

Smile. Sometimes it was best to play along. Pulaski stirred – which Cassel noted with amusement – but she said nothing. Sachs didn't need anybody to defend her honor.

With a sideways glance at the uniformed officer, Cassel continued, 'No, I'm afraid not. A friend stayed over. But she left about nine-thirty. Am I a suspect or anything?'

'We're just getting information at this point,' Pulaski said.

'Are you now?' He sounded condescending, as if he were talking to a child. 'Just the facts, ma'am. Just the facts.'

A line from an old TV show. Sachs couldn't remember which one.

Sachs asked where he'd been at the times of the other killings – the coin dealer, the earlier rape and the woman who'd owned the Prescott painting. He replaced the glasses and told her he didn't recall. He seemed completely at ease.

'How often do you go into the data pens?'

'Maybe once a week.'

'Do you take any information out?'

He frowned slightly. 'Well . . . you can't. The security system won't let you.'

'And how often do you download dossiers?'

'I don't know if I ever have. It's just raw data. Too noisy to be helpful for anything I do.'

'All right. Well, I appreciate your time. I think that'll do it for now.'

The smile and flirt faded. 'So is this a problem? Something I should be worried about?'

'We're just doing some preliminary investigation.'

'Ah, not giving anything away.' A glance at Pulaski. 'Play it close to the chest, right, Sergeant Friday?'

Ah, that was it, Sachs realized. *Dragnet*. The old police show she and her father would watch in rerun years ago.

After he'd left, another employee joined them. Wayne Gillespie, who oversaw the technical side of the company – the software and hardware. He didn't exactly fit Sachs's impression of a geek. Not at first. He was tanned and in good shape, wore an expensive silver – or platinum – bracelet. His grip was strong. But on closer examination she decided he was a classic techie after all, somebody dressed by his mother for class photographs. The short, thin man wore a rumpled suit and a tie that wasn't knotted properly. His shoes were scuffed, his nails ragged and not properly scrubbed. His hair could use a trim. It was as if he was playing the role of corporate exec but infinitely preferred to be in a dark room with his computer.

Unlike Cassel, Gillespie was nervous, hands constantly in motion, fiddling with three electronic devices on his belt – a BlackBerry, a PDA and an elaborate cell phone. He avoided eye contact – flirt was the last thing on his mind, though, like the sales director, his wedding ring finger was bare. Maybe Sterling preferred single men in positions of power at his company. Loyal princes rather than ambitious dukes.

Sachs's impression was that Gillespie had heard less than Cassel about their presence here and she snagged his attention when she described the crimes. 'Interesting. Okay, interesting. That's sleek, he's pianoing data to commit crimes.'

'He's what?'

Gillespie flicked his fingers together with nervous energy. 'I mean, he's finding data. Collecting it.'

No comment about the fact that people had been murdered. Was this an act? The real killer might have feigned horror and sympathy.

Sachs asked his whereabouts on Sunday and he too had no alibi, though he launched into a long story of code he was debugging at home and some role-playing computer game he was competing in.

'So there'd be a record of when you were online yesterday?'

A hesitation now. 'Oh, I was just practicing, you know. I wasn't online. I looked up and suddenly it was late. You're so nod, everything else kind of disappears.'

'Nod?'

He realized he was speaking a foreign language. 'Oh, I mean, like, you're in a zone. You get caught up in the game. Like the rest of your life dozes off.'

He claimed not to know Myra Weinburg either. And no

one could have gotten access to his passcodes, he assured her. 'As for cracking my words, good luck – they're all sixteen-digit random characters. I've never written them down. I'm lucky I've got a good memory.'

Gillespie was on his computer 'in the system' all the time. He added defensively, 'I mean, it's my job.' Though he frowned in confusion when asked about downloading individual dossiers. 'There's, like, no point. Reading about everything John Doe bought last week at his local grocery store. Hello . . . I've got better things to do.'

He also admitted that he spent a lot of time in the data pens, 'tuning the boxes.' Her impression was that he liked it there, found it comfortable – the same place that she couldn't escape from fast enough.

Gillespie too was unable to recall where he'd been at the times of the other killings. She thanked him and he left, pulling his PDA off his belt before he was through the doorway and typing a message with his thumbs faster than Sachs could use all her fingers.

As they waited for the next all-access suspect to arrive, Sachs asked Pulaski, 'Impressions?'

'Okay, I don't like Cassel.'

'I'm with you there.'

'But he seems too obnoxious to be Five Twenty-Two. Too yuppie, you know? If he could kill somebody with his ego, then, yeah. In a minute . . . As for Gillespie? I'm not so sure. He tried to seem surprised about Myra's death but I'm not sure he was. And that attitude of his – "pianoing" and "nod"? You know what those are? Expressions from the street. "Pianoing" means looking for crack, like your fingers are all over the place. You know, frantic. And "nod" means being drugged out on smack or a tranquilizer. It's how kids from the burbs talk trying to sound cool when they're scoring from dealers in Harlem or the Bronx.'

'You think he's into drugs?'

'Well, he seemed pretty twitchy. But my impression?'

'I asked.'

'It's not drugs he's addicted to, it's this—' The young officer gestured around him. 'The data.'

She thought about this and agreed. The atmosphere in SSD was intoxicating, though not in a pleasant way. Eerie and disorienting. It *was* like being on painkillers.

Another man appeared in the doorway. He was the Human Resources director, a young, trim, light-skinned African American. Peter Arlonzo-Kemper explained that he rarely went into the data pens but had permission to, so that he could meet with employees at their job stations. He did go online into innerCircle from time to time on personnel-related issues – but only to review data on employees of SSD, never the public.

So he *had* accessed 'closets,' despite what Sterling had said about him.

The intense man pasted a smile on his face and answered in monotones, frequently changing the subject, the gist of his message being that Sterling – always 'Andrew,' Sachs had noticed – was the 'kindest, most considerate boss anybody could ask for.' Nobody would ever think about betraying him or the 'ideals' of SSD, whatever those might be. He couldn't imagine a criminal within the hallowed halls of the company.

His admiration was tedious.

Once she got him off the worship, he explained that he had been with his wife all day on Sunday (making him the only married employee she'd talked to). And he'd been cleaning out his recently deceased mother's house in the Bronx on the date Alice Sanderson had been killed. He'd been alone but imagined he could find someone who'd seen him. Arlonzo-Kemper couldn't recall where he'd been during the times of the other killings.

When they had finished the interviews the guard escorted

Sachs and Pulaski back to Sterling's outer office. The CEO was meeting with a man about Sterling's age, solid and with combed-over dark blond hair. He sat slouching in one of the stiff wooden chairs. He wasn't an SSD employee: He wore a Polo shirt and a sports jacket. Sterling looked up and saw Sachs. He ended the meeting and rose, then escorted the man out.

Sachs looked at what the visitor was holding, a stack of papers with the name 'Associated Warehousing' on top, apparently the name of his company.

'Martin, could you call a car for Mr Carpenter?'

'Yes, Andrew.'

'We're all together, are we, Bob?'

'Yes, Andrew.' Carpenter, towering over Sterling, somberly shook the CEO's hand, then turned and left. A security guard led him down the hall.

The officers accompanied Sterling back into his office.

'What did you find?' he asked.

'Nothing conclusive. Some people have alibis, some don't. We'll keep pursuing the case and see if the evidence or witnesses lead us anywhere. There's one thing I was wondering. Could I get a copy of a dossier? Arthur Rhyme's.'

'Who?'

'He's one of the men on the list – one that we think was wrongly arrested.'

'Of course.' Sterling sat at his desk, touched his thumb to a reader beside the keyboard and typed for a few seconds. He paused, eyes on the screen. Then more keyboarding and a document began printing out. He handed the thirty or so pages to her – Arthur Rhyme's 'closet.'

Well, that was easy, she noted. Then Sachs nodded at the computer. 'Is there a record of you doing that?'

'A record? Oh, no. We don't log our internal downloads.' He looked over his notes again. 'I'll have Martin pull the client list together. It might take two or three hours.'

As they walked into the outer office, Sean Cassel stepped inside. He wasn't smiling. 'What's this about a list of clients, Andrew? You're going to give that to them?'

'That's right, Sean.'

'Why clients?'

Pulaski said, 'We were thinking that somebody who works for an SSD client got information he used in the crimes.'

The young man scoffed. 'Obviously that's what you *think* . . . But why? None of them has direct innerCircle access. They can't download closets.'

Pulaski explained, 'They might've bought mailing lists that had the information in them.'

'Mailing lists? Do you know how many times a client would have to be in the system to assemble all the information you're talking about? It'd be a full-time job. Think about it.'

Pulaski blushed and looked down. 'Well . . .'

Mark Whitcomb, of the Compliance Department, was standing near Martin's desk. 'Sean, he doesn't know how the business works.'

'Well, Mark, I'm thinking it's more about logic, really. Doesn't it seem? Each client would have to buy hundreds of mailing lists. And there are probably three, four hundred of them who've been in the closets of the sixteens they're interested in.'

'Sixteens?' Sachs asked.

'It means "people."' He waved vaguely toward the narrow windows, presumably suggesting humanity outside the Gray Rock. 'It comes from the code we use.'

More shorthand. Closets, sixteens, pianoing . . . There was something smug, if not contemptuous, about the expressions.

Sterling said coolly, 'We need to do everything we can to find the truth here.'

Cassel shook his head. 'It's not a client, Andrew. Nobody would dare use our data for a crime. It'd be suicide.'

'Sean, if SSD's involved in this we have to know.'

'All right, Andrew. Whatever you think best.' Sean Cassel ignored Pulaski, gave a cold, nonflirtatious smile to Sachs and left.

Sachs said to Sterling, 'We'll pick up that client list when we come back to interview the tech managers.'

As the CEO gave instructions to Martin, Sachs heard Mark Whitcomb whisper to Pulaski, 'Don't pay any attention to Cassel. He and Gillespie – they're the golden boys of this business. Young Turks, you know. I'm a hindrance. You're a hindrance.'

'Not a problem,' the young officer said noncommittally, though Sachs could see he was grateful. He has everything but confidence, she thought.

Whitcomb left, and the two officers said good-bye to Sterling.

Then the CEO touched her arm gently. 'There's something I want to say, Detective.'

She turned to the man, who stood with his arms at his side, feet spread, looking up at her with his intense green eyes. It was impossible to look away from his focused, mesmerizing gaze.

'I'm not going to deny that I'm in the knowledge service provider field to make money. But I'm also in it to improve our society. Think about what we do. Think about the kids who're going to get decent clothes and nice Christmas presents for the first time because of the money their parents save, thanks to SSD. Or about the young marrieds who can now find a bank that'll give them a mortgage for their first house because SSD can predict that in fact they'll be acceptable credit risks. Or the identity thieves that're caught because our algorithms see a glitch in your credit card spending patterns. Or the RFID tags in a child's bracelet or wristwatch that tell the parents where they are every minute of the day. The intelligent toilets that diagnose diabetes when you don't even know you're at risk.

'And take your line of work, Detective. Say you're investigating a murder. There're traces of cocaine on a knife, the murder weapon. Our PublicSure program can tell you who with a cocaine arrest in his background used a knife in the commission of a felony any time in the past twenty years, in any geographic area you like, and whether they were right- or left-handed and what their shoe sizes are. Before you even ask, their fingerprints pop up on the screen, along with their pictures, and details of their M.O.'s, distinguishing characteristics, disguises they've used in the past, distinctive voice patterns and a dozen more attributes.

'We can also tell you who bought that particular brand of knife – or maybe even that very knife. And possibly we know where the purchaser was at the time of the crime and where he is now. If the system can't find him, it can tell you the percentage likelihood of his being at a known accomplice's house and display *their* fingerprints and distinguishing characteristics. And this whole bundle of data comes to you in a grand total of about twenty seconds.

'Our society needs help, Detective. Remember the broken windows? Well, SSD is here to help . . .' He smiled. 'That's the wind-up. Here's the pitch. I'm asking that you be discreet in the investigation. I'll do whatever I can – especially if it seems this is somebody from SSD. But if rumors get started about breaches here, careless security, our competitors and critics would jump on that. And jump hard. It could badly interfere with SSD's job to fix as many windows as we can and make this world better. Are we in agreement?'

Amelia Sachs suddenly felt bad about this duplicitous mission, planting the seeds to encourage their perp to go after the trap without telling Sterling. She struggled to maintain eye contact as she said, 'I think we're in complete agreement.'

'Wonderful. Now, Martin, please show our guests out.'

Chapter
TWENTY-TWO

'Broken windows?'

Sachs was telling Rhyme about the SSD logo.

'I like that.'

'You do?'

'Yeah. Think about it. It's a metaphor for what we do here. We find the small bits of evidence and that leads us to the big answer.'

Sellitto nodded toward Rodney Szarnek, sitting in the corner, oblivious to everything but his computer and still whistling. 'Kid in the T-shirt's got the trap in place. And he's trying to hack in now.' He called, 'Any luck, Officer?'

'Heh – those folk know what they're doing. But I've got a dozen tricks up my sleeve.'

Sachs told them that the head of security didn't believe that anyone could hack into innerCircle.

'Only makes the game sweeter,' Szarnek said. He finished another coffee and resumed the faint whistling.

Sachs then told them about Sterling, the company and how the data-mining process worked. Despite what Thom had explained yesterday and despite their preliminary research, Rhyme hadn't realized how extensive the industry was.

'He acting fishy?' Sellitto said. 'This Sterling?'

Rhyme grunted at the, to him, pointless question.

'No. He's cooperative. And, good for us, he's a true believer. Data's his god. Anything that jeopardizes his company he wants to root out.'

Sachs then described the tight security at SSD, how very few people had access to all three data pens, and how it was impossible to steal data even if you got inside. 'They've had one intruder – a reporter – who was just after a story, not even stealing trade secrets. He did time and his career is over with.'

'Vindictive, hm?'

Sachs considered this. 'No. I'd say *protective* . . . Now, as for employees: I interviewed most of them who had access to people's dossiers. There are a few that weren't accounted for yesterday afternoon. Oh, and I asked if they log downloads; they don't. And we'll be getting a list of clients who've bought data about the vics and fall guys.'

'But the important thing is you let them know about an investigation and gave them all the name Myra Weinburg.'

'Right.'

Then Sachs took a document from her briefcase. Arthur's dossier, she explained. 'Thought it might be helpful. If nothing else, you might be interested in it. Seeing what your cousin's been up to.' Sachs removed the staple and mounted it on the reading frame near Rhyme – a device that turned pages for him.

He glanced at the document. Then back to the charts.

'Don't you want to look through it?' she asked.

'Maybe later.'

She returned to her briefcase. 'Here's the list of SSD employees who have access to the dossiers – they're called "closets."'

'As in secrets?'

'Right. Pulaski's out checking their alibis. We have to go back to talk to the two technical managers but here's what we have so far.' On a whiteboard she wrote their names and some comments.

Andrew Sterling, President, Chief Executive Officer
  Alibi – on Long Island, to be verified
Sean Cassel, Director of Sales and Marketing
  No alibi
Wayne Gillespie, Director of Technical Operations
  No alibi
Samuel Brockton, Director, Compliance Department
  Alibi – hotel records confirm presence in Washington
Peter Arlonzo-Kemper, Director of Human Resources
  Alibi – with wife, to be verified
Steven Shraeder, Technical Service and Support Manager,
  day shift
  To be interviewed
Faruk Mameda, Technical Service and Support Manager,
  night shift
  To be interviewed
Client of SSD (?)
  Awaiting list from Sterling

'Mel?' Rhyme called. 'Check NCIC and the department.'
Cooper ran the names through the National Crime Information Center and the NYPD equivalent, as well as the Justice Department's Violent Criminal Apprehension Program.
'Wait . . . may have a hit here.'
'What is it?' Sachs asked, moving forward.
'Arlonzo Kemper. Juvie in Pennsylvania. Assault twenty-five years ago. The record's still sealed.'
'The age would be right. He's about thirty-five. And he's light-skinned.' Sachs nodded at the 522 profile chart.

'Well, get the record unsealed. Or at least find out if it's the same guy.'

'I'll see what I can do.' Cooper typed some more.

'Any references to the others?' Rhyme nodded toward the suspect list.

'Nope. Just him.'

Cooper ran various state and federal database searches and checked some professional organizations. The tech shrugged. 'Went to UC-Hastings. No connection with Pennsylvania that I can find. Seems like a loner: Aside from college credentials, his only organization is the National Association of Human Resource Professionals. He was on the technology task force two years ago but hasn't done much since.

'Okay, here's what they have on the juvie. He attacked another kid in a detention home . . . Oh.'

'Oh what?'

'It's not him. No hyphen. The name's different. The juvenile was first name Arlonzo, last name Kemper.' He glanced at the chart. 'He's "Peter," last name "Arlonzo-Kemper." I typed it in wrong. If I'd included the hyphen, it wouldn't have shown up at all. Sorry.'

'Not the worst of sins.' Rhyme shrugged. This was a sobering lesson about the nature of data, he reflected. They seemingly had found a suspect and even Cooper's characterization of him suggested he might be the one – *He seems to be a loner* – yet the lead was completely wrong, due to the minuscule error of missing a single keystroke. They might have come down hard on the man – and misdirected resources – if Cooper hadn't realized his mistake.

Sachs sat down beside Rhyme, who, seeing her eyes, asked, 'What is it?'

'Funny, but now that I'm back, I feel like some kind of spell's been broken. I think I want an outside opinion. About

SSD. I lost perspective when I was there . . . It's a disorienting place.'

'How so?' Sellitto asked.

'You ever been to Vegas?'

Sellitto and his ex had. Rhyme gave a brief laugh. 'Las Vegas, where the only question is how *much* disadvantage you have. And why would I want to give money away?'

Sachs continued, 'Well, it was like a casino. The outside doesn't exist. Small – or no – windows. No watercooler conversation, nobody laughing. Everybody's completely focused on their jobs. It's like you're in a different world.'

'And you want somebody else's opinion on the place,' Sellitto said.

'Right.'

Rhyme suggested, 'Journalist?' Thom's partner, Peter Hoddins, was a former reporter for *The New York Times* and was now writing nonfiction books about politics and society. He'd probably know people from the business desk who covered the data-mining industry.

But she shook her head. 'No, somebody who's had first-hand contact with them. A former employee maybe.'

'Good. Lon, can you call somebody at Unemployment?'

'Sure.' Sellitto called the New York State unemployment department. After ten minutes or so of bouncing around from office to office he found the name of a former SSD assistant technical director. He'd worked for the data miner for a number of years but had been fired a year and a half ago. Calvin Geddes was his name and he was in Manhattan. Sellitto got the details and handed the note to Sachs. She called Geddes and arranged to see him in about an hour.

Rhyme had no particular opinion about her mission. In any investigation you need to cover all bases. But leads like Geddes and Pulaski's checking on alibis were, to Rhyme, like images seen in an opaque window's reflection – suggestions of the truth but not the truth itself. It was only the hard evidence, scant though it was, that held the real answer to who their killer was. And so he turned back to the clues.

Move . . .

Arthur Rhyme had given up being scared of the Lats, who were ignoring him anyway. And he knew the big fuck-you black guy wasn't any threat.

It was the tattooed white guy who bothered him. The tweaker – what meth-heads were apparently called – scared Arthur a lot. Mick was his name. His hands twitched, he scratched his welty skin and his eerie white eyes jumped like bubbles in boiling water. He whispered to himself.

Arthur had tried to avoid the man all yesterday, and last night he'd lain awake and in between bouts of depression spent a lot of time wishing Mick away, hoping that he'd go to trial today and vanish from Arthur's life forever.

But no such luck. He was back this morning and seemed to be staying close. He continued to glance at Arthur. 'You and me,' he once muttered, sending a chill right down to Arthur's tailbone.

Even the Lats didn't seem to want to hassle Mick. Maybe you had to follow certain protocols in jail. Some unwritten rules of right and wrong. People like this skinny tattooed druggie might not play by those rules, and everybody here seemed to know it.

Ever'body know ever'thing round here. 'Cept you. You don' know shit . . .

Once he laughed, looked at Arthur as if recognizing him and started to rise but then seemed to forget what he'd intended and sat down again, picking at his thumb.

'Yo, Jersey Man.' A voice in his ear. Arthur jumped.

The big black guy had come up behind him. He sat down next to Arthur. The bench creaked.

'Antwon. Antwon Johnson.'

Should he make a fist and tap it? Don't be a fucking idiot, he told himself and just nodded. 'Arthur—'

'I know.' Johnson glanced at Mick and said to Arthur, 'That tweaker fucked up. Don't do that meth shit. Fuck you up forever.' After a moment he said, 'So. You a brainy guy?'

'Sort of.'

'The fuck "sorta" mean?'

Don't play games. 'I have a physics degree. And one in chemistry. I went to M.I.T.'

'Mitt?'

'It's a school.'

'Good one?'

'Pretty good.'

'So you know science shit? Chemistry and physics and everything?'

This line of questioning wasn't at all like that of the two Lats, the ones who'd tried to extort him. It seemed like Johnson was really interested. 'Some things. Yeah.'

Then the big guy asked, 'So you know howta make bombs. One big enough to blow that motherfucking wall down.'

'I . . .' Heart thudding again, harder than before. 'Well—'

Antwon Johnson laughed. 'Fuckin' wit' you, man.'

'I—'

'Fuckin'. Wit. You.'

'Oh.' Arthur laughed and wondered if his heart would explode right at this moment or would wait till later. He hadn't gotten all of his father's genes, but had the faulty cardiac messages been included in the package?

Mick said something to himself and took an intense interest in his right elbow, scratching it raw.

Both Johnson and Arthur watched him.

Tweaker . . .

Johnson then said, 'Yo, yo, Jersey Man, lemme ask you somethin'.'

'Sure.'

'My momma, she religious, you know what I'm saying? And she tellin' me one time the Bible was right. I mean, all of it was exactly the way that shit was wrote. Okay but listen up: I'm thinking, where's the dinosaurs in the Bible? God created man and woman and earth and rivers and donkeys and snakes an' shit. Why don't it say God created dinosaurs? I mean, I seen their skeletons, you know. So they was real. So whatsa fuckin' truth, man?'

Arthur Rhyme looked at Mick. Then at the nail pounded in the wall. His palms were sweating and he was thinking that, of all the things that could happen to him in jail, he was going to get killed because he took a scientist's moral stand against intelligent design.

Oh, what the fuck?

He said, 'It would be against all the known laws of science – laws that have been acknowledged by every advanced civilization on earth – for the earth to be only six thousand years old. It would be like you sprouting wings and flying out that window there.'

The man frowned.

I'm dead.

Johnson fixed him with an intense gaze. Then he nodded. 'I fuckin' knew it. Didn't make no sense at all, six thousand years. Fuck.'

'I can give you the name of a book to read about it. There's this author Richard Dawkins and he—'

'Don' wanna read no fuckin' book. Take yo' word fo' it, Mr Jersey Man.'

Arthur really felt like tapping fists now. But he refrained. He asked, 'What's your mother going to say when you tell her?'

The round black face screwed up in astonishment. 'I ain' gonna tell her. That'd be fucked up. You never win no arguments 'gainst yo' mother.'

Or your father, Arthur said to himself.

Johnson then grew serious. He said, 'Yo. Word up you din't do what they busted you fo'.'

'Of course not.'

'But you got yo' ass collared anyway?'

'Yep.'

'The fuck that happen?'

'I wish I knew. I've been thinking about it since I got arrested. It's *all* I think about. How he could've done it.'

'Who's "he"?'

'The real killer.'

'Yo, like in *The Fugitive*. Or O.J.'

'The police found all kinds of evidence linking me to the crime. Somehow the real killer knew everything about me. My car, where I lived, my schedule. He even knew things I bought – and he planted them as evidence. I'm sure that's what happened.'

Antwon Johnson considered this and then laughed. 'Man. That yo' fucking problem.'

'What's that?'

'You went out an' you *bought* ever'thing. Shoulda just boosted it, man. Then nobody know shit what you about.'

Chapter
TWENTY-THREE

Another lobby.

But a lot different from SSD's.

Amelia Sachs had never seen anything quite so messy. Maybe when she was a beat officer, responding to domestics among druggies in Hell's Kitchen. But even then a lot of those people had had dignity; they made the effort. This place made her cringe. The not-for-profit organization Privacy Now, located in an old piano factory in the city's Chelsea district, won the prize for slovenly.

Stacks of computer printouts, books – many of them law books and yellowing government regulations – newspapers and magazines. Then cardboard boxes, which contained more of the same. Phonebooks too. Federal Registers.

And dust. A ton of dust.

A receptionist in blue jeans and a shabby sweater pounded furiously on an old computer keyboard and spoke, sotto voce, into a hands-free telephone. Harried people in jeans and T-shirts, or corduroys and wrinkled work shirts, walked into the office from up the hall, swapped files or picked up phone-message slips and disappeared.

Cheap printed signs and posters filled the walls.

BOOKSTORES: BURN YOUR CUSTOMERS' RECEIPTS, BEFORE THE GOVERNMENT BURNS THEIR BOOKS!!!

On one wrinkled rectangle of art board was the famous line from George Orwell's novel, *1984,* about a totalitarian society:

BIG BROTHER IS WATCHING YOU.

And sitting prominently on the scabby wall across from Sachs:

GUERRILLA'S GUIDE TO THE PRIVACY WAR

- Never give out your Social Security Number.

- Never give out your phone number.

- Hold loyalty card swap parties before you go shopping.

- Never volunteer for surveys.

- 'Opt out' every chance you can.

- Don't fill out product registration cards.

- Don't fill out 'warranty' cards. You don't need one for the warranty. They're information gathering devices!

- Remember – the Nazis' most dangerous weapon was information.

- Stay off the 'grid' as much as possible.

She was digesting this when a scuffed door opened and a short, intense-looking man with pale skin strode up to her, shook her hand and then led her back into his office, which was even messier than the lobby.

Calvin Geddes, the former employee of SSD, now worked

for this privacy rights organization. 'I went over to the dark side,' he said, smiling. He'd abandoned the conservative SSD dress code, and was wearing a yellow button-down shirt without a tie, jeans and running shoes.

The pleasant grin faded quickly, though, as she told him the story of the murders.

'Yep,' he whispered, his eyes hard and focused now. 'I *knew* something like this would happen. I absolutely knew it.'

Geddes explained that he had a technical background and had worked with Sterling's first company, SSD's predecessor, in Silicon Valley, writing code for them. He moved to New York and lived a nice life as SSD skyrocketed to success.

But then the experience had soured.

'We had problems. We didn't encrypt data back then and were responsible for some serious identity thefts. Several people committed suicide. And a couple of times stalkers signed up as clients – but only to get information from innerCircle. Two of the women they were looking for were attacked, one almost died. Then some parents in custody battles used our data to find their exes and kidnapped the children. It was tough. I felt like the guy who helped invent the atom bomb and then regretted it. I tried to put more controls in place at the company. And that meant that I didn't believe in the quote "SSD vision," according to my boss.'

'Sterling?'

'Ultimately, yes. But he didn't actually fire me. Andrew never gets his hands dirty. He delegates the unpleasantries. That way he can appear to be the most wonderful, kindest boss in the world . . . And as a practical matter there's less evidence against him if other people do his butchery . . . Well, when I left I joined Privacy Now.'

The organization was like EPIC, the Electronic Privacy Information Center, he explained. PN challenged threats to individuals' privacy from the government, businesses and financial institutions, computer providers, telephone companies, and commercial data brokers and miners. The organization lobbied in Washington, sued the government under the Freedom of Information Act to find out about surveillance programs, and sued individual corporations that weren't complying with privacy and disclosure laws.

Sachs didn't tell him about the data trap Rodney Szarnek had put together but explained in general terms how they were looking for SSD customers and employees who might be able to patch together dossiers. 'The security seems very tight. But that was what Sterling and his people told us. I wanted an outside opinion.'

'Happy to help.'

'Mark Whitcomb told us about the concrete firewalls and keeping the data divided up.'

'Who's Whitcomb?'

'He's with their Compliance Department.'

'Never heard of it. It's new.'

Sachs explained, 'The department is like a consumer advocate within the company. To make sure all government regulations are complied with.'

Geddes seemed pleased, though he added, 'That didn't come about out of the goodness of Andrew Sterling's heart. They probably got sued once too often and wanted to make a good show for the public and Congress. Sterling's never going to give one inch if he doesn't have to . . . But about the data pens, that's true. Sterling treats data like the Holy Grail. And hacking in? Probably impossible. And there is no way anybody could physically break in and steal data.'

'He told me that very few employees can log on and get dossiers from innerCircle. As far as you know, is that true?'

'Oh, yeah. A few of them have to have access but nobody else. *I* never did. And I was there from the beginning.'

'Do you have any thoughts? Maybe any employees with a troubling past? Violent?'

'It's been a few years. And I never thought anybody was particularly dangerous. Though, I've got to say, despite the big happy family façade Sterling likes to put on, I never really got to know anyone there.'

'What about these individuals?' She showed him the list of suspects.

Geddes looked it over. 'I worked with Gillespie. I knew Cassel. I don't like either of them. They're caught up in the whole data-mining curve, like Silicon Valley in the nineties. Hotshots. I don't know the others. Sorry.' Then he studied her closely. 'So you've been there?' he asked with a cool smile. 'What'd you think of Andrew?'

Her thoughts jammed as she tried to come up with a brief summary of her impressions. Finally: 'Determined, polite, inquisitive, smart but . . .' Her voice petered out.

'But you don't really know him.'

'Right.'

'Because he presents the great stone face. In all the years I worked with him I never really knew him. *Nobody* knows him. Unfathomable. I love that word. That's Andrew. I was always looking for clues . . . You notice something odd about his bookshelves?'

'You couldn't see the spines of the books.'

'Exactly. I snuck a peek once. Guess what? They weren't about computers or privacy or data or business. They were mostly history books, philosophy, politics: the Roman Empire, Chinese emperors, Franklin Roosevelt, John Kennedy, Stalin, Idi Amin, Khrushchev. He read a lot about the Nazis. Nobody used information the way they did and Andrew doesn't hesitate to tell you. First major use of computers to keep track of ethnic groups. That's how they consolidated power. Sterling's doing the same in the corporate world. Notice the company name, SSD? The rumor is he chose it intentionally. SS – for the Nazi elite army. SD – for their security and intelligence agency. You know what his competitors say it stands for? "Selling Souls for Dollars."' Geddes laughed grimly.

'Oh, don't get me wrong. Andrew doesn't dislike Jews. Or any other group. Politics, nationality, religion and race mean nothing to him. I heard him say once, "Data have no borders." The seat of power in the twenty-first century is information, not oil or geography. And Andrew Sterling wants to be the most powerful man on earth . . . I'm sure he gave you the data-mining-is-God speech.'

'Saving us from diabetes, helping us afford Christmas presents and houses and solving cases for the police?'

'That's the one. And all of it's true. But tell me if those benefits are worth somebody knowing every detail about your life. Maybe you don't care, provided you save a few bucks. But do you really want ConsumerChoice lasers scanning your eyes in a movie theater and recording your reactions to those commercials they run before the movie? Do you want the RFID tag in your car key to be available to the police to know that you hit a hundred miles an hour last week, when your route only took you along roads that were posted fifty? Do you want strangers knowing what kind of underwear your daughter wears? Or exactly when you're having sex?'

'What?'

'Well, innerCircle knows you bought condoms and KY this afternoon and your husband was on the six-fifteen E train home. It knows you've got the evening free because your son's at the Mets game and your daughter's buying clothes at The Gap in the Village. It knows you put on cable-TV porn at seven-eighteen. And that you order some nice tasty postcoital takeout Chinese at quarter to ten. That information is all there.

'Oh, SSD knows if your children are maladjusted in school and when to send you direct-mail flyers about tutors and child-counseling services. If your husband is having trouble in the bedroom and when to send him discreet flyers about erectile dysfunction cures. When your family history, buying patterns and absences from work put you in a presuicidal profile—'

'But that's good. So a counselor can help you.'

Geddes gave a cold laugh. 'Wrong. Because counseling potential suicide victims isn't profitable. SSD sends the name to local funeral homes and grief counselors – who could snag *all* of the family as customers, not just a single depressed person *after* he shoots himself. And, by the way, that was a very lucrative venture.'

Sachs was shocked.

'Did you hear about "tethering"?'

'No.'

'SSD has defined a network based just on you. Call it "Detective Sachs World." You're the hub and the spokes go to your partners, spouses, parents, neighbors, coworkers, anybody it might help SSD to know about and profit from that knowledge. Everybody who has any connection is "tethered" to you. And each one of them is his or her own hub, and there are dozens of people tethered to them.'

Another thought and his eyes flashed. 'You know about metadata?'

'What's that?'

'Data about data. Every document that's created by or stored on a computer – letters, files, reports, legal briefs, spreadsheets, Websites, emails, grocery lists – is loaded with hidden data. Who created it, where it's been sent, all the changes that have been made to it and who made them and when – all recorded there, second by second. You write a memo to your boss and for a joke you start out with "Dear Stupid Prick," then delete it and write it correctly. Well, the "stupid prick" part is still in there.'

'Seriously?'

'Oh, yes. The disk size of a typical word-processing report is much larger than the text in the document itself. What's the rest? Metadata. The Watchtower database-management program has special bots – software robots – that do nothing but find and store metadata from every document it collects. We called it the Shadow Department, because metadata's like a shadow of the main data – and it's usually much more revealing.'

Shadow, sixteens, pens, closets . . . This was a whole new world to Amelia Sachs.

Geddes enjoyed having a receptive audience. He leaned forward. 'You know that SSD has an education division?'

She thought back to the chart in the brochure that Mel Cooper had downloaded. 'Yes. EduServe.'

'But Sterling didn't tell you about it, did he?'

'No.'

'Because he doesn't like to let on that its main function is to collect everything it possibly can about children. Starting with kindergarten. What they buy, what they watch, what computer sites they go to, what their grades are, medical records from school . . . And that's very, very valuable information for retailers. But you ask me, what's scarier about EduServe is that school boards can come to SSD and run predictive software on their students and then gear educational programs to them – in terms of what's best for the community – or society, if you want to be Orwellian about it. Given Billy's background, we think he should go into skilled labor. Suzy should be a doctor but only in public health . . . Control the children and you control the future. Another element of Adolf Hitler's philosophy, by the way.' He laughed. 'Okay, no more lecturing . . . But you see why I couldn't stomach it anymore?'

But then Geddes frowned. 'Just thinking about your situation – we had an incident once at SSD. Years ago. Before the company came to New York. There was a death. Probably just a coincidence. But . . .'

'No, tell me.'

'In the early days we farmed out a lot of the actual data-collection part of the business to scroungers.'

'To what?'

'Companies or individuals who procure data. A strange breed. They're sort of like old-time wildcatters – prospectors, you could say. See, data have this weird allure. You can get addicted to the hunt. You can never find enough. However much they collect, they want more. And these guys are always looking for new ways to collect it. They're competitive, ruthless. That's how Sean Cassel started in the business. He was a data scrounger.

'Anyway, one scrounger was amazing. He worked for a small company. I think it was called Rocky Mountain Data in Colorado . . . What was his name?' Geddes squinted. 'Maybe Gordon somebody. Or that might've been his last name. Anyway, we heard that he wasn't too happy about SSD taking over his company. The word is he scrounged everything he could find about the company and Sterling himself – turned the tables on them. We thought maybe he was trying to dig up dirt and blackmail Sterling into stopping the acquisition. You know Andy Sterling – Andrew Junior – works for the company?'

She nodded.

'We'd heard rumors that Sterling had abandoned him years ago and the kid tracked him down. But then we also heard that maybe it was *another* son he abandoned. Maybe by his first wife, or a girlfriend. Something he wanted to keep secret. We thought maybe Gordon was looking for that kind of dirt.

'Anyway, while Sterling and some other people were out there negotiating the purchase of Rocky Mountain, this Gordon guy dies – an accident of some kind, I think. That's all I heard. I wasn't there. I was back in the Valley, writing code.'

'And the acquisition went through?'

'Yep. What Andrew wants, Andrew shall have . . . Now, let me throw out one thought about your killer. Andrew Sterling himself.'

'He has an alibi.'

'Does he? Well, don't forget he *is* the king of information. If you *control* data, you can *change* data. Did you check out that alibi real carefully?'

'We are right now.'

'Well, even if it's confirmed, he has men who work for him and would do whatever he wants. I mean anything. Remember, other people do his dirty work.'

'But he's a multimillionaire. What's his interest in stealing coins or a painting, then murdering the victim?'

'His interest?' Geddes's voice rose, as if he were a professor talking to a student who just wasn't getting the lesson. 'His interest is in being the most powerful person in the world. He wants his little collection to include everybody on earth. And he's particularly interested in law enforcement and government clients. The more crimes that are successfully solved using innerCircle, the more police departments, here and abroad, are going to sign on. Hitler's first task when he came to power was to consolidate all the police departments in Germany. What was our big problem in Iraq? We disbanded the army and the police – we should have used them. Andrew doesn't make mistakes like that.'

Geddes laughed. 'Think I'm a crank, don't you? But I live with this stuff all day long. Remember, it's not paranoia if somebody's really out there watching everything you do every minute of the day. And *that's* SSD in a nutshell.'

Chapter
TWENTY-FOUR

Awaiting Sachs's return, Lincoln Rhyme listened absently as Lon Sellitto explained that none of the other evidence in the earlier cases – the rape and coin theft – could be located. 'That's fucking weird.'

Rhyme agreed. But his attention veered from the detective's sour assessment to his cousin's SSD dossier, sitting beside him on the turning frame. He tried to ignore it.

But the document drew him, needle to magnet. Looking at the stark sheets, black type on white paper, he told himself that, as Sachs had suggested, perhaps something helpful could be found in it. Then he admitted that he was simply curious.

STRATEGIC SYSTEMS DATACORP, INC.
INNERCIRCLE® DOSSIERS

Arthur Robert Rhyme
SSD Subject Number 3480–9021–4966–2083

Lifestyle

Dossier 1A. Consumer products preferences

Dossier 1B. Consumer services preferences

Dossier 1C. Travel

Dossier 1D. Medical

Dossier 1E. Leisure-time preferences

Financial/Educational/Professional

Dossier 2A. Educational history

Dossier 2B. Employment history, w/ income

Dossier 2C. Credit history/current report and rating

Dossier 2D. Business products and services preferences

Governmental/Legal

Dossier 3A. Vital records

Dossier 3B. Voter registration

Dossier 3C. Legal history

Dossier 3D. Criminal history

Dossier 3E. Compliance

Dossier 3F. Immigration and naturalization

The information contained herein is the property of
Strategic Systems Datacorp, Inc. (SSD). The use hereof
is subject to the Licensing Agreement between SSD and
Customer, as defined in the Master Client Agreement.
© Strategic Systems Datacorp, Inc. All rights reserved.

Instructing the turning frame to flip through the pages, he skimmed the dense document, all thirty pages of it. Some categories were full, some sparse. The voter registration was redacted, and the compliance and portions of the credit history referred to separate files, presumably because of legislation limiting access to such information.

He paused at the extensive lists of the consumer products bought by Arthur and his family (they were described by the creepy phrase 'tethered individuals'). There was no doubt that anybody reading the dossier could have learned enough about his buying habits and where he shopped to implicate him in the murder of Alice Sanderson.

Rhyme learned about the country club Arthur belonged to, until he had quit several years ago, presumably because he'd lost his job. He noted the package vacations he'd bought; Rhyme was surprised he'd taken up skiing. Also, he or one of the children might have a weight problem; somebody had joined a dieting program. A health club membership for the entire family too. Rhyme saw a lay-away purchase for some jewelry around Christmastime; a chain jewelry store in a New Jersey mall. Rhyme speculated: small stones socketed in a large setting – a make-do gift, until times were better.

Seeing one reference, he gave a laugh. Like him, Arthur seemed to favor single-malt whisky – Rhyme's new favorite brand, in fact, Glenmorangie.

His cars were a Prius and a Cherokee.

The criminalist's smile faded at that reference, though, as he recalled another vehicle. He was picturing Arthur's red Corvette, the car he'd received from his parents on his seventeenth birthday – the car in which Arthur had driven off to Boston to attend M.I.T.

Rhyme thought back to the boys' respective departures for college. It was a significant moment for Arthur, and for his father too; Henry Rhyme was ecstatic that his son had been accepted by such a fine school. But the cousins' plans – rooming together, jousting over girls, outshining the other nerds – didn't work out. Lincoln wasn't accepted by M.I.T. but went instead to the University of Illinois-Champagne/Urbana, which offered Lincoln a full scholarship (and had some panache back then because it was located in the town where HAL, the narcissistic computer in Stanley Kubrick's *2001: A Space Odyssey*, was born).

Teddy and Anne were pleased their son was going to a home-state school, as was his uncle; Henry had told his nephew that he hoped the boy would return to Chicago often and continue to help him with his research, possibly even assist in his classes from time to time.

'Sorry you and Arthur won't be rooming together,' Henry said. 'But you'll see each other summers, holidays. And I'm sure your father and I can swing some trips out to Bean Town for a visit.'

'That might work out,' Lincoln had said.

Keeping to himself that while he was devastated he hadn't been accepted by M.I.T., there was an upside to the rejection – because he wanted never to see his goddamn cousin ever again.

All because of the red Corvette.

The incident had occurred not long after the Christmas Eve party at which he'd won the concrete piece of history, on a breathlessly cold day in February, which, sun or cloud, is Chicago's most heartless month. Lincoln was competing in a science fair at Northwestern in Evanston. He asked Adrianna if she wanted to accompany him, thinking that he might go for the marriage proposal afterward.

But she couldn't make it; she was going shopping with her mother at Marshall Field's department store in the Loop, lured by a big sale. Lincoln had been disappointed but thought nothing more of it and concentrated on the fair. He won first place in the senior division, then he and his friends packed up their projects and carted everything outside. Fingers blue and breath clouding around them in the painful air, they loaded the gear in the belly of the bus and sprinted for the door.

It was then that somebody called, 'Hey, check it out. *Excellent* wheels.'

A red Corvette was streaking through campus.

His cousin Arthur was at the wheel. Which wasn't odd; the family lived nearby. What did surprise Lincoln, though, was that the girl beside Arthur, he believed, was Adrianna.

Yes, no?

He couldn't be sure.

The clothes matched: a brown leather jacket and a fur hat, which looked identical to the one Lincoln had given her at Christmas.

'Linc, Jesus, get your ass in here. We gotta close the door.'

Still, Lincoln remained where he was, staring at the car as it fishtailed around the corner on the gray-white street.

Could she have lied to him? The girl he was considering marrying? It didn't seem possible. And cheating on him with *Arthur*?

Trained in science, he examined the facts objectively.

Fact One. Arthur and Adrianna knew each other. His cousin had met her months ago in the counselor's office where she worked after class at Lincoln's high school. They could very easily have exchanged phone numbers.

Fact Two. Arthur, Lincoln now realized, had stopped asking about her. This was odd. The boys had spent plenty of time talking about girls but recently Art hadn't once mentioned her.

Suspicious.

Fact Three. On reflection, he decided that Adie sounded evasive when she'd demurred about the science fair. (And he hadn't mentioned its site as Evanston, which meant she wouldn't hesitate to cruise around the gridded streets with Art.) Lincoln was slammed with jealousy. I was going to give her a piece of Stagg Field, for God's sake! A splinter of the true cross of modern science! He considered other times when she'd begged off seeing him under circumstances that, in retrospect, seemed strange. He counted three or four.

Still he refused to believe it. He crunched through the snow to a pay phone, and called her house and asked to speak to the girl.

'Sorry, Lincoln, she's out with friends,' said Adrianna's mother.

Friends . . .

'Oh. I'll try her later . . . Say, Mrs Waleska, did you two ever get downtown for that sale at Field's today?'

'No, the sale's next week . . . I have to get supper ready, Lincoln. You stay warm. It's freezing outside.'

'It sure is.' Lincoln knew this for a fact. He was standing at a phone kiosk, his jaw shivering, no desire to pick up the 60 cents that had leapt from his quivering hands into the snow after he'd tried repeatedly to feed the coins into the phone.

'Jesus Christ, Lincoln, get in the bus!'

Later that night he called and managed to maintain a normal conversation for a time, before asking how her day had gone. She explained that she'd enjoyed the shopping with Mom but the crowds were terrible. Garrulous, rambling, digressive. She sounded dead guilty.

Still, he couldn't take the matter on faith.

And so he kept up appearances. The next time Art was visiting he left his cousin in the rec room downstairs and slipped outside with a dog hair roller – exactly the sort used now by crime-scene teams – and collected evidence from the Corvette's front seat.

He slipped the tape into a Baggie and, when he saw Adrianna next, he took some samples of fur from her hat and coat. He felt cheap, scalded with shame and embarrassment but that didn't stop him from comparing the strands with one of the high school's compound microscopes. They were the same – both fur from the hat and synthetic fibers from the coat.

The girlfriend he was considering marrying had been cheating on him.

And from the quantity of fibers in Arthur's car he concluded she'd been there more than once.

Finally, a week later, he spotted them in the car, leaving no doubt.

Lincoln didn't bow out graciously or angrily. He just bowed out. Without the heart for a confrontation, he let his relationship with Adrianna wind down. The few times they went out were stiff and riddled with awkward silences. To his further dismay, she actually seemed upset about his growing distance. Damn it. Did she think she could have it both ways? *She* seemed mad at *him* . . . even while she was cheating.

He distanced himself from his cousin too. Lincoln's excuse was final exams, track meets and – the blessing in disguise: Lincoln's rejection by M.I.T.

The two boys saw each other occasionally – familial obligations, graduation ceremonies – but everything had changed between them, changed fundamentally. And of Adrianna neither boy had said a single word. At least not for many years after that.

My whole life changed. If it weren't for you, everything would've been different . . .

Even now Rhyme found his temple throbbing. He couldn't feel any coolness on his palms but he supposed they were sweating. These hard thoughts, though, were interrupted by Amelia Sachs, striding through the door.

'Any developments?' she asked.

A bad sign. If she'd had a breakthrough with Calvin Geddes she would have said so up front.

'No,' he admitted. 'Still waiting to hear from Ron about the alibis. And no bites on the trap that Rodney put together.'

Sachs took the coffee Thom offered and lifted half a turkey sandwich from a tray.

'The tuna salad's better,' said Lon Sellitto. 'He made it himself.'

'This'll do.' She sat beside Rhyme, offered him a bite. He had no appetite and shook his head. 'How's your cousin doing?' she asked, glancing at the open dossier on the turning frame.

'My cousin?'

'How's he doing in detention? This has to be hard for him.'

'Haven't had a chance to talk to him.'

'He's probably too embarrassed to contact you. You really should call.'

'I will. What'd you find out from Geddes?'

She admitted that the meeting had yielded no great revelations. 'Mostly it was a lecture on the erosion of privacy.' She gave him some of the more alarming bullet points: the personal data collected daily, the intrusions, the danger of EduServe, the immortality of data, the metadata records of computer files.

'Anything useful to *us*?' he asked acerbically.

'Two things. First, he's not convinced Sterling's innocent.'

'You said he's got an alibi,' Sellitto pointed out, taking another sandwich.

'Maybe not him personally. He might be using somebody else.'

'Why? He's a CEO of a big company. What's in it for him?'

'The more crime, the more society needs SSD to protect them. Geddes says he wants power. Described him as the Napoléon of data.'

'So he's got a hired gun breaking windows so he can step in and fix them.' Rhyme nodded, somewhat impressed with the idea. 'Only it backfired. He never thought we'd tip to the fact the SSD database was behind the crimes. Okay. Put it on the list of suspects. An UNSUB working for Sterling.'

'Now, Geddes also told me that a few years ago SSD acquired a Colorado data company. Their main scrounger – that's a data collector – was killed.'

'Any link between Sterling and the death?'

'No idea. But it's worth checking out. I'll make some calls.'

The doorbell rang and Thom answered. Ron Pulaski entered. He was grim-faced and sweaty. Rhyme sometimes had an urge to tell him to take it easier but since the criminalist himself didn't, he figured the suggestion would be hypocritical.

The rookie explained that most of the alibis for Sunday checked out. 'I checked with the E-ZPass people and they confirmed Sterling went through the Midtown Tunnel when he said. I tried his son to see if his dad called from Long Island just to double-check. But he was out.'

Pulaski continued, 'Something else – the Human Resources director? His only alibi was his wife. She backed him up but she was acting like a scared mouse. And she was like her husband: "SSD is the greatest place in the world. Blah, blah, blah . . ."'

Rhyme, distrustful of witnesses in any event, didn't make much of this; one thing he'd learned from Kathryn Dance, the body language and kinesics expert with the California Bureau of Investigation, was that even when people are telling the God's truth to police they often look guilty.

Sachs went to their suspect list and updated it.

Andrew Sterling, President, Chief Executive Officer
Alibi – on Long Island, verified. Awaiting son's
*   confirmation*
Sean Cassel, Director of Sales and Marketing
No alibi
Wayne Gillespie, Director of Technical Operations
No alibi

Samuel Brockton, Director, Compliance Department
Alibi – hotel records confirm presence in Washington
Peter Arlonzo-Kemper, Director of Human Resources
Alibi – with wife, verified by her (biased?)
Steven Shraeder, Technical Service and Support
    Manager, day shift
To be interviewed
Faruk Mameda, Technical Service and Support
    Manager, night shift
To be interviewed
Client of SSD (?)
Awaiting list from Sterling
UNSUB recruited by Andrew Sterling (?)

   Sachs looked at her watch. 'Ron, Mameda should be in by now. Could you go back and talk to him and Shraeder? See where they were yesterday at the time of the Weinburg murder. And Sterling's assistant should have the client list ready. If not, perch in his office until he gets it. Look important. Better yet, look impatient.'

'Go back to SSD?'

'Right.'

For some reason, he didn't want to, Rhyme could see.

'Sure. Just let me call Jenny and check up on things at home.' He pulled out his phone and hit speed dial.

Rhyme deduced from part of the conversation that he was talking to his young son, and then, sounding even more childish, presumably the baby girl. The criminalist tuned it out.

It was then that his own phone rang; 44 was the first number on caller ID.

Ah, good.

'Command, answer phone.'

'Detective Rhyme?'

'Inspector Longhurst.'

'I know you're working on that other case of yours but I thought you might like an update.'

'Of course. Please, go ahead. How's the Reverend Goodlight?'

'He's fine, if a bit scared. He's insisting that no new security people or officers come into the safe house. He only trusts the ones who've been with him for weeks.'

'Hardly blame him.'

'I have a man screening everyone who gets close. Former SAS chap. They're the best in the business . . . Now, we went through the Oldham safe house from top to bottom. Wanted to share with you what we found. Traces of copper and lead, consistent with bullets that had been milled or shaved. A few grains of gunpowder. And a few very small traces of mercury. My ballistics expert says he might be making a dum-dum bullet.'

'Yes, that's right. Liquid mercury's poured into the core. Causes hideous damage.'

'They also found some grease used in lubricating the receivers of rifles. And there were traces of hair bleach in the sink. And several dark gray fibers – cotton, quite thick with laundry starch. Our databases suggest they match the fabric in uniforms.'

'Do you think that the evidence was planted?'

'Our forensics people say not. The traces were quite minuscule.'

Blond, sniper, uniform . . .

'Now, one other incident set off alarms here: an attempted break-in at an NGO near Piccadilly – that's a nongovernmental organization. A nonprofit. The office was the East African Relief Agency, Reverend Goodlight's outfit. Guards came by and the culprit fled. He threw away his lock pick down the sewer. But we had a stroke of luck. Fellow on the street saw where. Well, to summarize, our people found it and discovered some soil on the tool. It contained a type of hop that's grown exclusively in Warwickshire. This hop had been processed for use in making bitter.'

'Bitter? Like beer?'

'Ale, yes. Now it so happens that we have a database of alcoholic drinks here at the Met. And their ingredients.'

Just like mine, he reflected. 'You do?'

'Put that together myself,' she said.

'Excellent. And?'

'The only brewery that uses this hop is near Birmingham. Now, we got an image of the NGO intruder on CCTV and, because of the hop, I thought I'd check the Birmingham CCTV tapes. Indeed, the same man arrived at New Street station several hours later, getting off the train with a large rucksack. We lost him in the crowds, I'm afraid.'

Rhyme considered this. The big question was: Were the hops planted on the tool to lead them off? That was the sort of thing that he could only get a feel for if he had examined the scene himself or had possession of the evidence. But now it was just down to what Sachs called a gut feel.

Planted or not?

Rhyme decided. 'Inspector, I don't believe it. I think Logan's pulling a double reversal. He's done this before. He wants us focused on Birmingham while he goes ahead with the hit in London.'

'I'm glad you say that, Detective. I was leaning that way myself.'

'We should play along. Where is everyone on the team?'

'Danny Krueger's in London with his people. So's your FBI man. The French agent and the Interpol chap were checking out leads in Oxford and Surrey. They didn't play out, though.'

'I'd get them all to Birmingham. Immediately. In a subtle but obvious way.'

The inspector laughed. 'Making sure Logan thinks we've swallowed the bait.'

'Exactly. I want him to think we believe we have a chance to catch him there. And send some tactical people too. Make a noise about it, make it look as if you're pulling them back from the shooting zone in London.'

'But in fact beef up the surveillance there.'

'Right. And tell them he's going for the long shot. He'll be blond and dressed in a gray uniform.'

'Brilliant, Detective. I'll get right to it.'

'Keep me posted.'

'Cheers.'

Rhyme ordered the phone to disconnect, just as a voice from across the room intruded. 'Heh, the long and the short of it is your friends at SSD are good. I can't get to first base, hacking in.' It was Rodney Szarnek. Rhyme had forgotten about him.

He rose and joined the officers. 'innerCircle's tighter than Fort Knox. And so is their database management system, Watchtower. I really doubt somebody could break in without a massive array of supercomputers, which you just aren't going to find at Best Buy or RadioShack.'

'But?' Rhyme could see that his face was troubled.

'Well, SSD's got some security on the system I've never seen before. It's pretty robust. And, I've got to say, scary. I had an anonymous ID and was wiping my tracks as I went. But what happens? Their security bot broke into *my* system and tried to identify me from what it found in the free space.'

'And, Rodney, what exactly does that mean?' Rhyme was trying to be patient. 'Free space?'

He explained that fragments of data, even deleted data, could be found in the empty space of hard drives. Software could often reassemble it into readable form. The SSD security system knew that Szarnek had covered his tracks so it had slipped inside his computer to read the data in the empty space and find out who he was. 'It's pretty freaky. I just happened to catch it. Otherwise . . .' He shrugged and took comfort in his coffee.

Rhyme had a thought. The more he considered the idea, the more he liked it. He looked over at the skinny Szarnek. 'Hey, Rodney, how'd you like to play real cop for a change?'

The carefree-geek visage disappeared. 'You know, I don't really think I'm up for that.'

Sellitto finished chewing the last of his sandwich. 'You haven't *lived* till a bullet breaks the sound barrier right next to your ear.'

'Wait, wait, wait . . . The only time I do any shooting is role-playing games and—'

'Oh, you wouldn't be the one at risk,' Rhyme said to the computer man, as his amused gaze slipped to Ron Pulaski, who was closing his phone.

'What?' the rookie asked with a frown.

Chapter
TWENTY-FIVE

'Anything else you need, Officer?'

Sitting in the SSD conference room, Ron Pulaski looked up into the emotionless face of Sterling's second assistant, Jeremy Mills. He was the 'outside' assistant, the young officer recalled. 'No, I'm fine, thanks. But I wonder if you could check with Mr Sterling about some files he was getting together for us. A list of clients. I think Martin was handling it.'

'I'd be happy to bring it up with Andrew when he's out of his meeting.' Then the broad-shouldered man walked around the room, pointing out the air-conditioning and light switches like the bellboy who'd escorted Jenny and Pulaski to their fancy room on their honeymoon.

Which reminded Pulaski again of how Jenny resembled Myra, the woman who'd been raped and killed yesterday. The way her hair lay, the slightly crooked smile he loved, the—

'Officer?'

Pulaski glanced up, realized his mind had been wandering. 'Sorry.'

The assistant was studying him as he pointed out a small refrigerator. 'Soda and water in here.'

'Thanks. I'm all set.'

Pay attention, he told himself angrily. Forget Jenny. Forget the children. People's lives are at stake here. Amelia thinks you can handle these interviews. So handle them.

You with us, rookie? I need you with us.

'If you want to make a call you can use this one. Dial nine for an outside line. Or you can just push this button, then speak the number. It's voice activated.' He pointed at Pulaski's cell phone. 'That probably won't work too well here. Lot of shielding, you know. For security.'

'Really? Okay.' Pulaski thought back; hadn't he seen somebody using a phone or BlackBerry here earlier? He couldn't recall.

'I'll have those employees come in. If you're ready.'

'That'd be great.'

The young man headed down the hall. Pulaski took his notebook out of his briefcase. Glanced at the names of the employees he had yet to interview.

Steven Shraeder, Technical Service and Support Manager, day shift.

Faruk Mameda, Technical Service and Support Manager, night shift.

He rose and peered into the hall. Nearby a janitor was emptying trash cans. He recalled he'd seen him yesterday, doing the same; it was as if Sterling was afraid that any brimming garbage would give the company a bad name. The solid man glanced at Pulaski's uniform without reaction and returned to his task, which he performed methodically. Looking farther down the immaculate corridor, the young cop could see a security guard standing at attention. Pulaski couldn't even get to the restroom without passing him. He returned to his seat to await the two men on the suspect list.

Faruk Mameda was first, a young man of Middle Eastern ancestry, Pulaski judged. He was very handsome, solemn-faced and confident. He held Pulaski's eye easily. The young man explained that he'd been with a small company SSD had acquired five or six years ago. His job was to supervise the technical-service staff. Single, with no family, he preferred working nights.

The cop was surprised that he didn't have a trace of foreign accent. Pulaski asked if Mameda had heard about the investigation. He claimed he hadn't heard the details – which could have been true, since he worked the night shift and had just gotten to work. All he knew was that Andrew Sterling had called and told him to speak to the police about a crime that had occurred.

He frowned as the police officer explained, 'There've been several murders recently. We think information from SSD was used in planning the crimes.'

'Information?'

'About the victims' whereabouts, some items they'd bought.'

Curiously Mameda's next question was 'Are you talking to all the employees?'

How much to tell, how much not to? That was one thing Pulaski never knew. Amelia always said it was important to grease the interview wheel, to keep the conversation going but never to give too much away. After the head injury, he believed his judgment had worsened and was nervous about what to say to wits and suspects. 'Not all of them, no.'

'Just certain ones who're suspicious. Or you've *decided* ahead of time are suspicious.' The employee's voice was defensive now, his jaw tight. 'I see. Sure. Happens a lot nowadays.'

'The person we're interested in is a man, and he has full access to innerCircle and Watchtower. We're talking to everyone who fits that description.' Pulaski had figured out Mameda's concern. 'Nothing to do with your nationality.'

The attempt at reassurance missed the mark. Mameda snapped, 'Ah, well, my nationality is American. I'm a U.S. citizen. Like you. That is, I *assume* you're a citizen. But maybe not. After all, very few people in this country were here originally.'

'I'm sorry.'

Mameda shrugged. 'Some things in life you have to get used to. It's unfortunate. The land of the free is also the land of the prejudiced. I . . .' His voice faded as he glanced past and above Pulaski, as if someone were standing behind him. The cop turned slightly. No one was there. Mameda said, 'Andrew said he wants full cooperation. So I'm cooperating. Could you ask me what you need to, please? It's a busy evening.'

'People's dossiers – closets, you call them?'

'Yes. Closets.'

'Do you ever download them?'

'Why would I download a dossier? Andrew wouldn't tolerate that.'

Interesting: the wrath of Andrew Sterling was the first deterrent. Not the police or the courts.

'So you haven't?'

'Never. If there's a bug of some sort or the data are corrupt or there's an interface problem, I may look at a portion of the entries or the headers but that's it. Only enough to figure out the problem and write a patch or debug the code.'

'Could somebody have found your passcodes and gotten into innerCircle? And downloaded dossiers that way?'

He paused. 'Not from me they couldn't. I don't have them written down.'

'And you go to the data pens frequently, all of them? And Intake too?'

'Yes, of course. That's my job. Repair the computers. Make sure the data are flowing smoothly.'

'Could you tell me where you were on Sunday afternoon between twelve and four?'

'Ah.' A nod. 'So that's what this is really about. Was I at the scene of the crime?'

Pulaski had trouble looking at the man's dark, angry eyes.

Mameda put his hands flat on the table, as if he were going to rise in anger and storm out. But he sat back and said, 'I had breakfast in the morning with some friends . . .' He added, 'They're from the mosque – you'll probably want to know.'

'I—'

'After that I spent the rest of the day alone. I went to the movies.'

'By yourself?'

'Fewer distractions. I usually go alone. It was a film by Jafar Panahi – the Iranian director. Have you ever see—' His mouth tightened. 'Never mind.'

'You have the ticket stub?'

'No . . . After that I did some shopping. I got home at six, I'd guess. Checked to see if they needed me here but the boxes were running smoothly so I had dinner with a friend.'

'In the afternoon did you buy anything with a credit card?'

He bristled. 'It was window-shopping. I got some coffee, a sandwich. Paid *cash* for it . . .' He leaned forward, whispered harshly, 'I don't really think you asked everybody all these questions. I know what you think of us. You think we treat women like animals. I can't believe you'd actually accuse me of raping someone. That's barbaric. And you're insulting!'

Pulaski struggled to look Mameda in the eye as he said, 'Well, sir, we *are* asking everybody with access to innerCircle about their whereabouts yesterday. Including Mr Sterling. We're just doing our job.'

He calmed slightly but continued to fume when Pulaski asked his whereabouts at the times of the other killings. 'I don't have any idea.' He refused to say any more and with a grim nod, stood and walked out.

Pulaski tried to figure out what had just happened. Was

Mameda acting guilty or innocent? He couldn't tell. Mostly he felt outmaneuvered.

Think harder, he told himself.

The second employee to be interviewed, Shraeder, was the opposite of Mameda: pure geek. He was gawky, the clothes ill-fitting and wrinkled, ink stains on his hands. His glasses were owlish and the lenses smeared. Definitely not in the SSD mold. While Mameda was defensive, Shraeder seemed oblivious: He apologized for being late – which he wasn't – and explained that he'd been in the middle of debugging a patch. He then embarked on the details, speaking as if the cop had a degree in computer science, and Pulaski had to steer him back on track.

His fingers twitching, as if he were typing on an imaginary keyboard, Shraeder listened in surprise – or feigned surprise – when Pulaski told him about the murders. He expressed sympathy and then, in answer to the young officer's questions, said he was in the pens frequently and *could* download dossiers, though he never did. He too expressed confidence that nobody could get access to his passcodes.

As for Sunday he had an alibi – he'd come into the office around 1 P.M. to follow up after a big problem on Friday, which he again tried to explain to Pulaski before the cop cut him off. The young man walked to the computer in the corner of the conference room, typed and then swiveled the screen for Pulaski to see. It was his time sheets. Pulaski looked over the entries for Sunday. He had indeed clocked in at 12:58 P.M. and didn't leave until after five.

Since Shraeder had been here at the time Myra was killed Pulaski didn't bother to ask about the other crimes. 'I think that'll be all. Thanks.' The man left and Pulaski sat back, staring out a narrow window. His palms were sweating, his stomach in a knot. He pulled his cell phone off its holster. Jeremy, the sullen assistant, was right. No damn reception.

'Hi, there.'

Pulaski jumped. Gasping, he looked up to see Mark Whitcomb in the doorway, several yellow pads under his arm and two cups of coffee in his hands. He lifted an eyebrow. Beside him was a slightly older man, with prematurely salt-and-pepper hair. Pulaski figured this had to be an SSD employee – since he was in the uniform of white dress shirt and dark suit.

What was this about? He struggled to put a casual smile on his face and nodded them in.

'Ron, wanted you to meet my boss, Sam Brockton.'

They shook hands. Brockton looked Pulaski over carefully and said, with a wry smile, 'So you were the one who had the maids checking up on me down at the Watergate hotel in D.C.?'

'Afraid so.'

'At least I'm off the hook as a suspect,' Brockton said. 'If there's anything we can do in the Compliance Department, let Mark know. He's brought me up to speed on your case.'

'Appreciate that.'

'Good luck.' Brockton left Whitcomb, who offered Pulaski a coffee.

'For me? Thanks.'

'How's it going?' Whitcomb asked.

'It's going.'

The SSD executive laughed and dusted a flop of blond hair off his forehead. 'You folks're as evasive as we are.'

'I guess we are. But I can say everybody's been cooperative.'

'Good. You finished?'

'Just waiting for something from Mr Sterling.'

He poured sugar into the coffee. He overstirred nervously, then stopped himself.

Whitcomb lifted his cup to Pulaski's as if toasting. He looked out at the clear day, the sky blue, the city rich green and brown. 'Never liked these small windows. Middle of New York and no views.'

'I was wondering. Why is that?'

'Andrew's worried about security. People taking pictures from outside.'

'Really?'

'It's not entirely paranoid,' Whitcomb said. 'Lot of money involved in data mining. Huge.'

'I suppose.' Pulaski wondered what kind of secrets somebody could see through a window from four or five blocks away, the closest office building this high.

'You live in the city?' he asked Pulaski.

'Yep. We're in Queens.'

'I'm out on the Island now but I grew up in Astoria. Off Ditmars Boulevard. Near the train station.'

'Hey, I'm three blocks from there.'

'Really? You go to St. Tim's?'

'St. Agnes. I've been to Tim's a few times but Jenny didn't like the sermons. They guilt you too much there.'

Whitcomb laughed. 'Father Albright.'

'Ooooo, yeah, he's the one.'

'My brother – he's a cop in Philly – he decided that all you had to do if you wanted a murderer to confess is to put him in a room with Father Albright. Five minutes and he'll confess to anything.'

'Your brother's a cop?' Pulaski asked, laughing.

'Narcotics task force.'

'Detective?'

'Yeah.'

Pulaski said, 'My brother's in Patrol, Sixth Precinct, down in the Village.'

'That's too funny. Both our brothers . . . So you went in together?'

'Yeah, we've kind of done everything together. We're twins.'

'Interesting. My brother's three years older. He's a lot bigger than I am. I might be able to pass the physical but I wouldn't want to have to tackle a mugger.'

'We don't do much tackling. It's mostly reasoning with the bad guys. Probably what you do in the Compliance Department.'

Whitcomb laughed. 'Yeah, pretty much.'

'I guess that—'

'Hey, look who it is! Sergeant Friday.'

Pulaski's gut thudded as he looked up to see slick, handsome Sean Cassel and his sidekick, the too-hip technical director, Wayne Gillespie, who joined the act by saying, 'Back to get more facts, ma'am? Just the facts.' He gave a salute.

Since he'd been talking to Whitcomb about church, the moment took Pulaski right back to the Catholic high school where he and his brother had been continually at war with the boys from Forest Hills. Richer, better clothes, smarter. And fast with the cruel snipes. ('Hey, it's the mutant brothers!') A nightmare. Pulaski sometimes wondered if he'd gone into police work simply for the respect a uniform and gun would bring him.

Whitcomb's lips tightened.

'Hey, Mark,' Gillespie said.

'How's it going, Sergeant?' Cassel asked the officer.

Pulaski had been glared at on the street, been sworn at, dodged spit and bricks, and sometimes hadn't dodged so well. None of those incidents had upset him as much as the sly words slung around like this. Smiling and playful. But playful the way a shark teases its meal before he devours it. Pulaski had looked up 'Sergeant Friday' on Google on his BlackBerry and learned this was a character from an old TV show called *Dragnet*. Even though Friday was the hero, he was considered a 'square,' which apparently meant a straight arrow, somebody extremely uncool.

Pulaski's ears had burned as he read the information on the tiny screen, realizing only then that Cassel had been insulting him.

'Here you go.' Cassel handed Pulaski a CD in a jewel box. 'Hope it helps, Sarge.'

'What's this?'

'The list of clients who've downloaded information about your victims. You wanted it, remember?'

'Oh. I was expecting Mr Sterling.'

'Well, Andrew's a busy man. He asked me to deliver it.'

'Well, thanks.'

Gillespie said, 'You've got your work cut out for you. Over three hundred clients in the area. And none of them got less than two hundred mailing lists.'

'That's what I was telling you,' Cassel said. 'You're gonna be burning the midnight oil. So do we get junior G-man badges?'

Sergeant Friday was often mocked by the people he interviewed . . .

Pulaski was grinning, though he didn't want to.

'Come on, guys.'

'Chill, Whitcomb,' Cassel said. 'We're joking around. Jesus. Don't be so uptight.'

'What're you doing down here, Mark?' Gillespie asked. 'Shouldn't you be looking for more laws we're breaking?'

Whitcomb rolled his eyes and gave a sour grin, though Pulaski saw he too was embarrassed – and hurt.

The officer said, 'You mind if I look it over here? In case I have some questions?'

'You go right ahead.' Cassel walked him to the computer in the corner and logged on. He put the CD in the tray, loaded it and stepped back, as Pulaski sat. The message on the screen asked what he wanted to do. Flustered, he found himself with a number of choices; he didn't recognize any of them.

Cassel stood over his shoulder. 'Aren't you going to open it?'

'Sure. Just wondering what program's best?'

'You don't have many options,' Cassel said, laughing, as if this were obvious. 'Excel.'

'X-L?' Pulaski asked. He knew his ears were red. Hated it. Just hated it.

'The spreadsheet,' Whitcomb offered helpfully, though to Pulaski that was no help whatsoever.

'You don't know Excel?' Gillespie leaned forward and typed so fast his fingers were a blur.

The program loaded and a grid popped up, containing names, addresses, dates and times.

'You've read spreadsheets before, right?'

'Sure.'

'But not Excel?' Gillespie's eyebrows were lifted in surprise.

'No. Some others.' Pulaski hated himself for playing right into their hands. Just shut up and get to work.

'Some others? Really?' Cassel asked. 'Interesting.'

'It's all yours, Sergeant Friday. Good luck.'

'Oh, that's E-X-C-E-L,' Gillespie spelled. 'Well, you can see it on the screen. You might want to check it out. It's easy to learn. I mean, a high school kid could do it.'

'I'll look into that.'

The two men left the room.

Whitcomb said, 'Like I said earlier – nobody around here likes them very much. But the company couldn't function without them. They're geniuses.'

'Which I'm sure they'll let you know.'

'You've got that right. Okay, I'll let you get to work. You all right here?'

'I'll figure things out.'

Whitcomb said, 'If you get back here to the snake pit, come by and say hi.'

'Will do.'

'Or let's meet in Astoria. Get some coffee. You like Greek food?'

'Love it.'

Pulaski flashed on an enjoyable time out. After his head injury the officer had let some friendships slide, uncertain if people would enjoy his company. He'd like hanging out with another guy, a beer, maybe catching an action flick, most of which Jenny didn't care for.

Well, he'd think about it later – after the investigation was over, of course.

When Whitcomb was gone, Pulaski looked around. No one was nearby. Still, he recalled Mameda glancing up uneasily behind and above Pulaski's shoulder. He thought of the special he and Jenny had recently seen about a Las Vegas casino – the 'eyes in the sky' security cameras everywhere. He recalled too the security guard up the hall and the reporter whose life had been ruined because he'd spied on SSD.

Well, Ron Pulaski sure hoped there was no surveillance here. Because his mission today entailed something much more than just collecting the CD and interviewing suspects; Lincoln Rhyme had sent him here to break into what was probably the most secure computer facility in New York City.

Chapter
TWENTY-SIX

Sipping strong, sweet coffee in the café across the street from the Gray Rock, thirty-nine-year-old Miguel Abrera was flipping through a brochure he'd received in the mail recently. It was yet another in a recent series of unusual occurrences in his life. Most were merely odd or irritating; this one was troubling.

He looked through it yet again. Then closed it and sat back, glancing at his watch. He still had ten minutes before he had to return to the job.

Miguel was a maintenance specialist, as SSD called it, but he told everybody he was a janitor. Whatever the title, the tasks he performed were a janitor's tasks. He did a good job and he liked the work. Why should he be ashamed of what he was called?

He could have taken his break in the building but the free coffee that SSD provided was lousy and they didn't even give you real milk or cream. Besides, he wasn't one for chitchat and preferred enjoying a newspaper and coffee in solitude. (He missed smoking, though. He'd bargained away cigarettes in the emergency room and even though God hadn't kept his side of the deal, Miguel had given up the habit anyway.)

He glanced up to see a fellow employee enter the café,

Tony Petron, a senior janitor who worked executive row. The men exchanged nods and Miguel was worried that the man would join him. But Petron went to sit in the corner by himself to read e-mail or messages on his cell phone and once again Miguel looked over the flyer, which was addressed to him personally. Then, as he sipped the sweet coffee, he considered the other unusual things that had happened recently.

Like his time sheets. At SSD you simply walked through the turnstile and your ID card told the computer when you entered and when you left. But a couple of times in the past few months his sheets had been off. He always worked a forty-hour week and was always paid for forty hours. But occasionally he'd happened to look at his records and saw that they were wrong. They said he came in earlier than he had, then left earlier. Or he missed a weekday and worked a Saturday. But he never had. He'd talked to his supervisor about it. The man had shrugged. 'Software bug maybe. As long as they don't short you, no problemo.'

And then there was the issue of his checking-account statement. A month ago, he'd found to his shock that his balance was ten thousand dollars higher than it should be. By the time he'd gone to the branch to have them correct it, though, the balance was accurate. And that had happened three times now. One of the mistaken deposits was for $70,000.

And that wasn't all. Recently he'd had a call from a company about his mortgage application. Only he hadn't applied for a mortgage. He rented his house. He and his wife had *hoped* to buy something but after she and their young son died in the auto accident he hadn't had the heart to consider a house.

Concerned, he checked his credit report. But no mortgage application was listed. Nothing out of the ordinary, though he noted that his credit rating had been raised – significantly. That too was odd. Though, of course, he didn't complain about this particular fluke.

But none of those things troubled him as much as this flyer.

Dear Mr Abrera:

As you are quite aware, at various times in our lives we go through traumatic experiences and suffer difficult losses. It's understandable that at moments like this, people have trouble moving on in life. Sometimes they even have thoughts that the burden is too great and they consider taking impulsive and unfortunate measures.

We, at Survivor Counseling Services, recognize the difficult challenges facing persons like you, who've suffered a serious loss. Our trained staff can help you get through the difficult times with a combination of medical intervention and one-on-one and group counseling to bring you contentment and remind you that life is indeed worth living.

Now, Miguel Abrera had never considered suicide, even at his worst, just after the accident eighteen months ago; taking his own life was inconceivable.

That he received the flyer in the first place was worrying. But two aspects of the situation really unnerved him. The first was that the brochure had been sent to him directly – not forwarded – at his new address. No one involved in his counseling or at the hospital where his wife and child died knew that he'd moved a month ago.

The second was the final paragraph:

Now that you've taken that vital first step of reaching out to us, Miguel, we'd like to set up a no-cost evaluation session at your convenience. Don't delay. We can help!

He had never taken *any* steps to contact the service.

How had they gotten his name?

Well, it was probably just an odd set of coincidences. He'd have to worry about it later. Time to get back to SSD. Andrew Sterling was the kindest and most considerate boss anybody could ask for. But Miguel had no doubt that the rumors were true: He reviewed every employee's time sheets personally.

Alone in the conference room at SSD, Ron Pulaski looked at the cell phone window, as he wandered frantically – walking in a grid pattern, he realized, not unlike searching a crime scene. But he had no reception, just like Jeremy had said. He'd have to use the landline. Was it monitored?

Suddenly he realized that although he'd agreed to help Lincoln Rhyme do this, he was at serious risk of losing the most important thing in his life after his family: his job as an NYPD cop. He was thinking now how powerful Andrew Sterling was. If he'd managed to ruin the life of a reporter with a major newspaper a young cop wouldn't stand a chance against the CEO. If they caught him he'd be arrested. His career would be over. What would he tell his brother, what would he tell his parents?

He was furious with Lincoln Rhyme. Why the hell hadn't he protested the plan to steal the data? He didn't *have* to do this. *Oh, sure, Detective . . . anything you say.*

It was totally crazy.

But then he pictured the body of Myra Weinburg, eyes gazing upward, hair teasing her forehead, looking like Jenny. And he found himself leaning forward, crooking the phone under his chin and hitting 9 for the outside line.

'Rhyme here.'

'Detective. It's me.'

'Pulaski,' Rhyme barked, 'where the hell have you been? And where are you calling from? It's a blocked number.'

'First time I've been alone,' he snapped. 'And my cell doesn't work here.'

'Well, let's get moving.'

'I'm on a computer.'

'Okay, I'll patch in Rodney Szarnek.'

The object of the theft was what Lincoln Rhyme had heard their computer guru comment on: the empty space on a computer hard drive. Sterling had claimed the computers didn't keep track of employees' downloading dossiers. But when Szarnek had explained about information floating around in the ether of SSD's computer, Rhyme had asked if that might include information about who had downloaded files.

Szarnek thought it was a real possibility. He said that getting into innerCircle would be impossible – he'd tried that – but there would be a much smaller server that handled administrative operations, like time sheets and downloads. If Pulaski could get into the system, Szarnek might be able to have him extract data from the empty space. The techie could then reassemble it and see if any employees had downloaded the dossiers of the victims and the fall guys.

'Okay,' Szarnek now said, coming on the phone. 'You're in the system?'

'I'm reading a CD they gave me.'

'Heh. That means they've only given you passive access. We'll have to do better.' The tech gave him some commands to type, incomprehensible.

'It's telling me I don't have permission to do this.'

'I'll try to get you root.' Szarnek gave the young cop a series of even more confusing commands. Pulaski flubbed them several times and his face grew hot. He was furious with himself for transposing letters or typing a backward slash instead of a forward.

Head injury . . .

'Can't I just use the mouse, look for what I'm supposed to find?'

Szarnek explained that the operating system was Unix, not the friendlier ones made by Windows or Apple. It required lengthy typed commands, which had to be keyboarded exactly.

'Oh.'

But finally the machine responded by giving him access. Pulaski felt a huge burst of pride.

'Plug the drive in now,' Szarnek said.

From his pocket the young officer took a portable 80-giga-byte hard drive and slipped the plug into the USB port on the computer. Following Szarnek's instructions, he loaded a program that would turn the empty space on the server into separate files, compress them and store them on the portable drive.

Depending on the size of the unused space, this could take minutes or hours.

A small window popped up and the program told Pulaski only that it was 'working.'

Pulaski sat back, scrolling through the customer information from the CD, which was still on the screen. In fact, the information on customers was mostly gibberish to him. The name of the SSD client was obvious, along with the address and phone number and names of those authorized to access the system, but much of the information was in .rar or .zip files, apparently compressed mailing lists. He scrolled to the end – page 1,120.

Brother . . . it would take a long, long time to pick through them and find if any customers had compiled information on the victims and—

Pulaski's thoughts were interrupted by voices in the hall, coming closer to the conference room.

Oh, no, not now. He carefully picked up the small, humming hard drive and slipped it into his slacks pocket.

It gave a clicking sound. Faint, but Pulaski was sure it could be heard across the room. The USB cable was clearly visible.

The voices were closer now.

One was Sean Cassel's.

Closer yet . . . Please. Go away!

On the screen in a small square window: *Working* . . .

Hell, Pulaski thought to himself and scooted the chair forward. The plug and the window would be clearly visible to anybody who stepped only a few feet into the room.

Suddenly a head appeared in the doorway. 'Hey, Sergeant Friday,' Cassel said. 'How's it going?'

The officer cringed. The man would see the drive. He had to. 'Good, thanks.' He moved his leg in front of the USB port to obscure the wire and plug. The gesture felt way obvious.

'How d'you like that Excel?'

'Good. I like it a lot.'

'Excellento. It's the best. And you can export the files. You do much PowerPoint?'

'Not too much of that, no.'

'Well, you might some day, Sarge – when you're police chief. And Excel is great for your home finances. Keep on top of all those investments of yours. Oh, and it comes with some games. You'd like 'em.'

Pulaski smiled, while his heart pounded as loudly as the hard drive whirred.

With a wink, Cassel disappeared.

If Excel comes with games, I'll eat the disk, you arrogant son of a bitch.

Pulaski wiped his palms on his dress slacks, which Jenny had ironed that morning, as she did every morning or the night before if he had an early tour or a predawn assignment.

Please, Lord, don't let me lose my job, he prayed. He thought back to the day when he and his twin brother had taken the police officer exam.

And the day they'd graduated. The swearing-in ceremony too, his mother crying, the look he and his father shared. Those were among the best moments of his life.

Would all that be wasted? Goddamnit. Okay, Rhyme's brilliant and no one cared more about collaring perps than he did. But breaking the law like this? Hell, he was home sitting in that chair of his, being waited on. Nothing would happen to him.

Why should Pulaski be the sacrificial lamb?

Nonetheless he concentrated on his furtive task. Come on, come on, he urged the collection program. But it continued to churn away slowly, assuring him only that it was on the job. No bar easing to the right, no countdown, like in the movies.

Working . . .

'What was that, Pulaski?' Rhyme asked.

'Some employees. They're gone.'

'How's it going?'

'Okay, I think.'

'You think?'

'It—' A new message popped up: *Completed. Do you want to write to a file?*

'Okay, it's finished. It wants me to write to a file.'

Szarnek came on the line. 'This is critical. Do exactly what I tell you.' He gave instructions on how to create the files, compress them and move them to the hard drive. Hands shaking, Pulaski did as instructed. He was covered in sweat. In a few minutes the job was done.

'Now you're going to have to erase your tracks, put everything back the way it was. To make sure nobody does what you just did and finds you.' Szarnek sent the officer into the log files and had him type more commands. Finally he got these taken care of.

'That's it.'

'Okay, get out of there, rookie,' Rhyme urged.

Pulaski hung up, unplugged the hard drive and slipped it back into his pocket, then logged off. He rose and walked outside, blinking in surprise to see that the security guard had moved closer. Pulaski realized he was the same one who'd escorted Amelia through the data pens, walking just behind her – as if he were taking a shoplifter to a store manager's office to await the police.

Had the man seen anything?

'Officer Pulaski. I'll take you back to Andrew's office.' His face was unsmiling and his eyes didn't reveal a thing. He led the officer up the hall. With every step the hard drive chafed against his leg and felt as if it were red hot. More glances at the ceiling. It was acoustic tile; he couldn't see any damn cameras.

Paranoia filled the halls, brighter than the stark white lighting.

When they arrived Sterling waved him into the office, turning over several sheets of paper he was working on. 'Officer, you got what you needed?'

'I did, yes.' Pulaski held up the client list CD like a kid at show-and-tell in school.

'Ah, good.' The CEO's bright green eyes looked him over. 'And how's the investigation going?'

'It's going okay.' These were the first words that came to Pulaski's mind. He felt like an idiot. What would Amelia Sachs have said? He had no clue.

'Is it now? Anything helpful in the client list?'

'I just looked through it to make sure we could read it okay. We'll go over it back at the lab.'

'The lab. In Queens? Is that where you're based?'

'We do work there, a few other places too.'

Sterling gave no response to Pulaski's evasion, just smiled pleasantly. The CEO was about four or five inches shorter but the young officer felt *he* was the one looking up. Sterling walked with him into the outer office. 'Well, if there's anything else, just let us know. We're one hundred percent behind you.'

'Thanks.'

'Martin, make those arrangements we talked about earlier. Then take Officer Pulaski downstairs.'

'Oh, I can find my way.'

'He'll show you out. You have a good night.' Sterling returned to his office. The door closed.

'I'll just be a few minutes,' Martin said to the policeman and picked up the phone and turned slightly, out of earshot.

Pulaski strolled to the door and looked up and down the hall. A figure emerged from an office. He was speaking in hushed tones on his mobile. Apparently in this part of the building cell phones worked fine. He squinted at Pulaski, said a brief farewell and flipped the phone shut.

'Excuse me, Officer Pulaski?'

He nodded.

'I'm Andy Sterling.'

Sure, Mr Sterling's son.

The young man's dark eyes confidently looked right into Pulaski's, though his handshake seemed tentative. 'I think you called me. And my father left a message that I was supposed to talk to you.'

'Yeah, that's right. You have a minute?'

'What do you need to know?'

'We're checking into certain people's whereabouts on Sunday afternoon.'

'I went hiking up in Westchester. I drove up there about noon and got back—'

'Oh, no, it's not you we're interested in. I'm just checking where your father was. He said he called you at around two from Long Island.'

'Well, yes, he did. I didn't take the call, though. I didn't want to stop on my hike.' He lowered his voice. 'Andrew has trouble separating business from pleasure and I thought he might want me to come into the office and I didn't want to screw up my day off. I called him back later, about three-thirty.'

'Do you mind if I take a look at your phone?'

'No, not at all.' He opened the phone and displayed the incoming-call list. He'd received and made several calls on Sunday morning but in the afternoon only one call was on the screen: from the number Sachs had given him – Sterling's Long Island house. 'Okay. That'll do it. Appreciate it.'

The young man's face was troubled. 'It's terrible, from what I've heard. Someone was raped and murdered?'

'That's right.'

'Are you close to catching him?'

'We have a number of leads.'

'Well, good. People like that should be lined up and shot.'

'Thanks for your time.'

As the young man walked off, Martin appeared and glanced at Andy's receding back. 'If you'd follow me, Officer Pulaski.' With a smile that might as well have been a frown, he walked toward the elevator.

Pulaski was being eaten alive by nervous energy, the disk drive filling his thoughts. He was sure everybody could see it outlined in his pocket. He began rambling. 'So, Martin . . . you been with the company long?'

'Yes.'

'You a computer person too?'

A different smile, which meant nothing more than the other one. 'Not really.'

Walking down the hallway, black and white, sterile. Pulaski hated it here. He felt strangled, claustrophobic. He wanted the streets, he wanted Queens, the South Bronx. Even the danger didn't matter. He wanted to leave, just put his head down and run.

A tickle of panic.

The reporter not only lost his job but was prosecuted under criminal trespass statutes. He served six months in state prison.

Pulaski was also disoriented. This was a different route from the one he'd taken to get to Sterling's office. Now Martin turned a corner and pushed through a thick door.

The patrolman hesitated when he saw what was ahead: a station manned by three unsmiling security guards, along with a metal detector and an X-ray unit. These weren't the data pens, so there was no data-erasing system, as in the other part of the building, but he couldn't smuggle out the portable hard drive without being detected. When he'd been here earlier with Amelia Sachs they hadn't passed through any security stations like these. He hadn't even seen any.

'Don't think we went through one of these last time,' he said to the assistant, trying to sound casual.

'Depends on whether people've been unattended for any period of time,' Martin explained. 'A computer makes the assessment and lets us know.' He smiled. 'Don't take it personally.'

'Ha. Not at all.'

His heart pounded, his palms were damp. No, no! He *couldn't* lose his job. He just couldn't. It was so important to him.

What the hell had he done, agreeing to do this? He told himself he was stopping the man who'd killed a woman who looked a lot like Jenny. A terrible man who had no problem with killing anyone if it suited his purpose.

Still, he reflected, this isn't right.

What would his parents say when he confessed to them that he was being arrested for stealing data? His brother?

'You have any data on you, sir?'

Pulaski showed him the CD. The man examined the case. He called a number, using speed dial. He stiffened slightly and then spoke quietly. He loaded the disk into a computer at his station and looked over the screen. The CD apparently was on a list of approved items; but still the guard ran it through the X-ray unit, studying the image of the jewel box and the disk inside carefully. It rolled on the conveyor to the other side of the metal detector.

Pulaski started forward but a third guard stopped him. 'Sorry, sir, please empty your pockets and put everything metal on there.'

'I'm a police officer,' he said, trying to sound amused.

The guard replied, 'Your department has agreed to abide by our security guidelines, since we're government contractors. The rules apply to everybody. You can call your supervisor to check, if you'd like.'

Pulaski was trapped.

Martin continued to watch him closely.

'Everything on the belt, please.'

Think, come on, Pulaski raged to himself. Figure something out.

Think!

Bluff your way through this.

I can't. I'm not smart enough.

Yes, you are. What would Amelia Sachs do? Lincoln Rhyme?

He turned away, knelt down and spent several moments carefully unlacing his shoes, slowly pulling them off. Standing, he placed the polished shoes on the belt and added his weapons, ammo, cuffs, radio, coins, phone and pens to a plastic tray.

Pulaski started through the metal detector and it went off with a squeal as the unit sensed the hard drive.

'You have anything else on you?'

Swallowing, shaking his head, he patted his pockets. 'Nope.'

'We'll have to wand you.'

Pulaski stepped out. The second guard passed the wand over his body and stopped at the officer's chest. The device gave a huge squeal.

The patrolman laughed. 'Oh, sorry.' He undid a button on his shirt and displayed the bulletproof vest. 'Metal heart plate. Forgot about it. Stops everything but a full-metal-jacket rifle slug.'

'Probably not a Desert Eagle,' the guard said.

'Now here's my opinion: A fifty-caliber handgun is just not natural,' Pulaski joked, finally drawing smiles from the guards. He started to remove the shirt.

'That's all right. I don't think we need to make you strip, Officer.'

With shaking hands Pulaski buttoned his shirt, right over the spot where the drive rested – between his undershirt and the vest; he'd stuffed it there when he'd bent down to unlace his shoes.

He gathered up his gear.

Martin, who'd bypassed the metal detector, guided him through another door. They were in the main lobby, a large, stark area in gray marble, etched with a huge version of the watchtower and window logo.

'Have a good day, Officer Pulaski,' Martin said, turning back.

Pulaski continued to the massive glass doors, trying to control the shaking of his hands. He was noticing for the first time the bank of TV cameras monitoring the lobby. His impression was of vultures, sitting serenely on the wall, waiting for wounded prey to gasp and fall.

Chapter
TWENTY-SEVEN

Even hearing Judy's voice, taking tearful comfort in its familiarity, Arthur Rhyme couldn't stop thinking about the tattooed white guy, the sizzling meth freak, Mick.

The guy kept talking to himself, he slipped his hands inside his pants every five minutes or so, and he seemed to turn his eyes to Arthur almost as frequently.

'Honey? Are you there?'

'Sorry.'

'I have to tell you something,' Judy said.

About the lawyer, about the money, about the children. Whatever it was, it would be too much for him. Arthur Rhyme was close to exploding.

'Go ahead,' he whispered, resigned.

'I went to see Lincoln.'

'You what?'

'I had to . . . You don't seem to believe the lawyer, Art. This isn't going to just fix itself.'

'But . . . I told you not to call him.'

'Well, there's a family involved here, Art. It's not just what *you* want. There's me and the children. We should've done it before.'

'I don't want him involved. No, call him back and tell him thanks but it's fine.'

'Fine?' Judy Rhyme blurted. 'Are you crazy?'

He sometimes believed she was stronger than he was – probably smarter too. She'd been furious when he'd stormed out of Princeton after being passed over for the professorship. She'd said he was behaving like a child having a tantrum. He wished he'd listened to her.

Judy blurted, 'You've got this idea that John Grisham is going to show up in court at the last minute and save you. But that's not going to happen. Jesus, Art, you ought to be grateful I'm doing *something*.'

'I am,' he said quickly, his words darting out like squirrels. 'It's just—'

'Just what? This is a man who nearly died, was paralyzed over his whole body and now lives in a wheelchair. And he's stopped everything to prove you're innocent. What the hell are you thinking of? You want your children to grow up with a father in prison for murder?'

'Of course not.' He wondered again if she really believed his denial that he hadn't known Alice Sanderson, the dead woman. She wouldn't think he'd killed her, of course; she'd wonder if they'd been lovers.

'I have faith in the system, Judy.' God, that sounded weak.

'Well, Lincoln *is* the system, Art. You should give him a call and thank him.'

Arthur hesitated, then asked, 'What does he say?'

'I just talked to him yesterday. He called to ask about your shoes – some of the evidence. But I haven't heard from him again.'

'Did you go see him? Or just call?'

'I went to his place. He lives on Central Park West. His town house is real nice.'

A dozen memories of his cousin came to mind, rapid-fire.

Arthur asked, 'How does he look?'

'Believe it or not, pretty much like when we saw him in Boston. Well, no, actually he looks in better shape now.'

'And he can't walk?'

'He can't move at all. Just his head and shoulders.'

'What about his ex? Do he and Blaine see each other?'

'No, he's seeing someone else. A policewoman. She's very pretty. Tall, redhead. I have to say, I was surprised. I shouldn't have been, I guess. But I was.'

A tall redhead? Arthur thought immediately of Adrianna. And tried to put that memory aside. It refused to leave.

Tell me why, Arthur. Tell me why you did it.

A snarl from Mick. His hand was back in his pants. His eyes flickered hatefully toward Arthur.

'I'm sorry, honey. Thanks for calling him. Lincoln.'

It was then that he felt hot breath on his neck. 'Yo, getoffadaphone.'

A Lat was standing behind him.

'Offadaphone.'

'Judy, I have to go. There's only one phone here. I've used up my time.'

'I love you, Art—'

'I—'

The Lat stepped forward and Arthur hung up, then slipped back to his bench in a corner of the detention area. He sat staring at the floor in front of him, the scuff in the shape of a kidney. Staring, staring.

But the distressed floor didn't hold his attention. He was thinking of the past. More memories joined those of Adrianna and his cousin Lincoln . . . Arthur's family's home on the North Shore. Lincoln's in the western suburbs. Arthur's stern king of a father, Henry. His brother, Robert. And shy, brilliant Marie.

Thinking too of Lincoln's father, Teddy. (There was an interesting story behind the nickname – his given name wasn't

Theodore; Arthur knew how it had come about but, curiously, he didn't think Lincoln did.) He'd always liked Uncle Teddy. A sweet guy, a little shy, a little quiet – but who wouldn't be in the shadow of an older brother like Henry Rhyme? Sometimes when Lincoln was out, Arthur would drive to Teddy and Anne's. In the small, paneled family room, uncle and nephew would watch an old movie or talk about American history.

The spot on the Tomb's floor now morphed into the shape of Ireland. It seemed to move as Arthur stared, eyes fixed on it, willing himself away from here, disappearing through a magic hole into the life Out There.

Arthur Rhyme felt complete despair now. And he understood how naive he'd been. There were no magical exit routes, and no practical ones either. He knew Lincoln was brilliant. He'd read all the articles in the popular press he could find. Even some of his scientific writing: 'The Biologic Effects of Certain Nanoparticulate Materials . . .'

But Arthur understood now that Lincoln could do nothing for him. The case was hopeless and he'd be in jail for the rest of his life.

No, Lincoln's role in this was perfectly fitting. His cousin – the relative he'd been closest to while growing up, his surrogate brother – ought to be present at Arthur's downfall.

A grim smile on his face, he looked up from the spot on the floor. And he realized that something had changed.

Weird. This wing of detention was now deserted.

Where had everybody gone?

Then approaching footsteps.

Alarmed, he glanced up and saw somebody moving toward him fast, feet scuffling. His friend, Antwon Johnson. Eyes cold.

Arthur understood. Somebody was attacking him from behind!

Mick, of course.

And Johnson was coming to save him.

Leaping to his feet, turning . . . So frightened he felt like crying. Looking for the tweaker, but—

No. No one was there.

Which is when he felt Antwon Johnson slip the garrote around his neck – homemade apparently, from a shirt torn into strips and twisted into a rope.

'No, wha—' Arthur was jerked to his feet. The huge man pulled him off the bench. And dragged him to the wall from which the nail protruded, the one he'd seen earlier, seven feet from the floor. Arthur moaned and thrashed.

'Shhhh.' Johnson looked around at the deserted alcove of the hall.

Arthur struggled but it was a struggle against a block of wood, against a bag of concrete. He slammed his fist point-lessly into the man's neck and shoulders, then felt himself lifted off the floor. The black man hefted him up and hooked the homemade hangman's noose to the nail. He let go and stood back, watching Arthur kick and jerk, trying to free himself.

Why, why, why? He was trying to ask this question but only wet sputtering came from his lips. Johnson stared at him in curiosity. No anger, no sadistic gleam. Just watching with mild interest.

And Arthur realized, as his body shivered and his vision went black, that this was all a setup – Johnson had saved him from the Lats for only one reason: He wanted Arthur for himself.

'Nnnnnn—'

Why?

The black man kept his hands at his sides and leaned close. He whispered, 'I'm doin' you a favor, man. Fuck, you'd do yourself in a month or two anyway. You ain't made for it here. Now jus' stop fightin' it. Go easier, you jus' give it up, you know what I'm sayin'?'

Pulaski returned from his mission at SSD and held up the sleek gray hard drive.

'Good job, rookie,' Rhyme said.

Sachs winked. 'Your first secret op assignment.'

He grimaced. 'It didn't feel much like an assignment. It felt more like a felony.'

'I'm sure we can find probable cause if we look hard enough,' Sellitto reassured him.

Rhyme said to Rodney Szarnek, 'Go ahead.'

The computer man plugged the hard drive into the USB port on his battered laptop and typed with firm, certain strikes on the keyboard, staring at the screen.

'Good, good . . .'

'You have a name?' Rhyme snapped. 'Somebody at SSD who downloaded the dossiers?'

'What?' Szarnek gave a laugh. 'It doesn't work that way. It'll take a while. I have to load it on the mainframe at Computer Crimes. And then—'

'How long a while?' Rhyme grumbled.

Szarnek once again blinked, as if seeing for the first time that the criminalist was disabled. 'Depends on the level of fragmentation, age of the files, allocation, partitioning, and then—'

'Fine, fine, fine. Just do the best you can.'

Sellitto asked, 'What else did you find?'

Pulaski explained about his interviews of the remaining technicians who had access to all of the data pens. He added that he'd talked to Andy Sterling, whose cell phone confirmed that his father had called from Long Island at the time of the killing. His alibi held up. Thom updated their suspect chart.

Andrew Sterling, President, Chief Executive Officer
    Alibi – on Long Island, verified. Confirmed by son
Sean Cassel, Director of Sales and Marketing
    No alibi
Wayne Gillespie, Director of Technical Operations
    No alibi
Samuel Brockton, Director, Compliance Department
    Alibi – hotel records confirm presence in Washington
Peter Arlonzo-Kemper, Director of Human Resources
    Alibi – with wife, verified by her (biased?)
Steven Shraeder, Technical Service and Support
    Manager, day shift
    Alibi – in office, according to time sheets
Faruk Mameda, Technical Service and Support
    Manager, night shift
    No alibi
Client of SSD (?)
    List provided by Sterling
UNSUB recruited by Andrew Sterling (?)

So now everyone at SSD who had access to innerCircle knew of the investigation . . . and still the bot guarding the NYPD 'Myra Weinburg Homicide' file had not reported a single attempted intrusion. Was 522 being cautious? Or did the concept of the trap miss the mark? Was the entire premise that the killer was connected to SSD completely wrong? It occurred to Rhyme that they'd been so awed by the power of Sterling and the company that they were neglecting other potential suspects.

Pulaski produced a CD. 'Here are the clients. I looked it over fast. There're about three hundred fifty of them.'

'Ouch.' Rhyme grimaced.

Szarnek loaded the disk and opened it up on a spreadsheet. Rhyme looked over the data on his flat-screen monitor – nearly a thousand pages of dense text.

'Noise,' Sachs said. She explained what Sterling had told her about data's being useless if it's corrupt, too sparse or too plentiful. The tech scrolled through the swamp of information – which clients had bought which lists of data-mined details . . . Too *much* information. But then Rhyme had a thought. 'Does it show the time and date of when the data was downloaded?'

Szarnek examined the screen. 'Yes, it does.'

'Let's find out who downloaded information just before the crimes.'

'Good, Linc,' Sellitto said. 'Five Twenty-Two'd want the most up-to-date data possible.'

Szarnek considered this. 'I think I can hack together a bot to handle it. Might take some time but, yeah, it's doable. Just let me know exactly when the crimes occurred.'

'We can get you those. Mel?'

'Sure.' The tech began to compile the details of the coin theft, the painting theft and two rapes.

'Hey, you're using that program Excel?' Pulaski asked Szarnek.

'That's right.'

'What is it, exactly?'

'Your basic spreadsheet. Mostly used for sales figures and financial statements. But now people use it for a lot of things.'

'Could I learn it?'

'Sure. You can take a course. Say, the New School or Learning Annex.'

'Should have boned up on it before now. I'll check them out, those schools.'

Rhyme believed he now understood Pulaski's reticence to go back to SSD. He said, 'Put that low on your list, rookie.'

'What's that, sir?'

'Remember, people hassle you in all sorts of different ways. Don't assume they're right and you're wrong just because they know something you don't. The question is: Do you *need* to know it to do a better job? Then learn it. If not, it's a distraction and to hell with it.'

The young officer laughed. 'Okay. Thanks.'

Rodney Szarnek took the CD and the portable hard drive and bundled up his computer to head down to the Computer Crimes Unit and its mainframe.

After he left, Rhyme glanced at Sachs, who was on the phone, tracking down information on the data scrounger killed in Colorado several years ago. He couldn't hear the words but she was clearly getting relevant information. Her head was forward, lips moist, and she tugged at a strand of hair. Her eyes were sleek and focused. The pose was extremely erotic.

Ridiculous, he thought. Concentrate on the goddamn case. He tried to push the sensation away.

He was only somewhat successful.

Sachs hung up the phone. 'Got something from the Colorado State Police. That data scrounger's name was P. J. Gordon. Peter James. Goes mountain biking one day and never comes home. They found his bike at the bottom of a cliff, battered up. It was beside a deep river. The body shows up twenty miles downstream a month or so later. Positive DNA match.'

'Investigation?'

'Not much of one. Kids're always killing themselves with bikes and skis and snowmobiles in that area. It was ruled accidental. But a few open questions remained. For one thing, it seemed that Gordon had tried to break into the SSD servers in California – not the database but the company's *own* files and some employees' personal ones. Nobody knows if he got inside or not. I tried to track down other people from the company, Rocky Mountain Data, to find out more. But nobody's around anymore. Looks like Sterling bought the company, took its database and let everybody go.'

'Anybody we can call about him?'

'No family that the state police could find.'

Rhyme was nodding slowly. 'Okay, this is an interesting premise, if I can use your flavor-of-the-week participle, Mel. This Gordon's doing his own data mining in SSD's files and finds something about Five Twenty-Two, who realizes he's in trouble, about to be found out. Then he kills Gordon and makes it look like an accident. Sachs, the police in Colorado have any case files?'

She sighed. 'Archived. They'll look for them.'

'Well, I want to find out who at SSD was with the company back then, when Gordon died.'

Pulaski called Mark Whitcomb at SSD. After a half hour he called back. A conversation with Human Resources revealed that dozens of employees were with the company at that time, including Sean Cassel, Wayne Gillespie, Mameda and Shraeder, as well as Martin, one of Sterling's personal assistants.

The large number meant that the Peter Gordon matter wasn't much of a lead. Rhyme hoped, though, that if they got the full Colorado State Police report, maybe he could find some evidence that pointed them toward one of the suspects.

He was staring at the list when Sellitto's phone rang. He took the call. The criminalist saw the detective stiffen. 'What?' he snapped, glancing at Rhyme. 'No shit. What's the story? . . . Call me as soon as you know.'

He hung up. His lips were pressed together and a frown crossed his face. 'Linc, I'm sorry. Your cousin. Somebody moved on him in detention. Tried to kill him.'

Sachs walked over to Rhyme, rested her hand on his shoulder. He could feel alarm in the gesture.

'How is he?'

'The director'll call me back, Linc. He's in the emergency clinic there. They don't know anything yet.'

Chapter
TWENTY-EIGHT

'Hey there.'

Pam Willoughby, ushered into the town house foyer by Thom, was smiling. The girl said hello to the crew there, who greeted her with smiles, despite the terrible news about Arthur Rhyme. Thom asked her how school had gone today.

'Great. Really good.' Then she lowered her voice and asked, 'Amelia, you have a minute?'

Sachs glanced at Rhyme, who nodded her toward the girl, meaning: There's nothing we can do about Art until we know more; go ahead.

She stepped into the hallway with the girl. Funny about young people, Sachs was thinking, you can read everything in their faces. The moods, at least, if not always the reasons behind them. When it came to Pam, Sachs sometimes wished she had more of Kathryn Dance's skill in reading how the girl felt and what she was thinking. This afternoon, though, she seemed transparently happy.

'I know you're busy,' Pam said.

'No problem.'

They walked into the parlor across the front foyer of the town house.

'So?' Sachs smiled conspiratorially.

'Okay. I did what you said, you know. I just asked Stuart about that other girl.'

'And?'

'It's just they *used* to go out – before I met him. He even told me about her a while ago. He ran into her on the street. They were just talking is all. She was kind of a clinger, you know. She was that way when they were going out and it's one of the reasons he didn't want to see her anymore. And she was holding on to him when Emily saw them – and he was trying to get away. That's all. Everything's, like, cool.'

'Hey, congrats. So the enemy is definitely out of the picture?'

'Oh, yeah. It has to be true – I mean, he *couldn't* date her, because he could lose his job—' Pam's voice came to an abrupt halt.

Sachs didn't need to be an interrogator to realize that the girl had stumbled. 'Lose his job? What job?'

'Well, you know.'

'Not exactly, Pam. Why would he lose his job?'

Blushing, she stared at the Oriental rug at their feet. 'Like, she's sort of in his class this year.'

'He's a *teacher*?'

'Kind of.'

'At your high school?'

'Not this year. He's at Jefferson. I had him last year. So it's okay if we—'

'Wait, Pam . . .' Sachs was thinking back. 'You told me he was in school.'

'I said I met him *at* school.'

'And Poetry Club?'

'Well—'

'He was the adviser,' Sachs said, grimacing. 'And he *coaches* soccer. He doesn't play it.'

'I didn't exactly lie.'

First, Sachs told herself, don't panic. That's not going to help anything. 'Well, Pam, this is . . .' And what the hell is it? She had so many questions. She asked the first one in her thoughts: 'How old is he?'

'I don't know. Not that old.' The girl looked up. Her eyes were hard. Sachs had seen her defiant and moody and determined. She'd never seen the girl this way – trapped and defensive, almost feral.

'Pam?'

'I guess, maybe, like forty-one or something.'

The no-panic rule was starting to crumble.

What the hell should she do? Yes, Amelia Sachs had always wanted children in her life – spurred by memories of the wonderful times she'd spent with her father – but she hadn't thought much about the tougher job of parenting.

'Be reasonable' was the guideline here, Sachs told herself. But it was about as effective as 'Don't panic' at the moment. 'Well, Pam—'

'I know what you're going to say. But it's not about *that*.'

Sachs wasn't so sure. Men and women together . . . To some extent it's always about *that*. But she couldn't consider the sexual aspect of the problem. It would only fuel the panic and destroy the reasonable.

'He's different. We have this connection . . . I mean, the guys in school, it's sports or video games. So boring.'

'Pam, there are plenty of boys who read poetry and go to plays. Weren't there any boys in Poetry Club?'

'It's not the same . . . I don't tell anybody what I went through, you know, with my mother and everything. But I told Stuart and he understood. He's had a tough time too. His father was killed when he was my age. He had to put himself through school, working two jobs or three.'

'It's just not a good idea, honey. There're problems you can't even imagine now.'

'He's nice to me. I love being with him. Isn't that the most important thing?'

'That's part of it but it's not everything.'

Pam's arms folded defiantly.

'And even if he's not your teacher now he could get into really bad trouble too.' Somehow, saying this made Sachs feel that she'd already lost the argument.

'He said I'm worth the risk.'

You didn't need to be Freud to figure it out: A girl whose father had been killed when she was young and whose mother and stepfather were domestic terrorists . . . she was primed to fall for an attentive, older man.

'Come on, Amelia, I'm not getting married. We're just dating.'

'Then why not take a break? A month. Go out with a couple other guys. See what happens.' Pathetic, Sachs told herself. Her arguments smacked of a losing rear-guard action.

An exaggerated frown. 'Like, why would I want to do that? I'm not out there trying to hook a boy, just to have somebody, like every other girl in my class.'

'Honey, I know you feel something for him. But just give it some time. I don't want you hurt. There are a lot of wonderful guys out there. They'll be better for you and you'll be happier in the long run.'

'I'm *not* breaking up with him. I love him. And he loves me.' She gathered up her books and said coolly, 'I better go. I have homework.' The girl started toward the door but then stopped and turned back. She whispered, 'When you started going out with Mr Rhyme, didn't somebody say it was a stupid idea? That you could find somebody who wasn't in a wheel-chair? That there were lots of "wonderful guys" out there? I bet they did.'

Pam held her eye briefly, then turned and left, closing the door behind her.

Sachs reflected that, yes, indeed, somebody had said just that to her, practically those very words.

And who else but Amelia Sachs's own mother?

Miguel Abrera 5465-9842-4591-0243, the 'maintenance specialist,' as the corporately correct say, left work at his usual time, around 5:00 P.M. He now gets out of the subway car near his home in Queens and I'm right behind him as he strolls home.

I'm trying to stay calm. But it's not easy.

They – the police – are close, close to *me*! Which has never happened before. In years and years of collecting, many dead sixteens, many ruined lives, many people in jail on my account, nobody has ever come close like this. Since I learned about the police suspicions, I've kept up a good facade, I'm sure. Still, I've been analyzing the situation frantically, picking through the data, looking for the lump of gold that tells me what They know and what They don't. How much at risk I really am. But I can't find the answer.

There's too much noise in the data!

Contamination . . .

I'm running through how I've behaved lately. I've been careful. Data certainly can work against you; they can pin you to the grid like a blue *Morpho menelaus* butterfly, smelling of cyanide's almond perfume, on a velvet board. But those of us in the know, we can use data for protection too. Data can be erased, can be massaged, can be skewed. We can add noise on purpose. We can place Data Set A right next to Data Set X to make A and X seem much more similar than they are. Or more different.

We can cheat in the simplest of ways. RFIDs, for instance. Slip a smart pass transponder into someone's suitcase and it will show your car's been in a dozen places over the weekend, while in fact it's actually been sitting in your garage the whole time. Or think about how easy it is to put your employee ID into an envelope and have it delivered to the office, where it sits for four hours until you ask somebody to collect the package and bring it to you in a restaurant downtown. Sorry, forgot to pick it up. Thanks. Lunch is on me. . . . And what do the data show? Why, that you were slaving away at work, while in reality you were wiping your razor clean as you stood over someone's cooling body during those hours in question. That nobody actually saw you at your desk is irrelevant. Here are my time sheets, Officer. . . . We trust data, we don't trust the human eye. There are a dozen more tricks I've perfected.

And now I have to rely on one of the more extreme measures.

Ahead of me now Miguel 5465 pauses and glances into a bar. I know for a fact that he drinks rarely and if he goes in for a *cerveza* it will throw off the timing a bit but that won't ruin my plans for this evening. He forgoes the drink, though, and continues along the street, head cocked to the side. I actually feel sorry that he didn't give in and indulge, considering he has less than an hour to live.

Chapter
TWENTY-NINE

Finally somebody from the detention center called Lon Sellitto.

He nodded as he listened. 'Thanks.' He disconnected. 'Arthur's going to be okay. He's hurt but not bad.'

'Thank God,' Sachs whispered.

'What happened?' Rhyme asked.

'Nobody can figure it out. The perp's Antwon Johnson, doing fed time for kidnapping and state lines. They moved him to the Tombs for trial on related state charges. He just kind of snapped, looks like, tried to make it look like Arthur hanged himself. Johnson denied it at first, then claimed Arthur wanted to die, asked him to help.'

'The guards found him in time?'

'No. Weird. Another prisoner went after Johnson. Mick Gallenta, two-timer in for meth and smack. He was half Johnson's size, took him on, knocked him out and got Arthur down from the wall. Nearly started a riot.'

The phone rang and Rhyme noticed a 201 area code.

Judy Rhyme.

He took the call.

'Did you hear, Lincoln?' Her voice was unsteady.

'I did. Yes.'

'Why would somebody do that? Why?'

'Jail's jail. It's a different world.'

'But it's just a holding cell, Lincoln. It's detention. I could understand if he were in prison with convicted murderers. But most of those people are awaiting trial, aren't they?'

'That's right.'

'Why would somebody risk his own case by trying to kill another prisoner there?'

'I don't know, Judy. It doesn't make sense. Have you talked to him?'

'They let him make a call. He can't speak very well. His throat was damaged. But it's not too bad. They're keeping him in for a day or two.'

'Good,' Rhyme said. 'Listen, Judy, I wanted more information before I called but . . . I'm pretty sure we'll be able to show that Arthur's innocent. It looks like there's someone else behind it. He killed another victim yesterday and I think we can tie him to the murder of the Sanderson woman.'

'No! Really? Who the hell is it, Lincoln?' No longer treading on ice, no longer carefully choosing words and worried about offending. Judy Rhyme had grown tough in the last twenty-four hours.

'That's what we're trying to find out now.' He glanced at Sachs then turned back to the speakerphone. 'And it doesn't look as if he had any connection with the victim. No connection at all.'

'You . . . ?' Her voice faded. 'Are you sure about that?'

Sachs identified herself and said, 'That's right, Judy.'

They could hear her inhaling. 'Should I call the lawyer?'

'There's nothing he can do. As things stand now, Arthur's still under arrest.'

'Can I call Art and tell him?'

Rhyme hesitated. 'Yes, sure.'

'He asked about you, Lincoln. In the clinic.'

'Did he?'

He sensed Amelia Sachs was looking at him.

'Yes. He said whatever came of it, thank you for helping.'

Everything would've been different . . .

'I should go, Judy. We have a lot to do. We'll let you know what we find.'

'Thank you, Lincoln. And everybody there. God bless you.'

A hesitation. 'Good-bye, Judy.'

Rhyme didn't bother with the voice command. He disconnected with his right index finger. He had better control with the ring finger of his left hand but the right moved fast as a snake.

Miguel 5465 is a survivor of tragedy and a dependable employee. He regularly visits his sister and her husband on Long Island. He wires Western Union money to his mother and sister in Mexico. He's a moral man. Once, a year after his wife and child died, he got a precious $400 out of an ATM machine in an area of Brooklyn known for its prostitutes. The janitor, though, balked. The money went back into his account the next day. Unfair he had to pay the $2.50 service charge at the ATM.

I know a lot more about Miguel 5465, more than most other sixteens in the database – because he's one of my escape hatches.

Which I desperately need now.

I've been grooming him as a surrogate for the past year. After he dies the diligent police will begin to put the pieces together. Why, we've found the killer/rapist/art-and-coin thief! He confessed in his suicide note – despondent and driven to murder by the death of his family. And in a box in his pocket, a fingernail from the victim Myra Weinburg.

And look at what else we have here: Sums of money passed through his account and vanished inexplicably. Miguel 5465 looked into getting a large mortgage to buy a house on Long Island, with a half million down, despite his salary of $46,000 a year. He went on art-dealer Web sites, inquiring about Prescott paintings. In the basement of his apartment building is a five-pack of Miller beer, Trojan condoms, Edge shave cream and a photo of Myra Weinburg's realm from OurWorld. Also hidden are books on hacking and thumb drives containing passcode-cracking programs. He's been depressed and even called a suicide counseling service just last week to ask for a brochure.

And then there are his time sheets, revealing that he was out of the office when the crimes occurred.

Slam dunk.

In my pocket is his suicide note, a reasonable facsimile of his handwriting, from the copies of his canceled checks and loan applications, conveniently scanned and obscenely available online. It's written on paper similar to what he bought a month ago at his neighborhood drugstore and the ink is from the same type of pen he owns a dozen of.

And since the last thing the police want is an extensive investigation into their prime data contractor, SSD, that will be the end of the matter. He'll die. Case closed. And I'll go back to my Closet, survey the mistakes I made and work on how to be more clever in the future.

But isn't that just a life lesson for us all?

As for the suicide itself, I looked at Google Earth and ran a basic prediction program, which suggested how he would get home from the subway station after leaving SSD. Miguel 5465 will most likely take a path through a small urban park here in Queens, right next to the expressway. The irritating rush of traffic and the gassy atmosphere from diesel exhaust mean the park is usually deserted. I'll come up fast behind him – don't want him to recognize me and grow cautious – and deliver a half dozen blows to the head with the BB-filled iron pipe. Then I'll slip the suicide note and box containing the fingernail into his pocket, drag him to the railing and over he goes onto the highway, fifty feet below.

Miguel 5465 is walking slowly, glancing into storefronts. And I'm thirty, forty feet behind, head down, inconspicuously lost in after-work music, like dozens of other commuters returning home, though my iPod is off (music is one thing I don't collect).

Now, the park is one block away. I—

But wait, something's wrong. He's not turning toward the park. He pauses at a Korean deli, buys some flowers and turns away from the commercial strip, heading toward a deserted neighborhood.

I'm processing this, running the behavior through my knowledge base. The prediction's not working.

A girlfriend? A relative?

How the hell can there be something about his life I don't know?

Noise in the data. I hate it!

No, no, this isn't good. Flowers for a girlfriend don't fit the profile of a suicidal killer.

Miguel 5465 continues down the sidewalk, the air fragrant with the spring smell of cut grass and lilac and dog urine.

Ah, got it now. I relax.

The janitor walks through the gate of a cemetery.

Of course, the dead wife and kid. We're doing fine. The prediction holds. We'll just have a brief delay. His path home will still take him through the park. This might be even better, a last visit to the wife. Forgive me for raping and murdering in your absence, dear.

I follow, keeping a safe distance, in my comfortable shoes, rubber-soled, making no sound whatsoever.

Miguel 5465 makes a direct line to a double grave. There he blesses himself, kneels in prayer. Then he leaves the flowers beside four other bouquets, in varying degrees of wilt. Why haven't the cemetery trips shown up on the grid?

Of course – he pays cash for the flowers.

He stands up and starts to walk away.

I begin to follow, breathing deeply.

When: 'Excuse me, sir.'

I freeze. Then turn slowly to the groundskeeper, who is talking to me. He's come up silently, treading over the carpet of short, dewy grass. And he looks from my face toward my right hand, which I slip into my pocket. He might or might not have seen the beige cloth glove I'm wearing.

'Hi,' I say.

'I saw you in the bushes there.'

How do I respond to that?

'The bushes?'

His eyes reveal to me that he's protective of his dead folks.

'Can I ask who you're visiting?'

His name is on the front of his overalls but I can't see it clearly. Stony? What kind of name is that? I'm riddled with anger. This is Their fault . . . Them, the people after me! They've made me careless. I'm addled by all the noise, all the contamination! I hate Them hate Them hate . . .

I manage a sympathetic smile. 'I'm a friend of Miguel's.'

'Ah. You knew Carmela and Juan?'

'Yes, that's right.'

Stony, or is it Stanley, is wondering why I'm still here since Miguel 5465 is gone. A shift in posture. Yes, it's Stony. . . . His hand moves closer to the walkie-talkie riding on his hip. I don't recall the names on the tombstones. I'm wondering if Miguel's wife was named Rosa and the boy Jose and I've just waltzed into a trap.

Other people's cleverness is so tedious.

Stony glances at his radio and when he looks up the knife is already halfway into his chest. One, two, three punches, careful around the bone – you can twist a finger if you're not careful, as I've learned the hard way. It's very painful.

The shocked groundskeeper is more resilient than I'd

expected, though. He lunges forward and grabs my collar with the hand not gripping the wound. We struggle, grappling and pushing and pulling, a macabre dance among the graves, until his hand falls away and he drops onto his back on the sidewalk, a snaky strip of asphalt that leads to the cemetery office. His hand finds the walkie-talkie at the same instant my blade finds his neck.

Zip, zip, two quiet slashes open the artery or vein or both and send a surprising torrent of blood into the sky.

I dodge it.

'No, no, why? *Why?*' He reaches for the wound, helpfully getting his hands out of the way and allowing me to do the same on the other side of his neck. Slash, slash, I can't stop myself. It's unnecessary but I'm mad, furious – at Them for throwing me off stride. They forced me to use Miguel 5465 as an escape. And now They've distracted me. I got careless.

More slashing . . . Then I stand back and in thirty seconds, after a few eerie kicks, the man is unconscious. In sixty, life becomes death.

I can only stand, numb from this nightmare, gasping from the effort. I'm hunched over and I feel like a miserable animal.

The police – They – will know I was the one, of course. The data are all there. The death happened at the gravesite of an SSD employee's family, and, after the wrestling match with the groundskeeper, I'm sure there's some evidence the clever police can trace to the other scenes. I don't have time to clean up.

They'll understand that I'd followed Miguel 5465 to fake his suicide and was interrupted by the groundskeeper.

Then a clatter from the walkie-talkie. Someone is asking for Stony. The voice isn't alarmed; it's a simple inquiry. But with no response they'll come looking for him soon.

I turn and leave quickly, as if I'm a mourner overcome with sorrow and bewildered by what the future holds.

But then, of course, that's exactly who I am.

Chapter
THIRTY

Another killing.

And there was no doubt that 522 had committed it.

Rhyme and Sellitto were on a hot list for immediate notification about any homicides in New York City. When the call arrived from the Detective Bureau, it took only a few questions to find out that the victim, a cemetery groundskeeper, had been murdered next to the grave of an SSD employee's wife and child, most likely by a man who'd followed the worker there.

Too much of a coincidence, of course.

The employee, a janitor, was not a suspect. He was talking to another visitor just outside the cemetery when they heard the groundskeeper's screams.

'Right.' Rhyme nodded. 'Okay, Pulaski?'

'Yes, sir.'

'Call somebody at SSD. See if you can find out where everybody on the suspect list was in the past two hours.'

'All right.' Another stoic smile. He sure didn't like the place.

'And, Sachs—'

'I'll run the scene at the cemetery.' She was already heading for the door.

After Sachs and Pulaski left, Rhyme called Rodney Szarnek at the NYPD Computer Crimes Unit. He explained about the recent killing and said, 'I'm guessing he's hungry for information about what we've learned. Have there been any hits on the trap?'

'Nothing outside the department. Just one search. Somebody from a Captain Malloy's office in the Big Building. Read through the files for twenty minutes then logged off.'

Malloy? Rhyme laughed to himself. Though Sellitto had been keeping the captain updated, as instructed, he apparently couldn't shake his nature as an investigator and was gathering as much information as he could – maybe intending to offer suggestions. Rhyme would have to call and tell him about the trap and that the bait files contained nothing helpful.

The tech said, 'I assumed it was okay for them to look it over, so I didn't call you.'

'It's fine.' Rhyme disconnected. He stared at the evidence boards for a long time. 'Lon, I've got an idea.'

'What?' Sellitto asked.

'Our boy's always one step ahead of us. We've been going about this like he's any other perp. But he's not.'

The man who knows everything . . .

'I want to try something a little different. I want some help.'

'From who?'

'Downtown.'

'Big area. Where exactly?'

'Malloy. And somebody at City Hall.'

'City Hall? The fuck for? Why do you think they'll even take your phone call?'

'Because they have to.'

'That's a reason?'

'You've gotta convince them, Lon. We need an edge on this guy. But you can do it.'

'Do what exactly?'

'I think we need an expert.'

'What kind?'

'Computer expert.'

'We've got Rodney.'

'He's not exactly what I have in mind.'

The man had been knifed to death.

Efficiently, yes, but also gratuitously, stabbed in the chest and then viciously slashed – in anger, Sachs assessed. This was another side to 522. She'd seen injuries like these at other scenes; the energetic and ill-aimed cuts suggested that the killer was losing control.

That was good for the investigators; emotional criminals are also careless criminals. They're more public and they leave more evidence than perps who exercise self-control. But, as Amelia Sachs had learned from her days on the street, the downside is that they're much more dangerous. People as crazed and dangerous as 522 drew no distinction among their intended victims, innocent bystanders and the police.

Any threat – any *inconvenience* – had to be dealt with instantly and fully. And to hell with logic.

In the harsh halogen lamps set up by the crime-scene team, bathing the graveyard in unreal light, Sachs looked over the victim, on his back, feet splayed where they'd danced outward in his death throes. A huge comma of blood leading away from the corpse stained the asphalt sidewalk in Forest Hills Memorial Gardens and a fringe of grass beyond.

None of the canvassers could find any witnesses, and Miguel Abrera, the SSD janitor, couldn't add anything. He was badly shaken both because he'd been a potential target of the killer and because his friend had died; he'd gotten to know the groundskeeper in his frequent visits to the graves of his wife and child. That night he'd had a vague feeling that someone had followed him from the subway and he'd even stopped and glanced into a bar window to look for reflections of a mugger tailing him. But the trick hadn't worked – he'd seen no one – and he'd continued on to the cemetery.

Now, in her white overalls, Sachs directed two crime-scene officers from the main CS operation in Queens to photograph and video everything. She processed the body and began to walk the grid. She was especially diligent. This was an important scene. The killing had happened fast and violently – the groundskeeper had obviously surprised 522 – and they had grappled, which meant more chances to find some evidence here that would lead to more information about the killer and his residence or place of work.

Sachs began on the grid – walking over the scene foot by foot in one direction and then turning perpendicular and searching the same area again.

Halfway through she stopped abruptly.

A noise.

She was sure it was the sound of metal against metal. A gun chambering a round? A knife opening?

She looked around quickly but saw only the dusk-blanketed cemetery. Amelia Sachs didn't believe in ghosts, and normally found resting grounds like this peaceful, even comforting. But now her teeth were clenched, her palms sweating in the latex gloves.

She'd just turned back to the body when she gasped, seeing a flash of light nearby.

Was it a streetlight through those bushes?

Or 522 moving closer, a knife in his hand?

Uncontrolled . . .

And she couldn't help but think he'd already tried once to kill her – the setup near DeLeon Williams's house with the federal agent – and failed. Maybe he was determined to finish what he'd started.

She returned to her task. But as she was nearly finished collecting evidence, she shivered. Movement again – this time on the far side of the lights, but still within the cemetery, which had been closed by patrol officers. She squinted through the glare. Had it been the breeze jostling a tree? An animal?

Her father, a lifer of a cop and a generous source of street wisdom, once told her, 'Forget the dead bodies, Amie, they're not going to hurt you. Worry about the ones who *made* 'em dead.'

Echoing Rhyme's admonition to 'search carefully, but watch your back.'

Amelia Sachs didn't believe in a sixth sense. Not in the way people think of the supernatural. To her, the whole natural world was so amazing and our senses and thought processes so complex and powerful that we didn't need superhuman skills to make the most perceptive of deductions.

She was sure somebody was there.

She stepped out of the crime-scene perimeter and strapped her Glock onto her hip. Tapped the grip a few times to orient her hand, in case she needed to draw fast. She went back to the grid, finished with the evidence and turned quickly in the direction where she'd seen the movement earlier.

The lights were blinding but she knew without doubt that a man was there, in the shadows of the building, studying her from the back of the crematorium. Maybe a worker but she wasn't taking any chances. Hand on her pistol, she strode forward twenty feet. Her white jumpsuit made a nice target in the failing light but she decided not to waste time stripping it off.

She drew her Glock and pushed fast through the bushes, starting a painful jog on arthritic legs toward the figure. But then Sachs stopped, grimacing, as she looked at the loading dock of the crematorium, where she'd seen the intruder. Her mouth tightened, angry at herself. The man, a silhouette against a streetlight outside the cemetery, was a cop; she could see the outline of the patrolman's hat and noted the slumped, bored posture of a man on guard duty. She called, 'Officer? You see anybody over there?'

'No, Detective Sachs,' he answered. 'Sure haven't.'

'Thanks.'

She finished with the evidence, then released the scene to the medical examiner tour doctor.

Returning to her car, she opened the trunk and began stripping off the white jumpsuit. She was chatting with the other officers from the CS main headquarters in Queens. They too had changed out of their own overalls. One frowned and was looking around for something he'd misplaced.

'Lose something?' she asked.

The man frowned. 'Yeah. It was right here. My hat.'

Sachs froze. 'What?'

'It's missing.'

Shit. She tossed the jumpsuit into the trunk and jogged fast to the sergeant from the local precinct, who was the immediate supervisor here. 'Did you have anybody secure the loading dock?' she asked breathlessly.

'Over there? Naw. I didn't bother. We had the whole area sealed and—'

Goddamnit.

Turning, she sprinted to the loading dock, her Glock in hand. She shouted to the officers nearby, 'He was here! By the crematorium. Move!'

Sachs paused at the old redbrick structure, noticing the open gate leading out to the street. A fast search of the grounds revealed no sign of 522. She continued on to the street and looked out fast, left and right. Traffic, curious onlookers – dozens of them – but the suspect was gone.

Sachs returned to the loading dock and wasn't surprised to find the police officer's hat lying nearby. It sat next to a sign, Leave Caskets Here. She collected the hat, slipped it into an evidence bag and returned to the other officers. Sachs and a local precinct sergeant sent officers around the neighborhood to see if anybody had spotted him. Then she returned to her car. Of course, he'd be far away by now but still she couldn't shake the raw uneasiness – which was due mostly to the fact that he hadn't tried to escape when he saw her walking toward the crematorium but casually stood his ground.

Though what chilled her the most was the memory of his casual voice – referring to her by name.

'Are they going to do it?' Rhyme snapped as Lon Sellitto walked through the door from his mission downtown with Captain Malloy and the deputy mayor, Ron Scott, about what Rhyme was calling the 'Expert Plan.'

'They're not happy. It's expensive and they—'

'Bull . . . shit. Get somebody on the phone.'

'Hold on, hold on. They'll do it. They're making the arrangements. I'm just saying they're grumbling about it.'

'You should have told me up front they agreed. I don't care how much they grumble.'

'Joe Malloy'll give me a call with the details.'

At around 9:30 P.M. the door opened and Amelia Sachs entered, carrying the evidence she'd collected at the groundskeeper's murder scene.

'He was there,' she said.

Rhyme didn't understand her.

'Five Twenty-Two. At the cemetery. He was watching us.'

'No shit,' Sellitto said.

'He was gone by the time I realized it.' She held up a patrolman's hat and explained that he'd been watching her in disguise.

'The fuck he'd do that for?'

'Information,' Rhyme said softly. 'The more he knows, the more powerful he is, the more vulnerable we become . . .'

'You canvass?' Sellitto asked.

'A team from the precinct did. Nobody saw anything.'

'He knows everything. We know zilch.'

She unpacked the crate as Rhyme's eyes took in each evidence-collection bag she lifted out. 'They struggled. Could be some good transfer trace.'

'Let's hope.'

'I talked to Abrera, the janitor. He said that for the past month, he's noticed some strange things. His time sheets were changed, there were deposits into his checking account he didn't make.'

Cooper suggested, 'Like Jorgensen – identity theft?'

'No, no,' Rhyme said. 'I'll bet Five Twenty-Two was grooming him to take the fall. Maybe a suicide. Plant a note on him . . . It was his wife and child's grave?'

'That's right.'

'Sure. He's despondent. Going to kill himself. Confesses to all the crimes in a suicide note. We close the case. But the groundskeeper interrupts him in the act. And now Five Twenty-Two's up a creek. He can't try this again; we'll be expecting a fake suicide now. He'll have to try something else. But what?'

Cooper had started going over the evidence. 'No hairs in the hat, no trace at all . . . But you know what I've got? A bit of adhesive. Generic though. Can't source it.'

'He removed the trace with tape or a roller before he left the hat,' Rhyme said, grimacing. Nothing 522 did would surprise him anymore.

Cooper then announced, 'From the other scene – by the grave – I've got a fiber. It's similar to the rope used in the earlier crime.'

'Good. What's in it?'

Cooper prepared the sample and tested it. A short time

later he announced, 'Okay, got two things. The most common is naphthalene in an inert crystal medium.'

'Mothballs,' Rhyme announced. The substance had figured in a poisoning case years ago. 'But they'd be old ones.' He explained that naphthalene had largely been abandoned in favor of safer materials. 'Or,' he added, 'from out of the country. Fewer safety codes on consumer products in a lot of places.'

'Then something else.' Cooper gestured at the computer screen. The substance it revealed was $Na(C_6H_{11}NHSO_2O)$. 'And it's bound with lecithin, carnauba wax, citrus acid.'

'What the hell's that?' Rhyme blurted.

Another database was consulted. 'Sodium cyclamate.'

'Oh, artificial sweetener, right?'

'That's it,' Cooper said, reading. 'Banned by the FDA thirty years ago. The ban's still under challenge but no products have been made with it since the seventies.'

Then Rhyme's mind made a few leaps, mimicking his eyes as they jumped from item to item on the evidence boards. 'Old cardboard. Mold. Desiccated tobacco. The doll's hair? Old soda? And boxes of mothballs? What the hell does it add up to? Does he live near an antiques store? Over one?'

They continued the analysis: minute traces of phosphorus sesquisulfide, the main ingredient in safety matches; more Trade Center dust; and leaves from a dieffenbachia, also called leopard lily. It was a common houseplant.

Other evidence included paper fibers from yellow legal pads, probably two different ones because of the color variations in the dyes. But they weren't distinctive enough to trace to a source. Also, more of the spicy substance that Rhyme had found in the knife used to murder the coin collector. This time they had enough to properly examine the grains and the color. 'It's cayenne pepper,' Cooper announced.

Sellitto mumbled, 'Used to be you could pin somebody to

a Latin neighborhood with that. Now, you can get salsa and hot sauce everywhere. Whole Foods to 7-Elevens.'

The only other clue was a shoeprint in the dirt of a recently dug grave near the site of the killing. Sachs deduced it was 522's because it appeared to have been left by someone running from that area toward the exit.

Comparing the electrostatic print with the database of shoe treadmarks revealed that 522's shoes were well-worn size-11 Skechers, a practical, though not particularly stylish, model often worn by workers and hikers.

While Sachs took a phone call, Rhyme told Thom to write the details on the chart as he dictated. Rhyme stared at the information – much more than when they'd started. Yet it was leading them nowhere.

UNSUB 522 PROFILE

- Male
- Possibly smokes or lives/works with someone who does, or near source of tobacco
- Has children or lives/works near them or near source of toys
- Interest in art, coins?
- Probably white or light-skinned ethnic
- Medium build
- Strong – able to strangle victims
- Access to voice-disguise equipment
- Possibly computer literate; knows OurWorld. Other social-networking sites?
- Takes trophies from victims. Sadist?
- Portion of residence/work-place dark and moist
- Lives in/near downtown Manhattan?
- Eats snack food/hot sauce
- Lives near antiques store?
- Wears size-11 Skechers work shoe

NONPLANTED EVIDENCE

- Old cardboard
- Hair from doll, BASF B35 nylon 6

- Tobacco from Tareyton cigarettes
- Old tobacco, not Tareyton, but brand unknown
- Evidence of Stachybotrys Chartarum mold
- Dust, from World Trade Center attack, possibly indicating residence/job downtown Manhattan
- Snack food/cayenne pepper
- Rope fiber containing:
- Cyclamate diet soda (old or foreign)
- Naphthalene mothballs (old or foreign)
- Leopard lily plant leaves (interior plant)
- Trace from two different legal pads, yellow colored
- Treadmark from size-11 Skechers work shoe

Chapter
THIRTY-ONE

'Appreciate you seeing me, Mark.'

Whitcomb, the Compliance Department assistant, smiled agreeably. Pulaski figured he must really love his job to be still working so late – just after nine-thirty. But then, the cop realized, he himself was still on the job.

'Another killing? And that same guy did it?'

'We're pretty sure.'

The young man frowned. 'I'm sorry. Jesus. When?'

'About three hours ago.'

They were in Whitcomb's office, which was a lot homier than Sterling's. And sloppier too, which made it more comfortable. He set aside the legal pad he was jotting on and gestured at a chair. Pulaski sat, noting pictures of family on his desk, some nice paintings on the walls, along with diplomas and some professional certificates. Pulaski had glanced up and down the quiet halls, extremely glad that Cassel and Gillespie, the school bullies, weren't here.

'Say, that your wife?'

'My sister.' Whitcomb gave a smile but Pulaski had seen that look before. It meant, this's a tough subject. Had the woman died?

No, it was the *other* answer.

'I'm divorced. Keep pretty busy here. Tough to have a family.' The young man waved his arm, indicating SSD, Pulaski supposed. 'But it's important work. Real important.'

'I'm sure it is.'

After trying to reach Andrew Sterling, Pulaski called Whitcomb, who had agreed to meet the cop and hand over the time sheets for that day – to see which of their suspects had been out of the office at the time the groundskeeper was killed.

'I've got some coffee.'

Pulaski noted that the man had a silver tray on his desk, with two china cups.

'I remembered how you liked it.'

'Thanks.'

The slim man poured.

Sipping the coffee. It was good. Pulaski was looking forward to the day when finances improved and he could afford a cappuccino maker. He loved his coffee. 'You work late every night?'

'Pretty often. Government regulations're tough in any industry but in the information business the problem is that nobody's quite sure what they want. For instance, states can make a lot of money selling driver's license information. Some places the citizens go ballistic and the practice's banned. But in other states it's perfectly okay.

'Some places, if your company gets hacked you have to notify the customers whose information gets stolen, whatever kind of data it is. In other states you only have to tell them if it's financial information. Some, you don't have to tell them anything. It's a mess. But we've got to stay on top of it.'

Thinking of security breaches, Pulaski was stabbed by guilt that he'd stolen the empty-space data from SSD. Whitcomb had been with him around the time he'd downloaded the files.

Would the Compliance officer get into trouble if Sterling found out about it?

'So here we go.' Whitcomb handed him about twenty pages of time sheets for that day.

Pulaski flipped through them, comparing the names with their suspects. First, he noted the time Miguel Abrera had left – a little after 5:00 P.M. Then Pulaski's heart jolted when he happened to glance down at the name Sterling. The man had left just seconds after Miguel, as if he were following the janitor . . . But then Pulaski realized that he'd made a mistake. It was *Andy* Sterling, the son, who'd left then. The CEO had left earlier – at about four – and had returned only about a half hour ago, presumably after business drinks and dinner.

Again, he was angry with himself that he hadn't read the sheet properly. And he'd nearly called Lincoln Rhyme when he'd seen the two departure times so close together. How embarrassing would *that* have been? Think better, he told himself angrily.

Of the other suspects, Faruk Mameda – the night-shift technician with the attitude – had been in SSD at the time of the killing. Technical Operations Director Wayne Gillespie's entries revealed that he'd left a half hour before Abrera but he'd returned to the office at six and stayed for several hours. Pulaski felt a petty disappointment that this seemed to take the bully off the list. All the others had left with enough time to follow Miguel to the cemetery or to precede him there and lie in wait. In fact, most employees were out of the office. Sean Cassel, he noticed, had been out for much of the afternoon but had returned – a half hour ago.

'Helpful?' Whitcomb asked.

'A little. You mind if I keep this?'

'No, go right ahead.'

'Thanks.' Pulaski folded the sheets and put them into his pocket.

'Oh, I talked to my brother. He's going to be in town next month. Don't know if you'd be interested but I was thinking you might like to meet him. Maybe you and your brother. You could swap cop stories.' Then Whitcomb smiled, embarrassed, as if that was the last thing police officers wanted to do. Which it wasn't, Pulaski could have told him; cops loved cop stories.

'If the case, you know, is solved by then. Or what do you say?'

'Closed.'

'Like that TV show. *The Closer,* sure . . . If it's closed. Probably can't have a beer with a suspect.'

'You're hardly a suspect, Mark,' Pulaski said, laughing himself. 'But, yeah, it's probably better to wait. I'll see if my brother can make it too.'

'Mark.' A soft voice spoke from behind them.

Pulaski turned to see Andrew Sterling, black slacks and a white shirt, sleeves rolled up. A pleasant smile. 'Officer Pulaski. You're here so often I should put you on payroll.'

A bashful grin.

'I called. The phone went to your voice mail.'

'Really?' The CEO frowned. Then the green eyes focused. 'That's right. Martin left early today. Anything we can help you with?'

Pulaski was about to mention the time sheets but Whitcomb jumped in fast. 'Ron was saying there's been another murder.'

'No, really? By the same person?'

Pulaski realized he'd made a mistake. Going around Andrew Sterling was stupid. It wasn't as if he thought Sterling was guilty or would try to hide anything; the cop just wanted the information quickly – and frankly, he also wanted to avoid running into Cassel or Gillespie, which might've happened if he'd gone to executive row for the time sheets.

But now he realized he'd gotten information about SSD

from a source that wasn't Andrew Sterling – a sin, if not an outright crime.

He wondered if the businessman could sense his discomfort. He said, 'We think so. Seems like the killer had originally targeted an SSD employee but ended up killing a bystander.'

'Which employee?'

'Miguel Abrera.'

Sterling immediately recognized the name. 'In maintenance, yes. Is he all right?'

'He's fine. A little shaken up. But okay.'

'Why was he targeted? Do you think he knows something?'

'I can't say,' Pulaski told him.

'When did this happen?'

'About six, six-thirty tonight.'

Sterling squinted faint wrinkles into the skin around his eyes. 'I've got a solution. What you should do is get your suspects' time sheets, Officer. That'd narrow down the ones with alibis.'

'I—'

'I'll take care of it, Andrew,' Whitcomb said quickly, sitting down at his computer. 'I'll get them from Human Resources.' To Pulaski he said, 'It shouldn't take long.'

'Good,' Sterling said. 'And let me know what you find.'

'Yes, Andrew.'

The CEO stepped closer, looking up into Pulaski's eyes. He shook his hand firmly. 'Good night, Officer.'

When he was gone, Pulaski said, 'Thanks. I should've asked him first.'

'Yeah, you should have. I assumed you did. The one thing that Andrew doesn't like is to be kept in the dark. If he has the information, even if it's bad news, he's happy. You've seen the reasonable side of Andrew Sterling. The unreasonable side doesn't *seem* much different. But it is, believe me.'

'You won't get in trouble, will you?'

A laugh. 'As long as he doesn't find out I got the time sheets an hour *before* he suggested it.'

As Pulaski walked toward the elevator with Whitcomb, he glanced back. There at the end of the corridor was Andrew Sterling, talking to Sean Cassel, their heads down. The sales director was nodding. Pulaski's heart bumped hard. Then Sterling strode off. Cassel turned and, polishing his glasses with the black cloth, looked directly at Pulaski. He smiled a greeting. His expression, the officer read, said the businessman wasn't the least surprised to see him there.

The elevator arrival bell dinged and Whitcomb gestured Pulaski inside.

The phone rang in Rhyme's lab. Ron Pulaski reported what he'd learned at SSD about the whereabouts of the suspects. Sachs transcribed the information on the suspects chart.

Only two were in the office at the time of the killing – Mameda and Gillespie.

'So it could be any one of the other half dozen,' Rhyme muttered.

'The place was virtually empty,' the young officer said. 'Not many people were in late.'

'They don't need to be,' Sachs pointed out. 'The computers do all the work.'

Rhyme told Pulaski to go on home to his family. He pressed back into his headrest and stared at the board.

Andrew Sterling, President, Chief Executive Officer
 Alibi – on Long Island, verified. Confirmed by son
Sean Cassel, Director of Sales and Marketing
 No alibi
Wayne Gillespie, Director of Technical Operations
 No alibi

Alibi for groundskeeper's killing (in office, according
    to time sheets)
Samuel Brockton, Director, Compliance Department
    Alibi – hotel records confirm presence in Washington
Peter Arlonzo-Kemper, Director of Human Resources
    Alibi – with wife, verified by her (biased?)
Steven Shraeder, Technical Service and Support
    Manager, day shift
    Alibi – in office, according to time sheets
Faruk Mameda, Technical Service and Support
    Manager, night shift
    No alibi
Alibi for groundskeeper's killing (in office, according to
    time sheets)
Client of SSD (?)
    Awaiting list from NYPD Computer Crimes Unit
UNSUB recruited by Andrew Sterling (?)

But was 522 one of them at all? Rhyme wondered once
again. He thought of what Sachs had told him about the
concept of 'noise' in data mining. Were these names just noise?
Distractions, keeping them from the truth?

Rhyme executed a smart turn on the TDX and again faced
the whiteboards. Something nagged. What was it?

'Lincoln—'

'Shh.'

Something he'd read, or heard about. No, a case – from
years ago. Hovering just out of memory. Frustrating. Like trying
to scratch an itch on his ear.

He was aware of Cooper looking at him. That irritated too.
He closed his eyes.

Almost . . .

Yes!

'What is it?'

Apparently he'd spoken out loud.

'I think I've got it. Thom, you follow popular culture, don't you?'

'What on earth does that mean?'

'You read magazines, newspapers. Look at ads. Are Tareyton cigarettes still made?'

'I don't smoke. I've *never* smoked.'

'I'd rather fight than switch,' Lon Sellitto announced.

'What?'

'That was the ad in the sixties. People with a black eye?'

'Don't recall it.'

'My dad used to smoke 'em.'

'Are they still made? That's what I'm asking.'

'I don't know. But you don't see 'em much.'

'Exactly. And the other tobacco we found was old too. So whether or not he smokes, it's a reasonable assumption he collects cigarettes.'

'Cigarettes. What kind of collector is that?'

'No, not just cigarettes. The old soda with the artificial sweetener. Maybe cans or bottles. And mothballs, matches, doll's hair. And the mold, the *Stachybotrys Chartarum*, the dust from the Trade Towers. I don't think it's that he's downtown. I think he just hasn't cleaned in years . . .' A grim laugh. 'And what other collection have we been dealing with lately? Data. Five Twenty-Two's obsessed with collecting . . . I think he's a hoarder.'

'A what?'

'He hoards things. He never throws anything away. That's why there's so much "old."'

'Yeah, I think I've heard of that,' Sellitto said. 'It's weird. Creepy.'

Rhyme had once searched a scene where a compulsive hoarder had died, crushed to death under a pile of books – well, he was immobilized and took two days to die of internal injuries. Rhyme described the cause of death as 'unpleasant.' He hadn't studied the condition much but he'd learned that New York had a task force to help hoarders get therapeutic assistance and protect them and their neighbors from their compulsive behavior.

'Let's give our resident shrink a call.'

'Terry Dobyns?'

'Maybe he knows somebody at the hoarding task force. Have him check. And get him over here in person.'

'At this hour?' Cooper asked. 'It's after ten.'

Rhyme didn't even bother to offer the punch line of the day: We're not sleeping; why should anyone else? A look conveyed the message just fine.

Chapter
THIRTY-TWO

Lincoln Rhyme had his second wind.

Thom had fixed food again and, although Rhyme generally took no particular pleasure in eating, he'd enjoyed the chicken club sandwiches with the aide's homemade bread. 'It's James Beard's recipe,' the aide announced, though the reference to the revered chef and cookbook author was utterly lost on Rhyme. Sellitto had wolfed down one sandwich and taken another with him when he left for home. ('Even better than the tuna,' he judged.) Mel Cooper asked for the bread recipe for Gretta.

Sachs was on the computer sending some e-mails. Rhyme was going to ask what she was doing when the doorbell rang.

A moment later Thom ushered into the lab Terry Dobyns, the NYPD behaviorist whom Rhyme had known for years. He was a little balder, a little thicker in the belly than when they'd first met – when Dobyns had sat with Rhyme for hours at a time, during that terrible time after the accident that left him paralyzed. The doctor still had the same kind, perceptive eyes that Rhyme recalled, and a calming, nonjudgmental smile. The criminalist was skeptical of psychological profiling, preferring forensics, but he had to admit that Dobyns had from time to time offered brilliant and helpful insights into the perps Rhyme pursued.

He now said hello to everyone, took coffee from Thom and declined food. He sat on a stool next to Rhyme's wheelchair.

'Good call, about the hoarding. I think you're right. And first, let me tell you that I checked with the task force and they looked into the known hoarders in the city. There aren't many and the odds are that it's none of them. I eliminated the women, since you told me about the rape. Of the men, most are elderly or nonfunctioning. The only two that fit the functioning profile are in Staten Island and the Bronx and they were accounted for by social workers or family members at the time of the killing on Sunday.'

Rhyme wasn't surprised – 522 was too smart not to cover his tracks. But he'd hoped for a small lead, at least, and scowled at the dead end.

Dobyns couldn't help but smile. This had been an issue they'd dealt with years ago. Rhyme had never been comfortable expressing personal anger and frustration. Professionally, though, he'd always been a master at it.

'But I can give you some insights that might be helpful. Now, let me tell you about hoarders. It's a form of obsessive-compulsive disorder. That occurs when a subject is faced with conflict or tensions they can't emotionally confront. Focusing on a behavior is much easier than looking at the underlying problem. Hand washing and counting are symptoms of OCD. So is hoarding.

'Now, it's rare for somebody who hoards to be dangerous per se. There are health risks – animal and insect infestation, mold and fire hazards – but essentially hoarders just want to be left alone. They'd live surrounded by their collection if they could and never go outside.

'But your fellow, well, he's a strange breed. A combination of narcissistic, antisocial personality and hoarding OCD. If he wants something – apparently collectible coins or paintings or sexual gratification – he *has* to have it. Absolutely has to. Killing is nothing to him if it helps him acquire what he wants and protect his collection. In fact, I'd go so far as to suggest that killing calms him down. Living humans give him stress. They would disappoint him, they'd abandon him. But inanimate objects – newspapers, cigar boxes, candy, even bodies – you can tuck away in your lair; they *never* betray you . . . I don't suppose you're interested in the childhood factors that may have made him that way?'

'Not really, Terry,' Sachs said. She was smiling at Rhyme, who was shaking his head.

'First, he's going to need space. A lot of it. And with the real estate prices here he's either very resourceful or very rich. Hoarders tend to live in big, older houses or town houses. They never rent. They can't stand the thought of a landlord with rights to come into their living area. And the windows will be painted black or taped over. He has to keep the outside world away.'

'How much space?' she asked.

'Rooms and rooms and rooms.'

'Some of the SSD employees would have plenty of money,' Rhyme speculated. 'The senior people.'

'Now, because your perp is so high functioning, he'll be leading two lives. We'll call them the "secret" life and the "façade." He needs to exist in the real world – to add to his collection and maintain it. And so he'll keep up appearances. He'll probably have a second house or a part of a single one that'll appear normal. Oh, he'd prefer to live in his secret place. But if he did, only there, people would start to take notice. So he'll also have a living space that seems like anybody in his socioeconomic situation would have. The residences might be connected or nearby. The ground floor could be normal, the upstairs where he keeps his collection. Or the basement.

'As for his personality, he'll play a role in his façade life that's almost the opposite of who he really is. Say the real Five Twenty-Two's personality is snide and petty. The public Five Twenty-Two will be measured, calm, mature, polite.'

'He could appear to be a businessman?'

'Oh, easily. And he'll play the part very, very well. Because he has to. It makes him angry, resentful. But he knows if he doesn't his trove could be endangered and that's simply not acceptable to him.'

Dobyns looked over the charts. He nodded. 'Now, I notice you're wondering about children? I really doubt he has any. He probably just collects toys. That again is something about his childhood. He'll be single too. It's rare to find a married hoarder. His obsession with collecting is too intense. He wouldn't want to share his time or space with another person – and frankly it's hard to find a partner who's so codependent she puts up with him.

'Okay, the tobacco and matches? He hoards cigarettes and matchbooks but I doubt very much he smokes. Most hoarders have huge stockpiles of papers and magazines, flammable objects. This perp isn't stupid. He'd never risk a fire because it could destroy his collection. Or at least expose him, when the fire department comes. And he probably has no particular interest in coins or art. He has an obsession with collecting for its own sake. *What* he collects is secondary.'

'So he probably doesn't live near an antiques store?'

Dobyns gave a laugh. 'That's exactly what his place'll *look* like. But, of course, without customers . . . Well, I can't think of much else. Except to tell you how dangerous he is. From what you've told me you've already stopped him several times. That makes him furious. He'll kill anybody who interferes with his trove, kill them without a second thought. I can't impress that on you enough.'

They thanked Dobyns. He wished them luck and the

psychologist left. Sachs updated the UNSUB list, based on what he'd told them.

UNSUB 522 PROFILE

- Male
- Probably nonsmoker
- Probably no wife/children
- Probably white or light-skinned ethnic
- Medium build
- Strong – able to strangle victims
- Access to voice-disguise equipment
- Possibly computer literate; knows OurWorld. Other social-networking sites?
- Takes trophies from victims. Sadist?
- Portion of residence/workplace dark and moist
- Eats snack food/hot sauce
- Wears size-11 Skechers work shoe
- Hoarder. Suffers from OCD
- Will have a 'secret' life and a 'façade' life
- Public personality will be opposite of his real self
- Residence: Won't rent, will have two separate living areas, one normal and one secret
- Windows will be covered or painted
- Will become violent when collecting or trove are threatened

'Helpful?' Cooper asked.

Rhyme could only shrug.

'What do you think, Sachs? Could it be anybody you talked to at SSD?'

She shrugged. 'I'd say Gillespie came the closest. He seemed just plain odd. But Cassel seemed the slickest – in terms of putting on a good façade. Arlonzo-Kemper's married, which takes him out of the running, according to Terry. I didn't see the technicians. Ron did.'

With an electronic trill, a caller ID box popped up on the screen. It was Lon Sellitto, back home but apparently still at work on the Expert Plan that Rhyme and the detective had put together earlier.

'Command, answer phone . . . Lon, how are we doing?'

'It's all set, Linc.'

'Where are we?'

'Watch the eleven o'clock news. You'll find out. I'm going to bed.'

Rhyme disconnected and turned on the TV in the corner of the lab.

Mel Cooper said good night. He was packing up his briefcase when his computer dinged. He looked over the screen. 'Amelia, you've got an e-mail here.'

She wandered over, sat down.

'Is it the Colorado State Police, about Gordon?' Rhyme asked.

Sachs said nothing but he noticed an eyebrow rise as she read through the lengthy document. Her finger disappeared into her long red hair, tied back in a ponytail, and worried her scalp.

'What?'

'I've got to go,' she said. She rose quickly.

'Sachs? What is it?'

'It's not about the case. Call me if you need me.'

And with that she was out the door, leaving behind a cloud of mystery as subtle as the aroma of the lavender soap she'd been favoring recently.

The 522 case was moving fast.

And yet cops always have to juggle other aspects of their lives.

Which was why she was now standing uneasily in front of a tidy detached house in Brooklyn, not far from her own home. The night was pleasant. A delicate breeze, fragrant with lilac and mulch, waltzed around her. It would be good to sit on the curb or a door stoop here and not do what she was about to.

What she *had* to do.

God, I hate this.

Pam Willoughby appeared in the doorway. She was wearing sweats and had her hair pulled back in a ponytail. She was talking to one of the other foster children, another teenager. Their faces had that conspiratorial yet innocent expression teenage girls wear like makeup. Two dogs played at their feet: Jackson, the tiny Havanese, and a much larger but equally exuberant Briard, Cosmic Cowboy, who lived with Pam's foster family.

The policewoman would meet the girl here occasionally, then they'd head off for a movie or Starbucks or ice cream. Pam's face usually brightened when she saw Sachs.

Not tonight.

Sachs got out of the car and leaned against the hot hood. Pam picked up Jackson and joined her as the other girl waved to Sachs and disappeared into the house with Cosmic Cowboy.

'Sorry to come by so late.'

'It's okay.' The girl was cautious.

'How's homework?'

'Homework's homework. Some's good, some sucks.'

True now, true in Sachs's day.

Sachs petted the dog, which Pam clutched possessively. She did this often with her things. The girl always refused offers to let someone else carry her book bag or groceries. Sachs guessed that so much had been taken away from her, she held tight to whatever she could.

'So. What's up?'

She could think of no way to ease gently into the subject. 'I talked to your friend.'

'Friend?' Pam asked.

'Stuart.'

'You *what*?' Light fragmented by leaves of a ginkgo tree fell on her troubled face.

'I had to.'

'No, you didn't.'

'Pam . . . I was worried about you. I had a friend in the department – somebody who does security checks – look him up.'

'No!'

'I wanted to see if there were any skeletons in his closet.'

'You didn't have any right to do that!'

'True. But I did anyway. And I just got an e-mail back.' Sachs felt her stomach muscles clench. Facing killers, driving 170 mph . . . those were nothing. She was shaken badly now.

'So is he a fucking murderer?' Pam snapped. 'A serial killer? A terrorist?'

Sachs hesitated. She wanted to touch the girl's arm. But didn't. 'No, honey. But . . . he's married.'

In the dappled light Sachs saw Pam blink.

'He's . . . married?'

'I'm sorry. His wife's a teacher too. A private school on Long Island. And he has two children.'

'No! You're wrong.' Sachs saw Pam's free hand was clenched so tightly the muscles had to be cramping. Anger filled her eyes, but there wasn't much surprise. Sachs wondered if Pam would be running through certain memories. Maybe Stuart had said he didn't have a home phone, only a mobile. Or maybe he'd asked her to use a particular e-mail account, not his general one.

And my house is such a mess. I'd be embarrassed for you to see it. I'm a teacher, you know. We're absentminded . . . I need to get a housekeeper . . .

Pam blurted, 'It's a mistake. You've got him mixed up with somebody else.'

'I went to see him just now. I asked him and he told me.'

'No, you didn't! You're making it up!' The girl's eyes flared and a cold smile crossed her face, cutting deep into Sachs's heart. 'You're doing just what my mother did! When she didn't want me to do something, she lied to me! Just like you're doing.'

'Pam, I'd never—'

'Everybody takes things away from me! You're not going to! I love him and he loves me, and you're not taking him away!' She wheeled and made for the house, the dog firmly under her arm.

'Pam!' Sachs's voice choked. 'No, honey . . .'

As the girl stepped inside she looked back once fast, hair swirling, posture stiff as iron, leaving Amelia Sachs grateful that the backlight prevented her from seeing Pam's face; she couldn't have stomached witnessing the hatred she knew was there.

The travesty at the cemetery still burns like fire.

Miguel 5465 should have died. Should be pinned to a velvet board for the police to examine. They'd say case closed and all would be well.

But he didn't. That butterfly got away. I can't try to fake a suicide again. They've learned something about me. They've collected some knowledge . . .

Hate Them hate Them hate Them hate Them . . .

I'm so close to taking my razor and storming out and . . .

Calm. Down. But it's becoming harder and harder to do that, as the years go by.

I've canceled certain transactions for this evening – I was going to celebrate the suicide – and now I head into my Closet. Being surrounded by my treasures helps. I wander through the fragrant rooms and hold several items close to me. Trophies from various transactions over the past year. Feeling the dried flesh and fingernails and hair against my cheek is such a comfort.

But I'm exhausted. I sit down in front of the Harvey Prescott painting, gaze up at it. The family looking back. As with most portraits their eyes follow you wherever you are.

Comforting. Eerie too.

Maybe one of the reasons I love his work so much is that these people were created fresh. They have no memories to plague them, to make them edgy, to keep them up all night and to drive them out into the streets, collecting treasures, and trophies.

Ah, memories:

June, five years old. Father sits me down, tucks his unlit cigarette away and explains to me I'm not theirs. 'We brought you into the family because we wanted you wanted you badly and we love you even if you aren't our natural son you understand don't you . . .' Not exactly, I don't. I stare at him blankly. Kleenex twisting in Mother's damp hands. She blurts that she loves me like a natural-born son. No, loves me more, though I don't understand why she would. It sounds like a lie.

Father leaves for his second job. Mother goes to take care of the other children, leaving me to consider this. My feeling is that something's been taken away from me. But I don't know what. I look out my window. It's beautiful here. Mountains and green and cool air. But I prefer my room and that's where I go.

August, seven years old. Father and Mother have been fighting. The oldest of us, Lydia, is crying. Don't leave don't leave don't leave . . . I myself plan for the worst, stocking up. Food and pennies – people never miss pennies. Nothing can stop me from collecting them, $134 worth of shiny or dull copper. Hide them in boxes in my closet . . .

November, seven years old. Father returns from where he's been for a month, 'scratching for the elusive dollar,' which he says a lot. (Lydia and I smile when he does.) He asks where the other children are. She tells him she couldn't handle all of them.

'Do the math. The fuck you thinking of? Get on the phone and call the city.'

'You weren't here,' she cries.

This mystifies Lydia and me but we know it's not good.

In my closet are $252 in pennies, thirty-three cans of tomatoes, eighteen of other vegetables, twelve of SpaghettiOs, which I don't even like but I have them. That's all that's important.

October, nine years old. More emergency foster placements. At the moment there are nine of us. We help, Lydia and me. She's fourteen and knows how to take care of the younger ones. Lydia asks Father to buy the girls dolls – because she never had one and it's important – and he said how can they make money from the city if they spend it on crap?

May, ten years old. I come back from school. It took all I could do to take some of the pennies and buy a doll for Lydia. I can't wait for her reaction. But then I see I made a mistake and left the closet door open. Father is inside, ripping open the boxes. The pennies are lying like dead soldiers on a battlefield. He fills his pockets and takes the boxes. 'You steal it you lose it.' I'm crying and telling him I found the pennies. 'Good,' Father says triumphantly. 'I found 'em too and that must mean they're mine . . . Right, young man? How can you argue with that? You can't. And, Jesus, almost five hundred bucks there.' And pulls the cigarette out from behind his ear.

Want to understand somebody taking your things away, your soldiers, your dolls, your pennies? Just close your mouth and pinch your nose. That's what's it like and you can't do it very long before something terrible happens.

October, eleven years old. Lydia's gone. No note. She doesn't take the doll. Fourteen-year-old Jason comes to live with us from Juvenile. He pushes into my room one night. He wants my bed (mine's dry and his isn't). I sleep in his wet one. Every night for a month. I complain to Father. He tells me to shut up. They need the money and they get a bonus for ED kids like Jason and

. . . He stops talking. Does he mean me too? I don't know what ED means. Not then.

January, twelve years old. Flashing red lights. Mother sobbing, the other foster children sobbing. The burn on Father's arm was painful but fortunately, the fireman says, the lighter fluid on the mattress didn't ignite fast. If it was gasoline he'd be dead. As they take Jason away, dark eyes under dark brows, he screams he didn't know how the lighter fluid and matches got into his book bag. He didn't do it, he didn't! And he didn't pin up those pictures of people burned alive in his classroom at school.

Father screams at mother, Look at what you did!

You wanted the bonus! she screams back.

The ED bonus.

Emotionally disturbed, I found out.

Memories, memories . . . Ah, some collections I would gladly give away, leave in a Dumpster if I could.

I smile up at my silent family, the Prescotts. Then I turn back to the problem at hand – Them.

I'm calmer now, the edginess dulled. And I'm confident that like my lying father, like panicked Jason Stringfellow led off by the police, like the sixteens screaming at the climax of a transaction, those pursuing me – They – will soon be dead and dust. And I'll be living out my days happily with my two-dimensional family and my treasures here in the Closet.

My soldiers, the data, are about to march into battle. I'm like Hitler in his Berlin bunker, ordering his Waffen-SS troops to meet the invaders. Data are invincible.

I see now that it's nearly 11:00 P.M. Time for the news. I need to see what They know about the death at the cemetery and what They don't. On goes the TV.

The station has 'gone live' to City Hall. Now the deputy mayor, Ron Scott, a distinguished-looking man, is explaining that the police have put together a task force to investigate a recent murder and rape, and a murder this evening in a Queens cemetery, which seems related to the earlier crime.

Scott introduces an NYPD inspector, Joseph Malloy, who 'will discuss the case more specifically.'

Though he doesn't, not really. He shows a composite of the perpetrator that resembles me only in the way it resembles about 200,000 other men in the city.

White or light-skinned? Oh, please.

He tells people to be cautious. 'We think the perpetrator has used techniques of identity theft to get close to his victims. Lower their defenses.'

Be wary, he goes on to say, of anyone you don't know but who has knowledge of your purchases, bank accounts, vacation plans, traffic violations. 'Even little things you wouldn't normally pay attention to.'

In fact, the city has just flown in an expert in information management and security from Carnegie Mellon University. Dr Carlton Soames will spend the next few days assisting the investigators and advising them on the issue of identity theft, which they believe is the best way to find the perpetrator.

Soames looks like a typical ruffled-haired small-town Midwest boy gone smart. An awkward grin. Suit a little off center, glasses a bit smudged, the asymmetrical glare tells me. And how much wear would that wedding ring show? Plenty, I'll bet. He looks like the sort who married early.

He doesn't say anything but gazes out like a nervous animal at the press and the camera. Captain Malloy continues, 'In an age when identity theft is increasing, and the consequences are increasingly grave—'

The pun, obviously unintentional, is unfortunate.

' – we take seriously our responsibility to protect the citizens of this city.'

The reporters jump into the fray, pelting the deputy mayor, captain and unsettled professor with questions a third-grader could have come up with. Malloy generally demurs. The word 'ongoing' is his shield.

Deputy Mayor Ron Scott reassures the public that the city is safe and everything is being done to protect them. The press conference ends abruptly.

We go back to the regular news, if you can call it that. Tainted veggies in Texas, a woman on a hood of a truck caught in a Missouri flood. The President has a cold.

I shut off the set and sit in my dim Closet, wondering how best to process this new transaction.

An idea occurs to me. It's so obvious, though, that I'm skeptical. But, surprise, it takes only three phone calls – to hotels close to One Police Plaza – to find the one where Dr Carlton Soames is registered.

IV

AMELIA 7303

TUESDAY, MAY 24

There was, of course, no way of knowing whether you were being watched at any given moment. How often, or on what system, the Thought Police plugged in on any individual wire was guesswork. It was even conceivable that they watched everybody all the time.

— GEORGE ORWELL, *1984*

Chapter
THIRTY-THREE

Amelia Sachs arrived early.

But Lincoln Rhyme had been awake earlier, unable to sleep soundly because of the plans unfolding presently, both here and in England. He'd had dreams about his cousin Arthur and his uncle Henry.

Sachs joined him in the exercise room, where Thom was getting Rhyme back into the TDX wheelchair after he'd done five miles on the Electrologic stationary bicycle, part of his regular exercise scheme to improve his condition and to keep his muscles toned for the day when they might once again begin to replace the mechanical systems that now ran his life. Sachs took over, while the aide went downstairs to fix breakfast. It was a hallmark of their relationship that Rhyme had long ago lost any qualms about her helping him with his morning routine, which many people would find unpleasant.

Sachs had spent the night at her place in Brooklyn, so now he updated her on the 522 situation. But she was distracted, he could see. When he asked why, she exhaled slowly and told him, 'It's Pam.' And she explained that Pam's boyfriend had turned out to be her former teacher. And a married one, at that.

'No . . .' Rhyme winced. 'I'm sorry. The poor kid.' His initial reaction was to threaten this Stuart into getting the hell out of the picture. 'You've got a shield, Sachs. Flash it. He'll head for the hills. Or I'll give him a call if you want.'

Sachs, however, didn't think that was the right way to handle the matter. 'I'm afraid if I'm too pushy or I report him, I'll lose her. If I don't do anything, she's in for a lot of grief. God, what if she wants to have his baby?' She dug a nail into her thumb. Stopped herself. 'It'd be different if I'd been her mother all along. I'd know how to handle it.'

'Would you?' Rhyme asked.

She considered this, then conceded with a smile, 'Okay, maybe not . . . This parent stuff. Kids ought to come with an owner's manual.'

In the bedroom, they had breakfast, which Sachs fed to Rhyme. Like the parlor and the lab downstairs, the bedroom was far homier than it had been when Sachs first saw it, years ago. Back then the place had been stark, the only decorations art posters, tacked up backward and used as impromptu white-boards for the first case they'd worked on together. Now those posters had been turned around and others added: of paintings that Rhyme enjoyed – impressionistic landscapes and moody urban scenes by artists like George Inness and Edward Hopper. Then she sat back, next to his wheelchair, and took his right hand, the one in which he'd recently regained some control and touch. He could feel her fingertips, though the sensation was odd, a step or two removed from the pressure he'd sense on his neck or face where the nerves worked normally. It was as if her hand were water trickling onto his skin. He willed his fingers to close on hers. And felt the pressure of her response. Silence. But he sensed, through her posture, that she wanted to talk about Pam, and he said nothing, waiting for her to continue. He watched the peregrine falcons on the ledge, aware, taut, the female larger. The pair were muscular bundles of readiness. Falcons hunt by day, and there were fledglings to feed.

'Rhyme?'

'What?' he asked.

'You still haven't called him, have you?'

'Who?'

'Your cousin.'

Ah, not Pam's situation. That she'd been thinking of Arthur Rhyme had never occurred to him. 'No. I haven't.'

'You know something else? I didn't even know you had a cousin.'

'Never mentioned him?'

'No. You talked about your uncle Henry and aunt Paula. But not Arthur. Why not?'

'We work too hard. No time for chitchat.' He smiled. She didn't.

Should he tell her? Rhyme debated. His first reaction was not to. Because the explanation reeked of self-pity. And that was poison to Lincoln Rhyme. Still, she deserved to know something. That's what happens in love. In the shaded portions where the two spheres of different lives meet, certain fundamentals – moods, loves, fears, angers – can't be hidden. That's the contract.

And so he told her now.

About Adrianna and Arthur, about the bitterly cold day of the science fair and the lies later, the embarrassing forensic examination of the Corvette and even the potential engagement present – a chunk of atomic-age concrete. Sachs nodded and Rhyme laughed to himself. Because he knew she'd be thinking: What was the big deal? A bit of teenage love, a little duplicity, a little heartbreak. Pretty small caliber in the arsenal of personal offenses. How did something so pedestrian ruin such a deep friendship?

You two were like brothers . . .

'But didn't Judy say you and Blaine used to visit them years later? That sounds like everything got patched up.'

'Oh, yep. We did. I mean, it was only a high school crush. Adrianna was pretty . . . a tall redhead, as a matter of fact.'

Sachs laughed.

'But hardly worth destroying a friendship over.'

'So there's more to the story, isn't there?'

Rhyme said nothing at first. Then: 'Not long before my accident, I went to Boston.' He sipped some coffee through a straw. 'I was speaking at an international conference on forensic science. I'd finished the presentation and was in the bar afterward. A woman came up to me. She was a retired professor from M.I.T. She'd been struck by my last name, and said that she'd had a student from the Midwest in her class years ago. His name was Arthur Rhyme. Was he any relation?

'My cousin, I told her. She went on to tell me what an interesting thing Arthur had done. He'd submitted a scientific paper with his application in lieu of an essay. It was brilliant, she said. Original, well researched, rigorous – oh, if you want to compliment scientists, Sachs, say that their research is "rigorous."' He fell silent briefly. 'Anyway, she encouraged him to flesh it out and publish it in a journal. But Arthur never pursued it. She hadn't stayed in touch with him and wondered if he'd done any research in the area since.

'I was curious. I asked her what the subject was. She actually remembered the title. "The Biologic Effects of Certain Nanoparticulate Materials" . . . Oh, and by the way, Sachs, I wrote it.'

'You?'

'It was a paper I'd written for a science fair project. Came in second in the state. It was some pretty original work, I will admit.'

'Arthur stole it?'

'Yep.' Even now, after all these years, the anger rippled within him. 'But it gets worse.'

'Go on.'

'After the conference I couldn't get what she'd told me out of my head. I contacted M.I.T.'s admissions. They kept all the applications on microfiche. They sent me a copy of mine. Something was wrong. My application was what I'd sent them, my signature. But everything sent by the *school,* from the counselor's office, had been altered. Art got a hold of my high school transcript and changed it. He gave me B's instead of the A's I really had. He'd forged new letters of recommendation, which were lukewarm. He made them sound like form letters. They were probably the ones *he*'d gotten from his teachers. My uncle Henry's recommendation wasn't included in my packet.'

'He took it out?'

'And he'd replaced my essay with some generic Why-I-want-to-go-to-M.I.T. crap. He even added some very choice typos.'

'Oh, I'm sorry.' She squeezed his hand harder. 'And Adrianna worked in the counselor's office, right? So she helped him.'

'No. I thought so at first but I tracked her down and called her.' He gave a cool laugh. 'We talked about life, our marriages, her kids, careers. Then the past. She always wondered why I'd cut things off the way I did. I said I thought she'd decided to go out with Arthur.'

That had surprised her and she'd explained that, no, she was only doing Art a favor – helping him with his college application. He'd come to her office a half dozen times simply to talk about schools, look at some samples of essays, letters of recommendation. He said his own college counselor was terrible and he was desperate to get into a good school. He asked her not to say anything to anyone, especially me; he was embarrassed that he needed the help, so they'd snuck off together a few times. She still felt guilty that Art had made her lie about it.

'And when she went to the bathroom or off to copy something he raided your file.'

'That's right.'

Why, Arthur never hurt a single soul in his life. He isn't capable of it . . .

Wrong, Judy.

'Are you absolutely sure?' Sachs asked.

'Yep. Because right after I hung up with her, I called Arthur.'

Rhyme could hear the conversation almost verbatim.

'Why, Arthur? Tell me why.' No greeting other than this.

A pause. Arthur's breathing.

And even though years had passed since the transgression his cousin knew immediately what he was referring to. No interest in how Rhyme had found out. No interest in denying or feigning ignorance or innocence.

His response: to go on the offensive. He'd blustered angrily, 'All right, you want to know the answer, Lincoln? I'll tell you. The prize at Christmas.'

Mystified, Rhyme had asked, 'The prize?'

'That my father gave you in the contest at the Christmas Eve party when we were seniors.'

'The concrete? From the Stagg Field stadium?' Rhyme had frowned in confusion. 'What do you mean?' There had to be more to it than winning a souvenir of significance to only a handful of people in the world.

'I deserved it!' His cousin had raged, acting as if he were the victim. 'Father named me after the man in charge of the atomic project. I knew he'd kept the memento. I knew he was going to give it to me when I graduated from high school or college. It was going to be my graduation present! I'd wanted it for years!'

Rhyme had been at a loss for words. There they were,

grown men, talking like children about a stolen comic book or piece of candy.

'He gave away the one thing that was important to me. And he gave it to *you*.' His voice was breaking. Was he crying?

'Arthur, I just answered some questions. It was a game.'

'A game? . . . What kind of fucking game was that? It was Christmas Eve! We should've been singing carols or watching *It's a Wonderful Life*. But, no, no, Father had to turn everything into a fucking classroom. It was embarrassing! It was boring. But nobody had the balls to say anything to the great professor.'

'Jesus, Art, it wasn't my fault! It was just a prize I won. I didn't steal anything from you.'

A cruel laugh. 'No? Well, Lincoln, it ever occur to you that maybe you did?'

'What?'

'Think about it! Maybe . . . my father.' He'd paused, breathing deeply.

'What the hell're you talking about?'

'You stole him! Did you ever wonder why I never tried out for varsity track? Because you had the lock on that! And academically? *You* were his other son, not me. You sat in on his classes at U of C. You helped him with his research.'

'This's crazy . . . He asked you to come to class too. I know he did.'

'Once was enough for me. He picked me apart until I wanted to cry.'

'He cross-examined *everybody*, Art. That's why he was so brilliant. He made you think, he pushed you until you got the right answer.'

'But some of us could *never* get the right answer. I was good. But I wasn't great. And the son of Henry Rhyme was supposed to be great. It didn't matter, though, because he had you. Robert went to Europe, Marie moved to California. And even then he didn't want me. He wanted you!'

The other son . . .

'I didn't ask for the role. I didn't sabotage you.'

'Didn't you? Ah, Mr Innocent. You didn't play the game? You just accidentally drove up to our house on weekends, even when I wasn't there? You didn't invite him to come to your track meets? Sure, you did. Answer me: Which of them would you really want for a father, mine or yours? Did your father ever fawn over you? Ever whistle for you from the stands? Give you that raised eyebrow of approval?'

'That's all bullshit,' Rhyme had snapped. 'You've got some issue with your father and what do you do? You sabotage *me*. I could've gotten into M.I.T. But you ruined that! And my whole life changed. If it weren't for you, everything would've been different.'

'Well, I can say the same about you, Lincoln. I can say the same . . .' A harsh laugh. 'Did you even try with *your* father? What do you think he felt, having a son like you, who was a hundred times smarter than he was? Going off all the time because he'd rather hang out with his uncle. Did you even give Teddy a chance?'

At that, Rhyme had slammed the phone into the cradle. It was the last time they talked. Several months later he was paralyzed at the crime scene.

Everything would've been different . . .

After he'd explained this to Sachs she said, 'That's why he never came to see you after you were hurt.'

He nodded. 'Back then, after the accident, all I could do was lie in bed and think that if Art hadn't changed the application I would have gotten into M.I.T. and maybe done graduate work at Boston University or joined the BPD or come to New York earlier or later. In any case I probably wouldn't've been at the subway crime scene and . . .' His voice dissolved to silence.

'The butterfly effect,' she said. 'A small thing in the past makes a big difference in the future.'

Rhyme nodded. And he knew that Sachs could take in this information with sympathy and understanding and make no judgments about the broader implications – which he would choose: walking and leading a normal life, or being a crip and perhaps a far better criminalist because of it . . . and, of course, being her partner.

This was the type of woman Amelia Sachs was.

He gave a faint smile. 'The funny thing is, Sachs . . .'

'There was something to what he said?'

'My own father never seemed to notice me at all. He certainly never challenged me the way my uncle did. I *did* feel like Uncle Henry's other son. And I liked it.' He'd come to realize that maybe, subconsciously, he *had* been pursuing boisterous, full-of-life Henry Rhyme. He was pelted with a dozen fast memories of the times he'd been embarrassed by his father's shyness.

'But it's no excuse for what he did,' she said.

'No, it's not.'

'Still,' she began.

'You're going to say that it happened a long time ago, let bygones be bygones, water over dams and under bridges?'

'Something like that,' she offered with a smile. 'Judy said he asked about you. He's reaching out. Forgive him.'

You two were like brothers . . .

Rhyme glanced over the still topography of his immobile body. Then back to Sachs. He said softly, 'I'm going to prove he's innocent. I'll get him out of jail. I'll give him his life back.'

'That's not the same, Rhyme.'

'Maybe not. But it's the best I can do.'

Sachs began to speak, perhaps to make her case again, but the subject of Arthur Rhyme and his betrayal vanished as the phone buzzed and on the computer screen came Lon Sellitto's number.

'Command, answer phone . . . Lon. Where are we?'

'Hey, Linc. Just wanted to let you know our computer expert's on his way.'

The guy was familiar, the doorman thought – the man who nodded pleasantly as he left the Water Street Hotel.

He nodded back.

The guy was on his cell phone and he paused near the door, as people eased around him. He was talking, the doorman deduced, to his wife. Then the tone changed. 'Patty, sweetheart . . .' A daughter. After a brief conversation about a soccer game he was back on with the wife, sounding more adult, but still adoring.

He fell into a certain category, the doorman knew. Been married fifteen years. Faithful, looked forward to getting home – with a bag of tacky, heartfelt presents. He wasn't like some guests: the businessman who'd arrive wearing his wedding ring and leave for dinner with finger naked. Or the tipsy businesswoman being escorted into the elevator by a hunky coworker (they *never* shed their rings; they didn't need to).

The things a doorman knows. I could write a book.

But the question nagged: Why was this guy so familiar?

And then he was saying to the wife, with a laugh, 'You saw me? It made the news there? Mom did too?'

Saw him. A TV celebrity?

Wait, wait. Almost there . . .

Ah, got it. Last night, watching the news on TV. Sure – this guy was a professor or doctor of some kind. Sloane . . . or Soames. A computer expert from some fancy school. The one that Ron Scott, the assistant mayor or whatever, was talking about. The prof was helping the police with that rape and murder on Sunday and some other crime.

Then the professor's face went still and he said, 'Sure, honey, don't worry. I'll be fine.' He disconnected and looked around.

'Hey, sir,' the doorman said. 'Saw you on TV.'

The professor smiled shyly. 'Did you?' He seemed embarrassed by the attention. 'Say, can you tell me how to get to One Police Plaza?'

'Right up there. About five blocks. By City Hall. You can't miss it.'

'Thanks.'

'Good luck.' The doorman was watching a limo approach, pleased that he'd had a brush with a semi-celebrity. Something to tell his own wife about.

Then he felt a thunk on his back, almost painful, as another man hurried out the door of the hotel and pushed past him. The guy didn't look back and said nothing by way of apology.

Prick, thought the doorman, watching the man, who was moving fast, head down, in the same direction as the professor. The doorman didn't say anything, though. However rude they were, you just put up with it. They could be guests or friends of guests or they could be guests next week. Or even executives from the home office, testing you.

Just put up and shut up. That was the rule.

The TV professor and the rude asshole faded from the doorman's thoughts as a limo stopped and he stepped forward to open the door. He got a nice view of soft cleavage as the guest climbed out; it was better than a tip, which he knew, absolutely knew, she wasn't going to give him anyway.

I could write a book.

Chapter
THIRTY-FOUR

Death is simple.

I've never understood why people complicate it. Movies, for instance. I'm not a fan of thrillers but I've seen my share. Sometimes I'll take a sixteen out on a date, to stave off boredom, to keep up appearances or because I'm going to kill her later, and we'll sit in a movie theater and it's easier than dinner; you don't have to talk so much. And I watch the film and think, What on earth is going on up there on the screen, setting up these contrived ways to kill?

Why use wires and electronics and elaborate weapons and plots when you can walk up to someone and beat them to death with a hammer in thirty seconds?

Simple. Efficient.

And make no mistake, the police are smart (and, how's this for irony, a lot of them have SSD and innerCircle helping them out). The more complicated the scheme, the more chance of leaving behind something they can use to track you down, the more chance for witnesses.

And my plans today for this sixteen I'm following through the streets of lower Manhattan are simplicity itself.

The failure at the cemetery yesterday is behind me now

and I'm exhilarated. I'm on a mission and, as part of it, I'll be adding to one of my collections.

As I follow my target I dodge sixteens right and left. Why, look at them all . . . My pulse is picking up. My head is throbbing at the thought that these sixteens are *themselves* collections – of their past. More information than we can comprehend. DNA is, after all, nothing more than a database of our bodies and genetic history, stretching back millennia. If you could plug that into hard drives, how much data could you extract? Makes innerCircle look like a Commodore 64.

Breathtaking . . .

But back to the task at hand. I maneuver around a young sixteen, smell her perfume, which she dabbed on this morning in her Staten Island or Brooklyn apartment in a sad attempt to exude competence and came off as cheaply seductive. I move closer to my target, feeling the comfort of the pistol against my skin. Knowledge may be one kind of power, but there are others that are nearly as effective.

'Hey, Professor, we've got some activity.'

'Uh-huh,' Roland Bell replied, his voice spilling from the speakers in the surveillance van, where sat Lon Sellitto, Ron Pulaski and several tactical officers.

Bell, an NYPD detective who worked with Rhyme and Sellitto occasionally, was on his way from the Water Street Hotel to One Police Plaza. He'd traded his typical jeans, work shirt and sports coat for a rumpled suit, since he was playing the role of the fictional professor Carlton Soames.

Or, as he'd put it in his North Carolina drawl, 'A stinkball on a hook and line.'

Bell now whispered into a lapel microphone as invisible as the tiny speaker in his ear, 'How close?'

'He's behind you about fifty feet.'

'Uhm.'

Bell was at the core of Lincoln Rhyme's Expert Plan, which was based on his increasing understanding of 522. 'He's not taking our computer trap but he's dying for information. I know it. We need a different sort of trap. Hold a press conference and lure him out into the open. Have them announce that we've hired an expert and get somebody undercover up onstage.'

'You're assuming he watches TV.'

'Oh, he'll be checking the media to see how we're handling the case, especially after the incident at the cemetery.'

Sellitto and Rhyme had contacted somebody not connected with the 522 case – Roland Bell was always game, if he wasn't on another assignment. Rhyme had then called a friend at Carnegie Mellon University, where he'd lectured several times. He told him about 522's crimes, and the authorities at the school, which was renowned for its work in high-technology security, agreed to help. Their webmaster added Carlton Soames, Ph.D., to the school's Web site.

Rodney Szarnek faked a résumé for Soames and sent it out to dozens of science Web sites, then cobbled together a credible site for Soames himself. Sellitto got a room for the professor at the Water Street Hotel, held the press conference and waited to see if 522 would take the bait in *this* trap.

Which apparently he had.

Bell had left the Water Street Hotel not long before and paused, carrying on a credible but fake phone call and standing in the open long enough to make sure he caught 522's attention. Surveillance showed that a man had quickly left the hotel just after Bell and was now following him.

'You recognize him from SSD? He one of the suspects on our list?' Sellitto asked Pulaski, sitting beside him, staring at the monitor. Four plainclothes officers were a block or so from Bell; two wore hidden video cameras.

On the crowded streets, though, it was hard to get a clear view of the killer's face. 'Could be one of the service techs. Or, weird, it almost looks like Andrew Sterling himself. Or, no, maybe it's that he kind of walks like him. I'm not sure. Sorry.'

Sweating heavily in the hot van, Sellitto wiped his face, then leaned forward and said into the mike, 'Okay, Professor, Five Twenty-Two's moving up. Maybe forty feet behind you. He's in a dark suit, dark tie. He's carrying a briefcase. His gait profile suggests that he's armed.' Most cops who've worked the street for a few years can recognize the difference in posture and walking patterns when a suspect is carrying a weapon.

'Gotcha,' commented the laconic officer, who carried two pistols himself and was ambidextrously talented with them.

'Man,' Sellitto muttered, 'I hope this works. Okay, Roland, go ahead with the right turn.'

'Uhm.'

Rhyme and Sellitto didn't believe that 522 would shoot the professor on the street. What would killing him accomplish? Rhyme speculated that the killer's intent was to abduct Soames, to learn what the police knew, then murder him later or perhaps threaten him and his family to have Soames sabotage the investigation. So the script called for Roland Bell to take a detour out of public view, where 522 would make his move and they'd nail him. Sellitto had found a construction site that would work well. It featured a long sidewalk, cordoned off to the public, that was a shortcut to One Police Plaza. Bell would ignore the *Closed* sign and head down the sidewalk, where he'd be lost to sight after thirty or forty feet. A team was hiding at the far end to move in when 522 approached.

The detective made the turn, stepping around the barrier tape and heading up the dusty sidewalk, while the rattle and slam of jackhammers and pile drivers filled the interior of the van from Bell's sensitive mike.

'We've got you on visual, Roland,' Sellitto said as one of the officers beside him hit a switch and another camera took up surveillance. 'You watching, Linc?'

'No, Lon, *Dancing with the Celebrities* is on. Jane Fonda and Mickey Rooney are up next.'

'It's *Dancing with the Stars,* Linc.'

Rhyme's voice clattered into the van. 'Is Five Twenty-Two going to make the turn? Or is he going to balk? . . . Come on, come on . . .'

Sellitto moved the mouse and double-clicked. Another image, on a split screen, popped up, from a Search and Surveillance team's video camera. It depicted a different angle: Bell's back moving down the sidewalk, away from the camera. The detective was glancing with curiosity at the construction site, as any normal passerby would. A moment later, 522 appeared behind him, keeping his distance, looking around too, though obviously with no interest in the workers; he was scanning for witnesses or the police.

Then he hesitated, looked around once more. And started to close the distance.

'Okay, everybody, heads up,' Sellitto called. 'He's moving up on you, Roland. We're going to lose you on visual in about five seconds so keep an eye out. You copy?'

'Yep,' said the easy-going officer. As if answering a bartender who'd asked if he wanted a glass with his bottle of Budweiser.

Chapter
THIRTY-FIVE

Roland Bell wasn't quite as calm as he sounded.

The widower father of two children, a nice house in the burbs and a sweetheart down in the Tarheel State he was getting pretty close to proposing to . . . All those domestic things tended to add up on the negative side when you were asked to be a sitting duck on an undercover set.

Still, Bell couldn't help but do his duty – particularly when it came to a perp like this 522, a rapist and killer, a species of criminal that Bell had a particular dislike for. And, truth be told, he didn't mind the rush from ops like this one.

'We all find our levels,' his daddy had often said, and once the boy realized that the man wasn't talking about misplaced tools he embraced that philosophy as a cornerstone of his life.

His jacket was unbuttoned and his hand poised to draw, aim and let fly with his favorite pistol, an example of Italy's finest firepower. He was glad Lon Sellitto had stopped his banter. He needed to hear this fellow's approach, and the *slam slam slam* of the pile driver was plenty loud. Still, concentrating hard, he heard a scrape of shoes on the sidewalk behind him.

Make it thirty feet.

Bell knew the takedown team was in front of him, though he couldn't see them, or they him, because of a sharp curve in the sidewalk. The plan was for them to take 522 as soon as the backdrop was safe and no bystanders were in danger. This portion of the sidewalk was still partly visible from a nearby street and the construction site and they'd been gambling that the killer wouldn't attack until Bell was closer to the tactical officers. But he seemed to be moving in more quickly than they'd planned on.

Bell hoped, though, that the man would hold off for a few minutes; a firefight here could endanger a number of passersby and construction workers.

But the logistics of the takedown vanished from his mind as he heard two things simultaneously: the sound of 522's footsteps breaking into a run toward him and, much more alarming, the cheerful Spanish chatter of two women, one pushing a baby carriage, as they emerged from the back of the building right next to Bell. The tac officers had sealed off the sidewalk but apparently nobody'd thought to notify the superintendents of the buildings whose rear doors faced it.

Bell glanced back and saw the women walk right in between him and 522, who was staring at the detective and running forward. In his hand was a gun.

'We've got trouble! Civvies between us. Suspect's armed! Repeat, he's got a weapon. Move in!'

Bell started for his Beretta but one of the women, seeing 522, screamed and jumped back, slamming into Bell, knocking him to his knees. His gun dropped to the sidewalk. The killer blinked in shock and froze, undoubtedly wondering why a college professor was armed, but he recovered fast and aimed at Bell, who was going for his second gun.

'No!' the killer shouted. 'Don't try it!'

The officer could do nothing but lift his hands. He heard Sellitto say, 'First team'll be there in thirty seconds, Roland.'

The killer said nothing, just snarled for the women to flee, which they did, and then he stepped forward, gun on Bell's chest.

Thirty seconds, the detective thought, breathing hard.

It might as well have been a lifetime.

Walking from the parking garage to One Police Plaza, Captain Joseph Malloy was irritated that he hadn't heard anything about the set involving Detective Roland Bell. He knew Sellitto and Rhyme were desperate to find this perp and he'd reluctantly agreed to the phony press conference but it really was over the line, and he wondered what the fallout would be if it didn't work.

Hell, there'd be fallout if it *did* work. One of the top rules in city government: Don't fuck with the press. Especially in New York.

He was just reaching into his pocket for his cell phone when he felt something touch his back. Insistent and purposeful. A pistol.

No, no . . .

His heart galloped.

Then came the voice, calm. 'Do not turn around, Captain. If you turn around, you'll see my face and that means you'll die. You understand?' He sounded educated, surprising Malloy for some reason.

'Wait.'

'Do you understand?'

'Yes. Don't—'

'At the next corner you're going to turn to the right into that alley and keep going.'

'But—'

'I don't have a silencer on the gun. But the muzzle is close enough to your body that nobody will know where the sound came from and I'll be gone before you hit the ground. And the bullet will go through you and with these crowds I'm sure it will hit somebody else. You don't want that.'

'Who are you?'

'You know who I am.'

Joseph Malloy had made a lifelong career in law enforcement, and after his wife was killed by a drug-crazed burglar the profession became more than a career; it was an obsession. Maybe he was brass, an administrator now, but he still had the instincts he'd honed on the streets of Midtown South precinct years ago. He understood instantly. 'Five Twenty-Two.'

'What?'

Calm. Stay calm. If you're calm you're in control. 'You're the man who killed that woman on Sunday and the groundskeeper in the cemetery last night.'

'What do you mean, "Five Twenty-Two"?'

'What the department's calling you internally. An unknown subject, UNSUB, number Five Twenty-Two.' Give him some facts. Make him relax too. Carry on a conversation.

The killer gave a brief laugh. 'A number? That's interesting. Now, turn to the right.'

Well, if he wanted you dead, you'd be dead. He just needs to know something, or he's kidnapping you for leverage. Relax. He's obviously not going to kill you – he doesn't want you to see his face. Okay, Lon Sellitto said they were calling him the man who knew everything? Well, get some information about him that *you* can use.

Maybe you can talk your way out.

Maybe you can lower his guard and get close enough to kill him with your bare hands.

Joe Malloy was perfectly capable of this, both mentally and physically.

After a brief walk 522 ordered him to stop in the alley. He put a stocking cap over Malloy's head and pulled it down over his eyes. Good. A huge relief. As long as I don't see him,

I'll live. Then his hands were taped and he was frisked. A firm hand on his shoulder, he was led forward and eased into a car trunk.

A drive in the stifling heat, the uncomfortable space, legs tucked up. A compact car. Okay, noted. No burning oil. And good suspension. Noted. No smell of leather. Noted. Malloy tried to keep track of the directions they turned but that was impossible. He paid attention to the sounds: traffic noises, a jackhammer. Nothing unique there. And seagulls and a boat horn. Well, how's that going to help pinpoint where you are? Manhattan is an island. Get something *useful*! . . . Wait – the car has a noisy power-steering belt. That's helpful. Tuck it away.

Twenty minutes later they came to a stop. He heard the rumble of a garage door closing, a big one, squeaky joints or wheels. Malloy gave a brief cry as the trunk popped, startling him. Musty but cool air embraced him. He gasped hard, sucking oxygen into his lungs through the damp wool of the cap.

'Out we go.'

'There are some things I'd like to talk to you about. I'm a captain—'

'I know who you are.'

'I have a lot of power in the department.' Malloy was pleased. His voice was steady. He was sounding reasonable. 'We can work something out.'

'Come on over here.' Five Twenty-Two helped him over the smooth floor.

Then he was seated.

'I'm sure you have grievances. But I can help you. Tell me why you're doing this, committing these crimes.'

Silence. What would happen next? Would he have a chance to fight physically? Malloy wondered. Or would he have to continue to work his way into the man's mind? By now he'd be missed. Sellitto and Rhyme might have figured out what happened.

Then he heard a noise.

What was it?

Several clicks, followed by a tinny electronic voice. The killer was testing a tape recorder, it seemed.

Then another: the clink of metal against metal, like tools being gathered up.

And finally the disturbing screech of metal on concrete as the killer scooted his chair so close to Malloy's that their knees touched.

Chapter
THIRTY-SIX

A bounty hunter.

They'd caught a goddamn bounty hunter.

Well, as the man corrected, a 'bond recovery specialist.'

'How the fuck did that happen?' was Lincoln Rhyme's question.

'We're checking,' Lon Sellitto said, standing dusty and hot beside the construction site where the man who'd been following Roland Bell sat in cuffs.

He wasn't exactly under arrest. In fact, he hadn't done anything wrong at all; he was licensed to carry a pistol and was merely trying to effect a citizen's arrest of a man he believed to be a wanted criminal. But Sellitto was pissed off and ordered him cuffed.

Roland Bell himself was on the phone, trying to find out if 522 had been spotted elsewhere in the area. But so far no one on the takedown teams had seen anyone fitting the scant profile of the killer. 'Might as well be in Timbuktu,' Bell drawled to Sellitto and folded up his phone.

'Look—' began the bounty hunter from his curb perch.

'Shut up,' the heavy detective barked for the third or fourth time. He returned to his conversation with Rhyme. 'He follows

Roland, moves in and looks like he's going to take him out. But seems he's just serving a warrant. He thought Roland was somebody named William Franklin. They look alike, Franklin and Roland. Lives in Brooklyn and missed a trial date on an assault with a deadly, and firearm possession. The bond company's been after him for six months.'

'Five Twenty-Two set it all up, you know. He found this Franklin in the system and sent the bondsman after him to keep us distracted.'

'I know, Linc.'

'Anybody see *anything* helpful? Somebody staking us out?'

'Nope. Roland just checked with all the teams.'

Silence. Then Rhyme asked, 'How did he know it was a trap?'

Though that wasn't the most important issue. There was really only one question they wanted the answer to and that was 'What the hell is he really up to?'

Do They think I'm stupid?

Did They think I wouldn't be suspicious?

They know about knowledge service providers at this point. About predicting how sixteens will act, based on past behavior and the behavior of others. This concept has been a part of my life for a long, long time. It should be part of everyone's. How will your next-door neighbor react if you do X? How will he react if you do Y? How will a woman behave when you're accompanying her to a car while you're laughing? When you're silent and fishing in your pocket for something?

I've studied Their transactions from the moment They became interested in me. I sorted them, analyzed Them. They've been brilliant at times – for instance, that trap of theirs: letting SSD employees and customers know about the investigation and waiting for me to peek at NYPD files on the Myra 9834 case. I almost did, came within an ENTER keystroke of searching but just had a feeling something was wrong. I know now I was right.

And the press conference? Ah, *that* transaction smelled off from the beginning. Hardly fit predictable and established patterns of behavior. I mean, for the police and the city to meet journalists at that time of night? And the particular assemblage up on the podium certainly didn't ring true.

Of course, maybe it was legit – even the best fuzzy logic and predictive behavior algorithms get it wrong occasionally. But it was in my interest to check further. I couldn't, even casually, talk to any of Them directly.

So instead, I did what I do best.

I looked into the closets, gazed through my secret window at the silent data. I learned more about the folks up there on the podium during the press conference: the deputy mayor, Ron Scott, and Captain Joseph Malloy – the man supervising the investigation against me.

And the third person, the professor. Carlton Soames, Ph.D.

Except . . . Well, he *wasn't*.

He was a cop decoy.

A search engine request *did* turn up hits for Professor Soames on the Carnegie Mellon Web site, and on his own site as well. His C.V. was also tucked away conveniently into various other sites.

But it took me only a few seconds to open up the coding of those documents and examine the metadata. Everything about the phony prof had been written and uploaded yesterday.

Do They think I'm stupid?

If I'd had time I could have learned exactly who the cop was. I could have gone to the TV network's Web site archive, found the press conference, frozen an image of the man's face and done a biometric scan. I'd compare that image to DMV records in the area and police and FBI personnel photos to come up with the man's real identity.

But that would have been a lot of work, and unnecessary. I didn't care who he was. All I needed was to distract the police and give myself time to locate Captain Malloy, the one who would be a veritable database of information about the operation.

I easily found an outstanding warrant for a man bearing a rough resemblance to the cop playing Carlton Soames – a white male in his thirties. Simple matter then to call the bail bondsman, claiming to be an acquaintance of the fugitive and reporting that I'd spotted him at the Water Street Hotel. I described what he was wearing and hung up fast.

Meanwhile I waited at the parking garage near Police Plaza where Captain Malloy parks his low-end Lexus (its oil change and wheel rotation long overdue, the dealer's data report) every morning between 7:48 and 9:02 A.M.

I engaged the enemy at exactly 8:35.

There followed the abduction, the drive to the warehouse on the West Side, and the judicious use of forged metal to execute a memory dump from the admirably courageous database. I'm feeling the inexplicable, more-than-sexual satisfaction of knowing I've completed a collection: the identities of all the sixteens who are after me, some of the people tethered to Them and how They're running the case.

Some information was particularly revealing. (The name Rhyme, for instance. That's the key as to why I'm in this fix, I now understand.)

My soldiers will soon be on their way, marching into Poland, marching into the Rhineland . . .

And, as I'd hoped, I got something for that collection of mine, one of my favorites, by the way. I should wait until I'm back in my Closet but I can't resist. I fish for the tape recorder and I hit REWIND then PLAY.

A happy coincidence: I find the exact spot where Captain Malloy's screams hit a crescendo. It chills even me.

* * *

He awoke from an uneasy sleep filled with bumpy nightmares. His throat hurt from the garrote, inside and out, though the stinging was worse in his mouth – from the dryness.

Arthur Rhyme glanced around at the dingy, windowless hospital room. Well, a *cell* in an infirmary inside the Tombs. No different from his own cell or that terrible common room where he'd almost been murdered.

A male nurse or orderly came into the room, examined an empty bed and wrote something down.

'Excuse me,' Arthur rasped. 'Can I see a doctor?'

The man looked his way – a large African American. Arthur felt a surge of panic, thinking this was Antwon Johnson, who'd stolen a uniform and snuck in here to finish what he'd started . . .

But, no, it was somebody else. Still, the eyes were just as cold and they spent no more time regarding Arthur Rhyme than they would glancing at a spill on the floor. He left without a word.

A half hour passed, Arthur dipping into and out of waking.

Then the door opened again and he glanced up, startled, as another patient was brought in. He'd had appendicitis, Arthur deduced. The operation was over and he was recovering. An orderly got him into bed. He handed the man a glass. 'Don' drink it. Rinse "n" spit.'

The man drank.

'No, I'm tellin' you—'

He threw up.

'Fuck.' The orderly tossed a handful of paper towels at him and left.

Arthur's fellow patient fell asleep, clutching the towels.

It was then that Arthur looked out the window in the door. Two men stood outside, one Latino, one black. The latter squinted, staring directly at him, then whispered something to the other, who briefly looked too.

Something about their posture and expressions told Arthur

their interest wasn't mere curiosity – seeing the con who'd been saved by Mick, the tweaker.

No, they were memorizing his face. Why?

Did *they* want to kill him too?

Another surge of panic. Was it only a matter of time until they were successful?

He closed his eyes but then decided he shouldn't sleep. He didn't dare. They'd move on him when he was asleep, they'd move on him if he closed his eyes, they'd move on him if he didn't pay complete attention to everything, everyone, every minute.

And now his agony was complete. Judy had said that Lincoln might have found something that could prove his innocence. She didn't know what, and so Arthur had no way to judge if his cousin was simply being optimistic, or if he'd discovered some concrete proof that he'd been wrongly arrested. He was furious at this ambiguous hope. Before he'd talked to Judy, Arthur Rhyme had resigned himself to a living hell and an impending death.

I'm doin' you a favor, man. Fuck, you'd do yourself in a month or two anyway . . . Now jus' stop fightin' it . . .

But now, realizing that freedom might be attainable, resignation blossomed into panic. He saw in front of him some hope that could be taken away.

His heart began its manic thudding again.

He grabbed the call button. Pushed it once. Then again.

No response. A moment later another pair of eyes appeared in the window. But they weren't a doctor's. Was it one of the cons he'd seen before? He couldn't tell. The man was looking directly at him.

Struggling to control the fear that trickled down his spine like electricity, he pressed the call button again, then held it down.

Still no response.

The eyes in the window blinked once, then vanished.

Chapter
THIRTY-SEVEN

'Metadata.'

On speakerphone Rodney Szarnek, in the NYPD computer lab, was explaining to Lincoln Rhyme how 522 most likely had learned that the 'expert' was in fact an undercover cop.

Sachs, standing nearby, with her arms crossed and fingers picking at her sleeve, reminded him of what she'd learned from Calvin Geddes of Privacy Now. 'That's data about data. Embedded in documents.'

'Right,' Szarnek confirmed, hearing her comment. 'He probably saw that we'd created the C.V. last night.'

'Shit,' Rhyme murmured. Well, you can't think of everything. Then: But you *have* to when you're up against the man who *knows* everything. And now the plan, which potentially could have netted him, had been wasted. The second time they'd failed.

And worse, they'd tipped their hand. Just like *they*'d learned about his suicide ploy, *he*'d learned how they operated and had a defense against future tactics.

Knowledge is power . . .

Szarnek added, 'I had somebody at Carnegie Mellon trace the addresses of everyone who was in their site this morning.

A half dozen hits originated in the city but they were from public terminals, no trace of the users. Two were from proxies in Europe, and I know the servers. They won't cooperate.'

Naturally.

'Now we've got some information from the empty-space files Ron got from SSD. It's taking some time. They were . . .' He apparently decided to avoid the technical explanation and said, '. . . pretty scrambled. But we've got fragments coming together. Looks like somebody *did* assemble dossiers and download them. We've got a nym – that's a screen name or code name. "Runnerboy." That's all so far.'

'Any idea who? An employee, customer, hacker?'

'Nope. I called a friend in the Bureau and checked their database for known nyms and e-mail addresses. They found about eight hundred Runnerboys. None in the metro area, though. We'll know more later.'

Rhyme had Thom write the name Runnerboy on the list of suspects. 'We'll check with SSD. See if that's a name anybody recognizes.'

'And the customer files on the CD?'

'I've got somebody going through it manually. The code I wrote only got us so far. There're too many variables – different consumer products, Metro fare cards, E-ZPasses. Most of the companies downloaded certain information from the victims but statistically nobody's jumping out as a suspect yet.'

'All right.'

He disconnected.

'We tried, Rhyme,' Sachs said.

Tried . . . He offered a lifted eyebrow, a gesture that meant absolutely nothing.

The phone buzzed and 'Sellitto' popped up on caller ID.

'Command, answer . . . Lon, any—'

'Linc.'

Something was wrong. The tone, through the speaker-phone, was hollow, the voice shaky.

'Another vic?'

Sellitto cleared his throat. 'He got one of us.'

Alarmed, glancing at Sachs, who was involuntarily leaning forward toward the phone, her arms unfolding. 'Who? Tell us.'

'Joe Malloy.'

'No,' whispered Sachs.

Rhyme's eyes closed and his head eased into the wheelchair's headrest. 'Sure, of course. That was the setup, Lon. He had it all planned.' His voice lowered. 'How bad was it?'

'What do you mean?' asked Sachs.

In a soft voice, Rhyme said, 'He didn't just kill Malloy, did he?'

Sellitto's quivering voice was wrenching. 'No, Linc, he didn't.'

'Tell me!' Sachs said bluntly. 'What are you talking about?'

Rhyme looked at her eyes, wide with the horror that they both felt. 'He set up the whole thing because he wanted information. He tortured Joe to get it.'

'Oh, God.'

'Right, Lon?'

The big detective sighed. He coughed. 'Yeah, got to say it was pretty bad. He used some tools. And from the amount of blood Joe held out for a long time. The prick finished him off with a gunshot.'

Sachs's face was red with anger. She kneaded the grip of her Glock. Through clenched jaws she asked, 'Did Joe have kids?'

Rhyme recalled that the captain's wife had been killed a few years ago.

Sellitto answered, 'A daughter in California. I made the call already.'

'You okay about it?' Sachs asked.

'Naw, I'm not.' His voice cracked again. Rhyme didn't think he'd ever heard the detective sound so upset.

In his mind he could hear Joe Malloy's voice when he was responding to Rhyme's 'forgetting' to share about the 522 case. The captain had looked beyond pettiness and backed them up, even after the criminalist and Sellitto hadn't been honest with him.

Policing came before ego.

And 522 had tortured and killed him simply because he needed information. Goddamn information . . .

But then, from somewhere, Rhyme summoned the stone that resided within him. The detachment that, as some people had said, meant he had a damaged soul, but that he believed allowed him to better do his job. He said firmly, 'Okay, you know what this means, don't you?'

'What?' Sachs asked.

'He's declaring war.'

'War?' It was Sellitto who asked this question.

'On us. He's not going underground. He's not running. He's telling us to go fuck ourselves. He's fighting back. And he thinks he can get away with it. Killing brass? Oh, yeah. He's drawn the battle line. And he knows all about us now.'

'Maybe Joe didn't tell him,' Sachs said.

'No, he told. He did everything he could to hold out but in the end he told.' Rhyme didn't even want to picture what the captain had been through as he'd tried to keep silent. 'It wasn't his fault . . . But we're all at risk now.'

'I've gotta go talk to the brass,' Sellitto said. 'They want to know what went wrong. They weren't happy about the plan in the first place.'

'I'm sure they weren't. Where did it happen?'

'A warehouse. Chelsea.'

'Warehouse . . . perfect for a hoarder. Was he connected to it? Work there? Remember his comfortable shoes? Or did he just find out about it from going through the data? I want to know all of the above.'

'I'll have it checked out,' Cooper said. 'Sellitto gave him the details.'

'And we'll get the scene searched.' Rhyme glanced at Sachs, who nodded.

After the detective disconnected, Rhyme asked, 'Where's Pulaski?'

'On his way back from the Roland Bell set.'

'Let's call SSD, find out where all our suspects were at the time Malloy was killed. Some of them must have been in the office. I want to know who *wasn't*. And I want to know about this Runnerboy. Think Sterling'll help?'

'Oh, definitely,' Sachs said, reminding him how cooperative Sterling had been throughout the investigation. She hit the speakerphone button and placed the call.

An assistant answered and Sachs identified herself.

'Hello, Detective Sachs. This is Jeremy. How can I help you?'

'I need to talk to Mr Sterling.'

'I'm afraid he's not available.'

'It's very important. There's been another killing. A police officer.'

'Yes, I heard that on the news. I'm very sorry. Hold on a moment. Martin just walked in.'

They heard a muffled conversation and then another voice came through the speaker. 'Detective Sachs. It's Martin. I'm sorry to hear, another killing. But Mr Sterling's off-site.'

'It's really important we talk to him.'

The calm assistant said, 'I'll relay the urgency.'

'What about Mark Whitcomb or Tom O'Day?'

'Hold for a moment, please.'

After a lengthy pause the young man's voice said, 'I'm afraid Mark is out of the office too. And Tom is in a meeting.

I've left messages. I have another call, Detective Sachs. I should go. And I am truly sorry about your captain.'

"You that shall cross from shore to shore years hence are more to me, and more to my meditations, than you might suppose."

Sitting on a bench, overlooking the East River, Pam Willoughby felt a thud in her chest and her palms began to sweat.

She looked behind her at Stuart Everett, lit brilliantly by the sun over New Jersey. A blue shirt, jeans, a sports coat, the leather bag over his shoulder. His boyish face, a flop of brown hair, narrow lips about to break into a grin that often never arrived.

'Hi,' she said, sounding cheerful. She was angry with herself, wanted to sound harsh.

'Hey.' He glanced north, toward the base of the Brooklyn Bridge. 'Fulton Street.'

'The poem? I know. It's "Crossing Brooklyn Ferry."'

From *Leaves of Grass,* Walt Whitman's masterpiece. After Stuart Everett had mentioned in class that it was his favorite anthology of poems, she'd bought an expensive edition. Thinking that somehow it made them more connected.

'I didn't assign that for class. You knew it anyway?'

Pam said nothing.

'Can I sit down?'

She nodded.

They sat in silence. She smelled his cologne. Wondered if his wife had bought it for him.

'Your friend talked to you, I'm sure.'

'Yeah.'

'I liked her. When she first called, okay, I thought she was going to arrest me.'

Pam's frown softened into a smile.

Stuart continued, 'She wasn't happy about the situation. But that was good. She was looking out for you.'

'Amelia's the best.'

'I couldn't believe she was a cop.'

And a cop who ran a check on my boyfriend. Being in the dark wasn't so bad, Pam reflected; having too much information sucked big-time.

He took her hand. Her impulse to pull it away vanished. 'Look, let's get this whole thing out in the open.'

She kept her eyes focused on the distance; looking into his brown eyes, under droopy lids, would be a way bad idea. She watched the river and the harbor beyond. Ferries still ran but most of the traffic was either private boats or cargo ships. She often sat near the river here and watched them. Forced to live underground, deep in the Midwest woods, with her crazy mother and a bunch of right-wing fanatics, Pam had developed a fascination with rivers and oceans. They were open and free and constantly in motion. That thought soothed her.

'I wasn't honest, I know. But my relationship with my wife isn't what it seems. I don't sleep with her anymore. Haven't for a long time.'

Was that the first thing a man said at a time like this? Pam wondered. She hadn't even considered the sex, just the married.

He continued, 'I didn't want to fall in love with you. I thought we'd be friends. But you turned out to be different from everybody else. You lit up something in me. You're beautiful, obviously. But you're, well, you're like Whitman. Unconventional. Lyrical. A poet in your own way.'

'You've got kids,' Pam couldn't stop herself from saying.

A hesitation. 'I do. But you'd like them. John's eight. Chiara's in middle school. She's eleven. They're wonderful kids. That's why Mary and I are together, the only reason.'

Her name's Mary. Was wondering.

He squeezed her hand. 'Pam, I can't let you go.'

She was leaning into him, feeling the comfort of his arm against hers, smelling the dry, pleasing scent, not caring who'd bought the aftershave. She thought: He was probably going to tell me sooner or later.

'I was going to tell you in a week or so. I swear. I was working up my courage.' She felt his hand trembling. 'I see my children's faces. I think, I can't break up the family. And then you come along. The most incredible person I've ever met . . . I've been lonely for a long, long time.'

'But what about holidays?' she asked. 'I wanted to do something on Thanksgiving or Christmas with you.'

'I can probably get away for one of them. At least part of the day. We just need to plan ahead of time.' Stuart lowered his head. 'Here's the thing. I can't live without you. If you can be patient, we'll make it work.'

She thought back to the one night they'd spent together. A secret night that nobody knew about. At Amelia Sachs's town house, when she was staying at Lincoln Rhyme's and Pam, and Stuart, had the place to themselves. It was magical. She wished every night of her life could be like that one.

She gripped his hand harder yet.

He whispered, 'I can't lose you.'

He inched closer on the bench. She found comfort in every square inch of contact. She actually had written a poem about him, describing their attraction as gravitational: one of the fundamental forces in the universe.

Pam rested her head against his shoulder.

'I promise I'll never hide anything from you again. But please . . . I have to keep seeing you.'

She thought of the wonderful times they'd had, times that would seem insignificant to anyone else, silly.

Nothing like it.

The comfort was like warm water on a wound, washing away the pain.

When they'd been on the run, Pam and her mother had lived with and around petty men who would strike them 'for their own good,' who didn't share a word with their wives or children except when correcting or silencing them.

Stuart wasn't even in the same universe with those monsters.

He whispered, 'Just give me a little while. It'll work out. I promise. We'll see each other like we have been . . . Hey, here's an idea. I know you want to travel. There's a poetry conference in Montreal next month. I could fly you there, get you a room. You could attend the sessions. And we'd have the evenings free.'

'Oh, I love you.' She leaned toward his face. 'I understand why you didn't tell me, really.'

He gripped her hard, kissed her neck. 'Pam, I'm so—'

Which is when she eased back and clutched her book bag to her chest like a shield. 'But no, Stuart.'

'What?'

Pam believed her heart was beating faster than it ever had. 'When you get divorced call me up and let's see. But until then, no. I can't see you anymore.'

She'd said what she thought Amelia Sachs would say at a time like this. But could she *behave* the same and not cry? Amelia wouldn't. No way.

She slapped a smile onto her face, struggling to control the pain as the loneliness and panic killed the comfort instantly. The warmth froze to icy shards.

'But, Pam, you're everything to me.'

'But what are *you* to *me*, Stuart? You can't be everything. And I'm not willing to take less than that.' Keep your voice steady, she told herself. 'If you get a divorce I'll be with you . . . Will you?'

Now the seductive eyes lowered. 'Yes.' A whisper.

'Now?'

'I can't just now. It's complicated.'

'No, Stuart. It's really, really simple.' She rose. 'If I don't see you again, have a nice life.' She began walking away quickly, heading for Amelia's town house, which was nearby.

Okay, maybe Amelia wouldn't cry. But Pam could no longer hold the tears back. She walked straight down the sidewalk, eyes streaming, and – afraid she'd weaken – not daring to look back, not daring to think about what she'd done.

Though she did have one thought about the encounter, which she supposed someday she'd consider pretty funny: What a sucky parting line that was. Wish I'd come up with something better.

Chapter
THIRTY-EIGHT

Mel Cooper was frowning.

'The warehouse? Where Joe was killed? Some publisher rents it to store paper there for recycling, though it hasn't been used actively for months. But what's strange is that the ownership's not clear.'

'What does that mean?'

'I've run all the corporate documents. It's leased to a chain of three companies and owned by a Delaware corporation – and *that*'s owned by a couple of New York corporations. The ultimate ownership seems to be in Malaysia.'

But 522 had known about it and that it was safe to torture a victim there. How? Because he's the man who knows everything.

The phone in the lab trilled and Rhyme glanced at caller ID. We've had such bad news in the 522 case, please let this be good. 'Inspector Longhurst.'

'Detective Rhyme, just to update you. It's looking rather productive here.' Her voice betrayed a rare excitement. She explained that d'Estourne, the team's French security service agent, had sped to Birmingham and contacted some Algerians in a Muslim community in West Bromwich, outside the city.

He'd learned that an American had commissioned a passport and transit papers to North Africa, traveling on to Singapore. He'd given them a large down payment and they promised the documents would be ready tomorrow evening. As soon as he picked them up he was heading for London to finish the job.

'Good,' Rhyme said, chuckling. 'That means Logan's *already* there, don't you think? In London.'

'Quite certain of it,' Longhurst agreed. 'Trying the shot tomorrow when our double meets the MI5 people at the shooting zone.'

'Exactly.'

So Richard Logan had ordered the papers, and paid a large price for them, to keep the team focused on Birmingham, while he hurried to London to complete his mission to kill the Reverend Goodlight.

'What do Danny Krueger's people say?'

'That a boat will be waiting on the south coast to spirit him away to France.'

Spirit him away. Rhyme loved it. Cops don't talk that way over here.

He thought again about the safe house near Manchester. And the break-in at Goodlight's NGO in London. Was there anything Rhyme might've seen if he had walked the grid at either of those locales via the high-definition video? Some tiny clue that they'd missed that might give them a clearer idea of exactly where and when the killer was going to strike? If so, the evidence was gone now. He'd just have to hope they'd made the right deductions.

'What do you have in place?'

'Ten officers around the shooting zone. All plainclothed or in camouflage.' She added that Danny Krueger, along with the French security man and another tactical team, were making themselves 'subtly visible' in Birmingham. Longhurst had also added an extra protection detail where the reverend was actually hiding; they had no evidence that the killer had learned the location but she didn't want to take any chances.

'We'll know something soon, Detective.'

Just as they disconnected, his computer dinged.

'mr Rhyme?'

The words appeared on the screen in front of him. A small window had opened. It was a webcam view of Amelia Sachs's living room. He could see Pam at the keyboard, instant messaging him.

He spoke to her through his voice-recognition system. *'Hello Pam owe are you dew in?'*

Goddamn computer. Maybe he should have their digital guru, Rodney Szarnek, install a new system.

But she deduced the message just fine.

'Good,' she typed. *'How R U?'*

'I am good.'

'Amelia there?'

'No. She is how on a case.'

':-(Bummer. Want 2 talk 2 her. Called but not picking up.'

'Any thing eye can dew—'

Damn. He sighed and tried again. *'Anything we can do here?'*

'No thx.' A pause and he saw her glance at her cell phone. She looked back at the computer. Typed, *'Rachel calling. Back in minute.'*

She left the webcam on but turned away, speaking into her mobile. She lugged a massive book bag onto her lap and dug through it, opened a text and found some notes inside. She read them aloud, it seemed.

Rhyme was about to turn to the whiteboards when he glanced at the webcam window.

Something had changed.

He frowned and maneuvered his chair closer, alarmed.

Someone else seemed to be in Sachs's town house. Could it be? It was hard to tell for certain but as he squinted he saw that, yes, a man was there, hiding in a dark hallway, only twenty feet or so from Pam.

Rhyme squinted, moving his head as far forward as he could. An intruder, his face hidden by a hat. And he was holding something. Was it a gun? A knife?

'Thom!'

The aide wasn't within earshot. Of course, he was taking the trash out.

'Command, dial Sachs, home.'

Thank God the ECU did exactly as instructed.

He could see Pam glance at the phone beside the computer. But she ignored the ringing; the house wasn't hers – she'd let voice mail take a message. She continued speaking into her mobile.

The man leaned out of the hallway, his face, obscured by the brim of his hat, aimed directly at her.

'Command, instant message!'

The box popped up on the screen.

'Command, type: "Pam exclamation point." Command, send.'

'Pamex lamentation point.'

Fuck!

'Command, type, "Pam danger leave now." Command, send.'

This message went through pretty much unchanged.

Pam, read it, please! Rhyme begged silently. Look at the screen!

But the girl was lost in her conversation. Her face was no longer so carefree. The discussion had turned serious.

Rhyme called 911, and the operator assured him that a police car would be at the town house in five minutes. But the intruder was only seconds away from Pam, who was completely unaware of him.

Rhyme knew it was 522, of course. He'd tortured Malloy to get information about all of them. Amelia Sachs was the first on the list to die. Only it wouldn't be Sachs. It would be this innocent girl.

His heart was pounding, a sensation registering as a fierce, throbbing headache. He tried the phone again. Four rings. *'Hi, this is Amelia. Please leave your message at the tone.'*

He tried again. 'Command, type, "Pam call me period. Lincoln period."'

And what would he tell her to do if he got through? Sachs had weapons in the place but he didn't know where she kept them. Pam was an athletic girl, and the intruder didn't seem much larger than she was. But he'd have a weapon. And, given where he was, he could get a garrote around her neck or a knife into her back before she was even aware of his presence.

And it would happen before his eyes.

Then at last she was swiveling toward the computer. She'd see the message.

Good, keep turning.

Rhyme saw a shadow on the floor across the room. Was the killer moving in closer?

Still talking on her phone, Pam moved toward the computer but she was looking at the keyboard, not the screen.

Look up! Rhyme urged silently.

Please! Read the goddamn message!

But like all kids today, Pam didn't need to look at the screen to make sure she'd typed correctly. With her cell held tight between cheek and shoulder, she glanced fast at the keyboard as she stabbed the letters with quick strokes.

'gotta go. bye mr Rhyme. C U :-)'

The screen went black.

Amelia Sachs was uncomfortable in the crime-scene Tyvek jumpsuit, with surgeon's hat and booties. Claustrophobic, nauseous from inhaling the bitter scent of damp paper and blood and sweat in the warehouse.

She hadn't known Captain Joseph Malloy well. But he was, as Lon Sellitto had announced, 'one of ours.' And she was appalled at what 522 had done to him, to extract the information he wanted. She was nearly finished running the scene and carried the evidence-collection bags outside, infinitely grateful for the air here, even though it reeked of diesel fumes.

She kept hearing the voice of her father. As a young girl she'd glanced into her parents' bedroom and found him in his dress patrolman's uniform, wiping tears. This had shaken her; she'd never seen him cry. He'd gestured her inside. Hermann Sachs always played straight with his daughter and he'd sat her down on a bedside chair and explained that a friend of his, a fellow officer, had been shot and killed while stopping a robbery.

'Amie, in this business, everybody's family. You probably spend more time with the guys you work with than you do with your own wife and kids. Every time somebody in blue dies, you die a little bit too. Doesn't matter, patrol or brass, they're all family and it's the same pain when you lose somebody.'

And she now felt the pain he'd been speaking of. Felt it very deeply.

'I'm finished,' she said to the crime-scene crew, who were standing beside their rapid response van. She'd searched the scene alone but the officers from Queens had videotaped and photographed it and walked the grid at the secondary scenes – the likely entrance and exit routes.

Nodding to the tour doctor and her associates from the M.E.'s office, Sachs said, 'Okay, you can get him to the morgue.'

The men, in their thick green gloves and jumpsuits, walked inside. Assembling the evidence in the milk crates for transport to Rhyme's lab, Sachs paused.

Someone was watching her.

She'd heard a tink of metal on metal or concrete or glass from up a deserted alleyway. A fast look, and she believed she saw a figure hiding near a deserted factory's loading dock, which had collapsed years ago.

Search carefully, but watch your back . . .

She remembered the scene at the cemetery, the killer, wearing the swiped police hat, watching her. Felt the same uneasiness she had there. She left the evidence bags and walked down the alley, hand on her pistol. She saw no one.

Paranoia.

'Detective?' one of the techs called.

She kept going. Was there a face behind that filthy window?

'Detective,' he persisted.

'I'll be right there.' A little irritation in her voice.

The crime-scene tech said, 'Sorry, it's a call. From Detective Rhyme.'

She always shut her phone off when she got to a scene to avoid distractions.

'Tell him I'll call him right back.'

'Detective, he says it's about somebody named Pam. There's been an incident at your town house. You're needed right away.'

Chapter
THIRTY-NINE

Amelia Sachs ran inside fast, oblivious to the pain in her knees.

Past the police at the door, not even nodding to them. 'Where?'

One officer pointed toward the living room.

Sachs hurried into the room . . . and found Pam on the couch. The girl looked up, her face pale.

The policewoman sat beside her. 'You're all right?'

'I'm fine. A little freaked out is all.'

'Nothing hurt? I can hug you?'

Pam laughed and Sachs flung her arms around the girl. 'What happened?'

'Somebody broke in. He was here while I was. Mr Rhyme could see him behind me on the webcam. He kept calling and on the, like, fifth ring or something, I picked up and he told me to start screaming and get out.'

'And you did?'

'Not really. I kind of ran into the kitchen and got a knife. I was pretty pissed. He took off.'

Sachs glanced at a detective from the local Brooklyn precinct, a squat African-American man, who said in a deep baritone, 'He was gone when we got here. Neighbors didn't see anything.'

So it *had* been her imagination at the warehouse crime scene where Joe Malloy was killed. Or maybe some kid or wino curious about what the cops were doing. After killing Malloy, 522 had come to her place – to look for files or evidence or to finish the job he'd started: kill her.

Sachs walked through the town house with the detective and Pam. The desk had been ransacked but nothing seemed to be missing.

'I thought maybe it was Stuart.' Pam took a breath. 'I kind of broke up with him.'

'You did?'

A nod.

'Good for you . . . But it wasn't him?'

'No. The guy here was wearing different clothes and wasn't built like Stuart. And, yeah, he's a son of a bitch but he's not going to break into somebody else's town house.'

'You get a look at him?'

'Naw. He turned and ran before I could see him real clearly.' She'd noticed only his outfit.

The detective explained that Pam had described the burglar as a male, white or light-skinned black or Latino, medium build, wearing blue jeans and a dark blue plaid sports jacket. He'd called Rhyme too, after he'd learned of the webcam, but the criminalist hadn't seen anything more than a vague form in the hallway.

They found the window through which he'd broken in. Sachs had an alarm system but Pam had shut it off when she'd arrived.

She looked around the place. The anger and dismay she'd felt at Malloy's horrible death faded, replaced by the same uneasiness, and vulnerability, that she'd been aware of at the cemetery, at the warehouse where Malloy had died, at SSD . . . in fact, *everywhere* since they'd started the pursuit of 522. Like at the scene near DeLeon's house: Was he watching her now?

She saw motion outside the window, a flash of light . . . Was it from the blowing leaves in front of nearby windows reflecting the pale sunlight?

Or was it 522?

'Amelia?' Pam asked in a soft voice, looking around uneasily herself. 'Everything okay?'

This brought Sachs back to reality. Get to work. And fast. The killer had been here – and not that long ago. Goddamnit, find out something useful. 'Sure, honey. It's fine.'

A patrol officer from the precinct asked, 'Detective, you want somebody from Crime Scene to look it over?'

'That's okay,' she said with a glance to Pam and a tight smile. 'I'll handle it.'

Sachs got her portable crime-scene kit from the trunk of her car, and she and Pam searched together.

Well, Sachs did the searching but Pam, standing clear of the perimeter, described exactly where the killer had been. Though her voice was unsteady, the girl was coolly efficient.

I kind of ran into the kitchen and got a knife.

Since Pam was here, Sachs asked a patrol officer to stand guard in the garden – where the killer had escaped. This didn't allay her concern completely, though, not with 522's uncanny ability to spy on his victims, to learn all about them, to get close. She wanted to search the scene and get Pam away as soon as she could.

With the teenager directing her, Sachs searched the places he'd stepped. But she found no evidence in the town house. The killer had either used gloves when he'd broken in or hadn't touched any receptive surfaces, and the adhesive rollers revealed no signs of foreign trace.

'Where did he go outside?' Sachs asked.

'I'll show you.' Pam glanced at Sachs's face, which was apparently revealing her reluctance to expose the girl to more danger. 'It'd be better than me just telling you.'

Sachs nodded and they walked into the garden. She looked around carefully. She asked the patrol officer, 'See anything?'

'Nope. But I've gotta say, when you think somebody's watching you, you see somebody watching you.'

'I hear that.'

He jerked a thumb toward a row of dark windows across the alley, then toward some thick azaleas and boxwood bushes. 'I checked them out. Nothing. But I'll keep on it.'

'Thanks.'

Pam directed Sachs to the path 522 had taken to escape and Sachs began walking the grid.

'Amelia?'

'What?'

'I was kind of a shit, you know. What I said to you yesterday. I felt, like, all desperate or something. Panicked . . . I guess what I'm saying is, I'm sorry.'

'You were the picture of restraint.'

'I didn't feel very restrained.'

'Love makes us weird, honey.'

Pam laughed.

'We'll talk about it later. Maybe tonight, depending on how the case goes. We'll get dinner.'

'Okay, sure.'

Sachs continued her examination, struggling to put aside her uneasiness, the sense that 522 was still here. But despite her effort the search wasn't very fruitful. The ground was mostly gravel and she found no footprints, except one near the gate through which he'd escaped from her yard into the alley. The only mark was the toe of a shoe – he'd been sprinting – and useless forensically. She found no fresh tire treadmarks.

But, returning to her yard, she saw a flash of white in the ivy and periwinkle covering the ground – exactly in the position where it would have landed after falling from 522's pocket as he'd vaulted the locked gate.

'You found something?'

'Maybe.' With tweezers, Sachs picked up a small piece of paper. Returning to the town house, she set up a portable examining table and processed the rectangle. She sprayed ninhydrin on it, then, after donning goggles, hit it with an alternative light source. She was disappointed that no prints were revealed.

'Is it helpful?' Pam asked.

'Could be. It's not going to point to his front door. But then evidence usually doesn't. If it did,' she added, smiling, 'they wouldn't need people like Lincoln and me, right? I'm going to go check it out.'

Sachs got her toolbox, took out the drill and screwed shut the broken window. She locked up, setting the alarm.

She had called Rhyme briefly earlier to tell him Pam was all right but she now wanted to let him know about the possible lead. She pulled out her cell phone but, before she called, she paused on the curb and looked around.

'What's the matter, Amelia?'

She put the phone back in its holster. 'My car.' The Camaro was gone. Sachs felt a surge of alarm. Her gaze swiveled up and down the street, her hand strayed to the Glock. Was 522 here? Had he stolen the car?

The patrol officer was just leaving the backyard and she asked if he'd seen anybody.

'That car, that old one? It was yours?'

'Yeah, I think the perp might've boosted it.'

'Sorry, Detective, I think it got towed. I woulda said something if I'd known it was yours.'

Towed? Maybe she'd forgotten to put the NYPD placard on the dash.

She and Pam walked up the street to the girl's beat-up Honda Civic and drove to the local precinct. The desk sergeant there, whom she knew, had heard about the break-in. 'Hi, Amelia. The boys canvassed the hood real careful. Nobody saw the perp.'

'Listen, Vinnie, my wheels're gone. They were by the hydrant across the street from my place.'

'Pool car?'

'No.'

'Not your old Chevy?'

'Yep.'

'Aw, no. That's lousy.'

'Somebody said it got towed. I don't know if I had the official-business sign on the dash.'

'Still, they ought to've run the plate, seen who it was registered to. Shit, that sucks. Sorry, miss.'

Pam smiled to show her immunity to words that she'd just uttered herself occasionally.

Sachs gave the sergeant the plate number and he made some calls, checked the computer. 'Naw, it wasn't Parking Violations. Hold on a second.' He made some other calls.

Son of a bitch. She couldn't afford to be without her wheels. She wanted desperately to check out the lead she'd found at her town house.

But her frustration became concern when she noticed the frown on Vinnie's face. 'You sure? . . . Okay. Where'd it go to? . . . Yeah? Well, gimme a call back as soon as you know.' He hung up.

'What?'

'The Camaro, you have it financed?'

'Financed? No.'

'This is weird. A repo team got it.'

'Somebody *repossessed* it?'

'According to them, you missed six months' payments.'

'Vinnie, it's a 'sixty-nine. My dad bought it for cash in the seventies. It's never had a lien on it. Who was the lender supposed to be?'

'My guy didn't know. He's going to check it out and call back. He'll find out where they took it.'

'Goddamn last thing I need. You have wheels here?'

'Sorry, nope.'

She thanked him and walked outside, Pam beside her. 'If there's one scratch on her, heads're going to roll,' she muttered. Could 522 have been behind the towing? It wouldn't have surprised her, though how he'd arrange it she couldn't imagine.

Another stab of uneasiness at how close he'd gotten to her, how much information about her he could access.

The man who knows everything . . .

She asked Pam, 'Can I borrow your Civic?'

'Sure. Only, can you drop me at Rachel's? We're going to do our homework together.'

'Tell you what, honey, how 'bout if I have one of the guys from the precinct run you into the city?'

'Sure. How come?'

'This guy knows way too much about me already. Think it's best just to keep a little distance.' She and the girl walked back into the precinct house to arrange for the ride. Outside once again, Sachs looked up and down the sidewalk. No sign of anyone watching her.

She glanced up fast at motion in a window across the street. She thought immediately of the SSD logo – the window in the watchtower. The person who'd glanced out was an elderly woman but that didn't stop the chill from trickling down Sachs's spine yet again. She walked quickly to Pam's car and fired it up.

Chapter
FORTY

With a snap of systems shutting down, deprived of their lifeblood, the town house went dark.

'What the hell is going on?' Rhyme shouted.

'The electricity's out,' Thom announced.

'That part I figured,' the criminalist snapped. 'What I'd like to know is why.'

'We weren't running the GC,' Mel Cooper said defensively. He looked out the window, as if checking to see if the rest of the neighborhood grid had gone down too, but since it was not yet dusk there were no ConEd references to tell the story.

'We can't afford to be offline now. Goddamnit. Get it taken care of!'

Rhyme, Sellitto, Pulaski and Cooper remained in the silent, dim room, while Thom walked into the hall and, on his cell phone, made a call. He was soon talking with somebody at the electric company. 'Impossible. I pay the bills online. Every month. Never missed one. I have receipts . . . Well, they're in the computer and I can't go online because there's no electricity, now can I? . . . Canceled checks, yes, but once again, how can I fax them to you if there's no electricity? . . . I don't know where there's a Kinko's, no.'

'It's him, you know,' Rhyme said to the others.

'Five Twenty-Two? He got your power shut off?'

'Yep. He found out about me and where I live. Malloy must've told him this is our command post.'

The silence was eerie. The first thing Rhyme thought of was how completely vulnerable he was. The devices that he relied on were useless now and he had no way to communicate, no way to lock or unlock the doors or use the ESU. If the blackout continued and Thom couldn't recharge his wheelchair's battery he'd be immobilized completely.

He couldn't remember that last time he'd felt so vulnerable. Even having others around didn't allay the concern; 522 was a threat to anybody, anywhere.

He was also wondering: Is the blackout a diversion, or the prelude to an attack?

'Keep an eye out, everybody,' he announced. 'He could be moving in on us.'

Pulaski glanced out the window. Cooper too.

Sellitto pulled out his cell phone and called someone downtown. He explained the situation. He rolled his eyes – Sellitto was never one for stoic faces – then ended the conversation with: 'Well, I don't care. Whatever it takes. This asshole's a killer. And we can't do a thing to find him without any fucking electricity . . . Thanks.'

'Thom, any luck?'

'No,' came the aide's abrupt reply.

'Shit.' Rhyme then reflected on something. 'Lon, call Roland Bell. I think we need protection. Five Twenty-Two went after Pam, he went after Amelia.' The criminalist nodded at a dark monitor. 'He knows about us. I want officers on Amelia's mother's place. Pam's foster home. Pulaski's house, Mel's mother's place. Your house too, Lon.'

'You think it's that much of a risk?' the big detective asked. Then shook his head. 'What the hell am I saying? Sure, it is.'

He got the information – addresses and phone numbers – then called Bell and had him arrange for officers. After hanging up he said, 'It'll take a few hours but he'll get it done.'

A loud knock on the door shattered the silence. Still clutching the phone, Thom started for it.

'Wait!' Rhyme shouted.

The aide paused.

'Pulaski, go with him.' Rhyme nodded at the pistol on his hip.

'Sure.'

They walked into the hallway. Then Rhyme heard a muted conversation and a moment later two men in suits, with trim hair and unsmiling faces, walked into the town house, looking around curiously – first at Rhyme's body, then at the rest of the lab, surprised either at the amount of scientific equipment or the absence of lights, or both, most likely.

'We're looking for a Lieutenant Sellitto. We were told he'd be here.'

'That's me. Who're you?'

Shields were displayed and ranks and names given – they were two NYPD detective sergeants. And they were with Internal Affairs.

'Lieutenant,' the older of the two said, 'we're here to take possession of your shield and weapon. I have to tell you that the results were confirmed.'

'I'm sorry. What're you talking about?'

'You're officially suspended. You're not being arrested at this time. But we recommend you talk to an attorney – either your own or one from the PBA.'

'The hell is going on?'

The younger officer frowned. 'The drug test.'

'*What?*'

'You don't have to deny anything to us. We just do the fieldwork, pick up shields and weapons and inform suspects of their suspension.'

'What fucking test?'

The older looked at the younger. This apparently had never happened before.

Naturally it hadn't, since whatever was going on had been ginned up by 522, Rhyme understood.

'Detective, really, you don't have to act—'

'Do I fucking look like I'm acting?'

'Well, according to the suspension order, you took a drug test last week. The results just came in, showing significant levels of narcotics in your system. Heroin, cocaine and psychedelics.'

'I took the drug test, like everybody in my department. It can't show up positive because I don't do any fucking drugs. I have *never* done any fucking drugs. And . . . Oh, shit,' the big man spat out, grimacing. He jabbed a finger at the SSD brochure. 'They've got drug-screening and background-check companies. He got into the system somehow and screwed up my file. The results were faked.'

'That would be very difficult to accomplish.'

'Well, it *got* accomplished.'

'And you or your attorney can bring up that defense at the hearing. Again, we really just need your shield and your weapon. And here's the paperwork on that. Now, I hope there's not going to be a problem. You don't want to add to your difficulties, do you?'

'Shit.' The big, rumpled man handed over his gun – an old-style revolver – and the shield. 'Gimme the fucking paper-work.' Sellitto snatched it out of the hand of the younger one, as the older wrote out a receipt and handed it to him, as well. He then unloaded the gun and placed it and the bullets in a thick envelope.

'Thank you, Detective. Have a good day.'

After they were gone, Sellitto flipped open his phone and called the head of IA. The man was out and he left a message.

Then he called his own office. The assistant he shared with several other detectives in Major Cases had apparently heard the news.

'I know it's bullshit. They what? . . . Oh, great. I'll call you when I find out what's going on.' He snapped the phone closed so hard Rhyme wondered if he'd broken it. He raised an eyebrow. 'They just confiscated everything in my desk.'

Pulaski asked, 'How the hell do you fight somebody like this?'

It was then that Rodney Szarnek called on Sellitto's mobile. He set it to speakerphone. 'What's wrong with the landline there?'

'The prick got the electricity shut off. We're working on it. What's up?'

'The list of SSD customers, from the CD. We found something. One customer downloaded pages of data about all victims and fall guys the *day* before each killing.'

'Who is it?'

'His name's Robert Carpenter.'

Rhyme said, 'Okay. Good. What's his story?'

'All I have is what's on the spreadsheet. He's got his own company in Midtown. Associated Warehousing.'

Warehousing? Rhyme was thinking of the place where Joe Malloy was murdered. Was there a connection?

'Have an address?'

The tech specialist recited it.

After disconnecting, Rhyme noted Pulaski was frowning. The young officer said, 'I think we saw him at SSD.'

'Who?'

'Carpenter. When we were there yesterday. A big, bald guy. He was in a meeting with Sterling. He didn't seem happy.'

'Happy? What does that mean?'

'I don't know. Just an impression.'

'Not helpful.' Rhyme said, 'Mel, check this Carpenter out.'

Cooper called downtown on his mobile. He spoke for a few minutes, moving closer to the window for the light, then jotted notes. He disconnected. 'You don't seem to like the word "interesting," Lincoln, but it is. I've got the NCIC and department database results. Robert Carpenter. Lives on the Upper East Side. Single. And, get this, he's got a record. Some credit card fraud and bad-check busts. Did six months in Waterbury. And he was arrested in a corporate extortion scheme. Those charges were dropped but he went nuts when they came to pick him up, tried to swing at the agent. They dropped those charges when he agreed to go into ED counseling.'

'Emotionally disturbed?' Rhyme nodded. 'And his company's in the warehousing business. Just the line of work for a hoarder . . . Okay, Pulaski, find out where this Carpenter was when Amelia's town house got broken into.'

'Yes, sir.' Pulaski was lifting his phone from its holster when the unit trilled. He glanced at caller ID. He answered. 'Hi, hon – What? . . . Hey, Jenny, calm down . . .'

Oh, no . . . Lincoln Rhyme knew that 522 had attacked on yet another front.

'*What*? Where are you? . . . Take it easy, it's just a mistake.' The rookie's voice was shaking. 'It'll all get taken care of . . . Give me the address . . . Okay, I'll be right there.'

He snapped shut the phone, closed his eyes momentarily. 'I have to go.'

'What's wrong?' Rhyme asked.

'Jenny's been arrested. By the INS.'

'Immigration?'

'She got put on a watch list at Homeland Security. They're saying she's illegal and a security threat.'

'Isn't she – ?'

'Our great-*grandparents* were citizens,' Pulaski snapped. 'Jesus.' The young officer was wild-eyed. 'Brad's at Jenny's mom's but she has the baby with her now. They're transporting her to detention – and they may take the baby. If they do that . . . Oh, man.' Pure despair filled his face. 'I have to go.' His eyes told Rhyme that nothing would stop him being with his wife.

'Okay. Go. Good luck.'

The young man sprinted out the door.

Rhyme closed his eyes briefly. 'He's picking us off like a sniper.' He grimaced. 'At least Sachs'll be here any minute. She can check out Carpenter.'

Just then another pounding shook the door.

Alarmed, his eyes jerked open. What now?

But this, at least, wasn't another disruption by 522.

Two crime-scene officers from the main facility in Queens walked inside, carrying a large milk crate, which Sachs had handed off to them before she'd raced to her town house. This would be the evidence from the scene of Malloy's death.

'Hi, Detective. You know your doorbell's not working.' One looked around. 'And your lights're off.'

'We're pretty aware of that,' Rhyme said coolly.

'Anyway, here you go.'

After the officers had left, Mel Cooper put the box on an examination table and extracted the evidence and Sachs's digital camera, which would contain images of the scene.

'Now, that's helpful,' Rhyme growled sarcastically, pointing his chin at the silent computer and its black screen. 'Maybe we can hold the memory chip up to the sunlight.'

He glanced at the evidence itself – a shoeprint, some leaves, duct tape and envelopes of trace. They had to examine it as soon as possible; since this wasn't planted evidence it might provide the final clue as to where 522 was. But without their equipment to analyze it and check the databases, the bags were nothing more than paperweights.

'Thom,' Rhyme called, 'the power?'

'I'm still on hold,' the aide shouted from the dark hallway.

He knew this was probably a bad idea. But he was out of control.

And it took a lot for Ron Pulaski to be out of control.

Yet he was furious. This was beyond anything he'd ever felt. When he'd signed up for the blue he'd expected to be beat up and threatened from time to time. But he'd never thought that his career would put Jenny at risk, much less his children.

So despite being straitlaced and by the book – Sergeant Friday – he was taking the matter into his own hands. Going behind the backs of Lincoln Rhyme and Detective Sellitto and even his mentor, Amelia Sachs. They wouldn't be happy at what he was going to do but Ron Pulaski was desperate.

And so on the way to the INS detention center in Queens, he'd made a call to Mark Whitcomb.

'Hey, Ron,' the man had said, 'what's going on? . . . You sound upset. You're out of breath.'

'I've got a problem, Mark. Please. I need some help. My wife's being accused of being an illegal alien. They say her passport's forged and she's a security threat. It's crazy.'

'But she's a citizen, isn't she?'

'Her family's been here for *generations*. Mark, we think this killer we've been after got into your system. He's had one detective fail a drug test . . . and now he's had Jenny arrested. He could do that?'

'He must've swapped her file with somebody who's on a watch list and then called it in . . . Look, I know some people at INS. I can talk to them. Where are you?'

'On my way to the detention center in Queens.'

'I'll meet you outside in twenty minutes.'

'Oh, thanks, man. I don't know what to do.'

'Don't worry, Ron. We'll get it worked out.'

Now, waiting for Whitcomb, Ron Pulaski was pacing in front of INS detention, beside a temporary sign indicating that the service was now operated by the Department of Homeland Security. Pulaski thought back to all the TV news reports he and Jenny had seen about illegal immigrants, how terrified they'd looked.

What was happening to his wife at the moment? Would she be stuck for days or weeks in some kind of bureaucratic purgatory? Pulaski wanted to scream.

Calm down. Handle it smart. Amelia Sachs always told him that.

Handle it smart.

Finally, thank you, Lord, Pulaski saw Mark Whitcomb walking quickly toward him, the expression one of urgent concern. He wasn't sure exactly what the man could do to help but he hoped that the Compliance Department, with its connections to the government, could pull strings with Homeland Security and get his wife and child released, at least until the matter was officially resolved.

Whitcomb, breathless, came up to him. 'Have you found out anything else?'

'I called about ten minutes ago. They're inside now. I didn't say anything. I wanted to wait for you.'

'You okay?'

'No. I'm pretty frantic here, Mark. Thanks for this.'

'Sure,' the Compliance officer said earnestly. 'It'll be okay, Ron. Don't worry. I think I can do something.' Then he looked up into Pulaski's eyes; the SSD Compliance officer was just slightly taller than Andrew Sterling. 'Only . . . it's pretty important for you to get Jenny out of there, right?'

'Oh, yeah, Mark. This's just a nightmare.'

'Okay. Come this way.' He led Pulaski around the corner

of the building, then into an alley. 'I've got a favor to ask, Ron,' Whitcomb whispered.

'Whatever I can do.'

'Really?' The man's voice was uncharacteristically soft, calm. And his eyes had a sharpness that Pulaski hadn't seen before. As if he'd dropped an act and was now being himself. 'You know, sometimes, Ron, we have to do things that we don't think are right. But in the end it's for the best.'

'What do you mean?'

'To help your wife out you might have to do something you might think isn't so good.'

The officer said nothing, his thoughts whirling. Where was this going?

'Ron, I need you to make this case go away.'

'Case?'

'The murder investigation.'

'Go away? I don't get it.'

'Stop the case.' Whitcomb looked around and whispered, 'Sabotage it. Destroy the evidence. Give them some false leads. Point them anywhere but at SSD.'

'I don't understand, Mark. Are you joking?'

'No, Ron. I'm real serious. This case's got to stop and you can do it.'

'I can't.'

'Oh, yes, you can. If you want Jenny out of there.' A nod toward the detention center.

No, no . . . *this* was 522. Whitcomb was the killer! He'd used the passcodes of his boss, Sam Brockton, to get access to innerCircle.

Instinctively Pulaski started for his gun.

But Whitcomb drew first, a black pistol appearing in his hand. 'No, Ron. That's not going to get us anywhere.' Whitcomb reached into the holster and pulled Pulaski's Glock out by the grip, slipped it into his waistband.

How could he have misjudged this so badly? Was it the head injury? Or was he just stupid? Whitcomb's friendship had been feigned, which hurt as much as it shocked. Bringing him the coffee, defending him to Cassel and Gillespie, suggesting they get together socially, helping with the time sheets . . . it was all a tactic to get close to the cop and use him.

'It's all a goddamn lie, isn't it, Mark? You didn't grow up in Queens at all, did you? And you don't have a brother who's a cop?'

'No to both.' Whitcomb's face was dark. 'I tried to reason with you, Ron. But you wouldn't work with me. Goddamnit! You could have. Now look what you've made me do.'

The killer pushed Pulaski farther into the alley.

Chapter
FORTY-ONE

Amelia Sachs was in the city, cruising through traffic, frustrated at the noisy, tepid response of the Japanese engine.

It sounded like an ice maker. And had just about as much horsepower.

She'd called Rhyme twice but both times the line went right to voice mail. This rarely happened; Lincoln Rhyme obviously wasn't away from home very much. And something odd was going on at the Big Building: Lon Sellitto's phone was out of order. And neither he nor Ron Pulaski was answering his mobile.

Was 522 behind this too?

All the more reason to move fast in following up on the lead she'd discovered at her town house. It was a solid one, she believed. Maybe it was the final clue, the one missing piece of the puzzle they needed to bring this case to its conclusion.

Now she saw her destination, not far away. Mindful of what had happened to the Camaro, and not wanting to jeopardize Pam's car too – if 522 had been behind the repossession, as she suspected – Sachs cruised around the block until she found the rarest of all phenomena in Manhattan: a legal, unoccupied parking space.

How 'bout that?

Maybe it was a good sign.

'Why are you doing this?' Ron Pulaski whispered to Mark Whitcomb as they stood in a deserted Queens alleyway.

But the killer ignored him. 'Listen to me.'

'We were friends, I thought.'

'Well, everybody thinks a lot of things that turn out not to be true. That's life.' Whitcomb cleared his throat. He seemed edgy, uncomfortable. Pulaski remembered Sachs saying that the killer was feeling the pressure of their pursuit, which made him careless. It also made him more dangerous.

Pulaski was breathing hard.

Whitcomb looked around again, fast, then back at the young officer. He kept the gun steady and it was clear he knew how to use it. 'Are you fucking listening to me?'

'Goddamnit. I'm listening.'

'I don't want this investigation to go any further. It's time for it to stop.'

'Stop? I'm in Patrol. How can I stop anything?'

'I was telling you: Sabotage it. Lose some evidence. Send people in the wrong direction.'

'I won't do that,' the young officer muttered defiantly.

Whitcomb shook his head, looking almost disgusted. 'Yes, you will. You can make this easy or hard, Ron.'

'What about my wife? Can you get her out of there?'

'I can do anything I want.'

The man who knows everything . . .

The young officer closed his eyes, grinding his teeth together the way he'd done as a kid. He looked at the building where Jenny was being held.

Jenny, the woman who looked just like Myra Weinburg.

Ron Pulaski now resigned himself to what he had to do.

It was terrible, it was foolish, but he had no choice. He was cornered.

His head down, he muttered, 'Okay.'

'You'll do it?'

'I said I would,' he snapped.

'That's smart, Ron. Very smart.'

'But I want you to promise' – Pulaski hesitated for a fraction of a second, glancing behind Whitcomb and then back—'that she and the baby'll be out today.'

Whitcomb caught the glance and quickly looked behind him. As he did, the muzzle of his gun moved slightly off target.

Pulaski decided he'd played it just right, and he struck fast. With his left hand the young officer shoved the gun farther away and lifted his leg, pulling a small revolver from an ankle holster. Amelia Sachs had instructed him always to have one with him.

The killer cursed and tried to back up but Pulaski kept a death grip on his shooting hand and he swung the pistol into Whitcomb's face hard, snapping cartilage.

The man gave a muffled scream, blood streaming. The Compliance officer went down and Pulaski managed to rip his pistol out of his fingers but he couldn't keep a grip on it himself. Whitcomb's black weapon went cartwheeling to the ground as the men locked together in a clumsy wrestling match. The gun clunked to the asphalt without discharging and Whitcomb, wide-eyed with panic and fury, shoved Pulaski into the wall and grabbed for his hand.

'No, no!'

Whitcomb snapped forward with a head butt and Pulaski, recalling the terror of the club hitting him in the forehead years ago, recoiled instinctively. Which gave Whitcomb just the chance he needed to shove Pulaski's backup toward the sky, and with his other hand draw the Glock, aiming it at the young officer's head.

Leaving him with only enough time to issue a sound bite of prayer and to fix on an image of his wife and children, a vivid portrait to carry with him to heaven.

Finally the electricity came back on, and Cooper and Rhyme quickly got back to work on the evidence from the Joe Malloy killing. They were alone in the lab; Lon Sellitto was downtown, trying to get his suspension overturned.

The pictures of the scene were unrevealing and the physical evidence wasn't extremely helpful. The shoeprint was clearly 522's, the same as they'd found earlier. The fragments of leaves were from houseplants: ficus and Aglaonema, or Chinese evergreen. The trace was unsourceable soil, more of the Trade Towers dust, and a white powder that turned out to be Coffee-mate. The duct tape was generic; no source could be located.

Rhyme was surprised at the amount of blood on the evidence. He thought back to Sellitto's description of the captain.

He's a crusader . . .

Despite his protests of detachment, he found himself very troubled by Malloy's death – and how vicious it had been. And Rhyme's anger burned hotter. His uneasiness too. Several times he glanced out the window, as if 522 were sneaking up at that moment, though he'd had Thom lock all the doors and windows and turn on the security cameras.

JOSEPH MALLOY HOMICIDE SCENE

- Size-11 Skechers work shoe
- Houseplant leaves: ficus and Aglaonema – Chinese evergreen
- Dirt, untraceable
- Dust, from Trade Center attack
- Coffee-mate
- Duct tape, generic, untraceable

'Add the plants and Coffee-mate to the nonplanted evidence chart, Mel.'

The technician walked to the whiteboard and penned in the additions.

'Not much. Damn, not much at all.'

Then Rhyme blinked. Another pounding on the door. Thom went to answer it. Mel Cooper moved away from the whiteboard and his hand slipped to the thin pistol on his hip.

But the visitor wasn't 522. It was an inspector with the NYPD, Herbert Glenn. A middle-aged man, with impressive posture, Rhyme observed. His suit was cheap but the shoes were polished to perfection. Several other voices sounded in the hallway, behind.

After introductions, Glenn said, 'I'm afraid I have to talk to you about an officer you work with.'

Sellitto? Or Sachs? What had happened?

Glenn said evenly, 'His name is Ron Pulaski. You do work with him, don't you?'

Oh, no.

The rookie . . .

Pulaski dead, and his wife in the bureaucratic hell of detention with her baby. What would she do?

'Tell me what happened!'

Glenn glanced behind him and gestured two other men into the room, a gray-haired man in a dark suit and a younger, shorter one, dressed similarly, but with a large bandage on his nose. The inspector introduced Samuel Brockton and Mark Whitcomb, employees of SSD. Brockton, Rhyme noted, was on the suspect list, though apparently he had an alibi for the rape/murder. Whitcomb, it turned out, was his assistant in the Compliance Department.

'Tell me about Pulaski!'

Inspector Glenn continued. 'I'm afraid—' His phone rang

and he took the call. Glenn glanced at Brockton and Whitcomb as he spoke in hushed tones. Finally he disconnected.

'Tell me what's happened to Ron Pulaski. I want to know now!'

The doorbell rang and Thom and Mel Cooper ushered more people into Rhyme's lab. One was a burly man with an FBI agent identification badge around his neck and the other was Ron Pulaski, who was in handcuffs.

Brockton pointed to a chair and the FBI agent deposited the young officer there. Pulaski was obviously shaken, and dusty and rumpled, flecked with blood, but otherwise unhurt, it seemed. Whitcomb too sat and gingerly touched his nose. He didn't look at anyone.

Samuel Brockton showed him his ID. 'I'm an agent with the Compliance Division of the U.S. Department of Homeland Security. Mark's my assistant. Your officer attacked a federal agent.'

'Who was threatening me at gunpoint without identifying himself. After he'd—'

Compliance Division? Rhyme had never heard of it. But within the complex warren of Homeland Security, organizations came and went like unsuccessful Detroit cars.

'I thought you were with SSD?'

'We have offices at SSD but we're federal government employees.'

And what the hell had Pulaski been up to? Relief now ebbing, while irritation flowed.

The rookie started to continue but Brockton silenced him. Rhyme, though, said sternly to the gray-suited man, 'No, let him talk.'

Brockton debated. His eyes revealed a patient confidence that suggested Pulaski, or anyone else, could say whatever he wanted and it wouldn't affect Brockton in the least. He nodded.

The rookie told Rhyme about meeting Whitcomb, in hopes

of getting Jenny released from INS detention. The man asked him to sabotage the 522 investigation, then pulled a gun and threatened him when he refused. Pulaski had struck Whitcomb in the face with his backup gun and they'd fought.

Rhyme snapped to Brockton and Glenn, 'Why're you interfering with our case?'

Brockton now seemed to notice that Rhyme was disabled, then disregarded the fact immediately. He said in a calm baritone, 'We tried it the subtle way. If Officer Pulaski had agreed we wouldn't have to crack the whip . . . This case has caused a lot of headaches for a lot of people. I was supposed to be meeting with Congress and Justice all week. Had to cancel everything and hightail it back up here to see what the hell was going on . . . All right, this is off the record. Everybody?'

Rhyme muttered agreement, and Cooper and Pulaski concurred.

'The Compliance Division does threat analysis and provides security to private companies that might be targets of terrorists. Big players in the country's infrastructure. Oil companies, airlines, banks. Data miners, like SSD. We have agents on site.'

Sachs had said Brockton spent a lot of time in Washington. That explained why.

'Then why lie about it, why say you're SSD employees?' Pulaski blurted. Rhyme had never seen the young man angry. He sure was now.

'We need to keep a low profile,' Brockton explained. 'You can see why pipelines and drug companies and food processors would be great targets for terrorists. Well, think what someone could do with the information that SSD has. The economy would be crippled if their computers were brought down. Or what if assassins learned details of executives' or politicians' whereabouts and other personal information from innerCircle?'

'Did you have Lon Sellitto's drug test report changed?'

'No, this suspect of yours — Five Twenty-Two — must've done that,' Inspector Glenn said. 'And had Officer Pulaski's wife arrested.'

'Why do you want the investigation stopped?' Pulaski blurted. 'Don't you see how dangerous this man is?' He was speaking to Mark Whitcomb but the Compliance assistant continued to examine the floor and remained silent.

'Our profile is that he's an outlier,' Glenn explained.

'A what?'

'An anomaly. He's a nonrecurring event,' Brockton explained. 'SSD has run an analysis of the situation. The profiling and predictive modeling told us that a sociopath like this will hit a saturation point any time now. He'll stop what he's doing. He'll simply go away.'

'But he hasn't, now has he?'

'Not yet,' Brockton said. 'But he will. The programs're never wrong.'

'They'll be wrong if one more person dies.'

'We have to be realistic. It's a balance. We can't let anybody know how valuable SSD is as a terrorist target. And we can't let anybody know about the Compliance Division of DHS. We have to keep SSD and Compliance off the grid as much as possible. A murder investigation puts them both *on* it in a very big way.'

Glenn added, 'You want to follow up conventional leads, Lincoln, go ahead. Forensics, wits, fine. But you'll have to keep SSD out of it. That press conference was a huge mistake.'

'We talked to Ron Scott in the mayor's office, we talked to Joe Malloy. They okayed it.'

'Well, they didn't check with the right people. It's jeopardized our relationship with SSD. Andrew Sterling doesn't *have* to provide us with computer support, you know.'

He sounded like the shoe-company president, terrified of upsetting Sterling and SSD.

Brockton added, 'Okay, now, the party line is that your killer didn't get his information from SSD. Actually, that's the only line.'

'Do you understand that Joseph Malloy is dead because of SSD and innerCircle?'

Glenn's face tightened. He sighed. 'I'm sorry about that. Very sorry. But he was killed in the course of an investigation. Tragic. But that's the nature of being a cop.'

The party line . . . the only line . . .

'So' Brockton said, 'SSD is no longer part of the investigation. Understood?'

A chill nod.

Glenn gestured to the FBI agent. 'You can let him go now.'

The man uncuffed Pulaski, who stood, rubbing his wrists.

Rhyme said, 'Get Lon Sellitto reinstated. And have Pulaski's wife released.'

Glenn looked at Brockton, who shook his head. 'Doing that at this point in time would be an admission that maybe data-mined information and SSD were involved in the crimes. We'll have to let those things go for the time being.'

'That is bullshit. You know Lon Sellitto's never done any drugs in his life.'

Glenn said, 'And the inquiry will clear him. We'll let the matter run its course.'

'No, goddamnit! According to the information the killer put into the system – he's *already* guilty. Just like Jenny Pulaski. All this is on their record!'

The inspector said calmly, 'This is how we'll have to leave it for now.'

The federal agents and Glenn walked to the door.

'Oh, Mark,' Pulaski called. Whitcomb turned back. 'Sorry.'

The federal officer blinked in surprise at the apology and touched his bandaged nose. Then Pulaski continued, 'That it was just your nose I broke. Fuck you, Judas.'

Well, the rookie's got some backbone after all.

After they'd left, Pulaski called his wife but couldn't get through. He angrily snapped his phone shut. 'I'll tell you, Lincoln, I don't care what they say, I'm not just packing up.'

'Don't worry. We'll keep right on going. Hey, they can't fire me – I'm a civilian. They can only fire you and Mel.'

'Well, I—' Cooper was frowning.

'Relax, Mel. I *do* have a sense of humor, despite what everybody thinks. Nobody'll find out – as long as the rookie here doesn't beat up any more federal agents. Okay, this Robert Carpenter, the SSD customer. I want him. Now.'

Chapter
FORTY-TWO

So I'm '522.'

I've been wondering why They picked that number. Myra 9834 wasn't my five hundred twenty-second victim (what a lovely thought!). None of the victims' addresses contained the number . . . Wait. The date. Of course. She was killed last Sunday – the twenty-second day of the fifth month – and that's when They started after me.

So to Them I'm a number. Just like They're numbers to me. I feel flattered. I'm in my Closet now, having completed most of my research. It's after work, people are heading home, out to dinner, off to see friends. But that's the great thing about data; they never sleep, and my soldiers can call in an air strike on anyone's life at any hour I choose, in any location.

At the moment the Prescott family and I are spending a few moments together before the attacks begin. The police will soon be guarding the houses of my enemies and their families . . . But they don't understand the nature of my weapons. Poor Joseph Malloy gave me plenty to work with.

For instance, this Detective Lorenzo – that is, Lon – Sellitto (he's taken great pains to conceal his real first name) is suspended but more awaits. That unfortunate incident a few years ago in which the perp was shot and killed during an arrest . . . new evidence will arise revealing that the suspect did not in fact have a gun – the witness was lying. The dead boy's mother will hear about that. And I'll send a few racist letters in his name to some right-wing Web sites. Then get the Reverend Al involved – that'll be the death knell. Poor Lon may actually do time.

And I've been checking Sellitto's tethered individuals. I'll dream up something for his teenage son by his first wife. A few drug charges, maybe. Like father, like son. Nice appeal to it.

That Polish fellow, Pulaski, well, he'll eventually be able to convince Homeland Security that his wife isn't a terrorist or an illegal. But won't they both be surprised when his child's birth records disappear and another couple, whose newborn vanished from the hospital a year ago, happens to learn that their missing boy might be Pulaski's? If nothing else the little guy'll be in foster-care limbo over the months it'll take to sort things out. That'll damage him forever. (I know this only too well.)

And then we come to Amelia 7303 and this Lincoln Rhyme. Well, just because I'm in a bad mood, Rose Sachs, who's scheduled for cardiac surgery next month, will lose her insurance due to – well, I think I'll make it past instances of fraud. And Amelia 7303's probably pissed off about her car but wait till she gets the really bad news: her careless consumer debt. Maybe $200,000 or so. With a nearly usurious rate of interest.

But those are simply appetizers. I've learned that a former boyfriend of hers was convicted of hijacking, assault, larceny and extortion. Some new witnesses will send anonymous e-mails that she was involved, too, and that there's hidden loot in her mother's garage, which I'll plant there before I call Internal Affairs.

She'll beat the charges – statute of limitations – but the publicity will ruin her reputation. Thank you, freedom of the press. God bless America . . .

Death is one type of transaction guaranteed to slow your pursuers down, but the nonlethal tactics can be just as effective and are, to me, far more elegant.

And as for this Lincoln Rhyme . . . Well, that's an interesting situation. Of course, I made the mistake of selecting his cousin in the first place. But, in fairness, I checked all of Arthur 3480's tethered individuals and didn't find any hits for his cousin. Which is curious. They're related by blood, yet they've had no contact in a decade.

I've made the mistake of stinging the beast awake. He's the best adversary I've ever been up against. He stopped me on the way to DeLeon 6832's house; he actually caught me in the act, which no one has ever done. And, according to Malloy's breathless account, he's getting closer all the time.

But, of course, I have a plan for this too. I don't have the benefit of innerCircle at the moment – have to be careful now – but journalists' articles and other sources of data are sufficiently illuminating. The problem, of course, is how to destroy the life of someone like Rhyme, whose physical life is largely destroyed anyway. Finally a solution occurs to me: If he's so dependent I'll destroy someone he's tethered to. Rhyme's caregiver, Thom Reston, will be my next target. If the young man dies – in a particularly unpleasant way – I doubt Rhyme will ever recover from that. The investigation will wither; no one else will pursue it the way he's been doing.

I'll get Thom into the trunk of my car and we'll head to another warehouse. There, I'll take my time with the Krusius Brothers razor. I'll record the whole session on tape and e-mail that to Rhyme. Being the hardworking criminalist that he seems to be, he'll have to view the gruesome tape carefully to look for clues. He'll have to watch it over and over again.

I guarantee it will ruin him for the case, if not destroy him altogether.

I go into room three of my Closet and find one of my video cams. Batteries are nearby. And in room two I collect the Krusius in its old box. There's still a brown wash of dried blood on the blade. Nancy 3470. Two years ago. (The court has just turned down the final appeal of her murderer, Jason 4971, the grounds for reversal being fabricated evidence, a claim that even his attorney probably found pathetic.)

The razor is dull. I remember meeting some resistance from Nancy 3470's ribs; she thrashed around more than I expected. No matter. A little work with one of my eight grinding wheels, then a leather strop and I'll be in business.

Now, the adrenaline from the hunt was flooding through Amelia Sachs.

The evidence in her garden had led her on a convoluted trail but she had a gut feeling – excuse me, Rhyme – that this present mission would be productive. She parked Pam's car along the city street and hurried to the address of the next person on her list of a half dozen, one of whom she desperately hoped would give her the final clue to 522's identity.

Two had been unsuccessful. Would the third one be the answer? Driving around town like this was a sort of macabre scavenger hunt, she reflected.

It was evening now and Sachs checked the address under a streetlight, found the town house and walked up the few steps to the front door. She was reaching for the bell when something began to nag.

She paused.

Was it the paranoia she'd been feeling all day? A sense of being watched?

Sachs glanced around fast – at the few men and women on the street; at the windows of the residences and small shops nearby . . . But nobody seemed threatening. Nobody seemed to be paying attention to her.

She began to press the buzzer again but lowered her hand. Something was off . . .

What?

Then she understood. It wasn't that she was being watched; it was a scent that troubled her. And with a jolt she knew what it was: mold. She was smelling mold, the scent coming from the very town house where she now stood.

Just a coincidence?

Sachs silently walked down the stairs and around to the side of the place into the cobblestoned alley. The building was very large – narrow from the front but quite deep. She moved farther into the alley and eased up to a window. Which was covered with newspaper. Scanning the side of the building; yes, they were all covered over. She recalled Terry Dobyns's words: *And the windows will be painted black or taped over. He has to keep the outside world away . . .*

She'd come here merely to get information – this *couldn't* be 522's place; the clues didn't add up. But she knew now that they'd been wrong; there was no doubt this was the killer's home.

She reached for her phone but suddenly heard a scuttling on the alley cobblestones behind her. Eyes wide, forsaking the phone for the gun, she turned fast. But before her hand made it to the Glock's grip, she was tackled hard. She slammed into the side of the town house. Stunned, she dropped to her knees.

Glancing up, gasping, she saw the hard dots of eyes in the killer's face, saw the stained blade of the razor he held as it began its journey to her throat.

Chapter
FORTY-THREE

'Command, call Sachs.'

But the phone went to voice mail.

'Damnit, where is she? Find her . . . Pulaski?' Rhyme wheeled his chair around to face the young man, who was on the phone. 'What's the story with Carpenter?'

He held up a hand. Then hung up. 'I finally got his assistant. Carpenter left work early, had some errands. He should be home by now.'

'I want somebody over there. Now.'

Mel Cooper tried paging Sachs and, when there was no response, said, 'Nothing.' He made a few other calls and reported, 'Nope. No luck.'

'Did Five Twenty-Two get her service dropped, like the electricity?'

'No, they say the accounts're active. It's just that the devices are disabled – broken or the batteries removed.'

'What? Are they sure?' The dread within him began to expand.

The doorbell rang and Thom went to answer it.

Lon Sellitto, his shirt half untucked and face sweaty, strode into the room. 'They can't do anything about the suspension.

It's automatic. Even if I take another test they have to keep it active until IA investigates. Fucking computers. I had somebody call PublicSure. They're quote "looking into it," which you know what that means.' He glanced at Pulaski. 'What happened with your wife?'

'Still in detention.'

'Jesus.'

'And it gets worse.' Rhyme told Sellitto about Brockton, Whitcomb and Glenn and the Compliance Division of Homeland Security.

'Shit. Never heard of it.'

'And they want us to hold off on the investigation, at least as far as SSD's involved. But we've got another problem. Amelia's missing.'

'What?' Sellitto barked.

'Looks that way. I don't know where she was going after she went to her town house. She never called . . . Oh, Christ, the power was out, the phones were off. Check voice mail. Maybe she called.'

Cooper dialed the number. And they learned that Sachs *had* called. But she'd said only that she was following up on a lead and said nothing more. She asked that Rhyme call her and she'd explain.

Rhyme jammed his eyes closed in frustration.

A lead . . .

To where? One of their suspects. He gazed at the chart.

Andrew Sterling, President, Chief Executive Officer
  Alibi — on Long Island, verified. Confirmed by son
Sean Cassel, Director of Sales and Marketing
  No alibi
Wayne Gillespie, Director of Technical Operations
  No alibi
Samuel Brockton, Director, Compliance Department

Alibi – hotel records confirm presence in Washington
Peter Arlonzo-Kemper, Director of Human Resources
Alibi – with wife, verified by her (biased?)
Steven Shraeder, Technical Service and Support
Manager, day shift
Alibi – in office, according to time sheets
Faruk Mameda, Technical Service and Support
Manager, night shift
No alibi
Alibi for groundskeeper's killing (in office, according to
time sheets)
Client of SSD (?)
Robert Carpenter (?)
UNSUB recruited by Andrew Sterling (?)
Runnerboy?

Did the lead involve one of them?

'Lon, go check out Carpenter.'

'What, like, "Hi, I used to be a cop but will you let me question you 'cause I'm such a nice person even though you don't have to"?'

'Yeah, Lon, just like that.'

Sellitto turned to Cooper. 'Mel, gimme your shield.'

'My shield?' the tech asked nervously.

'I won't get it scratched,' the big man muttered.

'I'm more worried about getting *me* suspended.'

'Welcome to the fucking club.' Sellitto took the badge and got Carpenter's address from Pulaski. 'I'll let you know what happens.'

'Lon, be careful. Five Twenty-Two's feeling cornered. He's going to hit back hard. And remember he's—'

'The son of a bitch who knows everything.' Sellitto stalked out of the lab.

Rhyme noticed Pulaski staring at the charts. 'Detective?'

'What?'

'There's something else I'm thinking of.' He tapped the whiteboard containing the suspects' names. 'Andrew Sterling's alibi. Well, when he was on Long Island he told me his son was hiking in Westchester. He'd called Andy from out of town, and we could see the time in his phone records. That checked out.'

'So?'

'Well, I remembered Sterling said his son took the train to Westchester. But when I talked to Andy, he said he *drove* up there.' Pulaski cocked his head. 'And there's something else, sir. The day the groundskeeper was killed, I checked the time sheets. I saw Andy's name. He left right after Miguel Abrera, the janitor. I mean, seconds afterwards. I didn't think about it because Andy wasn't a suspect.'

'But the son doesn't have any access to innerCircle,' Cooper said, nodding at the suspect chart.

'Not according to what his father said. But . . .' Pulaski shook his head. 'See, Andrew Sterling's been so helpful, we took whatever he told us at face value. He said that nobody but those people on the suspect list have access. But we don't know that independently. We never verified who could or couldn't log into innerCircle.'

Cooper offered, 'Maybe Andy went through his dad's PDA or computer to get a passcode.'

'You're on a roll, Pulaski. Okay, Mel, you're top dog now. Get a tactical team over to Andy Sterling's house.'

Even the best predictive analysis, powered by brilliant artificial brains like Xpectation, can't get it right all the time.

Who in a million years would have guessed that Amelia 7303, sitting stunned and handcuffed twenty feet away, would have come right to my door?

Some luck, I must say. I was just about to head off to get

Thom's vivisection under way when I noticed her through the window. My life seems to work that way, good fortune a trade-off for the edginess.

I consider the situation calmly. Okay, her colleagues at the police department don't suspect me; she only came here to show me the composite picture I found in her pocket, along with a list of six other people. Two at the top are crossed off. I'm unlucky number three. Someone will surely ask about her; when they do I'll say, yes, she came here to show me the composite and then left. And that'll be it.

I've dismantled her electronics and am placing them in appropriate boxes. I'd considered using *her* phone to record the final, thrashing moments of Thom Reston. It has a nice symmetry, an elegance. But, of course, she'll have to vanish completely. She'll go to sleep in my basement, next to Caroline 8630 and Fiona 4892.

Disappear completely.

Not as tidy as it could be – police do love to have the body – but it's good news for me.

I'll get to take a proper trophy this time. No mere fingernails from my Amelia 7303 . . .

Chapter
FORTY-FOUR

'Well, what's the goddamn story?' Rhyme snapped to Pulaski.

The rookie was three miles away, in Manhattan, at the Upper East Side town house of Andrew Sterling, Jr.

'Have you gone in? Is Sachs there?'

'I don't think Andy's the one, sir.'

'You *think*? Or he isn't the one?'

'He's not the one.'

'Explain.'

Pulaski told Rhyme that, yes, Andy Sterling had lied about his activities on Sunday. But not to cover up his role as a killer and rapist. He'd told his father he'd taken the train to Westchester to go hiking but the truth was that he'd driven, as he'd let slip when talking to Pulaski.

With two ESU officers and Pulaski in front of him, the flustered young man blurted out why he'd lied to his father when he said he'd been on Metro North. Andy himself didn't have a driver's license.

But his boyfriend did. Andrew Sterling might have been the world's number-one purveyor of information but he didn't know his son was gay, and the young man had never summoned the courage to tell him.

A call to Andy's boyfriend confirmed that they were both out of town at the time of the killings. The E-ZPass operations center confirmed that this was the case.

'Damn, okay, get on back here, Pulaski.'

'Yes, sir.'

Walking along the dusky sidewalk, Lon Sellitto was thinking, Shit, should've gotten Cooper's *gun* too. Of course, borrowing a shield was one thing if you were suspended but a weapon was something else. That would've moved the sorta bad into the shitstorm bad, if Internal Affairs found out.

And it'd give them grounds to legitimately suspend him, when the drug test came back clean.

Drugs. Shit.

He found the address he sought, Carpenter's, a town house on the Upper East Side in a quiet neighborhood. The lights were on but he saw no one inside. He strode up to the doorway and pressed the buzzer.

He believed he heard some noise from inside. Footsteps. A door.

Then nothing for a long minute.

Sellitto instinctively reached for where his weapon had once been.

Shit.

Finally the curtain on a side window parted and fell back. The door opened and Sellitto found himself looking at a solidly built man, hair combed over. He was gazing at the illicit gold shield. His eyes flickered with uncertainty.

'Mr Carpenter—'

He got nothing else out before the uneasiness vanished and the man's face screwed up in pure anger and he raged, 'Goddamn. Goddamnit!'

Lon Sellitto hadn't been in a fight with a perp for years, and he now realized that this man could easily beat him bloody and then cut his throat. Why the hell didn't I borrow Cooper's gun after all, whatever happened?

But, it turned out, Sellitto wasn't the source of the anger. It was, curiously, the head of SSD.

'That fucker Andrew Sterling did this, right? He called you? He's implicated me in those murders we keep hearing about. Oh, Christ, what'm I going to do? I'm probably already in the system and Watchtower's got my name on lists all over the country. Oh, man. What a fucking idiot I've been, getting caught up in SSD.'

Sellitto's concern diminished. He put away the badge and asked the man to step outside. He did.

'So I'm right – Andrew's behind this, isn't he?' Carpenter snarled.

Sellitto didn't reply but asked his whereabouts at the time Malloy had died earlier that day.

Carpenter thought back. 'I was in meetings.' He volunteered the name of several officials from a large bank in town, their phone numbers too.

'And Sunday afternoon?'

'My friend and I had some people over. A brunch.'

An easily verifiable alibi.

Sellitto phoned Rhyme to give him what he'd found. He got Cooper, who said he'd check the alibis. After he'd disconnected, the detective turned back to the agitated Bob Carpenter.

'He's the most vindictive prick I've ever done business with.'

Sellitto told him that, yes, his name had been provided by SSD. At this news Carpenter closed his eyes momentarily. The anger was lessening, replaced by dismay.

'What did he say about me?'

'It seems you downloaded information about the victims just before they were killed. In several murders over the past few months.'

Carpenter said, 'This's what happens when Andrew's upset. He gets even. I never thought it'd be like that . . .' Then he frowned. 'Over the past few months? This downloading – when was the most recent?'

'In the last couple weeks.'

'Well, it couldn't be me. I've been locked out of the Watchtower system since early March.'

'Locked out?'

Carpenter nodded. 'Andrew blocked me.'

Sellitto's phone trilled, Mel Cooper calling back. He explained that at least two of the sources had confirmed Carpenter's whereabouts. Sellitto had the tech call Rodney Szarnek to double-check the data on the CD Pulaski had been given. He snapped the phone shut and told Carpenter, 'Why were you blocked out?'

'See, what happened was I have a data-warehousing company, and—'

'*Data* warehousing?'

'We store data that companies like SSD process.'

'Not, like, a warehouse where you store merchandise?'

'No, no. It's all computer storage. On servers out in New Jersey and Pennsylvania. Anyway, I got . . . well, you could say I got seduced by Andrew Sterling. All his success, the money. I wanted to start *mining* the data too, like SSD, not just storing it. I was going to carve out a niche market in a few industries that SSD isn't that strong in. I wasn't really competing, it wasn't illegal.'

Sellitto could hear the desperation in the man's voice as he justified whatever he'd done.

'It was only nickel-and-dime stuff. But Andrew found out and locked me out of innerCircle and Watchtower. He threatened to sue me. I've been trying to negotiate but today he fired me. Well, terminated our contract. I really didn't do anything wrong.' His voice cracked. 'It was just business . . .'

'And you think Sterling changed the files to make it look like you were the killer?'

'Well, somebody at SSD had to.'

So the bottom line, Sellitto reflected, is that Carpenter's not a suspect and this was all a big fucking waste of time. 'I don't have any more questions. 'Night.'

But Carpenter was having a change of heart. The anger was gone completely, replaced by an expression that Sellitto decided was desperation, if not fear. 'Wait, Officer, don't get the wrong idea. I spoke too fast. I'm not suggesting it was Andrew. I was mad. But it was just a reaction. You won't tell him, will you?'

As he walked away the detective glanced back. The businessman actually looked like he was going to cry.

So yet another suspect was innocent.

First, Andy Sterling. Now, Robert Carpenter. When Sellitto returned he immediately called Rodney Szarnek, who said he'd find out what went wrong. The techie called back ten minutes later. The first thing he said was, 'Heh. Oops.'

Rhyme sighed. 'Go ahead.'

'Okay, Carpenter *did* download enough lists to give him the information he'd need to target the victims and fall guys. But it was over the course of two years. All part of legitimate marketing campaigns. And nothing since early March.'

'You said the information was downloaded just before the crimes.'

'That's what it said on the spreadsheet itself. But the metadata showed that somebody at SSD had changed the dates. The information on your cousin, for instance, he got two years ago.'

'And so somebody at SSD did that to point us away from him and toward Carpenter.'

'Right.'

'Now, the big question: Who the hell rearranged the dates? That's Five Twenty-Two.'

But the computer man said, 'There's no other information encoded in the metadata. The administrator and root-access logs aren't—'

'Just no. That's the short answer?'

'Correct.'

'You're sure?'

'Positive.'

'Thanks,' he muttered. They disconnected.

The son eliminated, Carpenter eliminated . . .

Where are you, Sachs?

Rhyme felt a jolt. He'd almost used her first name. But it was an unspoken rule between them, they used only their last names when referring to the other. Bad luck otherwise. As if the luck could get any worse.

'Linc,' said Sellitto, pointing at the board containing the list of suspects. 'The only thing I can think of is to check out every one of 'em. Now.'

'Well, how do we do that, Lon? We've got an inspector who doesn't even want this case to exist. We can't exactly . . .' His voice faded as his eyes settled on the profile of 522 and then the evidence charts.

His cousin's dossier too, on the turning frame nearby.

Lifestyle

Dossier 1A. Consumer products preferences

Dossier 1B. Consumer services preferences

Dossier 1C. Travel

Dossier 1D. Medical

Dossier 1E. Leisure-time preferences

Financial/Educational/Professional

Dossier 2A. Educational history

Dossier 2B. Employment history, w/income

Dossier 2C. Credit history/current report and rating

Dossier 2D. Business products and services preferences

Governmental/Legal

Dossier 3A. Vital records

Dossier 3B. Voter registration

Dossier 3C. Legal history

Dossier 3D. Criminal history

Dossier 3E. Compliance

Dossier 3F. Immigration and naturalization

Rhyme read through the document several times quickly. Then he looked at other documents taped up on the evidence boards. Something wasn't right.

He called Szarnek back. 'Rodney, tell me: How much storage space on a hard drive does a thirty-page document take up? Like that SSD dossier I have here.'

'Heh. A dossier? Text only, I assume.'

'Yes.'

'It'd be in a database so it'd be compressed . . . Make it twenty-five K, tops.'

'That's pretty small, right?'

'Heh. A fart in the hurricane of data storage.'

Rhyme rolled his eyes at the response. 'I've got one more question for you.'

'Heh. Shoot.'

*   *   *

Her head throbbed in agony and she tasted blood from the cut in her mouth after colliding with the stone wall.

With the razor at her throat, the killer had taken her gun and dragged her through a basement door then up steep stairs into the 'façade' side of the town house, the front, a modern, stark place echoing the black-and-white decor of SSD.

Then he led her to a door against the back wall in the living room.

It turned out to be, ironically, a closet. He pushed through some stale-smelling clothes and opened another door against the back wall, dragged her inside and relieved her of her pager, PDA, cell phone, keys and the switchblade knife in the back pocket of her slacks. He shoved her against a radiator, between tall stacks of newspaper, and cuffed her to the rusty metal. She looked around at the hoarder's paradise, moldy, dim, stinking of old, stinking of used, and filled with more junk and refuse than she'd ever seen in one place. The killer took all her gear to a large, cluttered desk. With her own knife he began to disassemble her electronics. He worked meticulously, savoring each component he extracted, as if dissecting a corpse for the organs.

Now she was watching the killer at his desk, typing on his keyboard. He was surrounded by huge stacks of newspapers, towers of folded paper bags, boxes of matches, glassware, boxes labeled 'Cigarettes' and 'Buttons' and 'Paper Clips,' old cans and boxes of food from the sixties and seventies, cleaning supplies. Hundreds of other containers.

But she wasn't paying attention to the inventory. She was reflecting, in shock, how he'd tricked them. Five Twenty-Two wasn't one of their suspects at all. They were wrong about the bullying executives, the techs, the clients, the hacker, Andrew Sterling's hired gun to drum up business for the company.

And yet he *was* an employee of SSD.

Why the hell hadn't she considered the obvious?

Five Twenty-Two was the security guard who'd taken her on a tour of the data pens on Monday. She remembered the name badge. John. His last name was Rollins. He must have seen her and Pulaski arrive at the guard station in the SSD lobby on Monday and moved in quickly to volunteer to escort them to Sterling's office. He'd then hovered nearby to find out about the purpose of their visit. Or maybe he'd even known ahead of time they were coming and arranged to be on duty that morning.

The man who knows everything . . .

Because he'd freely escorted her around the Gray Rock on Monday she should have known that the guards had access to all the pens and the Intake Center. She recalled that once you were in the pens, you didn't need a passcode to log on to innerCircle. She still wasn't sure how he'd smuggled out disks containing data – even he had been searched when they'd left the data pen – but somehow he'd managed to.

She squinted, hoping the pain in her skull would diminish. It didn't. She glanced up – to the wall in front of the desk, where a painting hung – a photorealistic portrait of a family. Of course: the Harvey Prescott he'd murdered Alice Sanderson for, her death blamed on innocent Arthur Rhyme.

Her eyes finally accustomed to the dim light, Sachs was looking over the adversary. She hadn't paid attention to him when he'd escorted her around SSD. But now she could see him clearly – a thin man, pale, a nondescript but handsome face. His hollow eyes moved quickly and his fingers were very long, his arms strong.

The killer sensed her scrutiny. He turned and looked her over with hungry eyes. Then he returned to the computer and continued typing furiously. Dozens of other keyboards, most of them broken or with the letters worn down, sat in piles on the floor. Useless to anybody else. But 522, of course, was incapable of throwing them away. Surrounding him were thousands of yellow legal pads, filled with minute, precise handwriting – the source of the flecks of paper they'd found at one of the scenes.

The smell of mold and unwashed clothing and linens was overwhelming. He must be so used to the stench he doesn't even notice it. Or maybe he enjoys it.

Sachs closed her eyes and rested her head against a stack of newspapers. No weapons, helpless . . . What could she possibly do? She was furious with herself for not leaving a more detailed message with Rhyme about where she was going.

Helpless . . .

But then some words came to her. The slogan of the entire 522 case: *Knowledge is power.*

Well, *get* some knowledge, damnit. Figure out something about him *you* can use for a weapon.

Think!

SSD security guard John Rollins . . . That name meant nothing to her. It had never come up during the investigation. What was his connection to SSD, to the crimes, to the data?

Sachs scanned the dark room around her, overwhelmed by the amount of junk she saw.

Noise . . .

Focus. One thing at a time.

And then she noticed something against the far wall that caught her attention. It was one of his collections: a huge stack of ski-resort lift tickets.

Vail, Copper Mountain, Breckinridge, Beaver Creek.

Could it be?

Okay, it was worth the gamble.

'Peter,' she said confidently, 'you and I have to talk.'

At the name, he blinked and looked her way. For an instant his eyes flickered with uncertainty. It was almost like a slap in the face.

Yes, she was right. John Rollins was – what else? – an assumed identity. In reality he was Peter Gordon, the famous data scrounger who'd died . . . who'd *pretended* to die when SSD took over the company he worked for in Colorado some years ago.

'We were curious about the faked death. The DNA? How'd you manage that?'

He stopped typing, staring up at the painting. Finally he said, 'Isn't it funny about data? How we believe them without question.' He turned to her. 'If it's in a computer, we know it has to be true. If it involves the DNA deity then it *definitely* has to be right. Ask no more. End of story.'

Sachs said, 'So you – Peter Gordon – go missing. The police find your bike and a decomposed body wearing your clothes. Not much left after the animals, right? And they take hair and saliva samples from your house. Yep, the DNA matches. No doubt in the world. You're dead. But it wasn't your hair or saliva in your bathroom, was it? The man you killed, you took some hair from him and left it in your bathroom. And brushed his teeth, right?'

'And a little blood on the Gillette. You police do love your blood, don't you?'

'Who was the man you killed?'

'Some kid from California. Hitchhiker on I-70.'

Keep him uneasy – information's your only weapon. Use it! 'We never knew why you did it, though, Peter. Was it to sabotage the SSD takeover of Rocky Mountain Data? Or was it more?'

'Sabotage?' he whispered in astonishment. 'You just don't get it, do you? When Andrew Sterling and his folks from SSD came to Rocky Mountain and wanted to acquire it, I scrounged every bit of data I could find on him and the company. And what I saw was breathtaking! Andrew Sterling is God. He's the future of data, which means he's the future of society.

He could find data that I couldn't even imagine existed, and use it like a gun, or like medicine, or like holy water. I *needed* to be part of what he was doing.'

'But you couldn't be a data scrounger for SSD. Not for what you had planned, right? For your . . . *other* collecting? And the way you lived.' She nodded at the filled rooms.

His face grew dark, his eyes wide. 'I wanted to be part of SSD. Do you think I didn't? Oh, the places I could have gone! But that's not the card I was dealt.' He fell silent, then he waved a hand around him, indicating his collections. 'You think living this way is what I'd choose? Do you think I like it?' He voice came close to cracking. Breathing hard, he gave a faint smile. 'No, my life has to be off the grid. That's the only way I can survive. Off. The. Grid.'

'So you faked your death and stole an identity. Got yourself a new name and Social Security number, somebody who'd died.'

The emotion was gone now. 'A child, yeah. Jonathan Rollins, three, from Colorado Springs. It's easy to get a new identity. Survivalists do it every day. You can buy books on the subject . . .' A faint smile. 'Just remember to pay cash for them.'

'And you got a job as a security guard. But wouldn't somebody from SSD recognize you?'

'I never met anybody at the company in person. That's the wonder of the data-mining business. You can collect data and never leave the privacy of your own Closet.'

Then his voice faded. He seemed uneasy, considering what she'd told him. Were they in fact getting close to matching Rollins with Peter Gordon? Would someone else come to the town house to check things out further? He apparently decided he couldn't take the chance. Gordon snatched up the key to Pam's car. He'd want to hide it. The killer examined the fob. 'Cheap. No RFIDs. But *everybody's* scanning the license plates now. Where'd you park?'

'You think I'd tell you?'

He shrugged and left.

Her strategy had worked, grabbing a bit of knowledge and using it as a weapon. Not much, of course, but at least she'd bought a little time.

Was it, however, enough to do what she planned: get to the handcuff key stuffed deep in her slacks pocket?

Chapter
FORTY-FIVE

'Listen to me. My partner's missing. And I need to look at some files.'

Rhyme was speaking to Andrew Sterling via a high-definition video link.

The head of SSD was back in his austere office in the Gray Rock. He sat completely upright in what seemed to be a plain wooden chair, ironically mimicking Rhyme's stiff posture in his TDX. Sterling said in a soft voice, 'Sam Brockton talked to you. Inspector Glenn too.' Not a splinter of uneasiness in the voice. No emotion at all, in fact, though a pleasant smile rested on his face.

'I want to see my partner's dossier. The officer you met, Amelia Sachs. Her *whole* dossier.'

'What do you mean, "whole," Captain Rhyme?'

The criminalist noted that Sterling had used his title, which wasn't common knowledge. 'You know exactly what I mean.'

'No, I don't.'

'I want to see her 3E Compliance dossier.'

Another hesitation. 'Why? It's nothing. Some technical government filing information. Privacy Act disclosures.'

But the man was lying. CBI agent Kathryn Dance had

given him some insights into kinesics – body language – and the analysis of how people communicate. A hesitation before answering is often a sign of coming deception, since the subject is trying to formulate a credible, but false, answer. One speaks quickly when telling the truth; there's nothing to fabricate.

'Why don't you want me to see it, then?'

'There's just no reason to . . . It wouldn't help you at all.'

Lie.

Sterling's green eyes remained calm, though once they flicked sideways, and Rhyme realized he'd glanced at where Ron Pulaski would appear on his screen; the young officer was back in the lab, standing behind Rhyme.

'Then answer me a question.'

'Yes?'

'I was just talking to an NYPD computer man. I had him estimate how big my cousin's SSD dossier was.'

'Yes?'

'He said a thirty-page dossier of text would be about twenty-five K in size.'

'I'm as concerned as you are about your partner's well-being but—'

'I doubt that very much. Now listen to me.' A slightly raised eyebrow was Sterling's only response. 'A typical dossier is twenty-five kilobytes of data. But your brochure says you have over five hundred *petabytes* of information. That's so much data most people can't even comprehend it.'

Sterling wasn't responding.

'If a dossier averages twenty-five K, then the database for every human being on *Earth* would take up maybe a hundred and fifty *billion* K, to be generous. But innerCircle has more than five hundred *trillion* K. What's in the rest of innerCircle's hard drive space, Sterling?'

Another hesitation. 'Well, lots of things . . . Graphics

and photographs, they take up a huge amount of space. Administrative data, for instance.'

Lie.

'And tell me why would somebody have a Compliance file in the first place? Who has to comply with what?'

'We make sure that everyone's file *complies* with the requirements of the law.'

'Sterling, if that file isn't on its way to my computer in five minutes I'm going straight to the *Times* with the story that you aided and abetted a criminal who used your information to rape and murder. The Compliance Division folks in Washington aren't going to save you from those headlines. And the story'll run above the fold. I guarantee that.'

Now Sterling simply laughed, his face exuding confidence. 'I don't think that will happen. Now, Captain, I'm going to say good-bye.'

'Sterling—'

The screen went black.

Rhyme closed his eyes in frustration. The criminalist maneuvered his chair to the whiteboards containing the evidence charts and the list of suspects. He stared at Thom's and Sachs's lettering, some scrawled fast, some penned methodically.

But no answers presented themselves.

Where are you, Sachs?

He knew she lived on the edge, that he would never suggest she avoid the high-risk situations she seemed drawn to. But he was furious that she'd followed up on her damn lead without backup.

'Lincoln?' Ron Pulaski asked softly. Rhyme glanced up to see the young officer's eyes unusually cold as he stared at the crime-scene pictures of Myra Weinburg's body.

'What?'

He turned to the criminalist. 'I have an idea.'

* * *

The face, with the bandaged nose, was now filling the high-def screen.

'You *do* have access to innerCircle, don't you?' Ron Pulaski asked Mark Whitcomb in a cool voice. 'You said you weren't cleared but you are.'

The Compliance assistant sighed. But finally he said, 'That's right.' Holding eye contact with the webcam briefly, then looking away.

'Mark, we have a problem. We need you to help us.'

Pulaski explained about Sachs's disappearance and Rhyme's suspicion that the Compliance file might help them figure out where she'd gone. 'What's in the dossier?'

'A Compliance dossier?' Mark Whitcomb whispered. 'It's absolutely forbidden to access one. If they find out, I could go to jail. And what Sterling's reaction will be . . . it'll be worse than jail.'

Pulaski snapped, 'You weren't honest with us and people died.' Then he added more softly, 'We're the good guys, Mark. Help us out. Don't let anybody else get hurt. Please.'

He said nothing more, letting the silence roll up.

Good job, rookie, thought Rhyme, who was content to take the copilot's seat on this one.

Whitcomb grimaced. He looked around and up at the ceiling. Was he afraid of listening devices or surveillance cameras? Rhyme wondered. It seemed so, because both resignation and urgency filled his voice as he said, 'Write this down. We won't have much time.'

'Mel! Get over here. We're going into SSD's system, innerCircle.'

'We are? Uh-oh, this doesn't sound good. First, Lon hijacks my shield, now this.' The tech hurried to a station next to Rhyme. Whitcomb recited a Web site address, which Cooper typed in. On the screen appeared some messages indicating that they'd made contact with SSD's secure server. Whitcomb gave Cooper a temporary user name and, after a moment of hesitation, three long random-character passcodes.

'Download the decryption file in the box in the center of the screen and hit EXECUTE.'

Cooper did and a moment later another screen appeared.

Welcome, NGHF235, please enter (1) the Subject's 16-digit SSD code; or (2) country and number of Subject's passport, or (3) Subject's name, current residence, Social Security number and one telephone number.

'Type in the information for the person you're interested in.'

Rhyme dictated the details about Sachs. On the screen appeared: *Confirm access to 3E Compliance Dossier? Yes No.*

Cooper clicked on the former and a box appeared, asking for yet another passcode.

With another glance at the ceiling, Whitcomb asked, 'You ready?'

As if something significant was about to happen. 'Ready.'

Whitcomb gave them another sixteen-digit passcode, which Cooper typed in. He hit ENTER.

As the text began filling the computer screen, the criminalist whispered an astonished, 'Oh, my God.'

And it took a lot to astonish Lincoln Rhyme.

R E S T R I C T E D

POSSESSION OF THIS DOSSIER BY ANY PERSON NOT HOLDING AN A-18 CLEARANCE OR HIGHER IS A VIOLATION OF FEDERAL LAW

Dossier 3E – Compliance
SSD Subject Number: 7303–4490–7831–3478

Name: Amelia H. Sachs
Pages: 478

TABLE OF CONTENTS

Click on topic to view
Note: Archived material may take up to five minutes to access

PROFILE

- Name/Aliases/Nics/Nyms/A.K.A.s
- Social Security Number
- Present address
- Satellite view of present address
- Prior addresses
- Citizenship
- Race
- Ancestral history
- National origin
- Physical description/distinguishing characteristics
- Biometric details
    Photographs
    Video
    Fingerprints
    Footprints
    Retinal scan
    Iris scan
    Gait profile
    Facial scan
    Voice pattern
- Tissue samples
- Medical history
- Political party affiliations
- Professional organizations
- Fraternal organizations
- Religious affiliations

- Military
  - *Service/discharge*
  - *DOD evaluation*
  - *National Guard evaluation*
  - *Weapons systems training*
- Donations
  - *Political*
  - *Religious*
  - *Medical*
  - *Philanthropic*
  - *Public Broadcasting System/National Public Radio*
  - *Other*
- Psychological/psychiatric history
- Myers-Briggs personality profile
- Sexual preference profile
- Hobbies/interests
- Clubs/fraternal organizations

INDIVIDUALS TETHERED TO SUBJECT

- Spouses
- Intimate relationships
- Offspring
- Parents
- Siblings
- Grandparents (paternal)
- Grandparents (maternal)
- Other blood relatives, living
- Other blood relatives, deceased
- Relatives related by marriage or tethering
- Neighbors
  - *Present*
  - *Past five years (archived, may be delay in accessing)*
- Co-workers, clients, etc.
  - *Present*

Past five years (archived, may be delay in accessing)
- Acquaintances
    - *In person*
    - *Online*
- Persons of Interest (PEOI)

FINANCIAL

- Employment – present
    - *Category*
    - *Salary history*
    - *Days absent/reasons for absence*
    - *Discharge/unemployment claims*
    - *Citations/reprimands*
    - *Title 7 discrimination incidents*
    - *OSHA incidents*
    - *Other actions*
- Employment – past (archived, may be delay in accessing)
    - *Category*
    - *Salary history*
    - *Days absent/reasons for absence*
    - *Discharge/unemployment claims*
    - *Citations/reprimands*
    - *Title 7 discrimination incidents*
    - *OSHA incidents*
    - *Other actions*
- Income – present
    - *IRS reported*
    - *Nonreported*
    - *Foreign*
- Income – past
    - *IRS reported*
    - *Nonreported*
    - *Foreign*

- Assets currently held
    - *Real property*
    - *Vehicles and boats*
    - *Bank accounts/securities*
    - *Insurance policies*
    - *Other*
- Assets, past twelve months, unusual disposition or acquisition of
    - *Real property*
    - *Vehicles and boats*
    - *Bank accounts/securities*
    - *Insurance policies*
    - *Other*
- Assets, past five years, unusual disposition or acquisition of (archived, may be delay in accessing)
    - *Real property*
    - *Vehicles and boats*
    - *Bank accounts/securities*
    - *Insurance policies*
    - *Other*
- Credit report/rating
- Financial transactions, U.S.-based institutions
    - *Today*
    - *Past seven days*
    - *Past thirty days*
    - *Past year*
    - *Past five years (archived, may be delay in accessing)*
- Financial transactions, foreign-based institutions
    - *Today*
    - *Past seven days*
    - *Past thirty days*
    - *Past year*
    - *Past five years (archived, may be delay in accessing)*

- Financial transactions, Hawala and other cash transactions, U.S. and foreign
  - *Today*
  - *Past seven days*
  - *Past thirty days*
  - *Past year*
  - *Past five years (archived, may be delay in accessing)*

COMMUNICATIONS

- Present phone numbers
  - *Mobile*
  - *Landline*
  - *Satellite*
- Prior phone numbers past twelve months
  - *Mobile*
  - *Landline*
  - *Satellite*
- Prior phone numbers past five years (archived, may be delay in accessing)
  - *Mobile*
  - *Landline*
  - *Satellite*
- Fax numbers
- Pager numbers
- Incoming/outgoing phone/pager calls – mobile/PDA
  - *Past thirty days*
  - *Past year (archived, may be delay in accessing)*
- Incoming/outgoing phone/pager/fax calls – landline
  - *Past thirty days*
  - *Past year (archived, may be delay in accessing)*
- Incoming/outgoing phone/pager/fax calls – satellite
  - *Past thirty days*
  - *Past year (archived, may be delay in accessing)*
- Wiretaps/intercepts

>   *Foreign Intelligence Surveillance Act (FISA)*
>   *Pen registers*
>   *Title 3*
>   *Other, warrants*
>   *Other, collateral*

- Web-based telephone activities
- Internet service providers, present
- Internet service providers, past 12 months
- Internet service providers, past five years (archived, may be delay in accessing)
- Favorite place/bookmarked Web sites
- E-mail addresses
    - *Present*
    - *Past*
- E-mail activity, past year
    - *TC/PIP history*
    - *Outgoing addresses*
    - *Incoming addresses*
    - *Content (warrant may be required to view)*
- E-mail activity, past five years (archived, may be delay in accessing)
    - *TC/PIP history*
    - *Outgoing addresses*
    - *Incoming addresses*
    - *Content (warrant may be required to view)*
- Web sites, present
    - *Personal*
    - *Professional*
- Web sites, past five years (archived, may be delay in accessing)
    - *Personal*
    - *Professional*
- Blogs, lifelogs, Web sites (See appendices for text of Passages of Interest (POI))

- Social Web site memberships (mySpace, Facebook, OurWorld, others) (See appendices for text of Passages of Interest (POI))
- Avatars/other personas online
- Mailing lists
- 'Buddies' on e-mail accounts
- Internet Relay Chat participation
- Web browsing and search engine requests/results
- Keyboarding technique profile
- Search engine grammar, syntax and punctuation profile
- Package delivery service history
- Postal boxes
- Express Mail/Registered/Certified USPS activity

LIFESTYLE ACTIVITIES

- Purchases today
    Threat-oriented items or commodities
    Clothing
    Vehicles and vehicle related
    Food
    Liquor
    Household items
    Appliances
    Other
- Purchases in past 7 days
    Threat-oriented items or commodities
    Clothing
    Vehicles and vehicle related
    Food
    Liquor
    Household items
    Appliances
    Other

- Purchases in past thirty days
    - *Threat-oriented items or commodities*
    - *Clothing*
    - *Vehicles and vehicle related*
    - *Food*
    - *Liquor*
    - *Household items*
    - *Appliances*
    - *Other*
- Purchases in past year (archived, may be delay in accessing)
    - *Threat-oriented items or commodities*
    - *Clothing*
    - *Vehicles and vehicle related*
    - *Food*
    - *Liquor*
    - *Household items*
    - *Appliances*
    - *Other*
- Books/magazines purchased online
    - *Suspicious/subversive*
    - *Others of interest*
- Books/magazines purchased in retail stores
    - *Suspicious/subversive*
    - *Others of interest*
- Books/magazines checked out from libraries
    - *Suspicious/subversive*
    - *Others of interest*
- Books/magazines observed by airport/airline personnel
    - *Suspicious/subversive*
    - *Others of interest*
- Other library activities
- Bridal/shower/anniversary gift registries
- Theatrical films

- Cable television programs/pay-per-view watched past thirty days
- Cable television programs/pay-per-view watched, past year (archived, may be delay in accessing)
- Subscription radio stations
- Travel
    Automotive
        Owned vehicles
        Rental
    Public transportation
    Taxis/limos
    Bus
    Trains
    Airplanes, commercial
        Domestic
        International
    Airplanes, private
        Domestic
        International
    TSA security screens
    Appearance on no-fly lists
- Presence in Locations of Interest (LOI)
    Local
        Mosques
    Other locations – U.S.
        Mosques
    Other locations – international
- Presence in or transit through Red Flag Locations (RFL): Cuba, Uganda, Libya, South Yemen, Liberia, Ghana, Sudan, Democratic Republic of Congo, Indonesia, Palestinian Territories, Syria, Iraq, Iran, Egypt, Saudi Arabia, Jordan, Pakistan, Eritrea, Afghanistan, Chechnya, Somalia, Sudan, Nigeria, Philippines, North Korea, Azerbaijan, Chile.

GEOGRAPHIC POSITIONING OF SUBJECT

- GPS devices (all positions today)
  - *Vehicular*
  - *Handheld*
  - *Mobile phones*
- GPS devices (all positions past seven days)
  - *Vehicular*
  - *Handheld*
  - *Mobile phones*
- GPS devices (all positions past thirty days)
  - *Vehicular*
  - *Handheld*
  - *Mobile phones*
- GPS devices (all positions past year) (archived, may be delay in accessing)
  - *Vehicular*
  - *Handheld*
  - *Mobile phones*
- Biometric observations
  - *Today*
  - *Past seven days*
  - *Past thirty days*
  - *Past year (archived, may be delay in accessing)*
- RFID reports, other than highway toll readers
  - *Today*
  - *Past seven days*
  - *Past thirty days*
  - *Past year (archived, may be delay in accessing)*
- RFID reports, highway toll readers
  - *Today*
  - *Past seven days*
  - *Past thirty days*
  - *Past year (archived, may be delay in accessing)*
- Traffic violation photos/video

- CCTV photos/video
- Warranted surveillance photos/video
- Collateral surveillance photos/video
- In-person financial transaction hits
    - *Today*
    - *Past seven days*
    - *Past thirty days*
    - *Past year (archived, may be delay in accessing)*
- Mobile phone/PDA/telecommunications hits
    - *Today*
    - *Past seven days*
    - *Past thirty days*
    - *Past year (archived, may be delay in accessing)*
- Incidents of proximity to security targets
    - *Today*
    - *Past seven days*
    - *Past thirty days*
    - *Past year (archived, may be delay in accessing)*

LEGAL

- Criminal history – U.S.
    - *Detention/questioning*
    - *Arrests*
    - *Convictions*
- Criminal history – foreign
    - *Detention/questioning*
    - *Arrests*
    - *Convictions*
- Watch lists
- Surveillance
- Civil litigation
- Restraining orders
- Whistleblower history

ADDITIONAL DOSSIERS

- Federal Bureau of Investigation
- Central Intelligence Agency
- National Security Agency
- National Reconnaissance Organization
- NPIA
- U.S. Military Intelligence Agencies
    Army
    Navy
    Air Force
    Marines
- State and local police intelligence departments

THREAT ASSESSMENT

- Assessment as security risk
    Private sector
    Public sector

And this was just the table of contents. Amelia Sachs's dossier itself was close to five hundred pages long.

Rhyme scrolled through the list and clicked on various topics. The entries were dense as wood. He whispered, 'SSD has this information? On everyone in America?'

'No,' Whitcomb said. 'For children under five there's very little, obviously. And with many adults, there're a lot of gaps. But SSD does the best they can. They're improving it every day.'

Improving? Rhyme wondered.

Pulaski nodded at the sales brochure Mel Cooper had downloaded. 'Four hundred million people?'

'That's right. And growing.'

'And it's updated hourly?' Rhyme asked.

'Often in real time.'

'So your government agency, Whitcomb, this Compliance

Division . . . it isn't about *guarding* the data; you're *using* it, right? To find terrorists?'

Whitcomb paused. But since he'd already sent the dossier to somebody who didn't have an A-18 clearance, whatever the hell that was, he must have figured that sharing a bit more wasn't going to make the consequences any worse. 'That's right. And it's not just terrorists. It's other criminals too. SSD uses predictive software to figure out who's going to commit crimes and when and how. A lot of the tips that go to police officials and intelligence departments come from what look like anonymous concerned citizens. They're actually avatars. Fictions. Created by Watchtower and innerCircle. Sometimes they even collect the rewards, which are then sent back to the government to be used again.'

It was Mel Cooper who asked, 'But if you're a government agency, why are you giving the job to a private company? Why not do it yourself?'

'We *have* to use a private company. The Defense Department tried to do something like this themselves after nine-eleven: the Total Information Awareness program. It was run by former National Security Advisor John Poindexter and an executive from SAIC. But it got closed down – violations of the Privacy Act. And the public thought it was too Big Brother. But SSD isn't subject to the same legal restrictions that the government is.'

Whitcomb gave a cynical laugh. 'Also, with all respect to my employer, Washington wasn't very talented. SSD is. The two main words in Andrew Sterling's vocabulary are "knowledge" and "efficiency." And nobody combines those better than him.'

'It's not illegal?' Mel Cooper asked.

'We're in some gray areas,' Whitcomb conceded.

'Well, can it help us? That's all I want to know.'

'Maybe.'

'How?'

Whitcomb explained, 'We'll run Detective Sachs's geographic-positioning profile for today. I'll take over the keyboarding.' He began to type. 'You'll see what I do on your screen in the box at the bottom.'

'How long will that take?'

A laugh, muted thanks to the broken nose. 'Not very long. It's pretty speedy.'

He hadn't finished speaking before text filled the screen.

GEOGRAPHIC POSITIONING PROFILE
SUBJECT 7303–4490–7831–3478

Time parameters: Past four hours.

- 1632 hours. Phone call. From subject's mobile phone to landline of Subject 5732-4887-3360-4759 (Lincoln Henry Rhyme) (tethered individual). 52 seconds. Subject was in her Brooklyn, NY, residence.
- 1723 hours. Biometric hit. CCTV, NYPD 84th Precinct, Brooklyn, NY. 95% probability match.
- 1723 hours. Biometric hit. Subject 3865-6453-9902-7221 (Pamela D. Willoughby) (tethered individual). CCTV, NYPD 84th Precinct, Brooklyn, NY. 92.4% probability match.
- 1740 hours. Phone call. From subject's mobile phone to landline of Subject 5732-4887-3360-4759 (Lincoln Henry Rhyme) (tethered Individual). 12 seconds.
- 1827 hours. RFID scan. Manhattan Style Boutique credit card, 9 West Eighth Street. No purchases.
- 1841 hours. Biometric hit. CCTV, Presco Discount Gas and Oil, 546 W. 14th Street, Pump 7, 2001 Honda Civic, NY License Number MDH459, registered to 3865-6453-9902-7221 (Pamela D. Willoughby) (tethered individual).
- 1846 hours. Credit card purchase. Presco Discount Gas

and Oil, 546 W. 14th Street. Pump 7. Purchase of 14.6 gallons, regular grade. $43.86 US.

- 1901 hours. License plate scan. CCTV, Avenue of the Americas and 23rd Street, Honda Civic MDH459 northbound.
- 1903 hours. Phone call. From subject's mobile phone to landline of Subject 5732-4887-3360-4759 (Lincoln Henry Rhyme) (tethered individual). Subject was at Avenue of the Americas and 28th Street. 14 seconds.
- 1907 hours. RFID scan, Associated Credit Union credit card, Avenue of the Americas and 34th Street. 4 seconds. No purchase.

'Okay, she's in Pam's car. Why's that? Where's hers?'

'What's the license?' Whitcomb asked. 'Never mind, it's faster just to use her code. Let's see . . .'

A window popped up and they could see a report that her Camaro had been impounded and towed from in front of her house. Nobody had any information on the pound it was destined for.

'Five Twenty-Two did that,' Rhyme whispered. 'He must have. Like your wife, Pulaski. And the electricity here. He's going after all of us, however he can.'

Whitcomb typed and the automobile information was replaced with a map, showing the hits on the geographic-positioning profile. It revealed Sachs's movement from Brooklyn to Midtown. But then the trail stopped.

'The last one?' Rhyme asked. 'The RFID scan. What was that?'

Whitcomb said, 'A store read the chip in one of her credit cards. But it was brief. Probably she was in the car. She'd have to be walking pretty fast for that short a reading.'

'Did she keep going north?' Rhyme mused.

'That's all the information we have. It'll update soon.'

Mel Cooper said, 'She might've taken Thirty-fourth Street to the West Side Highway. And gone north, out of the city.'

'There's a toll bridge,' Whitcomb said. 'If she crosses it we'll get a hit on the license plate number. The girl whose car it is – Pam Willoughby – doesn't have an E-ZPass. innerCircle would tell us if she did.'

At Rhyme's instruction, Mel Cooper – the senior police officer among them – had an emergency vehicle locator sent out on Pam's license number and car make.

Rhyme called the precinct house in Brooklyn, where he learned only that Sachs's Camaro had indeed been towed. Sachs and Pam had been there briefly but had left quickly and hadn't said where they were going. Rhyme called the girl on her mobile. She was in the city with a girlfriend. Pam confirmed that Sachs had discovered a lead after the break-in at her town house in Brooklyn but hadn't mentioned what it was or where she was going.

Rhyme disconnected.

Whitcomb said, 'We'll feed the geopositioning hits and everything we've got about her and the case through FORT, the obscure relationship program, then Xpectation. That's the predictive software. If there's any way to find out where she's gone, this'll do it.'

Whitcomb looked up at the ceiling again. Grimaced. He rose and walked to the door. Rhyme could see him lock it, then wedge a wooden chair under the knob. He gave a faint smile as he sat down at the computer. He began to type.

'Mark?' Pulaski asked.

'Yes?'

'Thanks. And this time, I mean it.'

Chapter
FORTY-SIX

Life is a struggle, of course.

My idol – Andrew Sterling – and I share the same passion for data, and we both appreciate their mystery, their allure, their immense power. But until I stepped into his sphere I never appreciated the full extent of using data as a weapon to expand your vision to every corner of the world. Reducing all of life, all of existence to numbers, then watching them billow into something transcendent.

Immortal soul . . .

I was in love with SQL, the workhorse standard for database management, until I was seduced by Andrew and Watchtower. Who wouldn't have been? Its power and elegance are enthralling. And I've come to fully appreciate the world of data, thanks to him – though indirectly. He's never given me more than a pleasant nod in the hall and a query about the weekend, though he knew my name without a glance at the ID on my chest (what a breathtakingly brilliant mind he has). I think of all the late nights I spent in his office, 2:00 A.M. or so, SSD empty, sitting in his chair and feeling his presence as I read through his spine-up library. Not a single one of those pedantic and silly businessman's self-help books, but volumes and volumes revealing a much greater vision: books about the collection of power and geographic territory: the continental U.S. under the Manifest Destiny doctrine in the 1800s, Europe under the Third Reich, *mare nostra* under the Romans, the entire world under the Catholic Church and Islam. (And they all appreciated the incisive power of data, by the way.)

Ah, the things I've learned just from overhearing Andrew, savoring what he's written in drafts of memos and letters and the book he's working on.

'Mistakes are noise. Noise is contamination. Contamination must be eliminated.'

'Only in victory can we afford to be generous.'

'Only the weak compromise.'

'Either find a solution to your problem, or stop considering it a problem.'

'We are born to battle.'

'He who understands wins; he who knows understands.'

I consider what Andrew would think about what I'm up to, and I believe he'd be pleased.

And now, the battle against Them moves forward.

On the street near my home I press the key fob again and finally a horn gives a muted bleep.

Let's see, let's see . . . Ah, here we go. Look at this piece of junk, a Honda Civic. Borrowed, of course, since Amelia 7303's car is now sitting in a pound – a coup I'm rather proud of. Never thought of trying that before.

My thoughts stray back to my beautiful redhead. Was she bluffing about what They knew? About Peter Gordon? That's the funny thing about knowledge; such a fine line between truth and a lie. But I can't take the chance. I'll have to hide the car.

My thoughts go back to her.

The woman's wild eyes, her red hair, the body . . . I'm not sure I can wait much longer.

Trophies . . .

A fast examination of the car. Some books, magazines, Kleenex, some empty Vitamin Water bottles, a Starbucks napkin, running shoes shedding rubber, a *Seventeen* magazine in the backseat and a textbook on poetry . . . And who owns this superb contribution to the world of Japanese technology? The registration tells me it's Pamela Willoughby.

I'll get a little more information on her from innerCircle then I'll pay her a visit. Wonder what she looks like? I'll check DMV to make sure she's worth the trouble.

The car starts up just fine. Ease out carefully, no upsetting other drivers. Don't want to make a scene.

A half block, into the alley.

What does Miss Pam like to listen to? Rock, rock, alternative, hip-hop, talk and NPR. Presets are extremely informative.

I'm already forming a game plan to arrange a transaction with the girl: getting to know her. We'll meet at Amelia 7303's memorial service (no body, no funeral). I'll offer sympathy. I met her during the case she was working on. I really liked her. Oh, don't cry, honey. It's okay. Tell you what. Let's get together. I can tell you all about the stories Amelia shared with me. Her father. And the interesting story of her grandfather's coming to this country. (After I learned she was snooping around, I checked out her dossier. What an interesting history.) We got to be good friends. I'm really devastated . . . How about coffee? You like Starbucks? I always go there after my run in Central Park every evening. No! You too?

We sure seem to have something in common.

Oh, there's that feeling again, thinking about Pam. How ugly can she be?

It might be a wait to get her into my trunk . . . I have to take care of Thom Reston first – and a few other things. But at least I have Amelia 7303 for tonight.

I drive into the garage and ditch the car – it'll rest here

until I swap plates and it goes to the bottom of the Croton reservoir. But I can't think about that now. I'm pretty consumed, planning out the transaction with my red-haired friend, waiting back home in my Closet, like a wife for her husband after a really tough day at the office.

Sorry, no prediction can be made at this time. Please input more data and try your request again.

Despite drawing from the world's largest database, despite the state-of-the-art software examining every detail of Amelia Sachs's life at the speed of light, the program struck out.

'I'm sorry,' Mark Whitcomb said, dabbing his nose. The high-def system on the video-conferencing system displayed the nasal injury quite prominently. It looked bad; Ron Pulaski had really slammed him.

The young man continued, sniffing, 'There just aren't enough details. What you get out is only as good as what you put in. It works best with a pattern of behaviors. All it tells us is that she's going someplace she's never been before, at least not on that route.'

Right to the killer's house, Rhyme reflected in frustration. Where the hell was she?

'Hold on a minute. The system's updating . . .'

The screen flickered and changed. Whitcomb blurted, 'I've got her! Some RFID hits twenty minutes ago.'

'Where?' Rhyme whispered.

Whitcomb put them on the screen. They were in a quiet block on the Upper East Side. 'Two hits at stores. The duration of the first RFID scan was two seconds. The next was slightly longer, eight seconds. Maybe she was pausing to check an address.'

'Call Bo Haumann now!' Rhyme shouted.

Pulaski hit speed dial and a moment later the head of Emergency Service came on the phone.

'Bo, I've got a lead on Amelia. She went after Five Twenty-Two and she's disappeared. We've got a computer monitoring her whereabouts. About twenty minutes ago she was near six forty-two East Eighty-eighth.'

'We can be there in ten minutes, Linc. Hostage situation?'

'That's what I'd say. Call me when you know something.'

They disconnected.

Rhyme thought back to her message on voice mail. It seemed so fragile, that tiny bundle of digital data.

In his mind he could hear her voice perfectly: *I have a lead, a good one, Rhyme. Call me.*

He couldn't help wondering if it would be their last communication.

Bo Haumann's Emergency Service Unit A Team was standing near a doorway of a large town house on the Upper East Side: four officers in full body armor, holding MP-5s, compact, black machine guns. They were carefully staying clear of the windows.

Haumann had to admit he hadn't seen anything like this in all his years in the military or the police department. Lincoln Rhyme was using some kind of computer program that had tracked Amelia Sachs to this area, only it wasn't through her phone or a wire or GPS tracker. Maybe this was the future of police work.

The device hadn't given the actual location where the teams now were – a private residence. But a witness had seen a woman pause at both shops where the computer had spotted her, then she'd headed to this town house across the street.

Where she was presumably being held by the perp they were calling 522.

Finally, the team in the back called in. 'B Team to One. We're in position. Can't see anything. Which floor is she on, K?'

'No idea. We just go in and sweep. Move fast. She's been

in there a while. I'll hit the bell and when he comes to the door, we move in.'

'Roger, K.'

'Team C. We'll be on the roof in three or four minutes.'

'Move it!' Haumann grumbled.

'Yes, sir.'

Haumann had worked with Amelia Sachs for years. She had more balls than most of the men who served under him. He wasn't sure he *liked* her – she was pigheaded and abrupt and often bluffed her way onto point when she should have held back – but he sure as hell respected her.

And he wasn't going to let her go down to a rapist like this 522. He nodded an ESU detective up to the porch – dressed in a business suit so that when he knocked on the door, a glance through the peephole wouldn't tip off the killer. Once he opened the door, officers crouching against the front of the town house would leap up and rush him. The officer buttoned his jacket and nodded.

'Goddamnit,' Haumann radioed impatiently to the team in the back. 'You in place yet or not?'

Chapter
FORTY-SEVEN

The door opened and she heard the killer's footsteps enter the stinking, claustrophobic room.

Amelia Sachs was in a crouch, her knees in agony, struggling to get to the handcuff key in her front pocket. But surrounded by the towering stacks of newspapers, she hadn't been able to turn far enough to reach into her front pocket. She'd touched it through the cloth, felt its shape, tantalizing, but couldn't slip her fingers into the slit.

She was racked with frustration.

More footsteps.

Where, where?

One more lunge for the key . . . Almost but not quite.

Then his steps moved closer. She gave up.

Okay, it was time to fight. Fine with her. She'd seen his eyes, the lust, the hunger. She knew he'd be coming for her at any moment. She didn't know how she'd hurt him, with her hands cuffed behind her and the terrible pain in her shoulder and face from the fight earlier. But the bastard'd pay for every touch.

Only, where was he?

The footsteps had stopped.

Where? Sachs had no perspective on the room. The corridor

he'd have to come through to get to her was a two-foot-wide path through the towers of moldy newspapers. She could see his desk and the piles of junk, the stacks of magazines.

Come on, come for me.

I'm ready. I'll act scared, shy away. Rapists are all about control. He'll be empowered – and careless – when he sees me cower. Then when he leans close, I'll go for his throat with my teeth. Hold on and don't let go, whatever happens. I'll—

It was then that the building collapsed, a bomb detonated.

A massive crushing tide tumbled over her, slamming her to the floor and pinning her immobile.

She grunted in pain.

Only after a minute did Sachs realize what he'd done – maybe anticipating that she was going to fight, he'd simply pushed over stacks of the newspapers.

Legs and hands frozen, her chest, shoulders and head exposed, she was trapped by hundreds of pounds of stinking newspaper.

The claustrophobia grabbed her, the panic indescribable, and she barked a scream with staccato breath. She struggled to control the fear.

Peter Gordon appeared at the end of the tunnel. She saw in one of his hands the steel blade of a razor. In the other was a tape recorder. He studied her closely.

'Please,' she whimpered. The panic was only partly feigned.

'You're lovely,' he whispered.

He began to say something else but the words were lost in the sound of a doorbell, which chimed in here as well as the main part of the town house.

Gordon paused.

Then the bell rang again.

He rose and walked to the desk, typed on the keyboard and studied the computer screen – probably a security camera showing the image of the visitor. He frowned.

The killer debated. He glanced at her and carefully folded the razor, then slipped it into his back pocket.

He walked to the closet door and stepped through it. She heard the click of the latch behind him. Once more her hand began to worm closer to her pocket and the tiny bit of metal inside.

'Lincoln.'

Bo Haumann's voice was distant.

Rhyme whispered, 'Tell me.'

'It wasn't her.'

'What?'

'The hits – from that computer program – they were right. But it wasn't Amelia.' He explained that she gave her friend, Pam Willoughby, her credit card to buy groceries in hopes they could have dinner that night and talk about some 'personal stuff.' 'That's what the system read, I guess. She went to a store, did some window-shopping and then she stopped here – it's a friend's house. They were doing their homework.'

Rhyme's eyes closed. 'Okay, thanks, Bo. You can stand down. All we can do is wait.'

'I'm sorry, Lincoln,' Ron Pulaski said.

A nod.

His eyes strayed to the mantel, where sat a picture of Sachs wearing a black crash helmet, in the cage of a NASCAR Ford. Beside it was a photo of them together, Rhyme in his chair, Sachs hugging him.

He couldn't look at it. His eyes strayed to the whiteboards.

UNSUB 522 PROFILE

- Male
- Probably nonsmoker
- Probably no wife/children
- Probably white or light-skinned ethnic
- Medium build
- Strong – able to strangle victims
- Access to voice-disguise equipment
- Computer literate; knows

OurWorld. Other social-networking sites?

- Takes trophies from victims
- Eats snack food/hot sauce
- Wears size-11 Skechers work shoe
- Hoarder. Suffers from OCD
- Will have a 'secret' life and a 'façade' life
- Public personality will be opposite of his real self
- Residence: won't rent, will have two separate living areas, one normal and one secret
- Windows will be covered or painted
- Will become violent when collecting or trove are threatened

NONPLANTED EVIDENCE

- Old cardboard
- Hair from doll, BASF B35 nylon 6
- Tobacco from Tareyton cigarette

- Old tobacco, not Tareyton, but brand unknown
- Evidence of Stachybotrys Chartarum mold
- Snack food/cayenne pepper
- Dust, from World Trade Center attack, possibly indicating residence/job downtown Manhattan
- Rope fiber containing:
- Cyclamate diet soda (old or foreign)
- Naphthalene (mothballs, old or foreign)
- Leopard lily plant leaves (interior plant)
- Trace from two different legal pads, yellow colored
- Treadmark from size-11 Skechers work shoe
- Houseplant leaves: ficus and Aglaonema – Chinese evergreen
- Coffee-mate

Where are you, Sachs? Where are you?

He stared at the charts, hypnotically, willing them to speak. But these scanty facts offered no more insights to Rhyme than had the innerCircle data to the SSD computer.

Sorry, no prediction can be made at this time . . .

FORTY-EIGHT

A neighbor.

My visitor is a neighbor who lives up the block at number 697 West Ninety-first Street. He'd just gotten home from work. A package was supposedly dropped off but it wasn't there. The store thinks it might have been delivered to 679, my address. A misread of the numbers.

I frown and explain that nothing's been delivered. He should check with the store again. I want to cut his throat for interrupting my tryst with Amelia 7303 but, of course, I smile sympathetically.

He's sorry he's bothered me. Have a good day you too glad they've finished that street work aren't you . . .

And now I'm back to thinking about my Amelia 7303. But, closing the front door, I feel the jolt of panic. I've suddenly realized that I took everything from her – phone and weapons and MACE and knife – except the handcuff key. It must be in her pocket.

This neighbor has distracted me. I know where he lives and he'll pay for it. But now I hurry back toward my Closet, pulling the razor from my pocket. Hurry! What's she doing inside? Is she making a call to tell Them where to find her?

She's trying to take it all away from me! I hate her. I hate her so much . . .

The only progress Amelia Sachs had made in Gordon's absence was to control the panic.

She'd tried desperately to reach the key but her legs and arms remained frozen in the vise of newspaper and she couldn't get her hips in position to slip her hand inside her pocket.

Yes, the claustrophobia was at bay, but pain was rapidly replacing it. Cramps in her bent legs, a sharp corner of paper digging into her back.

Her hopes that the visitor was a source of salvation died. The door to the killer's hideaway opened once more. And she heard Gordon's footsteps. A moment later she looked up from her spot on the floor and saw him gazing at her. He walked around the mountain of paper, to the side, and squinted, noting that the cuffs were still intact.

He smiled in relief. 'So I'm Number Five Twenty-Two.'

She nodded, wondering how he'd found out their designation for him. Probably from torturing Captain Malloy, which made her all the angrier.

'I prefer a number that has a connection to something. Most digits are just random. There's too much randomness in life. That's the date you caught on to me, isn't it? Five Twenty-Two. That has significance. I like it.'

'If you come in we'll cut a deal.'

'"Cut a deal"?' He gave an eerie, knowing laugh. 'What kind of deal could anyone "cut" me? The murders were premeditated. I'd never get out of jail. Come on.' Gordon disappeared momentarily and returned with a plastic tarp, which he spread out on the floor in front of her.

Sachs stared at the brown-bloody sheet, heart thudding. Thinking of what Terry Dobyns had explained about hoarders, she realized he was worried about getting his collection stained with her blood.

Gordon got his tape recorder and set it on a nearby stack of papers, a short one, only three feet high. The top one was yesterday's *New York Times*. A number had been written precisely in the upper left-hand corner, 3,529.

Whatever he tried, he was going to hurt. She'd use her teeth or knees or feet. He was going to hurt bad. Get him close. Look vulnerable, look helpless.

Get him in close.

'Please! It hurts . . . I can't move my legs. Help me straighten them out.'

'No, you *say* you can't move your legs so I get close and you try to rip my throat out.'

Exactly right.

'No . . . Please!'

'Amelia Seven Three Oh Three . . . Do you think I didn't look you up? The day you and Ron Forty-Two Eighty-Five came to SSD I went into the pens and checked you out. Your record's pretty revealing. They like you, by the way, in the department. I think you also scare them. You're independent, a loose cannon. You drive fast, you shoot well, you're a crime-scene specialist and yet somehow you've made it onto five tactical teams in the past two years . . . So it wouldn't make much sense for me to get close without taking precautions, would it?'

She hardly heard his rambling. Come on, she thought. Get close. Come on!

He stepped aside and returned with a Taser stun gun.

Oh, no . . . no.

Of course. Being a security guard, he had a full arsenal of weapons. And he couldn't miss from this distance. He clicked the safety off the weapon and was stepping forward . . . when he paused, cocking his head.

Sachs too had heard some noise. A trickle of water?

No. Breaking glass, like a window shattering somewhere in the distance.

Gordon frowned. He took a step toward the door that led to the entryway closet – and suddenly flew backward as it crashed open.

A figure, holding a short metal crowbar, charged into the room, blinking to orient himself to the darkness.

Falling hard, the wind knocked from his lungs, Gordon dropped the Taser. Wincing, he climbed to his knees and reached for the weapon but the intruder swung the metal bar hard and caught him on the forearm. The killer screamed as bone cracked.

'No, no!' Then Gordon's eyes, tearing in pain, narrowed as he gazed at his attacker.

The man cried, 'You're not so godlike now, are you? You motherfucker!' It was Robert Jorgensen, the doctor, the identity theft victim from the transient hotel. He brought the crowbar down hard on the killer's neck and shoulder, two-handed. Gordon's head slammed into the floor. His eyes rolled back and he collapsed, lying completely still.

Sachs blinked in astonishment at the doctor.

Who is he? He's God, and I'm Job . . .

'Are you all right?' he asked, starting forward.

'Get these papers off me. Then take the cuffs off and put them on him. Hurry! The key's in my pocket.'

Jorgensen dropped to his knees and began pulling the papers off.

'How did you get here?' she asked.

Jorgensen's eyes were wide, just like she remembered from the cheap hotel on the Upper East Side. 'I've been following you ever since you came to see me. I've been living on the street. I *knew* you'd lead me to him.' A nod back at Gordon, still immobile, breathing shallowly.

Jorgensen was gasping as he grabbed huge handfuls of paper and flung them away.

Sachs said, '*You* were the one following me. At the cemetery and the loading dock on the West Side.'

'That was me, yes. Today I followed you from the warehouse to your apartment and the police station and then to that office building in Midtown, the gray one. Then here. I saw you go into the alley and then when you didn't come out, I wondered what had happened. I knocked on the door and he answered. I told him I was a neighbor looking for a delivery. I looked inside. I didn't see you. I pretended to leave but then I saw him go through the door in the living room with a razor.'

'He didn't recognize you?'

A sour laugh as Jorgensen tugged his beard. 'He probably only knew me from my driver's license photo. And that was taken when I bothered to shave – and could afford haircuts . . . God, these are heavy.'

'Hurry.'

Jorgensen continued, 'You were my best hope of finding him. I know you have to arrest him but I want some time with him first. You have to let me! I'm going to make him undo every bit of agony he's put me through.'

The sensation began to return to her legs. She glanced toward where Gordon lay. 'My front pocket . . . can you reach the key?'

'Not quite. Let me get some more off you.'

More papers flew to the floor. One headline: DAMAGE FROM BLACKOUT RIOTS IN MILLIONS. Another: NO PROGRESS IN HOSTAGE CRISIS. TEHRAN: NO DEALS.

Finally she squirmed out from underneath the papers. She clumsily rose, on aching legs, as far as the cuffs would allow. She leaned unsteadily against another tower of paper and turned toward him. 'The cuff key. Fast.'

Reaching into her pocket, Jorgensen found the key and

reached behind her. With a faint click one of the cuffs unlatched and she was able to stand. She turned to take the key from him. 'Fast,' she said. 'Let's—'

A stunning gunshot sounded and she felt simultaneous taps on her hands and face as the bullet – fired by Peter Gordon from her own gun – struck Jorgensen in the back, spattering her with blood and tissue.

He cried out and slumped into her, knocking her backward and saving her from the second slug, which zipped past and cracked into the wall inches from her shoulder.

Chapter
FORTY-NINE

Amelia Sachs had no choice. She had to attack. Immediately. Using Jorgensen's body as a shield, she lunged toward hunched-over, bleeding Gordon, grabbed the Taser from the floor and fired it in his direction.

The probes don't have the velocity of bullets and he fell backward just in time; the barbs missed. She snatched Jorgensen's metal bar and charged toward him. Gordon rose to one knee. But when she was just ten feet away he managed to bring the gun up and fire a round directly at her, just as she flung the bar at him. The bullet slammed into the American Body Armor vest. The pain was stunning but the round had struck her well below the solar plexus, where a hit would have knocked the breath from her lungs and paralyzed her.

The crowbar spun into his face, colliding with a nearly silent *thonk*, and he cried out in pain. He didn't go down, though, and still held the gun firmly. Sachs turned in the only direction she could flee – to her left – and sprinted through a canyon of artifacts filling the creepy place.

'Maze' was the only way to describe it. A narrow path through his collections: combs, toys (a lot of dolls – one of which had probably sloughed off the hair recovered at an early crime scene), old toothpaste tubes, carefully rolled up; cosmetics, mugs, paper bags, clothing, shoes, empty food cans, keys, pens, tools, magazines, books . . . She'd never seen so much junk in her life.

Most of the lamps were off here, though a few faint bulbs cast a yellow pall on the place, and pale illumination from streetlights filtered in through stained shades and newspapers taped over the glass. The windows were all barred. Sachs stumbled several times and caught herself just before sprawling into a stack of china or a massive bin of clothespins.

Careful, careful . . .

A fall would be fatal.

Close to vomiting from the blow to her belly, she turned between two towering stacks of *National Geographic*s and gasped, ducking just in time as Gordon turned the corner forty feet away, spotted her and, wincing in pain from his shattered arm and the blow to the face, fired two shots, left-handed. Both went wide. He started forward. Sachs wedged her elbow behind a tower of the glossy magazines and sent them cascading into the aisle, blocking it completely. She scrabbled away, hearing two more shots.

Seven fired – she always counted – but it was a Glock, still fat with eight rounds. She looked for any exit, even an unbarred window she could fling herself through, but this side of the town house had none. The walls contained shelves filled with china statuettes and knickknacks. Sachs could hear him furiously kicking aside the magazines, muttering to himself.

His face emerged over the piles as he tried to climb over the stack but the coated covers were slick as ice and he slipped twice, crying out as he used his broken arm to steady himself. Finally he scrabbled to the top. But before he could raise the gun he froze in horror, gasping. He shouted, 'No! Please, no!'

Sachs had both hands on a bookcase filled with antique vases and china figurines.

'No, don't touch it. Please!'

She had recalled what Terry Dobyns had said about losing anything in his collection. 'Throw the gun out here. Do it now, Peter!'

She didn't believe he would but, faced with the horror that he was about to lose what was on the shelf, Gordon was actually debating.

Knowledge is power.

'No, no, please . . .' A pathetic whisper.

Then his eyes changed. In an instant, they turned to dark dots and she knew he was going to go for the shot.

She shoved the shelf into another and two hundred pounds of ceramics turned to shards on the floor, a painful cacophony – which Peter Gordon's eerie, primal howl drowned out.

Two more shelves of ugly figurines and cups and saucers joined the destruction.

'Throw the gun down or I'll break every goddamn thing in here!'

But he'd lost control completely. 'I'll kill you I'll kill you I'll kill you I'll—' He fired twice more but by then Sachs had dived for cover. She knew he'd be coming after her as soon as he surmounted the pile of *National Geographics* and she assessed their positions. She'd circled back toward the closet door at the front, while he was still at the back of the town house.

But to make it to the door and safety would mean a run past the doorway of the room where he was now – to judge from the sound – scrabbling over the shelves and shattered ceramics. Did he realize her predicament? Was he waiting, gun aimed at the shooting gallery she'd have to traverse in order to make it to the closet door and safety?

Or had he bypassed the roadblock and snuck around her via a route she didn't know about?

Creaks sounded throughout the murky place. Were they his footsteps? The wood settling?

Panic tickled and she spun around. She couldn't see him. She knew she had to move, fast. Go! Now! She took a deep, silent breath, willed away the pain in her knees and, keeping low, charged forward, directly past the blockade of magazines.

No shots.

He wasn't there. She stopped fast, pressing her back against the wall and forcing herself to calm her breathing.

Quiet, quiet . . .

Hell. Where, where, where? Down this aisle of shoe boxes, down this one of canned tomatoes, down this one of neatly folded clothing?

More creaks. She couldn't tell where they were coming from.

A faint sound like the wind, like a breath.

Finally Sachs made a decision – just run for it. Now! All out for the front door!

And hope he's not behind you or hasn't snuck toward the front via a different passageway.

Go!

Sachs pushed off, sprinting past more corridors, canyons of books, glassware, paintings, wires and electronic equipment, cans. Was she going the right way?

Yes, she was. Ahead of her was Gordon's desk, surrounded by the yellow pads. Robert Jorgensen's body was on the floor. Move faster. Move! Forget the phone on the desk, she told herself after briefly considering calling 911.

Get out. Get out now.

Speeding toward the closet door.

The closer she got, the more fierce the panic. Waiting for the gunshot, any moment.

Only twenty feet now . . .

Maybe Gordon believed she was hiding in the back. Maybe he was on his knees, mourning madly the destruction of his precious porcelain.

Ten feet . . .

Around a corner, pausing only to grab the crowbar, slick with his blood.

No, out the door.

Then she stopped, gasping.

Directly in front of her, she saw him, in silhouette, backlit by the glare from the closet doorway. He apparently *had* taken another route here, she realized in despair. She lifted the heavy iron rod.

For a moment, he didn't see her but her hope of going undetected vanished as he turned her way and dropped to the floor, lifting the gun her way, as an image of her father, then one of Lincoln Rhyme, filled her thoughts.

There she is, Amelia 7303, clear in my sights.

The woman who destroyed hundreds of my treasures, the woman who would take everything away from me, deprive me of all my future transactions, expose my Closet to the world. I have no time for fun with her. No time for recorded screams. She has to die. Now.

I hate her I hate her I hate her I hate her I hate her I hate her I hate her I hate her I hate her . . .

No one is going to take anything away from me, never again.

Aim and squeeze.

Amelia Sachs stumbled backward as the gun in front of her fired.

Then another shot. Two more.

As she fell to the floor, she covered her head with her arms, numb at first, then aware of growing pain.

I'm dying . . . I'm dying . . .

Only . . . only the only painful sensation was in her arthritic knees, where she'd landed hard on the floor, not from where the bullets must have struck her. Her hand rose to her face, her neck. No wound, no blood. He *couldn't* have missed her from this range.

But he had.

Then he was running forward toward her. Her eyes cold, her muscles tense as iron, Sachs gasped and gripped the crowbar.

But he continued past her, not even glancing her way.

What was this? Sachs slowly rose, wincing. Without the backlight of glare from the open closet door she saw the silhouette become distinct. It wasn't Gordon at all but a detective she knew from the nearby 20th Precinct – John Harvison. The detective held his Glock steady as he moved cautiously to the body of the man he'd just shot to death.

Peter Gordon, Sachs now understood, had been moving up silently behind her and been about to shoot her in the back. From where he'd been stalking her, he hadn't seen Harvison, low in the closet doorway.

'Amelia, you all right?' the detective called.

'Yeah. Fine.'

'Other shooters?'

'Don't think so.'

Sachs rose and joined the detective. All the rounds from his gun had apparently hit their target; one of them had struck Gordon's forehead directly. The resulting wound was massive. Blood and brain matter flecked Prescott's American Family painting above the desk.

Harvison was an intense man in his forties who'd been decorated several times for courage under fire and collaring major drug dealers. He was pure professional now and paid no attention to the bizarre setting as he secured the scene. He lifted the Glock out of Gordon's bloody hand and locked it open, slipping the gun and clip into his pocket. He moved the Taser safely aside too, though it was unlikely there'd be any miraculous resurrections.

'John,' Sachs whispered, staring at the killer's ruined body. 'How? How on earth did you find me?'

'Got an any-available squawk about an assault in progress at this address. I was a block away on a drug thing so I headed over.' He glanced at her. 'It was that guy you work with who called it in.'

'Who?'

'Rhyme. Lincoln Rhyme.'

'Oh.' The answer didn't surprise her, though it left more questions than it settled.

They heard a faint gasp. They turned. The sound had come from Jorgensen. Sachs bent down. 'Get an ambulance here. He's still alive.' She put pressure on the bullet wound.

Harvison pulled out his radio and called for medics.

A moment later two other officers, from Emergency Service, burst through the doorway, guns drawn.

Sachs instructed, 'The main perp's down. Probably no others. But clear the place just to make sure.'

'Sure, Detective.'

One ESU cop joined Harvison and they started through the packed corridors. The other paused and said to Sachs, 'This is a goddamn spook house. You ever see anything like this, Detective?'

Sachs wasn't in the mood for banter. 'Find me some bandages or towels. Hell, with everything he's got here, I'll bet there's a half dozen first aid kits. I want something to stop the bleeding. Now!'

v

THE MAN WHO KNOWS EVERYTHING

WEDNESDAY, MAY 25

The privacy and dignity of our citizens [are] being whittled away by sometimes imperceptible steps. Taken individually, each step may be of little consequence. But when viewed as a whole, there begins to emerge a society quite unlike any we have seen – a society in which government may intrude into the secret regions of a [person's] life.

– SUPREME COURT JUSTICE
WILLIAM O. DOUGLAS

Chapter
FIFTY

'Okay, the computer helped,' Lincoln Rhyme acknowledged.

He was referring to innerCircle, the Watchtower database management program and SSD's other programs. 'But it was mostly the evidence,' he said stridently. 'The computer pointed me in a *general* direction. That's all. We took over from there.'

It was well after midnight and Rhyme was speaking to Sachs and Pulaski, both seated nearby in the lab. She'd returned from 522's town house, where the medics had reported that Robert Jorgensen would survive; the bullet had missed major organs and blood vessels. He was in the Columbia-Presbyterian intensive care facility.

Rhyme continued his explanation of how he'd found out that Sachs was in an SSD security guard's town house. He told her about her massive Compliance dossier. Mel Cooper called it up on the computer for her to look at. She scrolled through it, her face ashen at the amount of information inside. Even as they watched, the screen flickered as it updated.

'They know everything,' she whispered. 'I don't have a single secret in the world.'

Rhyme went on to tell her how the system had compiled a list of her positions after she had left the precinct house in

Brooklyn. 'But all the computers could do was give a rough direction of your travel. It came up blank for a destination. I kept looking at the map and realized that you were headed in the general direction of SSD – which, by the way, their *own* goddamn computer didn't figure out. I called and the lobby guard said that you'd just spent a half hour there, asking about employees. But nobody knew where you'd gone after that.'

She explained how her lead had taken her to SSD: The man who'd broken into her town house had dropped a receipt from a coffee shop next to the company. 'That told me the perp had to be an employee or somebody connected to SSD. Pam got a look at the guy's clothes – blue jacket, jeans and a cap – and I figured the security guards might know of employees who'd worn that outfit today. The ones who were on duty didn't remember seeing anyone like that so I got the names and addresses of guards who were off duty. I started canvassing them.' A grimace. 'Never occurred to me that Five Twenty-Two *was* one of them. How'd *you* know he was a guard, Rhyme?'

'Well, I knew you were looking for an employee. But was it one of the suspects or somebody else? The goddamn computer wasn't any help so I turned to the evidence. Our perp was an employee who wore unstylish work shoes and had traces of Coffee-mate on him. He was strong. Did those mean he had some physical job in the lower rungs of the company? Mailroom, deliveryman, janitor? Then I recalled the cayenne pepper.'

'Pepper spray,' Sachs said, sighing. 'Of course. It wasn't food at all.'

'Exactly. A security guard's main weapon. And the voice-disguise box? You can buy them at stores that sell security equipment. Then I talked to the head of security at SSD. Tom O'Day.'

'Right. We met him.' A nod at Pulaski.

'He told me a lot of security guards worked only part-time, which'd give Five Twenty-Two plenty of time to practice his hobby outside the office. I ran the other evidence past O'Day. The bits of leaf we found could've come from the plants in the security guards' lunch room. And they have Coffee-mate there, not real milk. I told him Terry Dobyns's profile and asked for a list of all the guards who were single and had no children. Then he cross-referenced their time sheets with the times of the killings for all the crimes going back two months.'

'And you found one who was out of the office at the time – John Rollins, aka Peter Gordon.'

'No, I found that John Rollins was *in* the office every time the crime occurred.'

'*In* the office?'

'Obviously. He got into the office management system and changed the time sheets to give himself an alibi. I had Rodney Szarnek check the metadata. Yep, he was our man. I called it in.'

'But, Rhyme, I don't understand how Five Twenty-Two got the dossiers. He had access to all the data pens but everybody was searched when they left, even him. And he didn't have online access to innerCircle.'

'That was the one stumbling block, yep. But we have Pam Willoughby to thank. She helped me figure it out.'

'Pam? How?'

'Remember she told us that nobody could download the pictures from the social-networking site, OurWorld, but the kids just took pictures of the screen?'

Oh, don't worry, Mr Rhyme. A lot of times people miss the obvious answer . . .

'I realized that's how Five Twenty-Two could get his information. He didn't *need* to download thousands of pages of dossiers. He just copied what he needed about the victims and the fall guys, probably late at night when he was one of the only people in the pens. Remember we found those flecks from yellow pads? And at the security station the X-ray or metal detectors wouldn't pick up paper. Nobody'd even think about it.'

Sachs said that she'd seen maybe a thousand yellow pads surrounding his desk in his secret room.

Lon Sellitto arrived from downtown. 'The fucker's dead,' he muttered, 'but I'm still in the system for being a goddamn crackhead. All I can get out of them is, "We're working on it."'

But he did have some good news. The district attorney would reopen all the cases in which 522 had apparently fabricated evidence. Arthur Rhyme had been released outright, and the status of the others would be reviewed immediately, the likelihood being that they'd be released within the next month.

Sellitto added, 'I checked on the town house where Five Twenty-Two was living.'

The Upper West Side residence had to be worth tens of millions. How Peter Gordon, employed as a security guard, had been able to afford it was a mystery.

But the detective had the answer. 'He wasn't the owner. Title's held by a Fiona McMillan, an eighty-nine-year-old widow, no close relatives. She still pays the taxes and utility bills. Never misses a payment. Only, funny thing – nobody's seen her in five years.'

'About the time SSD moved to New York.'

'I figure he got all the information he needed about assuming her identity and killed her. They're going to start searching for the body tomorrow. They'll start with the garage and then try the basement.' The lieutenant then added, 'I'm putting together the memorial service for Joe Malloy. It's on Saturday. If you want to be there.'

'Of course,' Rhyme said.

Sachs touched his hand and said, 'Patrol or brass, they're all family and it's the same pain when you lose somebody.'

'Your father?' Rhyme asked. 'Sounds like something he'd say.'

A voice from the hallway intruded: 'Heh. Too late. Sorry. Just got word you closed the case.' Rodney Szarnek was strolling into the lab, ahead of Thom. He was holding a stack of print-outs and once again was speaking to Rhyme's computer and ECU system, the equipment, not the human beings.

'Too late?' Rhyme asked.

'The mainframe finished assembling the empty-space files that Ron stole. Well, that he *borrowed*. I was on the way here to show them to you and heard that you nailed the perp. Guess you don't need them now.'

'Just curious. What'd you find?'

He walked forward with a number of printouts and displayed them to Rhyme. They were incomprehensible. Words, numbers and symbols, and large gaps of white space in between.

'I don't read Greek.'

'Heh, that's funny. You don't read Geek.'

Rhyme didn't bother to correct him. He asked, 'What's the bottom line?'

'Runnerboy – that nym I found earlier – *did* download a lot of information from innerCircle secretly and then he erased his tracks. But they weren't the dossiers of any of the victims or anybody else connected with the Five Twenty-Two case.'

'You got his name?' Sachs asked. 'Runnerboy's?'

'Yeah. Somebody named Sean Cassel.'

The policewoman closed her eyes. 'Runnerboy . . . And he said he was training for a triathlon. I didn't even think about it.'

Cassel was the sales director and one of their suspects, Rhyme reflected. He now noticed that Pulaski was reacting to the news. The young officer blinked in surprise and glanced at Sachs with a lifted eyebrow and a faint but dark smile of recognition. He recalled the officer's reluctance to return to SSD and his embarrassment at not knowing about Excel. A run-in between Pulaski and Cassel was a credible explanation.

The officer asked, 'What was Cassel up to?'

Szarnek flipped through the printouts. 'I couldn't tell you exactly.' He stopped and proffered the page to the young cop, shrugging. 'Take a look, if you want. Here are some of the dossiers he accessed.'

Pulaski shook his head. 'I don't know any of these guys.' He read some names out loud.

'Wait,' Rhyme barked. 'What was the last one?'

'Dienko . . . Here, it's mentioned again. Vladimir Dienko. You know him?'

'Shit,' said Sellitto.

Dienko – the defendant in the Russian organized crime investigation, the one whose case had been dropped because of witness and evidentiary problems. Rhyme said, 'And the one just before him?'

'Alex Karakov.'

This was an informant against Dienko who had been in hiding, under an assumed identity. He'd disappeared two weeks before trial, presumed dead, though no one could figure out how Dienko's men had gotten to him. Sellitto took the sheets from Pulaski and flipped through them. 'Jesus, Linc. Addresses, ATM withdrawals, car registrations, phone logs. Just what a hitman would need to get close for a clip . . . Oh, and get this. Kevin McDonald.'

'Wasn't he the defendant in some RICO case you were working on?' Rhyme asked.

'Yep. Hell's Kitchen, arms dealing, conspiracy. Some drugs and extortion. He got off too.'

'Mel? Run all the names on that list through our system.'

Of the eight names that Rodney Szarnek had found in the reassembled files, six had been defendants in criminal cases over the past three months. All six had either been acquitted or had had serious charges against them dropped at the last minute because of unexpected problems with witnesses and evidence.

Rhyme gave a laugh. 'This's pretty serendipitous.'

'What?' Pulaski asked.

'Buy a dictionary, rookie.'

The officer sighed and said patiently, 'Whatever it means, Lincoln, it's probably not a word I'll ever want to use.'

Everybody in the room laughed, Rhyme included. 'Touché. What I mean is we've coincidentally stumbled on something very *interesting*, if you will, Mel. NYPD has files on the SSD servers, through PublicSure. Well, Cassel's been downloading information about the investigation, selling it to the defendants and erasing all traces of it.'

'Oh, I can see him doing it,' Sachs said. 'Don't you think, Ron?'

'Don't doubt it for a minute.' The young officer added, 'Wait . . . Cassel was the one who gave us the CD of the customers' names – he's the one who fingered Robert Carpenter.'

'Of course,' Rhyme said, nodding. 'He changed the data to implicate Carpenter. He needed to point the investigation away from SSD. Not because of the Five Twenty-Two case. But because he didn't want anybody looking over the files and finding that he'd been selling police records. And who better to give to the wolves than somebody who'd tried to become a competitor?'

Sellitto asked Szarnek, 'Anybody else involved from SSD?'

'Not from what I found. Just Cassel.'

Rhyme then looked at Pulaski, who was staring at the evidence board. His eyes displayed the same hard edge Rhyme had seen earlier that day.

'Hey, rookie? You want it?'

'Want what?'

'The case against Cassel?'

The young officer considered this. But then his shoulders slumped and, laughing, he said, 'No, I don't think so.'

'You can handle it.'

'I know I can. I just . . . I mean, when I run my first case solo I want to make sure I'm doing it for the right reasons.'

'Well said, rookie,' Sellitto muttered, lifting his coffee mug toward the young man. 'Maybe there's hope for you after all . . . All right. If I'm suspended at least I can finish up that work around the house that Rachel's been nagging me to do.' The big detective grabbed a stale cookie and ambled out the door. ''Night, everybody.'

Szarnek assembled his files and disks and placed them on a table. Thom signed the chain-of-custody card as the criminalist's attorney-in-fact. The techie left, reminding Rhyme, 'And when you're ready to join the twenty-first century, Detective, give me a call.' A nod at the computers.

Rhyme's phone rang – it was a call for Sachs, whose dismembered mobile wouldn't be operative any time soon. Rhyme deduced from the conversation that the caller was in the precinct house in Brooklyn and that her car had been located at a pound not far away.

She made plans with Pam to drive to the place tomorrow morning in the girl's car, which had been found in a garage behind Peter Gordon's town house. Sachs went upstairs to get ready for bed, and Cooper and Pulaski left.

Rhyme was writing a memo for the deputy mayor, Ron Scott, describing 522's M.O. and suggesting they look for other instances in which he'd committed crimes and framed somebody for them. There'd be other evidence in the hoarder's town house, of course, but he couldn't imagine the amount of work involved in searching *that* crime scene.

He finished the e-mail, sent it on its way and was speculating what Andrew Sterling's reaction might be to one of his underlings' selling data on the side, when his phone rang. An unknown number on caller ID.

'Command, answer phone.'

Click.

'Hello?'

'Lincoln. It's Judy Rhyme.'

'Well, hello, Judy.'

'Oh, I don't know if you heard. They dropped the charges. He's out.'

'Already? I knew it was in the works. I thought it might take a little longer.'

'I don't know what to say, Lincoln. I guess, I mean: thank you.'

'Sure.'

She said, 'Hold on a minute.'

Rhyme heard a muted voice, her hand over the mouthpiece, and supposed she was talking to one of the children. What were their names again?

Then he heard: 'Lincoln?'

How curious that his cousin's voice was instantly familiar to him, a voice he hadn't heard for years. 'Well, Art. Hello.'

'I'm downtown. They just released me. All the charges are dropped.'

'Good.'

How awkward is this?

'I don't know what to say. Thank you. Thank you so much.'

'Sure.'

'All these years . . . I should have called before. I just . . .'

'That's okay.' What the hell's that supposed to mean? Rhyme wondered. Art's absence from his life wasn't okay, it wasn't not okay. His responses to his cousin were mere filler. He wanted to hang up.

'You didn't have to do what you did.'

'There were some irregularities. It was an odd situation.'

Which meant absolutely nothing either. And Lincoln Rhyme wondered too why he was deconstructing the conversation. It was some defense mechanism, he supposed – and this thought was as tedious as the others. He wanted to hang up. 'You're okay, after what happened in detention?'

'Nothing serious. Scary, but this guy got to me in time. Helped me down off the wall.'

'Good.'

Silence.

'Well, thanks again, Lincoln. Not a lot of people would have done this for me.'

'I'm glad it worked out.'

'We'll get together. You and Judy and me. And your friend. What's her name?'

'Amelia.'

'We'll get together.' A long silence. 'I'd better go. We have to get home to the kids. Okay, you take care.'

'You too . . . Command, disconnect.'

Rhyme's eyes settled on his cousin's dossier from SSD. *The other son . . .*

And he knew that they'd never 'get together.' So it ends, he thought. Feeling at first troubled – that with the click of a disconnecting phone something that might have been now would not be. But Lincoln Rhyme concluded that this was the only logical end to the events of the past three days.

Thinking of SSD's logo, he reflected that, yes, their lives had coincided once again after all these years, but it was as if the two cousins remained separated by a sealed window. They'd observed each other, they'd shared some words, but that was to be the extent of their contact. It was now time to return to their different worlds.

Chapter
FIFTY-ONE

At 11:00 A.M. Amelia Sachs stood in a scruffy lot in Brooklyn. Choking back tears, she was gazing at the corpse.

The woman who had been shot at, who had killed in the line of duty, who talked her way onto point in dynamic hostage-rescue ops was now paralyzed with grief.

Rocking back and forth, her index finger digging into the quick of her thumb, nail against nail, until a minor stain of blood appeared. She glanced down at her fingers. Saw the crimson but didn't stop the compulsion. She couldn't.

Yes, they'd found her beloved 1969 Chevrolet Camaro SS.

But what the police apparently hadn't known was that the car had been sold for scrap, not just impounded for missed payments. She and Pam were standing in the car impound lot, which could have been a set in a Scorsese film, or *The Sopranos,* a junkyard stinking of old oil and smoke from a trash fire. Loud, mean gulls hovered nearby, white vultures. She wanted to draw her weapon and empty the clip into the air to send them fleeing in terror.

A crushed metal rectangle was all that remained of the car, which had been with her since her teenage days. The vehicle was one of her father's three most important legacies to her, the others being his strength of character and his love of police work.

'I got the paperwork. It's all, you know, in order.' The uneasy head of the scrap yard was brandishing the limp printouts that had turned her car into an unrecognizable cube of steel.

'Sold for the basket' was the expression; it meant selling a car for parts and, whatever was left, for scrap. Which was idiotic, of course; you're not going to make any money selling forty-year-old pony car parts from a gray-market yard in the South Bronx. But as she'd learned all too well in the course of this case, when a computer in authority gives instruction, you do as you're told.

'I'm sorry, lady.'

'She's a police officer,' Pam Willoughby said harshly. 'A detective.'

'Oh,' he said, considering the further implications of the situation and not liking them much. 'Sorry, Detective.'

Still, he had his in-order paperwork shield. He wasn't all that sorry. The man stood beside them for a few minutes, rocking from one foot to another. Then wandered away.

The pain within her was far worse than the greenish bruise from the 9-millimeter slug that had punched her belly last night.

'You okay?' Pam asked.

'Not really.'

'Like, you don't get freaked much.'

No, I don't, Sachs thought. But I'm freaked now.

The girl twined her red-streaked hair around her fingers, perhaps a tame version of Sachs's own nervous touch. She looked once more at the ugly square of metal, about three by four feet, sitting amid a half dozen others.

Memories were reeling. Her father and teenage Amelia, sharing Saturday afternoons in their tiny garage, working on a carburetor or clutch. They'd escaped to the back for two reasons – for the pleasure of the mechanical work in each other's company, and to escape the moody third party in the family: Sachs's mother.

'Gaps?' he'd asked, playfully testing her.

'Plug,' teenage Amelia had replied, 'is zero three five. Points, thirty to thirty-two dwell.'

'Good, Amie.'

Sachs recalled another time – a date, her first year in college. She and a boy who went by the name of C.T. had met at a burger place in Brooklyn. Their vehicles surprised each other. Sachs in the Camaro – yellow at the time, with tar black stripes for accent – and he atop a Honda 850.

The burgers and sodas vanished fast, since they were only a few miles from an abandoned airstrip and a race was inevitable.

He was off the line first, given that she was inside a ton and a half of vehicle, but her big block caught him before the half mile – he was cautious and she wasn't – and she steered into the drift on the curves and kept ahead all the way to the finish.

Then her favorite drive of all time: After they'd concluded their first case together, Lincoln Rhyme, largely immobilized, strapped in beside her, windows down and wind howling. She rested his hand on the gearshift knob as she shifted and she remembered him shouting over the slipstream, 'I think I can feel it. I think I can!'

And now the car was gone.

Sorry, lady . . .

Pam climbed down the embankment.

'Where are you going?'

'You shouldn't go down there, miss.' The owner, outside the office shack, was waving the paperwork like a warning semaphore.

'Pam!'

But she wouldn't be stopped. She walked up to the mass of metal and dug around inside. She tugged hard and pulled out something, then returned to Sachs.

'Here, Amelia.' It was the horn button emblem, with the Chevrolet logo.

Sachs felt the tears but continued to will them away. 'Thanks, honey. Come on. Let's get the hell out of here.'

They drove back to the Upper West Side and stopped for recuperative ice cream; Sachs had arranged for Pam to take the day off from school. She didn't want her to be around Stuart Everett, and the girl was only too happy to agree.

Sachs wondered if the teacher would take no for an answer. Thinking of the trashy flicks – à la *Scream* and *Friday the 13th* – that she and Pam sometimes watched late at night, fortified with Doritos and peanut butter, Sachs knew that old boyfriends, like horror movie killers, sometimes have a way of rising from the dead.

Love makes us weird . . .

Pam finished her ice cream and patted her stomach. 'I so needed that.' Then she sighed. 'How could I be so stupid?'

In the girl's ensuing laugh – eerily adult – Amelia Sachs heard what she believed was the final shovel of earth on the grave of the hockey-masked killer.

They left Baskin-Robbins and walked toward Rhyme's town house, several blocks away, planning a girls' night out, along with another friend of Sachs's, a policewoman she'd known for years. She asked the girl, 'Movie or play?'

'Oh, a play . . . Amelia, when does an off-Broadway play become an off-off-Broadway play?'

'That's a good question. We'll Google it.'

'And why do they call them Broadway plays when there aren't any theaters on Broadway?'

'Yeah. They should be "near Broadway" plays. Or "right around the corner from Broadway" plays.'

The pair walked along the east-west side street, approaching Central Park West. Sachs was suddenly aware of a pedestrian nearby. Somebody was crossing the street behind them, moving in their general direction, as if following them.

She felt no alarm, putting the breeze of concern down to the paranoia from the 522 case.

Relax. The perp's dead and gone.

She didn't bother to look back.

But Pam did.

And screamed shrilly, 'It's him, Amelia!'

'Who?'

'The guy who broke into your town house. That's him!'

Sachs spun around. The man in the blue plaid jacket and baseball cap. He moved toward them fast.

She slapped her hip, going for her gun.

Which wasn't there.

No, no, no . . .

Since Peter Gordon had fired the weapon, the Glock was now evidence – as was her knife – and both were at Crime Scene Unit in Queens. She hadn't had the chance to go downtown and do the paperwork for a replacement.

Sachs now froze, recognizing him. It was Calvin Geddes, an employee of Privacy Now. She couldn't make sense of this, and wondered if they'd been wrong. Were Geddes and 522 in on the murders together?

He was now just yards away. Sachs could do nothing but step between Geddes and Pam. She balled her fists up as the man stepped close and reached into his jacket.

Chapter
FIFTY-TWO

The doorbell rang, and Thom went to answer it.

Rhyme heard some heated words from the front entryway. A man's voice, angry. A shout.

Frowning, he glanced at Ron Pulaski, who had his weapon out of his high-riding holster, and pointed it up, ready to fire. He held it expertly. Amelia Sachs was a good mentor.

'Thom?' Rhyme called.

He didn't answer.

A moment later a man appeared in the doorway, wearing a baseball cap, jeans and an ugly plaid jacket. He blinked in shock as Pulaski aimed the gun toward him.

'No! Wait!' the man cried, ducking and lifting a hand.

Then Thom, Sachs and Pam entered immediately behind him. The policewoman saw the weapon and said, 'No, no, Ron. It's okay . . . He's Calvin Geddes.'

It took Rhyme a moment to recall. Ah, that's right: with the Privacy Now organization, and the source of the lead about Peter Gordon. 'What's this all about?'

Sachs said, 'He's the one who broke into my place. It wasn't Five Twenty-Two.'

Pam nodded, confirming this.

Geddes stepped closer to Rhyme and reached into his jacket pocket and extracted some blue-backed documents. 'Pursuant to New York State civil procedure laws, I'm serving you this subpoena in connection with *Geddes et al. versus Strategic Systems Datacorp, Inc.*' He held them out.

'I got one too, Rhyme.' Sachs held up her own copy.

'And I'm supposed to do *what* with those?' Rhyme asked Geddes, who continued to proffer the documents.

The man frowned, then looked down at the wheelchair, aware of Rhyme's condition for the first time. 'I, well—'

'He's my attorney-in-fact.' Rhyme nodded to Thom, who took the papers.

Geddes began, 'I'm—'

'You mind if we read it?' Rhyme asked acerbically, with a nod toward his aide.

Thom did so, aloud. It was a subpoena requesting all the paper and computer files, notes and other information that Rhyme had in his possession that related to SSD, its Compliance Division and evidence of SSD's connections with any governmental body.

'She told me about Compliance.' Geddes nodded toward Sachs. 'It didn't make any sense at all. Something was fishy about it. No way would Andrew Sterling volunteer to work with the government on privacy issues if he didn't get something big out of the arrangement. He'd fight them tooth and nail. That made me suspicious. Compliance is about something else. I don't know what. But we're going to find out.'

He explained that the suit was under federal and state privacy acts and for various civil violations of common law and constitutional rights of privacy.

Rhyme reflected that Geddes and his attorneys would have a pretty pleasant surprise when they had a look at the Compliance dossiers. One of which he just happened to have in a computer not ten feet from where Geddes now stood.

And which he would be more than delighted to hand over, given Andrew Sterling's refusal to help find Sachs after she'd disappeared.

He wondered which would be in worse trouble, Washington or SSD, when the press learned of the Compliance operation.

Dead heat, he concluded.

Sachs then said, 'Of course, Mr Geddes here will have to juggle the case with his own trial.' Giving him a dark look. She was referring to the break-in at her town house in Brooklyn, whose mission presumably was to find information about SSD. She explained that, ironically, it had been Geddes, not 522, who'd dropped the receipt that had led her to SSD. He regularly hung out at the coffee shop in Midtown, from which he kept up a furtive surveillance of the Gray Rock, noting the comings and goings of Sterling and other employees and customers.

Geddes said fervently, 'I'll do whatever's necessary to stop SSD. I don't care what happens to me. I'll happily be the sacrificial lamb if it brings back our individual rights.'

Rhyme respected his moral courage but decided he needed more quotable lines.

The activist began to lecture them now – reiterating much of what Sachs had reported earlier – about the arachnid sweep of SSD and other data miners, the death of privacy in the country, the risk to democracy.

'Okay, we've got the paperwork,' Rhyme interrupted the tiresome rant. 'We'll have a little talk with our own lawyers and, if they say everything's in order, I'm sure you'll be getting a care package by your deadline.'

The doorbell rang. Once, twice. Then loud knocking.

'Oh, brother. Goddamn Grand Central Station . . . What now?'

Thom went to the door. He returned a moment later with a short, confident-looking man in a black suit and white shirt. 'Captain Rhyme.'

The criminalist turned his wheelchair to face Andrew Sterling, whose calm green eyes registered no surprise whatsoever at the criminalist's condition. Rhyme suspected that his own Compliance dossier documented the accident and his life afterward in considerable detail, and that Sterling would have boned up on the particulars before he arrived here.

'Detective Sachs, Officer Pulaski.' He nodded to them, then returned to Rhyme.

Behind him were Sam Brockton, the SSD Compliance director, and two other men, who were dressed conservatively. Neat hair. They could have been congressional aides or corporate middle managers, though Rhyme was not surprised to learn they were lawyers.

'Hello, Cal,' Brockton said, looking over Geddes wearily. The Privacy Now man glared back.

Sterling said in a soft voice, 'We found out what Mark Whitcomb did.' Despite his diminutive stature, Sterling was imposing in person, with the vibrant eyes, the perfectly straight posture, the unflappable voice. 'I'm afraid he's out of a job. For starters.'

'Because he did the right thing?' Pulaski snapped.

Sterling's face continued to show no emotion. 'And I'm afraid too the matter's not over with yet.' A nod to Brockton.

'Serve them,' the Compliance director snapped to one of the attorneys. The man handed out his own batch of blue-backed documents.

'*More?*' Rhyme commented, nodding at the second set of paperwork. 'All this reading. Who's got the time?' He was in a good mood, still elated that they'd stopped 522 and that Amelia Sachs was safe.

The sequel turned out to be a court order forbidding them to give Geddes any computers, disks, documents or any material of any kind relating to the Compliance operation.

And to turn over to the government any such material in their possession.

One hired gun said, 'Failure to do so will subject you to civil and criminal penalties.'

Sam Brockton offered, 'And believe me, we will pursue all remedies available to us.'

'You can't do this,' Geddes said, angry. His eyes shone and sweat dotted his dark face.

Sterling counted the computers in Rhyme's lab. There were twelve. 'Which one has the Compliance dossier that Mark sent you, Captain?'

'I forget.'

'Did you make any copies?'

Rhyme smiled. 'Always back up your data. And store it in a separate, secure location. Off site. Isn't that the message of the new millennium?'

Brockton said, 'We'll just get another order to confiscate everything and search all the servers you've uploaded data to.'

'But that'll take time and money. And who knows what could happen in the meantime? E-mails or envelopes might get sent to the press, say. Accidentally, of course. But it could happen.'

'This has been a very trying time for everyone, Mr Rhyme,' Sterling said. 'No one's in the mood for games.'

'We're not playing games,' Rhyme said evenly. 'We're negotiating.'

The CEO gave what appeared to be his first genuine smile. He was on his home turf now and he pulled up a chair next to Rhyme. 'What do you want?'

'I'll give you everything. No court battles, no press.'

'No!' Geddes was enraged. 'How can you cave in?'

Rhyme ignored the activist as efficiently as Sterling did and continued, 'Provided you get my associates' records cleared up.' He explained about Sellitto's drug test and Pulaski's wife.

'I can do that,' Sterling said as if it were no more trouble than turning up the volume on a TV.

Sachs said, 'And you have to fix Robert Jorgensen's life too.' She told him about how 522 had virtually destroyed the man.

'Give me the details and I'll make sure it's taken care of. He'll have a clean slate.'

'Good. As soon as everything's cleared up you'll have what you want. And nobody will see a single piece of paper or file about your Compliance operation. I give you my word.'

'No, you have to fight it!' Geddes said bitterly to Rhyme. 'Every time you don't stand up to them, everybody loses.'

Sterling turned to him and said in a voice just a few decibels above a whisper, 'Calvin, let me tell you something. I lost three good friends in the Trade Towers on September eleventh. Four more were badly burned. Their lives'll never be the same. And our country lost thousands of innocent citizens. My company had the technology to find some of the hijackers and the predictive software to figure out what they were going to do. We – I – could have prevented the whole tragedy. And I regret every single day that I didn't.'

He shook his head. 'Oh, Cal. You and your black-and-white politics . . . Don't you see: *That*'s what SSD is about. Not about the thought police kicking in your door at midnight because they don't like what you and your girlfriend are doing in bed or arresting you because you bought a book about Stalin or the Koran or because you criticized the President. The mission of SSD is to guarantee that you're free and safe to enjoy the privacy of your home and to buy and read and say whatever you want to. If you're blown up by a suicide bomber in Times Square, you won't have any identity to protect.'

'Spare us the lectures, Andrew,' Geddes raged.

Brockton said, 'Cal, if you don't calm down, you're going to find yourself in a lot of trouble.'

Geddes gave a cold laugh. 'We're already in a lot of trouble. Welcome to the brave new world . . .' The man spun around and stormed out. The front door slammed.

Brockton said, 'I'm glad you understand, Lincoln. Andrew Sterling is doing very good things. We're all safer because of it.'

'I'm so happy to hear it.'

Brockton missed the irony entirely. But Andrew Sterling didn't. He was, after all, the man who knew everything. But his reaction was a humorous, self-assured smile – as if he knew that the lectures eventually got through to people, even if they didn't appreciate the message just yet. 'Good-bye, Detective Sachs, Captain. Oh, and you too, Officer Pulaski.' He glanced wryly at the young cop. 'I'll miss seeing you around the halls. But if you want to spend any more time honing your computer skills, our conference room'll always be available to you.'

'Well, I . . .'

Andrew Sterling gave him a wink and turned. He and his entourage left the town house.

'You think he knew?' the rookie asked. 'About the hard drive?'

Rhyme could only shrug.

'Hell, Rhyme,' Sachs said, 'I suppose the order's legit but after all we've been through with SSD, did you have to cave so quickly? Brother, that Compliance dossier . . . I'm not happy all that information's out there.'

'A court order's a court order, Sachs. Not much we can do about it.'

Then she looked at him closely and must have noticed the glimmer in his eyes. 'Okay, what?'

Rhyme asked his aide, 'In your lovely tenor read me that order again. The one our SSD friends just delivered.'

He did.

Rhyme nodded. 'Good . . . There's a Latin phrase I'm thinking of, Thom. Can you guess what it is?'

'Oh, you know, I *should,* Lincoln, considering all those hours I have free here, sitting in the parlor and studying the classics. But I'm afraid I'm drawing a blank.'

'Latin . . . what a language that is. Admirable precision. Where else can you find five declensions of nouns, and those amazing verb conjugations? . . . Well, the phrase is *Inclusis unis, exclusis alterius.* It means that by including one category you automatically exclude other, related categories. Confused?'

'Not really. To be confused you have to be paying attention.'

'Excellent riposte, Thom. But I'll give you an example. Say you're a congressman and you write a statute that says, "No raw meat shall be imported into the country." By choosing those particular words you're automatically giving permission to import canned or cooked meat. See how it works?'

'Mirabile dictu,' said Ron Pulaski.

'My God,' Rhyme said, truly surprised. 'A Latin speaker.'

He laughed. 'A few years. In high school. And, being a choirboy, you tend to pick things up.'

'Where are we going with this, Rhyme?' Sachs asked.

'Brockton's court order only bars giving Privacy Now information about the Compliance Division. But Geddes asked for everything we have about SSD. Therefore – ergo – anything else we have on SSD is fair to release. The files Cassel sold to Dienko were part of PublicSure, not Compliance.'

Pulaski laughed. But Sachs was frowning. 'They'll just get another court order.'

'I'm not so sure. What're the NYPD and the FBI going to say when they find out that somebody who works for their own data contractor has been selling out high-profile cases? Oh, I've got a feeling the brass'll back us on this one.' This thought led to another. And the conclusion was alarming. 'Wait, wait, wait . . . In detention – that man who moved on my cousin. Antwon Johnson?'

'What about him?' Sachs asked.

'It never made any sense that he'd try to kill Arthur. Even Judy Rhyme mentioned that. Lon said he was a federal prisoner temporarily in state detention. I wonder if somebody from Compliance cut a deal with him. Maybe he was there to see if Arthur thought somebody was getting consumer information about him to use in the crimes. If so, Johnson was supposed to clip him. Maybe for a reduction in his sentence.'

'The government, Rhyme? Trying to take out a witness? That's a bit paranoid, don't you think?'

'We're talking about five-hundred-page dossiers, chips in books and CCTVs on every street corner in the city, Sachs . . . But, okay, I'll give them the benefit of the doubt: Maybe somebody from SSD contacted Johnson. In any case we'll call Calvin Geddes and give him all that information too. Let the pit bull run with it if he wants. Only wait until everybody's files are cleaned up. Give it a week.'

Ron Pulaski said good-bye and left to see his wife and baby daughter.

Sachs walked up to Rhyme and bent down to kiss him on the mouth. She winced, probing her belly.

'You okay?'

'I'll show you tonight, Rhyme,' she whispered flirtatiously. 'Nine-millimeter slugs leave some interesting bruises.'

'Sexy?' he asked.

'Only if you think purple Rorschachs are erotic.'

'As a matter of fact, I do.'

Sachs gave a subtle smile to him, then walked into the hallway and called to Pam, who'd been in the front parlor, reading. 'Come on. We're going shopping.'

'Excellent. What for?'

'A car. Can't be without wheels.'

'Neat, what kind? Oh, a Prius'd be *way* cool.'

Both Rhyme and Sachs laughed hard. Pam smiled uncertainly and Sachs explained that though her life was green in many ways, gasoline mileage didn't figure into her love of the environment. 'We're going to get a muscle car.'

'What's that?'

'You'll find out.' She brandished a list of potential vehicles she'd downloaded from the Internet.

'You going to get a new one?' the girl asked.

'Never, ever buy a new car,' Sachs lectured.

'Why?'

'Because cars today are just computers with wheels. We don't want electronics. We want mechanics. You can't get grease on your hands with computers.'

'Grease?'

'You'll love grease. You're a grease kind of girl.'

'You think so?' Pam seemed pleased.

'You bet. Let's go. Later, Rhyme.'

Chapter
FIFTY-THREE

The phone trilled.

Lincoln Rhyme glanced up at a nearby computer screen, where caller ID displayed '44.'

At last. This was it.

'Command, answer phone.'

'Detective Rhyme,' said the impeccable British voice. Longhurst's alto never gave anything away.

'Tell me.'

A hesitation. Then: 'I'm so sorry.'

Rhyme closed his eyes. No, no, no . . .

Longhurst continued, 'We haven't made the official announcement yet but I wanted to tell you before the press reported it.'

So the killer had succeeded after all. 'He's dead then, Reverend Goodlight?'

'Oh, no, he's fine.'

'But—'

'But Richard Logan got his intended target, Detective.'

'He got . . . ?' Rhyme's voice faded as the pieces began coming together. The *intended* target. 'Oh, no . . . Who was he really after?'

'Danny Krueger, the arms dealer. He's dead, two of his security people too.'

'Ah, yes, I see.'

Longhurst continued, 'Apparently after Danny went straight, some cartels in South Africa, Somalia and Syria felt he was too great a risk to stay alive. A conscience-stricken arms dealer made them nervous. They hired Logan to kill him. But Danny's security network in London was too tight so Logan needed to draw him out into the open.'

The reverend had been merely a diversion. The killer himself had planted the rumor that there was a contract out on Goodlight. And he'd forced the British and the Americans to turn to Danny for help to save the reverend.

'And it's worse, I must say,' Longhurst went on. 'He got all of Danny's files. All his contacts, everybody who's been working for him – informants, warlords who could be turned, mercenaries, bush pilots, sources of funds. All the potential witnesses will go to ground now. The ones who aren't killed outright, that is. A dozen criminal cases'll have to be dismissed.'

'How'd he do it?'

She sighed. 'He was masquerading as our French liaison, d'Estourne.'

So the fox had been in the henhouse from the beginning.

'I would guess he intercepted the real d'Estourne in France on the way to the Chunnel, killed him and buried the body or dumped it at sea. It was brilliant, I must say. He researched everything about the Frenchman's life and his organization. He spoke perfect French – and English with a perfect French accent. Even the idioms were spot-on.

'A few hours ago some chap shows up at a building in the London courtyard shooting zone. Logan had hired him to deliver a package. He worked for Tottenham Parcel Express; they wear gray uniforms. Remember the fibers we found? And the killer had requested a particular driver he claimed he'd used before – who happened to be blond.'

'The hair dye.'

'Exactly. Dependable fellow, Logan said. Which is why he wanted him in particular. Everyone was so focused on the operation there, tracking this fellow through the shooting zone, looking for accomplices, worried about diversionary bombs, that the people in Birmingham lowered their guard. The killer just knocked on the door to Danny's room in the Hotel Du Vin, while most of his security team were down in the champagne bar having a pint. He started shooting – with those dum-dum bullets. The wounds were horrible. Danny and two of his men were killed instantly.'

Rhyme closed his eyes. 'So no fake transit papers.'

'All a diversion . . . It's a bloody awful mess, I'm afraid. And the French – they're not even returning my calls . . . I don't even want to think about it.'

Lincoln Rhyme couldn't help but wonder what would have happened if he'd stuck with the case, searched the scene outside Manchester with the high-def video system. Would he have seen something that revealed the true nature of the killer's plan? Would he have decided that the Birmingham evidence too was planted? Or was there something that might have led him to conclude that the person who'd rented the room – the man he was so desperate to catch – was masquerading as the French security agent?

Was there something he might have seen at the NGO office break-in in London?

'And the name Richard Logan?' Rhyme asked.

'Wasn't his, apparently. A complete alias. He stole somebody's identity. It's surprisingly easy to do, apparently.'

'So I've heard,' Rhyme said bitterly.

Longhurst continued, 'One rather odd thing, though, Detective. That bag that was to be delivered in the shooting zone by the Tottenham chap? Inside was—'

' – a package addressed to me.'

'Why, yes.'

'Was it a watch or clock, by any chance?' Rhyme asked.

Longhurst barked an incredulous laugh. 'A rather posh table clock, Victorian. How on earth did you possibly know?'

'Just a hunch.'

'Our explosives people checked it. It's quite safe.'

'No, it wouldn't be an IED . . . Inspector, please seal it in plastic and ship it over here overnight. And I'd like to see your case report when it's finished.'

'Of course.'

'And my partner—'

'Detective Sachs.'

'That's right. She'll want to video interview everybody involved.'

'I'll put together a dramatis personae.'

Despite his anger and dismay, Rhyme had to smile at the expression. He loved the Brits.

'It's been a privilege to work with you, Detective.'

'And with you too, Inspector.' He disconnected, sighed.

A Victorian clock.

Rhyme looked at the mantelpiece, on which was displayed a Breguet pocket watch, old and quite valuable, a gift from the very same killer. The watch had been delivered here just after the man had escaped from Rhyme on a cold, cold day in December not so long ago.

'Thom. Scotch. Please.'

'What's wrong?'

'There's nothing wrong. It's not breakfast time and I want some scotch. I passed my physical with flying colors and the last time I looked you weren't a Bible-thumping, teetotaling Baptist. Why the hell do you think there's something wrong?'

'Because you said "please."'

'Very funny. Quite the wit today.'

'I try.' But he frowned as he studied Rhyme and read something in his expression. 'Maybe a double?' he asked softly.

'A double would be lovely,' Rhyme said, lapsing into Brit English.

The aide poured a large tumblerful of Glenmorangie and arranged the straw near his mouth.

'Join me?'

Thom blinked. Then he laughed. 'Maybe later.' It was the first time, Rhyme believed, that he'd ever offered his aide a drink.

The criminalist sipped the smoky liquor, staring at the pocket watch. He thought of the note the killer had included with the timepiece. Rhyme had long ago memorized it.

The pocket watch is a Breguet. It is the favorite of the many timepieces I have come across in the past year. It was made in the early 1800s and features a ruby cylinder escapement, perpetual calendar and parachute anti-shock device. I hope you appreciate the phases-of-the-moon window, in light of our recent adventures together. There are few specimens like this watch in the world. I give it to you as a present, out of respect. In my years at this profession, no one has ever stopped me from finishing a job; you're as good as they get. (I would say you're as good as I, but that is not quite true; you did not, after all, catch me.)

Keep the Breguet wound (but gently); it will be counting out the minutes until we meet again.

Some advice – If I were you, I would make every one of those seconds count.

You're good, Rhyme spoke silently to the killer.

But I'm good too. Next time, we finish our game.

Then his thoughts were interrupted. Rhyme squinted,

looking away from the watch and focusing out the window. Something had caught his eye.

A man in casual clothing was dawdling on the sidewalk across the street. Rhyme maneuvered his TDX to the window and looked out. He sipped more whisky. The man stood beside a dark overpainted bench in front of the stone wall bordering Central Park. He was staring at the town house, hands in his pockets. Apparently he couldn't see that he was being observed from inside the town house's large window.

It was his cousin, Arthur Rhyme.

The man started forward, nearly crossing the street. But then he stopped. He walked back to the park and sat on one of the benches facing the town house, beside a woman in a running suit, sipping water and bobbing her foot as she listened to her iPod. Arthur pulled a piece of paper out of his pocket, looked at it and put it back. His eyes returned to the town house.

Curious. He looks like me, Rhyme reflected. In all their years of comradeship and separation, he'd never realized it.

Suddenly, for some reason, his cousin's words from a decade ago filled his mind:

Did you even try with your father? What do you think he felt, having a son like you, who was a hundred times smarter than he was? Going off all the time because he'd rather hang out with his uncle. Did you even give Teddy a chance?

The criminalist shouted, 'Thom!'

No response.

A louder summons.

'What?' the aide asked. 'You finished the scotch already?'

'I need something. From the basement.'

'The basement?'

'I just said that. There're a few old boxes down there. They'll have the word "Illinois" on them.'

'Oh, those. Actually, Lincoln, there are about thirty of them.'

'However many.'

'Not a few.'

'I need you to look through them and find something for me.'

'What?'

'A piece of concrete in a little plastic box. About three by three inches.'

'Concrete?'

'It's a present for someone.'

'Well, I can't *wait* for Christmas, to see what's in *my* stocking. When would you – ?'

'Now. Please.'

A sigh. Thom disappeared.

Rhyme continued to watch his cousin, staring at the front door of the town house. But the man wasn't budging.

A long sip of scotch.

When Rhyme looked back, the park bench was empty.

He was alarmed – and hurt – by the man's abrupt departure. He drove the wheelchair forward quickly, getting as close to the window as he could.

And he saw Arthur, dodging traffic, making for the town house.

Silence for a long, long moment. Finally the doorbell buzzed.

'Command,' Rhyme said quickly to his attentive computer. 'Unlock front door.'

Author's Note

Calvin Geddes's comment about a 'brave new world' is, of course, a reference to the title of Aldous Huxley's 1932 futuristic novel about the loss of individual identity in a supposedly utopian society. The book remains as harrowing as ever, as does George Orwell's *1984*.

Readers wishing to know more about the issue of privacy might want to peruse some of the following organizations' websites: Electronic Privacy Information Center (www.epic.org); Global Internet Liberty Campaign (www.gilc.org); In Defense of Freedom (www.indefenseoffreedom.org); Internet Free Expression Alliance (www.ifea.net); The Privacy Coalition (www.privacycoalition.org); Privacy International (www.privacyinternational.org); Privacy.org (www.privacy.org); and the Electronic Frontier Foundation (www.eff.org).

I think you'll also enjoy – and be unnerved by – the excellent book from which I borrowed several quotations to use as epigrams, *No Place to Hide,* by Robert O'Harrow, Jr.

Those who'd like to know more about how Amelia Sachs came to meet Pam Willoughby might wish to read *The Bone Collector,* and their follow-up story in *The Cold Moon*. Similarly, *The Cold Moon* describes Lincoln Rhyme's first meeting with the killer whom he and Inspector Longhurst try to capture in this novel.

Oh, and be sure to keep an eye on your identity. If you don't, there're plenty of people out there who will.

Acknowledgments

My thanks to a great crew: Will and Tina Anderson, Louise Burke, Luisa Colicchio, Jane Davis, Julie Deaver, Jamie Hodder-Williams, Paolo Klun, Carolyn Mays, Deborah Schneider, Vivienne Schuster, Seba Pezzani, Betsy Robbins, David Rosenthal, Marysue Rucci . . . and, of course, Madelyn Warcholik.

About the Author

A former journalist, folksinger and attorney, Jeffery Deaver is an international number-one best-selling author. His novels have appeared on a number of best-seller lists around the world, including *The New York Times, The Times* of London and *The Los Angeles Times*. His books are sold in 150 countries and translated into 25 languages. The author of twenty-three novels and two collections of short stories, he's been awarded the Steel Dagger and Short Story Dagger from the British Crime Writers' Association, is a three-time recipient of the Ellery Queen Reader's Award for Best Short Story of the Year and is a winner of the British Thumping Good Read Award. He's been nominated for six Edgar Awards from the Mystery Writers of America, an Anthony Award and a Gumshoe Award. His book *A Maiden's Grave* was made into an HBO movie starring James Garner and Marlee Matlin, and his novel *The Bone Collector* was a feature release from Universal Pictures, starring Denzel Washington and Angelina Jolie. His most recent books are *The Sleeping Doll, The Cold Moon, The Twelfth Card* and *More Twisted: Collected Stories, Volume II*. And, yes, the rumors are true, he did appear as a corrupt reporter on his favorite soap opera, *As the World Turns*.

Deaver is presently writing the second in the Kathryn Dance series, who had her book-length debut in last year's *The Sleeping Doll*, and the next Lincoln Rhyme novel for 2010.

Readers can visit his website at www.jefferydeaver.com.

The BODIES LEFT BEHIND

Jeffery DEAVER

THE SUSPENSE IS KILLING

A spring night in a small town in Wisconsin.
A call to police emergency from a distant lake house is cut short.
A phone glitch or something more sinister?
Off-duty deputy Brynn McKenzie leaves her family's dinner table and
drives up to the lake to find out.

And stumbles onto the scene of a murder. Before she can call for backup,
she finds herself the next potential victim. Deprived of her phone, weapon
and car, Brynn flees, along with the only survivor of the crime.

These unlikely allies – women from city and small town – can survive only
by escaping into the dense, deserted woods, on a desperate trek to safety.
And ultimately to a life or death choice: flight or fight?

Out now in hardback

HODDER &
STOUGHTON

The
SLEEPING DOLL

Jeffery
DEAVER

YOU CAN TELL A LIAR BY HIS EYES.
Special Agent Kathryn Dance reads people the
way other investigators read crime scenes.
But she's never seen eyes like Daniel Pell's.
YOU CAN CATCH A KILLER BY HIS SMILE.

In 1999, Daniel Pell murdered an entire family.
Only one little girl survived, asleep in her bed
and hidden by her dolls.

When Kathryn Dance interrogates Pell, he's serving
a life sentence for the murders. Moments later, he's
on the run, a trail of death and mayhem in his wake.

To catch him, Dance must draw on every clue from
their brief meeting. And her fear that they share a common
aim: to find the girl they call the Sleeping Doll . . .

'Deaver is a terrific storyteller, and he takes the reader
on a rollercoaster of suspense, violence and mystery'
Daily Telegraph

Out now in Hodder paperback

HODDER